KARL'S KINGDOM

BOOK 1: THE FOUR WALLS

MARK BOUTROS

Wonderful cover illustrated by Ivan via Miblart

Awesome map design by Tania Gomes
www.mystic-wings.com

Proofread by Nick Hodgson
www.root-and-branch-editing.com

ISBN: 978-1-9162974-7-0

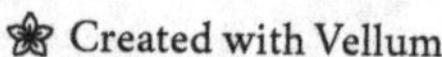 Created with Vellum

ABOUT THE AUTHOR

Mark Boutros is an International Emmy nominated and PAGE International award-winning writer, creative writing teacher and mentor.

He lives in London and dreams of leaving it for a mountain where he can grow his own food and not be asked to do things.

If you want to know more about Mark visit www.mark-boutros.com

Instagram: @markboutroswrites
Facebook: www.facebook.com/MarkBoutrosWrites
Not on Twitter/ Threads because it's mostly people shouting at each other and misery

This book is dedicated to Cinthia, the kindest and most interesting human I've ever met

CONTENTS

CURRENTLY KNOWN MAP OF HASTOVIA

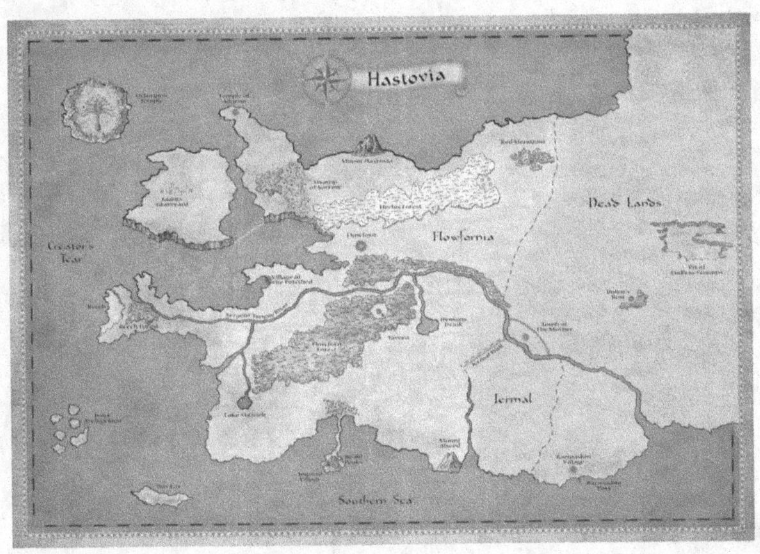

PROLOGUE

The world of Hastovia was full of idiots. From the Giant's Graveyard in the west, to the suffocating Dead Lands in the east – idiots, idiots, and more idiots.

There were bad idiots: tyrants who, perhaps, never processed the trauma of their childhood, when their mother forbade them from playing with an axe. Now, they marched from kingdom to kingdom, slashing and hacking, determined to never be told "no" again.

There were harmless idiots: those who drifted through their days, never questioning anything and working themselves to the bone to earn a few coins, only to repeat the cycle until they died with an irrelevant whimper.

And then there were the good idiots: those who lived to help others but, deep down, did it for their own legacy. They had good intentions, but were blind to the impact of their plans. Yet, on they went, idioting for the betterment of the world.

King Sastin of Flowforn was one such idiot.

He stood at the edge of the King's Tower, gazing over his kingdom under the night sky, as the wind teased his beard. Beneath him, Flowforn buzzed with life: outside the tavern, several drunks threw boots at each other. In the alleys, a seamstress chased a man, trying to force a lacy vest over his head. In the courtyard, a horn player blew his instrument in a sleeping guard's ear.

The king inhaled the chaos and joy, but his guilt nibbled at him. 'I think it's time to tell the boy,' he told his rotund aide, Lombus.

Lombus raised a bushy eyebrow. 'You told me you wanted to come up here to admire the view.'

King Sastin smirked. 'Yes. And to reveal my intention.'

Lombus chuckled and shook his head. 'Are you actually going to tell him this time?'

King Sastin shrugged and dragged his feet to the King's Eye Bridge, connecting the King's Tower to the Lookout Tower. It stretched over the administration building that housed the Great Hall, stone store, planning rooms, and other places nobody cared about. 'I think so. Maybe it will have a profound impact on him. Make him less useless.'

Lombus joined King Sastin and placed a hand on his shoulder. 'Do you really want to risk all of this? Look at what you've built within these four walls – everyone has all they need and lives their dreams because of you.'

King Sastin watched a baker in a loin cloth trying to stuff as many rolls of bread as possible into a horse's mouth. 'Some dreams are more bizarre than others.' It warmed his heart.

Lombus chuckled. 'The boy could react badly. Can you afford a damaged reputation?'

King Sastin scoffed, but Lombus had a point. 'Perhaps you're right. The sacrifices could become worthless.' His gaze lingered on the cemetery, beyond the farms. A boy, Karl, sat hunched over a couple of stones. Karl didn't know it, but he carried a resemblance – her cheekbones, and the way she slumped as though the world weighed too much. However, while she was extraordinary, Karl was average, painfully so. Yet, he was a part of King Sastin's greatest mistake. 'Maybe I'll talk to Sabrinia first. See what she thinks.' His daughter was wiser than he was, even if she didn't realise it.

Lombus patted King Sastin on the back. 'I look forward to us having this conversation again tomorrow.'

King Sastin sighed and followed Lombus down the Lookout Tower, to join the free people who chanted the name of their great king, but he didn't feel so great. The idiotic choice he had made to wreck a life all those years ago to save his kingdom would haunt him forever.

There was no life in Hastovia that was free from idiocy, even when they had the best intentions.

Idiots came in all shapes, sizes, and moods. Yet, the worst idiots of all were those who were useless at everything. They weren't malicious, but their incompetence and inability to fit were truly rare. They were one in a million: A nothing idiot.

If anyone ever came across a nothing idiot they would do well to walk away. Nothing idiots were worthless to the world, and would most likely do something annoying like accidentally knock a table of food over, or stumble onto someone's toe, but precisely on the nail to crack it.

Karl, the young boy in the cemetery, was one such idiot.

DAY TO DAY

Karl sat cross-legged in front of two blue stones the size of his head and stared at the carved names of Polward and Ansel. He blew his greasy brown hair away from his bony face, dropped a handful of honey-covered beans into his mouth and sipped ale from a pouch.

'Things are… okay, I guess. I sleep. I eat.' He counted himself lucky to have lived in Flowforn for all of his nineteen years. Here, there was no expectation on anyone to do anything they didn't want to.

He poured water from a flask over the stones. 'I got dismissed from another task today. Building.' He wiped his runny nose on his shabby sleeve. 'There was a new tower, supposed to house fifty more people. They'd spent a year building it and carved all sorts of nice-looking creatures into the stone. I misjudged where to hammer a steel spike…' He shook his head. 'So now the builders hate me.' He sighed. 'So that's cleaner, blacksmith, builder, baker, farmer, jester…'

He picked up a twig and scratched at the soil with it, but it snapped. 'All I do is fail. If that was work I'd be the best. The supreme failure. I could go from kingdom to kingdom, teaching people how to be master failures.' He drank more ale. 'I like to imagine what you were like. Dad, I think you were hard-working, and that you liked beans too. And Mum, I imagine you were funny, always telling stories and people loved you.'

He patted the stones, the silence reminding him this was a one-way conversation.

The creaking of the cemetery gate broke his thoughts. Two brutes armed with hammers were blocking the entrance, staring at him.

Karl stood. 'I'd better go. I love you.' It always felt odd to say that to stones, to people he'd never met.

Karl turned to sprint away, but a wide, bald man gripping a hammer stepped in front of him. 'Proster...' Karl said. 'How are you?'

'Worthless runt!' Proster squeezed Karl's arm so tightly that he felt the brute's thumb against his bone. 'You visit here a lot. Maybe I'll make it your new home.'

The other brutes closed in and smirked.

Karl, panicked, thought it might help to lighten the situation. 'I guess you could build me one with some of the leftover stone from that tower.' Karl smiled, but it wasn't reciprocated. 'Too soon?'

Proster's face darkened and he raised his weapon. 'I'll show you what a real swing of a hammer looks like.' Karl braced himself.

'What's going on?' a familiar voice asked, and Karl's body relaxed.

Princess Sabrinia stood behind the brutes. Her kind face countered by her folded arms.

'Nothing, Princess.' Proster released Karl. 'We were on our way to rebuild the tower when we ran into our friend. I was showing him the proper technique for striking spikes through wood.'

She nodded. 'Well, good luck rebuilding.'

Proster's irritated gaze rested on her a moment too long. He reluctantly bowed his head and then stomped away. His fellow brutes followed.

'Are you okay, Karl?' Sabrinia held his wrist.

'I am now. Thanks for getting me work with them. I'm sorry it didn't come to anything.'

She waved his apology away. 'We'll find the right thing one day.' She pulled at her dress, averting Karl's gaze. 'Are you busy?'

Karl shrugged. 'I was going to sit in my room and stare at the bricks like I do most nights, so yes.'

She smiled. 'Walk with me then.'

They left the cemetery, passing the pile of rubble that would have been a glorious tower had Karl not touched it.

He appreciated Sabrinia's company and her protection. Karl had been lucky enough to spend time with her when they were younger, when King Sastin took him in as a baby. Now, she was always busy being a princess and he was busy being Karl.

She seemed bothered. 'Is everything okay?' Karl asked.

Sabrinia took a moment to answer. 'Yes, fine.' She scratched her nose. 'You know, it would do you good to venture outside of Flowforn one day. The world is far more exciting than staring at bricks, and you'd find it invigorating.'

'How so?' Karl asked, failing to see how anything new could be good.

Sabrinia's eyes lit up. 'There are endless discoveries. Before Father shut the world away, we would visit other kingdoms. Once, we got lost, but came to a cliff with a stunning view over Flowfornia and beyond. The way the sunset empowered everything it touched made me feel a warmth that nothing within these four walls could recreate. I felt so insignificant that I realised I'm a tiny part of something so much bigger and incredible.' She clasped her hands. 'I can convince Father to let you out.'

Karl swallowed. She probably didn't realise that a big part of her joy was sharing that moment with a parent, a sensation he would never feel. 'That sounds great. But, I'm fine with the sun setting over these walls. At least in here I know the dangers. I've no need for discoveries. I know what I'm part of. Besides, King Sastin made all this so we never have to leave.'

He caught the disappointment in her eyes. 'My father's grief made him want to never have to rely on other kingdoms, and I understand that. But, if you don't look beyond these four walls, then you'll only ever know who you are within them.'

He nodded. 'I guess,' he said, wanting to move the conversation on, but not sure how.

They entered the quiet gardens, where bright blue and white vines choked imposing columns, and water flowed from the symmetrical fountains sculpted in the shape of children of no significance. King Sastin's statue stood in the middle, a reminder of the kind of person Karl could never be – someone with purpose.

Sabrinia looked at Karl but then gazed at her feet.

'What? You looked like you were about to say something,' Karl said.

'No, no...' She bit her lip. 'Do you want to play three-word monster slayer?'

'Aren't we a bit too old for that?'

'That's the point. It's nice to do some of the things that used to make us happy.' A small smile broke through her concerned expression.

'Before you had to do all the things a princess does?' Karl asked.

Sabrinia huffed. 'Exactly. There's only so much smiling and waving at people you can do before you lose any sense of joy.'

Karl chuckled. 'Okay.' He took a few steps ahead and then turned around. 'Leaf. Fire. And... donkey-sloth.'

Sabrinia tapped her fingers against the side of her head. 'This is a tricky one.'

'I'm happy to help if it's too much of a struggle.' He smirked.

She tutted. 'Got it! There's an evil donkey-sloth and it travels on a giant, flying leaf to swoop down and bite people. The only way to defeat it is to set the leaf on fire, as the creature can't move independently.' She smiled.

'Very good,' Karl said. 'Okay, give me my three.' He was excited to impress her with the monster he could come up with the first two words, and the solution to defeat it with the third.

She stopped and sat on a stone bench. She looked at him as though she was about to apologise for something. 'To be truthful, Karl, I came to tell you something. I'm just not sure how.' She patted the empty space on the bench next to her.

Karl sat, worried. 'Nobody ever struggles to give good news, so if it is something bad, don't tell me. Let whatever it is just happen. That way I don't have to spend time thinking about it.'

She smiled sympathetically and took his hand in hers.

Karl swallowed, despite the comfort of her touch. 'Definitely bad news.'

She chuckled and her eyes met his, but before she could speak, Lombus rushed up to them panting, his face pale. 'Princess. We… we need… talk.'

Sabrinia hung her head, frustrated. 'Hold on, Karl. I probably waved too aggressively at someone so now must write a letter of apology.'

Karl smiled at her.

Lombus walked her far enough away that Karl couldn't hear them.

Karl stared at his tatty shoes, trying to convince himself that the news might be something between good and bad. Maybe it was average, nothing-to-be-worried-about news. He peeled sticky beans from the inside of his pocket and ate them.

Sabrinia wrapped her arms around Lombus and her raw, haunting scream ripped through the quiet garden. Her pain pierced through Karl right to his bones.

ASHES UPON ASHES

King Sastin was dead.

The king who had taken Karl into Flowforn when he was fifty sunsets old and parentless, was dead.

Karl dragged himself into the crowded courtyard as the last of the ten bells of goodbye rang through the kingdom.

Everyone from Flowforn must have been there. The collective sadness hung over everything, from the walls lined with statues of former kings, to the waste well in the middle of the courtyard. For the first time in Karl's life, the flames above Flowforn Arch did not burn.

Karl struggled to understand that King Sastin was definitely dead. He possessed so many strengths: his kindness, his approachable authority, and his vision for a contained world where people had free will. But, he had one great weakness – love.

He loved fish.

He would spend a large part of his day by the stream scooping fish into his mouth. However, he got bored by the selection, and had heard of a special fish that a pig-shark would swallow whole. The fish would then pass through the pig-shark's intestines completely intact, but the intestinal fluids would add a tangy flavour to it, making it extra delicious.

Turned out it was poisonous.

What a miserable way to die.

Karl wanted to get closer to Sabrinia, but spotted Proster across the crowd so stopped by a barrel. One funeral was enough.

Sabrinia's tears fell onto her black mourning armour. She stared at King Sastin's straw-covered body, which rested in a pit under his statue.

Sabrinia's skinny aide, Questions, pulled on her loose-fitting, shabby clothes that matched her messy red hair. She placed the last of the straw on the king's torso, followed by three clear stones in a line from his chest to his waist. They represented peace, light, and spirit. She hugged Sabrinia and Lombus, then pushed the creaking straw-filled wheelbarrow towards the alleys.

Lombus handed Sabrinia a torch.

She dropped it into the hole. The sparkle in her eyes dwindled behind fear, sadness, and the reflection of the flames devouring her father.

A Flowfornian band played their violins. That was it, a life dedicated to improving the world reduced to ash in the time it took to play a few tunes.

'It would have touched him to know how much you all loved him.' Sabrinia's eyes followed the rising smoke. 'And at least now Mother's soul no longer needs to wander Hastovia alone.'

'Are you okay, Karl?' Questions had returned from the alleys and stood next to him.

'Sort of.' He was glad to have someone to talk to.

'Are you sad?'

Karl swallowed. 'King Sastin and Sabrinia have always been good to me.'

Questions scratched her arm. 'Does death make you think of your parents?'

Karl nodded. 'It's strange. I didn't think you could miss people you've never met, but I do.' He sighed.

'Why do you think people get sad?' Questions asked.

'I don't know.' He wished he did.

'Is sadness an invisible monster?'

'I don't know.' Karl kept his focus on Sabrinia.

'Is it in clouds?'

'I have no idea.' He bit his lip, hoping she'd stop asking questions now. A momentary silence suggested she might.

'Why don't you know?' she asked.

Karl huffed. Questions' tribe, the Inquisos, were honest and had kind hearts, but they could only ask questions, and they liked to ask lots of them, about everything.

He stared ahead, bracing himself for another question, but hoping it would not arrive.

Distant, up-tempo drum and horn music disrupted the crackling of flames and halted the violins. The tap, tap, tap pierced by intermittent toots turned mourners towards Flowforn Arch to seek the source.

'Probably just more condolence gifts being delivered,' Sabrinia said. 'They'll leave them at the gate.'

Karl gazed towards the arch but saw nothing of note.

'Father would want us to not dwell on his death…' Sabrinia's words battled the drums and horns, now accompanied by marching. She raised her voice. 'He would want—'

'Quiet!' A whiny, nasal voice interrupted. The drum and horn music stopped.

The voice didn't match the cloaked man dominating the arch. Muscles fought for space on his body and a layer of rock covered his fists as though sculpted around them.

Some mourners scurried off.

Questions turned to Karl. 'Are we in trouble?'

'I hope not. But his face looks like it's never met a smile.'

The crowd backed away from the visitors.

The man stood around eight feet tall, twice the size of the four drum-and-horn-wielding creatures next to him. Behind them, there must have been near a hundred creatures armed with spears, spiked clubs and steel swords. Some sat on horned wolves that scanned the Flowfornians for their next meal. They all had grey, wrinkly skin, beady eyes and wore shoddy leather armour. They had different sized noses and ears, the only things to tell them apart.

Karl's heart pounded. Was this what an invasion looked like? He watched Sabrinia, still focused on her father while Flowfornians mumbled among themselves.

'Quiet!' the voice repeated, and from behind the large man a short cross between a man and a hawk emerged.

Karl raised an eyebrow. The feathery thing had a human's torso and limbs, but a hawk's head and wings. It had talons for feet and claws for hands. It was as though someone had taken a man and a hawk and smashed them together, creating a mess of a creature.

'Is anyone going to open this?' The creature tapped his shiny, silver axe against the iron bars. He stroked his copper-plated armour, etched with the sigil of whatever creature he was, using its talons to crush a skull.

Sabrinia remained fixated on the king. 'We're not taking visitors until tomorrow. Now if you don't mind, I'd like to finish watching my father become ash.'

The creature looked to the large man and nodded.

The large man punched through the iron bars as though they were no tougher than twigs.

Karl's jaw dropped. The crowd backed towards the alleys.

'I think you should go and hide,' Karl told Questions, partly being considerate, but mainly wanting to avoid any more questions.

'But what about Sabrinia?'

'She'd want you to be safe, and it's better you look after others.'

Questions nodded at Karl and snuck away with other Flowfornians.

The feathered creature strutted towards Sabrinia as though the world had stopped to watch him.

Sabrinia refused to acknowledge him.

Lombus stood in front of her and folded his arms.

The creature coughed. 'I'm sure you've all heard of me. I'm—' he wheezed, struggling to breathe. 'The Supreme Man-Hawk, Arazod.' He looked over the crowd, but nobody reacted. 'No? What about my axe? You must have heard of the Soul Bleeder? The sharpest axe in all of Hastovia?'

Still no reaction.

'I go from kingdom to kingdom, destroying things? For fun!'

Still nothing.

Sabrinia lifted her head and turned to Arazod. 'I know who you, your large associate, Lord Ragnus, and your army of Fools are. If you want to destroy things please return tomorrow. Or consider not destroying us. We're no threat to anyone.'

Arazod's beak curled into a smug smirk. 'Yes, but, you might become a threat tomorrow.'

Sabrinia shook her head. 'We won't. Please be on your way.' She turned back to her father.

Arazod stared at the back of her head. He coughed and opened one of his wings. The other twitched as though wounded. 'You say you won't, but I can't guarantee that. So, I have to act in self defence.'

Arazod swung his axe and sliced off a Flowfornian man's arm.

Karl retched.

Flowfornians screamed and fled.

'Fools, kill them all!' Arazod commanded.

Yellow flickered in each of the Fools' eyes. Fools and horned wolves chased the innocent.

'Stop!' Sabrinia demanded.

A wolf drove its horn through a baker's back.

A Fool slashed a woman's stomach.

Lord Ragnus stepped forward, playing with a green horn on his necklace, no doubt a trophy from an unfortunate creature.

Lombus charged at Lord Ragnus. 'For my king!'

Lord Ragnus punched him. The crack sickened Karl and he turned away from the dented mess that was once Lombus' head.

'Lombus!' Sabrinia's face turned pale.

Lord Ragnus brushed his bloody knuckles on his trousers as though denting heads was as normal as eating.

Karl wanted to help Sabrinia, but took cover behind a tipped-over barrel and watched.

'Please stop!' Sabrinia pleaded. 'We'll give you gold!'

Arazod was too busy inhaling the battle to listen.

A Fool stomped on the back of a man's neck.

'Food. Have it all,' Sabrinia offered.

Arazod kicked pebbles into a fleeing Flowfornian's face.

'I'll marry you!' Sabrinia blurted.

Karl wondered if he was hearing correctly.

'What?' Arazod replied.

'What if I marry you?' she repeated.

Arazod turned to Lord Ragnus. 'Is she doing that witchcraft thing I keep hearing about?'

Lord Ragnus stared Sabrinia down.

She stepped closer to Arazod. 'You go from kingdom to kingdom, burning and killing. Yet that obviously isn't satisfying whatever urge you have. What if I marry you? What if you stay here, and instead of destroying as a tyrant, you rule, and build, and become an eternally *loved* king?' She pointed to the ashes of her father. 'In life, and death.'

Arazod's eyes narrowed.

Karl studied the situation. There was a clear run to the alleys and back to his hut, but he had to help Sabrinia like she had always helped him.

He could leap over the well. Sure, he'd never jumped half that distance, but that didn't mean it was impossible. He could land behind Arazod, then threaten to snap his neck unless they all left.

Maybe this was his moment; the moment he would do something worthy and be remembered and accepted by other Flowfornians. Maybe that's why he was bad at so many things. Everything he had failed at, that long list including baker, builder, and jester. They were all just stepping stones towards this great moment. His moment of heroism.

A warm energy filled Karl's body. He stepped out of hiding, puffed out his chest, clenched his fists and steadied himself. 'Right—'

The butt of a spear smacked the back of his head. He slumped over the well, facing the murky waste. Blood warmed his neck.

He lifted his throbbing head towards a blurry Sabrinia. On the well tiles, the shadow of the Fool's long nose and its spear were about to come down on his worthless existence. He'd never know what Sabrinia had wanted to tell him. His life flashed before his eyes, mostly images of people disappointedly shaking their heads at him.

Sabrinia opened her palms. 'Maybe a different approach would make being a tyrant more fun.'

Arazod raised an arm. 'Fools, stop!' He pointed to Lord Ragnus' side.

Yellow flickered in their eyes. They stopped mid-destruction and returned to Lord Ragnus.

Karl's breathing slowed. The shadow moved away.

'I am a bit—' Arazod gasped, 'sick of dragging all these items around.' He gestured to carts full of supplies. 'And since I turned thirty it takes longer to recover my energy from conquering.'

Sabrinia nodded. 'My one request is that you allow my people to live as they are, free within these walls.'

Arazod laughed through a wheeze. 'You're in no position to make requests, but very well, I'll rule the free people—' he gasped, 'apart from those who fought back. Lock them up!' Arazod commanded.

Yellow flickered in the Fools' eyes once more.

Arazod kicked up pebbles and clapped. 'I'm the King of Flowforn! Now kneel!'

Flowfornians followed Sabrinia's lead, bowed their heads and dropped to one knee.

A Fool grabbed Karl by the ankles and dragged him towards the dungeons. He looked around to see if anyone was joining him, but it seemed he was the only one foolish enough to have fought back.

Karl could now add hero to his list of failures.

IS AN IDIOT IN A CAGE STILL AN IDIOT?

'Let me out!' Karl groaned. He yanked against the iron chains that bound his limbs to the rank cell stones. He convinced himself that he could break free, but all he did was hurt his bony wrists.

'Sorry, Karl. Arazod's orders,' Hargon, the plump guard said, as he brushed his long red hair from his face. He dipped his paintbrush in a clay bowl and stroked it against the stone slab on his lap. 'Now, would you say your hair is more tree bark or filth brown?'

'I'd rather you didn't immortalise this moment,' Karl replied. 'It's been seven sunsets. When am I getting out of here?' He swallowed, tasting the stale bread that formed his daily meal.

'I have no idea.'

All Karl knew about the last seven sunsets was what Hargon had told him, which was that there had been many parties to celebrate Arazod's coronation. That meant one night for the actual event, then as was Flowfornian custom, they celebrated anything they could think of. They toasted the sun rising until it set. Then, they celebrated someone finding a hat that had been missing for three sunsets. Big news. To top it off, a bald bird simply being a bald bird inspired everyone to drink more. The bird didn't even bother to stick around for the party.

'Look, Hargon, they seem to have forgotten about me. So why not just let me out?'

'I'd love to, Karl. But if I let you out, I'll end up taking your place. If you were me, what would you do?'

'I'd free me, obviously.'

'Sorry. If one of us has to die...' Hargon shrugged and continued painting.

Karl hung his head.

Hargon shuffled. 'Ooh, actually, hold that disappointed look. Really complements the ambience of the piece.'

Karl sighed and pulled himself a few steps away from the wall, as far as the chains would allow. 'Hargon, we've known each other a very long time, right?'

Hargon nodded.

'Remember when we were little and you couldn't catch up with the thief who stole your music stick?'

'Yeah. I still hate him for that.'

'Remember who caught him?' Karl smiled, hopeful.

Hargon lifted his paintbrush and pointed it at Karl. 'He tripped over you because you were passed out on the ground from eating too many beans.' Hargon continued painting.

Karl cursed his luck and slumped back down.

Toot, toot, toot. Tap, tap, boom!

The drum and horn music invaded the dungeon.

Karl groaned. 'I'd rather someone jammed a hot sword in my ear.'

Hargon placed his paintbrushes and stone slab on a stool. He stood. 'All hail King Arazod, the Supreme Man-Hawk, and his future queen, Princess Sabrinia!' Hargon bowed his head to Sabrinia and stepped back on seeing Lord Ragnus.

Sabrinia gazed at the floor. Maybe she knew Karl was about to die.

Arazod spun his axe and turned his beak up at the surroundings. With a nod, Hargon opened the cell door.

'This is Karl.' Hargon turned to Karl. 'You should stand.'

Karl stood reluctantly. He waited for Arazod to speak, but the Man-Hawk stepped in and locked his beady, yellowy-green eyes on Karl and scratched axe lines into the stone floor.

Sabrinia and Hargon shrugged.

Karl remembered King Sastin's advice to him when he was a child. "Never show weakness to strangers, as they will think themselves above you." Karl took a breath. 'I'd do a twirl, but I'm a bit restricted.' Karl shook his chains. 'Maybe if you free—'

Arazod raised a claw to cut Karl off. Karl wanted to kick it, but that would be foolish, and he couldn't lift his foot that high.

'Karl.' Arazod studied him, probably for signs of fear. 'I'm here to give you a choice. You see, I've killed seven thousand and eighty-two beings of all sorts in my life.'

Karl considered asking Arazod what that had taught him, but thought better of it.

Arazod wheezed. 'And it can get boring, so now I toy with people. So—' Arazod gasped, 'I either kill you, or you choose someone, any Flowfornian to swap places with. All you have to do is watch me kill them and you can have your life back.'

Karl's face dropped.

'Look at that reaction!' Arazod turned to Sabrinia. 'His face! Great, isn't it? That's why I always do this in person.'

She nodded, humouring him. She seemed as lost as Karl was.

Hargon squeezed his eyes shut, likely regretting not freeing Karl and now hoping for mercy.

Karl thought about all those who disliked him. Pretty much everyone he had worked for. There was a long list of people he wouldn't miss, like Proster and his stupid brutes. Karl smiled, but then realised those people probably had families, loved ones, friends; people who would miss them if they died. Karl had nobody. He was an irrelevance to the world, good at nothing, good for nothing. His body weakened. 'Just kill me.'

The colour drained from Sabrinia's face.

Arazod's beak twitched. Confused, he turned to Lord Ragnus, then back to Karl. 'Very well. I sentence you to—' he wheezed, 'to… to… t… to transformation!' Arazod coughed in Karl's face and laughed.

Sabrinia's eyes widened.

Karl wiped his eyes and mouth. 'Isn't that a bit extreme?'

Arazod stopped laughing. He fanned out his one working wing. The other wing twitched. 'Are you calling me extreme?'

Hargon and Sabrinia glared at Karl.

He shrugged. 'Yes, because you're being extreme.'

Hargon and Sabrinia shook their heads.

'What? He is! All I did was try to defend the place I live in.'

Lord Ragnus stepped forward. 'He talks too much. Shall I just end him?'

Karl gazed at Lord Ragnus' stone fists. 'Transformation is fine.'

Arazod pointed a claw at Karl. 'Tonight, you shall be trans-formed into—' Arazod turned to his Conjurer Fool. A miniature spiked hat looked like it grew out of its head and an orb hung around its neck.

'A flying elephant,' it said.

'A flying… is that all you have?' Arazod asked. 'Always with the flying elephant. What happened to your other spells?'

'It's my old rotting brain. I've forgotten them. Or so I've been told.'

Lord Ragnus backhanded Conjurer Fool against the wall.

Arazod pointed at Karl. 'You shall be turned into a flying elephant, and fed to the Great Dragon!'

Karl imagined sharp teeth shredding the flesh off his bones. His eyes welled up and he gestured to Lord Ragnus. 'Actually, I'm happy for you to end me.'

Arazod smiled as if he was absorbing Karl's regret. 'You will be taken to the top of Mount Hastovia, and it'll probably be a moment before you're caught and devoured.'

'Wait,' Sabrinia pleaded. 'Why don't you think about it for a while?'

'Think about it?' Arazod scratched his axe handle against his head.

'Yes, think about it.'

'But, I've just made my decision.'

'And you might think of a better one. Sometimes waiting allows you to think of a far more interesting alternative. What's the rush?'

Arazod turned to Lord Ragnus. 'Is this normal?' He wheezed. 'Do other kings think about it?'

'Weak ones do,' Lord Ragnus stated.

'Kinder ones do, too,' Sabrinia countered. 'And it often helps them to be loved by their people.' Her hand brushed Arazod's arm.

His feathers fluttered. 'Hmm, I'll try it this once. How long am I supposed to think about it for?'

'I guess a day is normally good,' Sabrinia said.

'So be it. Tomorrow, I'll make a decision.'

Karl appreciated Sabrinia's attempt to help, but he knew he was dead, only now he had more time to dwell on it.

'Right. Enough of him.' Arazod spun on his talons and left the cell. His band started their tune and followed him out of the dungeon. The music faded along with Karl's hopes of seeing a twentieth year.

Sabrinia held her sympathetic gaze on Karl, and then she disappeared around the corner. Karl realised he would probably never see her again or find out what she had wanted to tell him. For a moment, among hundreds of scenarios, he had convinced himself she was going to ask him to spend more time with her, but why would she? He was worthless.

He closed his eyes, slipping into his final sleep before the eternal rest.

* * *

KARL AWOKE startled and he wondered if he had died. When the light of Sabrinia's lantern allowed his eyes to focus, the fear melted. 'Here to say goodbye?'

'In a way.' Sabrinia pulled a key from the pocket of her blue cloak.

Karl's body tingled with hope.

She unlocked his chains. 'You have to go. And whatever you do, never return.'

'But I've never left Flowforn. I'll die out there.' Karl's eyes shot around Sabrinia's face, hoping she'd recognise his desperation and offer another solution.

'Out there, you might die. In here, you will absolutely, definitely die in some bizarre and horrific way.' She pulled him to his feet. 'It's time to be brave.'

'That didn't go so well at the burial.' His head still throbbed.

Sabrinia turned to the cell door and listened. When there was only silence she checked the corridors. 'Hurry. Before Fools see us.' She grabbed his arm and led him to the stairs. 'When you get out of Flowforn, pick a direction and keep going. But not east, that just leads to desert.'

He swallowed. 'Okay.'

'Oh, and not west. Best to avoid the tribes.'

'So, south or north?'

'Actually, no. Not north. Lionbears have been spotted in the northeast so it's too risky.'

'Lionbears?' A lump formed in Karl's throat.

'I showed you a sketch of one when I returned from a visit to the northeast coast.'

'You mean that horrible devil of a monster with teeth like spikes and claws like scythes?'

'Yes. That's a Lionbear.'

'The beast more solid than a tree, with death in its eyes?'

'The sketch made it look a touch more menacing than it is, but yes.'

Karl welled up. 'I've spent my life calling them demon beasts.' His legs felt like sacks of stones.

'If you see one, just don't provoke it.' Sabrinia handed Karl a pouch of gold. 'I'm not sure what's going on in the south, but it's probably best you go that way. This gold will help, and when you're outside so will my dear, loyal parrot, Peezant.'

'Okay.' Karl knew Peezant. He regularly squawked outside his window to wake him up.

'Peezant has the message I wanted to give you before my father passed.'

Karl nodded. 'Can't I just use this gold to pay some unhappy Fools to turn against Arazod?'

Sabrinia shook her head. 'The Fools are born with a curse to do exactly what their leader says. I doubt he's told them to kill him if the right offer comes along.'

'Lord Ragnus?' Karl asked more out of hope than expectation.

Sabrinia raised an eyebrow.

Karl shook his head at the hopelessness. Despite never fitting in, this was the only place he had ever called home.

Sabrinia gave him a long hug, confirming their goodbye.

Karl squeezed her. 'I hope you find a way out of marrying that idiot.'

Sabrinia released the hug and her shoulders slumped. 'I have no choice. It's the only way to limit innocent deaths.'

It wasn't fair. 'This is Flowforn. The point is nobody has to do anything they don't want to.'

'Things don't always work out as planned, it seems.' The hopelessness in her voice made Karl's heart clench.

He couldn't believe she would have to bind her soul to Arazod's and be tormented by him in life and death. 'Thank you for everything you've done for me.'

She placed a hand on his shoulder. 'I'll miss you.'

'Will I ever see you again?' He knew it depended on him staying alive.

'Who knows?' She shrugged. 'Good luck, and be careful. It's a strange world out there.'

A SPECIAL KIND OF CLUELESS

Karl stood in the doorway to the courtyard and watched Sabrinia walk out of his life. Just like that, gone. She would only exist in his memory – one of the few good ones.

He sighed and stared across the courtyard at the arch to uncertainty.

Two Fools rolled a rock towards the alleys.

Karl waited until they passed and then sprinted to the arch. Fools approached from outside the castle, so Karl pressed his back against the cold stone wall next to the arch pier, trying to hide.

Karl stared at the statue of King Sastin, back in the courtyard. He cursed his luck at being born useless while King Sastin had entered the world heroic.

Karl poked his head out, but Arazod and Lord Ragnus stood in the arch. Karl waited, steadying his breath.

Lord Ragnus turned to Arazod. 'I think it's time you gave me command of the Fool army.'

'Soon,' Arazod replied. 'Once I get everything I–' he wheezed. 'I want.'

'And what is it that you want?' Lord Ragnus scanned the trees, probably seeking something to punch.

'I'll know when I have it.'

Lord Ragnus folded his arms. 'I need the Fools to help me to explore the land for relics and fighters.'

Arazod scratched his talons against the ground. 'Very well, Ragnus. Fools! Wherever you are, on one knee!'

Whether they were lifting stones, patrolling the alleys or eating, all the Fools Karl could see dropped to one knee.

'If I die, I want you all to kill yourselves,' Arazod ordered.

Their eyes flickered, accepting the command.

'What?' Lord Ragnus clenched his terrifying stone fists.

Arazod chuckled. 'And if Lord Ragnus kills me or threatens me, you will never serve him, and will make it your life's mission to kill him.'

'What are you doing?' Lord Ragnus complained.

'I enjoy our alliance. But I need to make sure there are no surprises.' Arazod kicked dirt at the Fools near him. 'Back to work.'

The Fools returned to their duties.

'It's nothing personal,' Arazod wheezed. 'I just want to make sure you remain properly motivated.' He shrugged. 'You'd do the same.'

Lord Ragnus scoffed. 'What if someone else kills you?'

'Well. If you don't want the Fools to kill themselves you'd better make sure nobody does.'

Lord Ragnus huffed and the pair turned to face the capital.

Karl pressed himself against the wall, waiting for his moment to flee.

Arazod coughed. 'I'll try this marriage and ruling thing, see what it's like. Then you can have them.'

Hargon had given Karl some background on Arazod while he was in the dungeon. His father, Supreme Man-Hawk Sarzo, was said to be brutal, but was loved by all Man-Hawks. Arazod seemed to be good at the conquering thing, but he had no love, just Lord Ragnus, who clearly wanted his Fools, and Fools who he ordered to follow him, so that didn't count.

'And when is the wedding?' Lord Ragnus pressed.

'It was meant to be yesterday, but Sabrinia—' he gasped, 'said it wasn't warm enough.'

'Then make her wear a scarf.'

'If it turns out this isn't what I want—' he coughed, 'we'll burn this place down, then find a new kingdom across the sea to destroy as part of a farewell conquering celebration. Then I'll keep some Fools and the rest will be yours.'

'Perfect.'

'Now, let's go and can kill that idiot, Karl.'

Karl's body tensed.

'Nothing like killing before bed to help one sleep soundly,' Lord Ragnus said.

'It is already tomorrow, so Sabrinia can't complain.' Arazod chuckled. 'And now I've thought about it, transformation is boring—' Arazod gasped, 'maybe I'll run my axe down his spine. Then you can choose stage two of death.'

Karl's chest tightened as if it were trying to crush his heart to protect him from a worse death.

'Marvellous,' Lord Ragnus replied. 'I've recently been enjoying punching the sides of people's heads with both fists. You get the crushing of the hard skull followed by the cushioning of the brain. It's quite a soothing sensation.'

Sickness rose in Karl's throat. As soon as he saw them enter the dungeons, he peered through the arch to the forest. Behind him was imprisonment and death, and in the wild was mystery and a high chance of death.

He waited for patrolling Fools to be far enough away, and then ran into the unknown.

The dull green and red-leaved trees of Flowforn Forest

twisted around each other, fighting for space. Any clear path was buried under a knot of roots bursting through the mud.

When Flowforn was far enough away, on top of its hill, Karl stopped. He rested his weary body against a broken tree, which had been snapped by the weight of two others wrestling to grow either side of it. He placed his hand on a dry, dull leaf. He'd noticed the colour in the leaves had faded into a ghostly grey as he progressed through the forest, as though a sickness had swept through it.

There was no way Sabrinia's situation would end well.

The Fools carried stones across the King's Eye towards a statue of Arazod being built on the King's Tower.

'Peezant!' A chubby, dirt-orange parrot squawked and swooped down. He pecked around in tree cavities for nothing in particular.

'Peezant. What's the message you have for me?' Karl asked.

Peezant stopped pecking. 'Feed me, I'm tired.'

'You've only flown down the hill. You probably just glided.'

'When tired, I'm hungry. When hungry, I'm not in the mood to deliver messages. Especially ones this important.'

'Fine.' Karl, annoyed, searched his surroundings. He collected a handful of rotten berries scattered on the dirt and stretched his palm out. 'Here, these look good for a parrot.'

Peezant flicked the berries out of Karl's hand with his wing. 'No! Gold feed,' he squawked.

'I need this gold to survive!'

The royal trumpet alarm sounded. Karl guessed that meant Arazod knew he had escaped and Fools would be hunting him.

Peezant licked his beak.

'Fine.' Karl gritted his teeth and shoved coins into Peezant's mouth to feel as if he'd achieved a minor victory. 'Speak.'

Peezant's voice changed into Sabrinia's. 'Karl, now that you are free, there's something you must know. After my mother died, for a while Father would write letters to her in the hope her soul would read them.'

Karl scratched his head.

'He would write to her about everything. The reason I wanted to speak to you, was because Father shared these letters with me recently. It's hard for me to say, but it turns out your parents weren't your parents, or even real people.'

'What?' Karl scrunched his eyebrows and sat up.

'One letter tells of Father finding you in a heap of Lionbear dung while visiting a burned-down village. He took you in and then sent word to all corners of Hastovia, offering gold to those who could claim you. But only thieves came forward. When they couldn't identify your name, which was embroidered on your sock, Father knew they were just after riches.'

'Is this the part where you tell me this is a joke, Peezant?'

Peezant pecked under his wing and took out a tiny, singed sock with Karl's name embroidered on it.

Karl held it in his hands and stared, possibilities of a past overwhelming him.

'When nobody legitimate came forward, Father made up your parents and their story, so that you never felt abandoned, and he made sure we looked after you until you were old enough to make your own way.'

Tears tickled Karl's eyes. He had spent so much time building up his supposed parents that they were very much real. He had imagined scenarios where they cooked beans together, had bow and arrow contests, and simply went for walks where they could be seen as a family, even if they weren't saying much and were wishing they could be elsewhere.

Peezant coughed and Sabrinia's voice broke. 'I think there's more to it, Karl. I believe you are from another world.'

Karl scoffed, struggling to process the first revelation. 'I think the grief is messing with her.' He tapped his head.

'You've always been a bit different. Struggling to do any kind of work, not fitting in...'

Karl folded his arms. 'That doesn't mean I'm from another world. It just means me and the world aren't yet aligned.'

'However, the main reason is your name has no roots in Hastovian history. I studied all the History Orbs on all the families, and there is nothing linking your name to any of them, not even to the animals. No other Karl's ever. Nothing.'

Karl stared ahead, feeling a sense of emptiness. No roots. No attachments.

Peezant's voice returned to normal. 'There's more,' he squawked.

Karl's shoulders slumped. 'Does there have to be?'

A Fool patrol left Flowforn, but thankfully walked in the opposite direction.

Karl stood. 'Maybe let's do this while moving.' He sped away from Flowforn.

Peezant perched on Karl's shoulder and his voice changed back to Sabrinia's. 'In Hastovian history, it has been documented that portals appeared between our world and another. A story tells of a great beast appearing from one. Father sent a group of mages to find and destroy the monster and the portals, but they must not have found them all, because you must have come from one. Father told me to talk to him once I had read the letters, but he died before I could. I'm certain he was going to mention this. You need to find any remaining portal and get home before Arazod catches you. Good luck, and be careful. It's a strange world out there.'

It had just gotten stranger.

Karl ran his thumb over the wool sock. He had felt worthless before, having a dead family and no place, but now he felt lower than worthless, whatever that was. He leaned against a tree and went over what he'd heard, while Peezant unhelpfully pecked his ear.

'I've got no parents, and I'm from another world?'

'Yep.'

'So my entire life has been a lie?'

'Yep.'

Karl sighed into his hands and his stomach cramped.

The royal trumpets invaded the air.

Karl gazed at his feathered companion. 'What do I do, Peezant?'

Then, like most living beings put under unwanted pressure, Peezant did what came naturally.

He flew away.

Karl stared as Peezant disappeared into the distance. He was alone.

WHAT ARE THE ALTERNATIVES?

Karl lay in the shade of a dead bush and closed his eyes. He had spent two sunsets lost in the forest, trying to understand everything. He would walk, and then a wave of grief would wash over him. He would sit to think, and then a gust of anger would smack him. Emotions surrounded his brain and took turns punching it. Could Sabrinia be sure? Was there any point in running? Why did his parents abandon him?

Sleep was the only time he was at peace, and with Fools hunting him, he didn't get much of that. Every noise shook him, from unknown creatures howling to his stomach rumbling for food.

Growing up in Flowforn, the only danger was figuring out what to do with his life. In the wild, the danger was the endless number of things that could end it.

Splat, splat.

Footsteps slapped against the wet mud. Karl forced his eyes open and listened.

Splat, splat.

He sat up and peeked through the twigs. Three armed Fools

searched for him. One had a dart shooter while the others wielded spears.

Karl scrambled behind an ashen tree, but the branches above him rustled. A purple ant the size of a barrel leapt from the branches and landed in front of him.

Karl's neck stiffened. It was as though this ant had eaten all of the other ants. Karl smiled at it and waved, hoping it would understand a friendly gesture.

It clicked violently and stood on its back legs, aiming its abdomen at Karl. Perhaps ants found smiling and waving offensive. Its body throbbed, stretched and cracked.

Karl ran.

'It's him!' a Fool yelled. A dart whistled past Karl's ear and chipped the side of a tree. 'It's ugly Karl. Must capture ugly Karl.'

The other two Fools repeated the order. 'Must capture ugly Karl.'

The ant's abdomen exploded. The force knocked Karl to the mud and the air abandoned his lungs. A dull purple mess burned the trees and singed Karl's trousers.

The ant, now tiny, burrowed into the dirt.

Karl took deep breaths, stood and then stumbled through the forest rubbing his sore chest. He refused to look back or dwell on being called ugly.

Another dart whizzed past his left arm. He came to a steep slope. He steadied himself, confident that if he ran down he would maintain his balance. His confidence was misplaced. He fell and rolled through the mud, hitting rocks and sticks, and making more noise than he should.

He took a moment to gather his strength, then noticed faint puffs of smoke rising above some jagged trees. Karl limped towards the source and found a tavern with a sign on a pole that read:

'This is a tavern. If you haven't already figured

that out by the generic tavern look of the place then you aren't welcome.'

He hoped for help, or a hiding place.

Karl pushed the poorly fitted wooden door open and scanned the dimly lit tavern for Fools.

Two old figures sat by a fireplace and drank from stone steins. One was a round man with a chaotic beard that didn't match the peace in his eyes, while the other, a slender man, appeared shrivelled, as though he had sat on that stool for years and consumed ale for every meal.

By the dirt-covered windows that shut out the forest, a large, cloaked beast sat slumped with his back to Karl.

A small stage suggested the tavern was once lively. No sign of that now.

The Bar Witch, wearing a long, ale-stained green tunic, stood behind the bar opposite the entrance. Messy black hair obscured her gaunt, pale face, and her unwelcoming eyes suggested she was in the wrong job.

'Please. You have to hide me,' Karl pleaded.

'I don't have to do anything.' Bar Witch crossed her arms. 'Especially for someone in your state.'

Karl noticed that his shabby trousers were torn and burnt, and his shirt was stained with sweat, filth, mud and tears he dared not tell anyone he had cried. 'Please. They want to kill me.'

'Stop babbling. Order a drink or get out,' Bar Witch said.

The cloaked beast dragged his feet into the toilet bucket stalls.

Muffled conversation came from outside.

The Fools.

Karl ran and cowered behind the bar.

'Oi! No coming back here!' Bar Witch nudged him away with her foot.

'Please. You can't let them find me. I've done nothing wrong.'

'I'll be the judge of that.' Bar Witch switched her attention to the door.

The Fools entered.

Karl squeezed himself between two ale barrels; the stale scent stung his nostrils. He peeked through a crack in the bar wood.

Without a word, the Fools searched the tavern. One of them ran its spear along the wall, scraping the wood. It pried the point in between planks to see if there was anything behind the wall.

Bar Witch smacked the bar. 'Oi! You here for something, or just trying to vandalise my tavern?'

The Fool with the dart shooter held up a parchment with a likeness of Karl sketched on it. 'We're looking for this man. His nose is a bit bigger.'

Another Fool used its spear to scratch an itch on its cheek, drawing blood but not noticing.

'And what do you want him for?' Bar Witch asked.

'He was rude to King Arazod.'

Bar Witch chuckled. 'Oh. What a terrible crime. Who would be stupid enough to be rude about that idiot?'

The Fool pointed to the parchment. 'Him. So has he been in here? There's gold in it for you.'

'Gold?' Bar Witch looked down.

Karl stretched out his palm and showed her three gold pieces.

'Lots of gold,' the Fool said.

Karl closed his fist and returned his pathetic offer to his pouch. Sweat dotted his forehead.

'Hmm. I could really use some gold,' Bar Witch said. 'It would help me give this place a bit of a lift. Might bring some business back in.'

Karl scanned for a weapon, but the only thing within reach was the tiny, hairy foot of a long-perished creature.

'So have you seen him?' the Fool asked.

'Sadly not,' Bar Witch replied.

Relief flooded Karl's body and he almost passed out.

'Frong?' Bar Witch asked the filthy-bearded one.

'No. Not seen anyone like that in a while,' Frong replied in a slow, thoughtful voice. 'What about you, Sags?' Frong rubbed his shrivelled companion's shoulder.

Sags grunted.

'That's a no from him too,' Frong said.

'Hmm.' The Fool looked at its fellow hunters, then back towards Bar Witch. 'If you do see him, stick him with this.' It took a dart from its belt and slammed it on the bar, above where Karl hid. 'It'll send him sleepy. Then tie him up, get word to Flowforn and we'll come back. King Arazod wants him alive.'

Karl wasn't sure if that was a good or a bad thing.

'Of course,' Bar Witch said.

The Fools turned to leave. 'Actually, must check everywhere.' The leader pointed at the wooden door to the toilet buckets.

'I wouldn't,' Bar Witch warned.

'Ha! I knew it. You're hiding him in there. Ooh, you tried to trick me, but no, no, no!'

The Fool pushed the door open.

'Fools!' a voice boomed.

'Run!' the Fool yelled.

The cloaked beast chased them out of the tavern.

Bar Witch kicked the barrels for Karl to come out.

'Thank you, thank you, thank you.' Karl stood.

'I didn't do it for you. This place used to be full of people to entertain before Arazod destroyed the villages around here. So you're lucky. He's the only person I like less than strangers.'

'Well, I'd like to give you something to show my appreciation.' Karl offered her the three gold coins, hoping it would buy him an ally.

'No. Clear off. I don't want you bringing more mess through my door.'

'Please, you have to let me stay. I don't know what I'm supposed to do out there.' He dreaded being back in the forest.

'Not my problem. Now go before we think about their reward.'

Karl hoped for understanding from Frong and Sags, but they turned away.

Karl made his way towards the door. He turned back, but they had already forgotten about him. He took a few more steps and looked back again, but they still didn't care. He pushed the door open.

'Hold on,' Frong said. 'I'd like to invite him to have a drink,' he told Bar Witch.

'Really? Why?' she asked.

'It's nice to have someone new to talk to.'

'Fine, but if he says one thing that's annoying, he's out.' She grabbed a cloth, wiped the bar and mumbled, 'Coming in here making demands, bringing chaos, stinking of mud.'

Karl offered Frong an appreciative smile. 'Thank you.'

'Our only rule is you have to tell us your story.' Frong pulled up a stool.

Karl told them everything. He hoped for sympathy, but mostly got laughter from Bar Witch, who grabbed a stool and joined them. Karl considered leaving out the bit about being found in Lionbear dung and being from another world, but thought he had nothing to lose. 'So, any of you have any idea where there might be a portal to another world?'

Sags grunted. Karl's lack of mastery over the languages left him thinking that response was as useful as a hat at the bottom of the sea.

'Any translators in the room?' Karl asked.

'He and me are the greatest adventurers in all of this land,' Frong said with pride.

Bar Witch laughed. 'You're the only adventurers!'

Frong raised a finger. 'Which, if you look in any rule book written on any topic, by definition, makes us the greatest.'

Karl thought he could win Bar Witch's approval. 'It looks like the greatest adventure you've had is to the bottom of an ale barrel.' He looked at her, but she simply spat at his feet and dipped her cup in the barrel of ale by the table.

'We're retired.' Frong looked at Sags, who exhaled. They touched foreheads and Frong grabbed the back of Sags' neck. 'To Marlens,' Frong said.

Sags grunted.

Karl was about to ask a question, but Bar Witch shook her head and leaned into him. 'Their third member died in a volcano accident so they hung up the adventures. Don't prod.'

Karl nodded, appreciating the kindness.

'As a two we're not so good, but when we had Marlens we were incredible. My strength, Sags' agility, and her potions and planning. She was one of the finest alchemists you could meet.' Frong lowered his head.

'I'm sorry,' Karl said.

Frong took a long swig of ale, then looked Karl in the eyes as though the next words would be important. 'But… as Sags was saying, there is a portal.'

Karl leaned forward. 'So, they've not all been sealed by mages?'

Frong chuckled. 'Have you ever known anyone, anywhere, unless it involved counting or spelling, to do anything perfectly? Even if it's nearly perfect, it's still not perfect, so there is still an error somewhere.'

'Mages sound pretty thorough, though.'

'Like everyone else they got tired, hungry, cranky. They were made to work every day and with no extra reward. Maybe they pictured going on a boat trip to another land and just wanted to finish the job so lied about it.'

'So you're saying—'

'If the stories are true, they did miss one.'

Karl's eyes widened, his heart filled with hope. 'Where do I find it?'

Sags grunted and Frong nodded in response. 'Information like that comes at a price.' Frong bit into his beard.

Karl huffed. 'Of course it does.' He slammed gold coins on the table. 'There.'

'No. Sags would be most grateful if you could scrape his feet.' Frong gestured to the disgusting task.

'You're joking?'

Sags shook his head, lifted his feet onto a stool and wiggled his toes. Little patches of hair broke out of cracked skin and there were bumps of different, gloomy colours. It was as if all the disease and filth from the world had congregated on this tiny surface.

'I'd do it, but my arms aren't what they used to be,' Frong said. 'And I can't stand to see him in pain.' He squeezed Sags' hand.

'I hate my life.' Karl shuffled up to Sags' feet. The thick, damp smell tickled his nose hairs and stung his eyes.

Frong reached behind himself and dragged a wooden box of implements in front of Karl, ranging from sharp knives to a shovel. 'Don't enjoy it too much.'

Karl thought about smashing the hammer through his own skull, when a shuffling outside caught everyone's attention.

The door opened and Karl had no chance of hiding. He grabbed the hammer, ready to defend himself, but terrified of doing so. He hoped it was the cloaked beast returning.

His heart relaxed.

Questions stood there in her shabby clothes and smiled at him. 'Am I saying hello, Karl?'

'Questions! Yes you are! Hello.' Karl smiled and placed the hammer down.

She approached Karl and held out a letter. 'Do you want this?'

'I guess I do.' He took it and unfolded it. 'It's from Princess Sabrinia.' He hoped it was good news and read:

'Dearest Karl, I've sent Questions to keep an eye on

*you and to help you on your quest. She's the person
I trust most, has read books on most of Hastovia
and she'll help you to find allies. She's amazing,
incredibly loyal, and has promised to do anything to
help you and to keep you safe.'*

Questions smiled, touched by the words.
Karl continued reading:

*'I'm sorry to have delivered the news the way I
did. I wish I could have done it in person. Good
luck, and be careful. It's a strange world out
there.'*

Karl's eyes welled up. Sabrinia's words made it feel as if she
was present in his life again.

'Is there anything I can help with?' Questions asked.

Karl rubbed his eyes. 'To be honest, I'm exhausted, and I could
really use someone to scrape this creature's feet in my place. I'm
sorry. I wouldn't normally ask.'

Questions took a fork from the box. She didn't complain
about the horror-drenched feet in front of her. She sat and
scraped.

'Are we going to go on an adventure, Karl?'

'Unfortunately.'

'Are we going to go on lots of adventures?'

'Ideally not.'

'Where are we going to go?'

'I don't know yet.'

'Why?'

Karl refused to answer, hoping she'd stop.

'Are we going to see the Dead Lands?'

Karl huffed. 'I'm not an adventure planner.'

Questions pulled some shreds of loose skin from Sags' foot. 'Why is your shirt so dirty, Karl?'

This was going to take a while…

* * *

THE ORIGIN OF QUESTIONS

All the Inquisos ever wanted was knowledge, acceptance, and love. They were puny, harmless people who lived in the tiny village of Inquiso, high on Mount Brohl in southernmost Flowfornia. Nobody ever bothered them, as there was nothing of note to see, nothing of value to steal and, most off-putting, it was far.

If anyone accidentally ended up in Inquiso, they would find themselves lost in a maze of innocent questioning that would dizzy them to the point of passing out or sometimes madness. On a list of destinations to visit, Inquiso didn't even make the list.

The cold season approached, and Questions' father, the High Inquiso, Quizmal, a wiry and affectionate man, asked people to prepare. The cold season in Inquiso was terrible, and it had grown colder over the last few years. Wind made the cold cling onto people like a net and would freeze them solid if they weren't wrapped up warm enough. The Inquisos had always managed by adding layers of wood to their homes, but this cold season, the Fools, under Arazod's father's rule, had spread their territories, destroying the woodland. Supreme Man-Hawk Sarzo wanted to see everything as he flew. To him, trees were a cover that needed removing.

Without the woodland, the Inquisos couldn't get the materials to repair their homes or light fires. Also, with the Fools roaming below they'd have to go further afield to find wood, increasing the risk of capture. Matters were made worse because by only talking in questions everything took twice as long.

Quizmal rang the Inquiso Bell, summoning everyone to the dining hut for a meeting. The winds already nipped at them.

'Quizzical, can you go and get enough wood to burn until the hot times return?' Quizmal ordered through a question.

'Shall I?' Quizzical asked, down on one knee to show his respect.

'Can you?'

'Would you like me to?'

'Will you go now?'

'Can I?'

This continued for nine sunsets, and the winds grew colder. The Inquisos historically lacked confidence, and thus could never make a statement. Nods and shakes of the head worked for general conversation, but not when it came to official orders. The laws could have benefited from a rewrite.

Quizzical and Quizmal were in a deadly spiral of questioning. You could look back through history orbs to find there was never a mention of an Inquiso making a statement. They thought Quizzy-bell once did, but it turned out to be a long coughing fit. She died.

Food supplies were low, and they were out of wood. Questions, at seven years old, could see what was coming and tried to help.

'Should we be finding supplies to protect us?' she asked.

'Can you get that wood, Quizzical?' Quizmal asked.

Quizzical remained on one knee and didn't respond. Questions nudged him and he fell to the floor, now an ice sculpture. It was too late. The Inquisos would perish. Most tribes and species fell to disease, invasion, or famine, but the Inquisos' death would come due to their inability to make a statement.

Questions loved her father dearly, and he loved her even more. He would do anything to protect her and give her the knowledge she craved. From old tales of monsters that roamed the land, to ancient foods that people once ate, Questions was never short of stories when her father was near. She wrote her favourites in her book called *Is This the Book of Tales?* so his words were always close. The tales were more a stream of questions than coherent stories, but Questions understood them. She often looked out across Flowfornia from the peaks, imagining other lives in Hastovia through the tales she'd heard.

As more Inquisos perished, Questions lay shivering in her hut. She feared she'd die before ever knowing a life outside of Inquiso.

Quizmal knelt beside her, his skin blue. Old age was already against him, and he complained about the chill creeping through his veins, closing in on his heart. He likened it to a fleet of ships approaching a small island from all sides to attack. It was just a matter of time.

'Do you know I love you, Questions?' Quizmal wrapped his arms around her.

She nodded. 'Are we going to die, Daddy?'

Quizmal looked into her eyes. 'Can you stay alive?' He'd obviously meant to say, 'Of course you won't die.' But that flaw struck again. No matter, Questions understood.

She nodded again. 'Can you not die too, please?'

Quizmal took the blanket from around his shoulders and covered Questions with it. He carried Questions to a part of the hut where the draft was weakest.

'Daddy, can you answer me, please?' Questions asked.

Smiling, he put Questions down in the corner. 'Can you wait a moment?'

He removed his cloak and threw it over Questions, ripping little eyeholes and a mouth hole for her. The wind beat against the hut.

Quizmal removed what clothes he had left and wrapped them

around Questions until she was a little ball of warmth. Only one of her hands, her eyes and mouth were visible.

'Do you promise me that when you find people you love, you will always look after them?' He often reminded her that there was nothing more powerful than loyalty and love in the world.

She touched his hand and blinked. 'Where are you going?'

Quizmal walked towards the hut entrance and stood there, blocking as much of the outside as he could. Questions knew what he was doing and tried to stand, but she was too heavy from all the clothes so could only roll around. She tried to call to him but couldn't. Quizmal stared out at his village, wide-eyed, defiant. The wind did not take his life. He gave it up to protect his daughter.

Questions cried and cried and then cried some more. The only thing keeping her going was that she didn't want her father's sacrifice to be for nothing. But the hunger, and the cold…

Powerful winds split sections of the hut, like an icy giant ripping wood from the ground and throwing it off the cliffs.

The wind carried her favourite books away. *Is This the Book of Tales?* shook and threatened to take flight. Questions was too stiff to move, but she couldn't let her father's words and, with them, his soul be carried away. She rocked, exhausted, until she rolled over. The winds tried to force the book through a stubborn plank wedged in the ground. She was close. Her tiny hand froze and the wind chilled her eyes. She stretched her fingers out. The plank left the floor, but she grabbed the book by its corner and smothered it to protect it.

The cold surrounded her and she closed her eyes, falling asleep on her father's precious stories.

Questions woke to the sound of marching and carriage wheels bumping on the ice-covered, rocky ground. Could she make a noise to get their attention? She tried to move, tried to force a sound, but her limbs were stiff and her lips bound by frost. All she could move was one eye. Could they hear her blink?

The wooden wheels cracking ice faded with the marching. Questions closed her one working eye for what she thought would be the final time.

Giggling filled her brain. Childish giggling. She thought she was slipping into a happy memory of her father, but the sound grew closer.

'Stop, Sabrinia!' boomed an authoritative voice.

A tiny girl, surely not much older than her, wrapped from head to toe in fur ran in. The girl saw Questions and stopped. Curious, she approached.

Questions was terrified, but Sabrinia smiled at her and she felt safe.

'Pa, I found a fat girl!'

'Leave her. She probably wants to die with her people,' King Sastin said. The thud of his boots broke the ice on the wooden remains.

He studied Questions and turned to Sabrinia. 'You know people outside of the castle have strange customs. The last thing we want is someone declaring war because in trying to help we misunderstood the situation.'

King Sastin took Sabrinia in his arms and walked her out of the hut, but she kicked free and ran back to Questions. 'No. We're taking her with us! Please, Pa.'

'But—'

'There's nobody left to declare war even if we break a custom.'

King Sastin huffed. 'Hard to refuse when you have a valid point. Guards!' he called out. 'Bring her with us.'

Questions sat in the carriage with Sabrinia and King Sastin all the way to Flowforn. She turned to look back at the peaks of Mount Brohl, once her home, now a frosty cemetery. She vowed to return one day, and to travel the world to finish writing *Is This the Book of Tales?* for her father.

Sabrinia gave Questions her furs and explained what everything was on the way to Flowforn. Questions blinked her responses at Sabrinia. She would have cried if she could. Sabrinia showed Questions the sort of kindness she had only felt from her father, and from that day forward Questions knew that no matter what, she would always do what Sabrinia asked...

* * *

... EVEN IF IT meant scraping the most disgusting feet in Hastovia.

Questions dug the fork into the crusts of filth. She dripped with sweat and her arms shook.

Karl paced, eating bread, his first familiar meal since he had fled Flowforn. 'She's been scraping long enough for you to give me information now.'

Frong nodded. 'Well—'

'What is all this stuff?' Questions blew flakes off Sags' feet. She took *Is This the Book of Tales?* from the leather pouch on her belt and prepared to note down the answer.

'Ah,' Frong clicked, excited to share. 'There's a lot of horse-mole hair. It has a life of its own so burrows into the skin and causes great pain. It's what gives him his limp. And that layer of crust is formed from all the different dirt in the land. That yellow one is sea dragon phlegm, over fourteen thousand and one hundred sunsets old.'

'What's that in years?' Questions asked.

'Oh, we don't do years. You see, we like to live sunset by sunset.' He pointed to Sags' feet. 'It's developed a sort of casing, as you can see. You've got to really dig in. It even blunted my sword so I used my teeth, but look what happened.' He showed her his yellow-brown, blunt teeth.

Questions grimaced.

'Does any of this relate to the portal?' Karl prodded.

'Youth, so impatient.' Frong took a long swig of his drink.

Karl closed his eyes to contain his frustration.

'You've given it a good go,' Frong said to Questions. 'Maybe we can do more scraping later.'

Sags retracted his foot and smiled at Questions.

Frong looked at Karl to get his attention. 'An angry, drunk knight once told me the story of a lady who used to live in Flowforn, roughly between seven and ten thousand sunsets ago, when Flowforn was not such a nice place to live.'

'Okay.' Karl hoped this backstory was relevant.

'Once, when King Sastin was off getting a hair and beard trim, the lady put on his crown and made orders to the servants. She told them to throw some left-over food at a passing carriage for a joke, thinking it was her friend inside.' Frong pulled his beard, distracted by a thought. 'You know, they should really have training schools for servants. They can do things like protocol, food handling—' Frong chuckled to himself. 'That's actually a great idea.'

Karl tapped his foot against the floorboards.

'Anyway. Being stupid, the servants followed these orders. Turned out the carriage contained a warlord on his way to discuss peace. Not the nicest of welcomes, and war was declared. To avoid it, Flowforn had to pay a lot of gold and resources, and King Sastin had to make an example of the lady by sentencing her to rot in a cell for all eternity.'

'King Sastin wouldn't have done that, he's a hero,' Karl said.

'This was when he was still learning what being a good king meant. Plus, being in a cell for all eternity sounds worse than it is. In those times all cells were pretty luxurious and had doors instead of bars, so at least there was privacy. People hadn't quite gotten the hang of punishment. You see, the first form of punishment was just to ignore someone so they felt like they didn't exist, then came the idea of imprisonment, followed by brutal—'

'The portal,' Karl said through gritted teeth. He would've choked Frong if it didn't mean he'd release information even slower. 'Please. Time is important.'

'Relax. We're there,' Frong assured Karl. 'One hundred and fifty-nine sunsets into her sentence, when the guards decided to go in and poke her for fun, she was completely gone. No sign of escape, no rotting corpse. Just gone. They decided to make Cell Two B a storage room and assumed that a spirit had devoured her. But if you ask me, that's where the mages missed a portal. You see, spirits always leave something behind to scare people, like a nail, a tooth, blood or some air that chills you when you pass through it, but there was nothing.'

'But you're not completely sure?'

'Flowforn castle is one of the few places we've not explored in Flowfornia. To be honest, when they turned us away we decided it wasn't worth our time.'

'Why did they turn you away?' Questions asked.

'We wanted to live there, in your free kingdom, but your great hero king rejected us because we aren't a conventional coupling.'

'But he welcomed everyone,' Karl said.

'Everyone who falls into a comfortable category. He was a king, so even if he wanted to, he still had to do what made his people happy, and there are a lot of people in this world who don't accept what we are.'

Sags squeezed Frong's thigh.

'That's why popular kings aren't always the best. They're scared to teach people new ways of thinking,' Frong said.

'I'm sorry,' Karl said.

Frong shrugged. 'We're happy living here. We did think about sneaking in and kissing in the middle of the courtyard for a challenge, but then, well...' Frong and Sags raised their drinks to Marlens once again. 'I'd bet my beard your portal is in that cell. It all makes sense.'

'So, more in the hope of a story being true, I have to go back to the place I've just escaped, where someone wants to, at the very least, horrifically torture me.'

'Sounds about right,' Frong said.

Bar Witch laughed at Karl's predicament.

'Thanks.' He needed an alternative, but he wasn't exactly presented with several options. 'You know what? I'll just live out my life here.'

Frong waved his finger. 'Surely the Fools will return. And what's to stop them being a bit more thorough next time?'

Karl huffed.

'Do you want to go home and find out who you really are?' Questions asked.

'I do. And I want to learn about my parents, who they really were. But if the cost is my life, I'll gladly wait until the price comes down.' Karl scratched his neck.

'When you think about it, the word "home" is misleading. It suggests a place, but in fact, home is the place where you feel most, at home,' Frong said.

Karl stared at him then looked at Bar Witch. 'Could you just magic me into the cell?'

'Nope.'

'But you're a witch.'

'I'm a *Bar* Witch. It's all party magic and showpieces, like animals.'

She rolled her eyes into the back of her head and a light blue glow pulsed through her veins. 'Beakesto!' Her breath heavy, she pulled a two-beaked crow out of her sleeve. It flew into the wall and fell to the floor. Bar Witch dabbed her forehead with a cloth. 'Sorry I can't help.' It seemed to take a lot out of her.

Karl hung his head.

Questions handed him a parchment.

'There's another engagement party in two nights.' Karl shook his head, amazed anything ever got done in Flowforn. 'But all are welcome.'

'You could sneak in.' Frong turned to Questions. 'You know, engagement parties used to be surprises, where people would find out on the day that a couple were to wed. Now they've become less special because everyone wants gifts. And it all began with the first king of Barma, a poor kingdom—'

'Nobody cares,' Karl said, before raising an apologetic hand to Frong. 'But you're right, they'll just come back. I could stay, and they might find me, or I can run and they might find me. Or I can go to the portal where they might find me, but at least there's a way out there.'

'That's the spirit,' Frong said. 'Often the hardest choice, the one you are most resistant to, carries the greatest reward.'

Karl nodded. 'I'll sneak into the castle. Work my way down to Cell Two B, trick a guard into giving me the keys and—' he banged the table. 'Vanish. Hopefully into my parents' home.' Despair became hope. In his mind he was already hugging his mother and father. The news that had previously been devastating now gave him hope. His real home and parents would be a fresh start. Maybe that's where the real Karl would emerge.

Questions' leg shook. 'Do you know that Arazod has a Fool holding the keys? Do you know it's stood by him at all times?'

Karl hung his head and squeezed his eyes shut. He needed a plan, but right now, he mostly needed to rest.

THE TEAM

The night sun's rays bounced off the grey leaves of the forest, and the chilly air gave the trees a smoke-like gloss.

Karl had whined for the sunset and a half they'd travelled, unable to formulate a plan and fighting scenarios in his mind that ended with his death.

'Do you hear that?' Questions asked.

Karl shook his head. 'It's just the wind blowing through the leaves.'

'Are you sure?'

'Yes. Like I was a moment ago, and the moment before that.'

Mount Hastovia's spikes crept over the horizon, the stars dancing above it. Questions stopped to open her *Is This the Book of Tales?* She took a quill from her inside pocket.

'Why are stars so bright, Karl?' She dipped the quill into a tiny bottle of ink.

'I don't know, Questions, but we should keep walking.'

'Why are they so still, Karl?'

Karl took a breath. 'I don't know, Questions, but please stop, I need to think.' They passed an abandoned cart, covered with patches of straw and stained with blood. Karl's eyes shot around the forest.

A twig snapped, accompanied by a thud and a smack.

'Okay, I heard that,' Karl said.

Questions walked towards the noise.

'No, Questions, move away from the noise.' He looked around for a weapon, but found only rocks that wouldn't do much.

'Did I promise Sabrinia I'd protect you?'

'Yes, but you never walk towards the scary noise. You run away from it. Away.'

Questions gasped and stiffened. She waved Karl over and he reluctantly joined her. His eyes widened and a metallic taste filled his mouth. At the bottom of a slope were thirteen Fools punching the beast from the tavern. Blood ran down the beast's sad face, dotting the cloak hanging over his grass-green tough frame.

'Shall we help the creature?' Questions whispered.

Karl tapped a knuckle against his teeth. He turned to look at Flowforn castle on the horizon. 'It's only us two, Questions. We don't stand a chance.' He grimaced. The Fools had the numbers, the weapons and the will to harm. 'I think we need to pick our battles. Come on.'

They turned, but a groan filled the air.

'Are they going to kill him?' Questions' eyes welled up. She clasped her hands together.

Karl turned back. One Fool took out its bow and arrow. The others tried to tie the bloodied, struggling beast to a tree, but he shook them off. His strength was incredible, but there were too many Fools and they eventually held him down. Karl tried to convince himself that the beast had the strength to overcome the odds, but he knew that wouldn't happen. The beast looked only slightly older than him.

Karl couldn't abandon a life. He'd be no better than those who had discarded him. He ran over to the cart and pushed it down the slope. 'Hopefully this works.'

The Fool drew its arm back to release the arrow that would end the beast's life, but the cart smashed into the Fool, knocking the shot wayward.

'It worked, Questions!'

The other Fools looked up the slope and saw Karl and Questions. One Fool took a parchment from its leather pouch. 'That's ugly Karl! Must capture ugly Karl!'

Their facial expressions shifted to dull and focused. It was as though they lost control of themselves. They left the beast and chased Karl.

Questions and Karl ran, weaving in and out of trees.

'They're after me, Questions. You run that way.' Karl pointed towards a stream, but she wouldn't go.

'Did I promise Sabrinia I'd protect you?'

'Stop saying that. Just go.'

She shook her head.

Karl's legs throbbed and he couldn't keep running. He stopped and turned in the hope that the Fools had given up, but they closed in.

'Must capture ugly Karl,' they repeated.

'Seriously, Questions, just go. Get over that tree.' A fallen tree, not far, bridged a river that the stream fed into.

She stood by his side and clenched her fists.

He appreciated her dedication, even if it would amount to both of them dying. 'I don't agree with your decision, but thank you.'

Ten Fools closed in, but the cloaked beast punched the tenth in the back. Then the ninth, eighth and seventh were all knocked out. He bashed his way through all of them and stood by Karl and Questions.

'Follow, before they recover.' The cloaked beast ran towards the tree bridging the banks of the river. Questions carefully walked across it.

'Go on,' he told Karl.

Karl stared at the violent water and froze.

The beast shoved him. 'Look forward and take it foot by foot.'

Karl turned back. The mob of Fools had recovered and was gaining ground.

'Hurry!' the beast said.

Karl's legs shook.

'Can you look at me?' Questions asked.

Karl took a breath.

The beast grabbed him. 'No time for fear.' He flung Karl across, his face crashing against the mud.

The beast joined them and pushed the tree into the river, stopping the Fools from following.

Karl rubbed his jaw. 'You could've warned me.' He noticed all thirteen Fools stood on the opposite riverbank staring at him.

'Must capture ugly Karl,' one said. It stepped into the water and was swept away.

'What are they doing?' Questions asked.

Karl caught his breath. 'They're cursed to follow orders, and it seems that when they can identify me, catching me is all that matters.'

Another Fool walked into the water.

'Stop!' Karl yelled, sad to see the loss of life.

Another Fool with tears in its eyes walked forward as though knowing it would die, but unable to stop itself. 'Must capture ugly Karl.' It walked through the river until it was neck deep. Its eyes locked on Karl. The water consumed it.

'Good…' the beast said. He hung his head as though disappointed with himself for saying it.

The Fool with the dart shooter took aim.

'Let's go,' Karl said.

Away from the river, they rested under a tree with Flowforn

in full view. Questions studied her book, and then grabbed a plant with circular leaves. She squeezed a gloopy liquid from a leaf, directly onto the beast's wound.

'Thank you for saving me,' the beast said.

'Thank you for saving us.' Karl stared at the soil, angry that living things had died because of him. How could Arazod discard life so thoughtlessly?

'I'm Oaf.' The cloaked beast extended his huge hand.

Questions shook it and smiled. 'Am I Questions?'

'I don't know,' Oaf answered.

'She is,' Karl said. 'She's from the Inquiso tribe. They can only speak in questions.'

Oaf nodded. 'Well then, nice to meet you, Questions.'

'And I'm Karl.' He shook Oaf's hand. 'I'm trying to find out what tribe I'm from.' He half-smiled.

'Why are they so desperate to catch you?'

'Because I escaped before Arazod and Lord Ragnus could kill me.'

'Lord Ragnus?' Oaf's voice hardened, and in his brown eyes Karl saw a sea of sadness, with more turbulent waters than his own.

'Yes. Overly aggressive. Seems to have an issue with smiles.'

'Where is he?' Oaf asked.

'In that castle over there.' Karl pointed towards Flowforn.

'He destroyed my people. I'm going to become the first Oaf to ever kill by snapping him in half.'

Karl swallowed. 'I'm… that's awful.'

Questions scratched her arm. 'Am I sorry, too?'

'Thanks.' Oaf stared at Flowforn. 'I'm coming with you.'

Karl stood. 'Actually, I was going to sneak in. That's a bit tricky with a creature as large as yourself.'

Oaf frowned.

'Is a team a good thing?' Questions smiled at Oaf.

Oaf nodded. 'And how do you expect to sneak in the castle with all the Fools trying to catch you? You'll need my help.'

Karl huffed. They had a point, and Oaf's strength was something unique. Also, Oaf was the last of his kind, and so was Questions, and Karl didn't know what his kind was, so it seemed like a good fit.

Karl nodded. 'Looks like we're a team.'

THERE'S GOOD IN EVERYONE

$\mathcal{T}$he smoky smell of fire-cooked meats blew through the courtyard. Friends and enemies united under one common joy – free food and wine. However, the buzz Sabrinia was used to on such an occasion was non-existent. Instead of relaxing, people whispered and watched Arazod in case he erupted into a fury for no reason.

A circle of Fools surrounded Arazod's table, preventing anyone from getting too close to him, Sabrinia, and the Fool with the keys on its belt.

Sabrinia noticed Fools guarding a structure covered by a huge silk sheet near the wall. She imagined it was a giant lava pit for Arazod to push people into, or a cage with some violent creature waiting to be released onto the innocent. Either of those sounded likely.

Fools played their dull horns, providing an unpleasant, tinny soundtrack to the evening, while Lord Ragnus sat on a hunched over Cyclops, keeping watch by the alley to the gardens.

Arazod stared at Sabrinia with the tenderness of a predator. 'When you are my bride—' He coughed. 'You will have to wear less revealing outfits. I want nobody else to set eyes upon you.' Arazod wheezed.

Sabrinia blinked to mask her frustration at being stuck in an eternal cycle of wheezing.

'In fact, maybe I'll just scratch everyone's eyes out.' Arazod laughed.

Sabrinia covered the top of her low-cut dress with her silk scarf. 'Don't you think that's a bit...'

Arazod's eyes narrowed.

'That it's a bit too much work for you?' she finished. She tried to read his reactions, but he was so strange, a tyrant with child-like tendencies, desperate for approval.

'Good point.' Arazod glanced at a chef. The chef hurried to the kitchen.

The circle of Fools opened. A Fool on a horned wolf rode through, dragging a rope-bound prisoner with a grey sack over his head. 'I found him, Supreme Man-Hawk,' the Fool said.

A lump formed in Sabrinia's throat.

'Show me,' Arazod commanded.

Sabrinia wasn't sure whether to open or close her eyes, so she settled on a squint.

The Fool lifted the grey sack. The gagged man only looked like Karl. Sabrinia's breathing calmed, but now she worried for the new victim.

'Nope. Not ugly enough,' Arazod groaned. 'End him.'

The man pleaded through his gag.

'Wait!' Sabrinia said. 'He's done no wrong.'

'But he's annoyed me by not being Karl. Surely that is something wrong?' Arazod said.

Such muddled logic. 'If you kill people for not doing anything, then they won't be as obedient. They will think there is no point, because they could die at any moment.' She watched him, his mind turning.

Arazod tapped his claws on the table. 'Very well. Get him out of—' he wheezed. 'My sight. But no killing.'

The Fool nodded and took the man away.

'Thank you.' Sabrinia smiled. 'Why is it you are so eager to kill Karl? He'll likely die in the wild anyway.'

Arazod's beak twitched. 'Of the many prisoners I've given the choice to, he's the only one to not save himself.'

Sabrinia scratched her arm, proud of her friend.

'My world has no place for people like him.'

Good people, Sabrinia thought. 'And what world is it you want to create?'

Arazod pulled a feather out of his neck. 'I plan to make sure peace is maintained, as that is what my future bride would like, no?' Arazod smiled.

'That's good to hear... my dear. And one of the reasons our marriage is so important. A representation of peace.'

'As well as... love.' Arazod scratched the feathers under his chin.

'Yes. Of course. Love.' Sabrinia politely smiled. She hoped she could trick herself into at least liking him. Despite his thirst for violence, he did, when prompted, show mercy. Perhaps there was hope and being bound to him for eternity wouldn't be so awful. Perhaps love would calm him down and her people would be spared.

Perhaps...

OVERCOOKED PLAN

Karl, hiding in a bush, watched, baffled, as Oaf and Questions devised a plan to get through Flowforn Arch.

'Can we make a ladder out of these branches to climb the wall?' She held three pathetic branches.

'Or I can throw you and Karl over the wall, then you can both make a ladder, then sneak back out of the castle with the ladder, then we all climb back over.'

Karl stared at them, thinking he was better off on his own. 'I can't listen to any more of this nonsense. I'm just going to cover my face and walk in. After all, everyone is welcome, right?'

Oaf pointed to the spear-wielding Fools guarding the entrance.

'Look,' Oaf said. 'Let's watch their movements first.'

A woman with markings all over her arms and legs approached the Fools.

They crossed their spears. 'Gift.'

She bowed her head. 'I am Syla of Klesper. I bring these throwing daggers with golden handles forged of Klesperian gold.' She opened a golden box to show the Fools.

Just what Arazod needed, more things to kill people with.

The Fools took the box and stood aside.

Oaf turned to Karl and Questions. 'Okay, so we need a gift, then when they're looking at it, you can sneak in Karl. What can we offer them?'

'Do they want my socks?' Questions asked.

'I can give them a piece of my cloak.'

Karl zoned out as they debated more pointless items that would likely get them turned away. He gazed at the trees and spotted another purple ant. He left Questions and Oaf to their debate, unaware he had gone, and stood beneath the ant.

It dropped down and stared at him, so he pulled his collar over his face and ran towards Flowforn Arch and it followed.

'Halt. Gift,' the Fools said, crossing spears.

Karl stopped and listened for the ant scurrying. 'Let me just check where I put it.' He patted himself down, pretending he'd misplaced an object.

'Show your face,' a Fool commanded.

'Found the gift.' Karl dropped his collar and leapt aside as the ant's abdomen exploded and purple mess covered the Fools.

'My eyes!' one screamed, while the other was knocked back into the wall.

Karl rushed through the arch, passing the bald woman who had gifted the daggers. She eyed him suspiciously.

'Enjoy the party,' Karl said. He turned back to see Questions and Oaf stood over the unconscious Fool holding their offering – a leaf. He shook his head. 'Come on.'

They entered and stood out of sight, by several tied up carriages.

'What do we do now?' Questions asked.

Oaf huffed. 'I can't go storming in there. Six to ten Fools I can handle. Maybe eleven. But any more than that and I'm done. I'm going to find somewhere and wait for Lord Ragnus to come to me.'

Karl frowned, sad to lose Oaf's strength, but he understood. 'Well, I guess this is goodbye. Thank you.'

Oaf removed his cloak, revealing his leather vest, trousers and a circular scar on his right shoulder. He handed the cloak to Karl. 'You'll need this.'

Karl held it and stared at it. 'It's a bit big, and the blood stains might draw more attention to me than my own face.'

Oaf chuckled. He took the cloak, turned it inside out and tore the bottom off it.

Karl put it on. 'Thanks.'

Questions smiled at Oaf.

He smiled back, turned and walked towards the gardens.

'What's the plan, Karl?' Questions asked.

'I have no idea.' He pulled the hood over his head and he and Questions crept closer to the celebrations, keeping to the wall.

'There they are.' Karl pointed to Arazod and Sabrinia, surrounded by Fools who only allowed other Fools and chefs with food and drink into their inner circle.

Arazod took a plate of dead rabbit-mice from the chef and handed it to the Fool with the keys.

The Fool tried the food and nodded.

Arazod took the plate to eat.

'I've got it,' Karl said. 'Next time a dish is delivered and the circle of Fools opens, I'll leap in, snatch the keys, leap out, and run.'

'Is that a terrible plan?' Questions asked.

'Well, yes. Have you got a better one?'

She smiled. 'Can we make a big stick? Can we use it to reach over the circle of Fools? Can we snatch the keys with it?'

Karl stared at her. 'How have you come up with a plan that's worse than mine?' He thought for a moment, but had no idea what to do. Then he looked at Sabrinia and it came to him. 'I've got it. I need to borrow your quill.'

* * *

KARL AND QUESTIONS stood among the crowd, close enough to see Sabrinia, but a safe distance away from any Fools.

'I hope this works,' Karl said. 'Otherwise I'm two gold down and out of ideas.'

'What did you write on the parchment?' Questions asked.

'Help.'

'What else?' Questions asked.

'Should there have been more?' Karl asked.

Questions bit her lip.

Karl sighed.

The muscly chef he had bribed delivered meals to Arazod and Sabrinia's table. 'Here you are, Supreme Man-Hawk.' She placed a bowl of lumpy liquid in front of him, and a plate of chicken-cow leg and Bickle leaf in front of Sabrinia. 'And for you, Princess.' She bowed her head and left.

The Fools closed the circle behind her.

'My favourite; tortured souls.' Arazod pointed at his bowl. 'When Lord Ragnus tortures something, this is what it becomes.'

Sabrinia looked into the bowl and didn't seem impressed. She stared at her chicken-cow leg. Karl hoped she would notice the parchment.

'Come on, come on, come on.' He clasped his hands together.

Sabrinia used her fork to lift the meat, paused for a moment and looked confused, almost disappointed at the lack of information. She scanned the courtyard. Karl waved but she couldn't see him. he edged closer to the circle. Questions reluctantly followed.

Arazod coughed. 'You see, Lord Ragnus can easily kill anything, but sometimes he feels people deserve torturing. Some victims do die from the agony, but the stronger ones, their souls twist from fighting back and they burst into these little soul puffs.' He wheezed and cackled.

Karl could tell that Sabrinia's smile was forced. He edged into her eyeline. She spotted him and her eyes widened, before she caught herself and continued nodding along to Arazod's nonsense.

Karl pointed to the Fool holding the keys and gestured keys to Sabrinia, but it looked like he was telling her to stab the Fool.

She looked appalled.

Arazod continued. 'It's their inner strength that ends up being their curse! He learned it from some tribe!' Arazod laughed and pointed to the bowl.

Questions joined Karl and gestured knocking, then unlocking and opening a door.

Sabrinia nodded, getting it.

Karl turned to Questions. 'That's what I did.'

Arazod waved at the tortured souls in the bowl. 'One of them is a king from across the sea, but I can't say his name to him or he'll turn back into his true self.' Arazod clapped, beside himself. 'They have no memory, although after a long time they remember tiny, insignificant details. They never last that long, though.'

Arazod ordered the Fool holding the keys to come and take the bowl, but as it touched the bowl, Sabrinia gestured, knocking it over.

'Oh no!' she said.

The bowl smashed and tortured souls scurried everywhere. Arazod leapt off his chair and stomped on them, but one got away, running towards the gardens.

Arazod turned to his Fool and scratched its face. 'You idiot!'

'It's my fault,' Sabrinia said to the Fool. 'I'm so sorry. Why don't you go and get Arazod another bowl?'

Karl turned to Questions. 'She's a genius.'

Arazod's beak twitched. 'Yes. Fine. Get the chefs to speed it up though.'

The Fool left the circle and rushed towards the kitchen. Karl and Questions followed it out of the crowd, but before it could get to the kitchen Karl stepped in front of it. 'Sorry.'

'For what?' The Fool asked.

He whacked it over the head with a rock, knocking it unconscious. He felt awful, but it had to be done.

He removed the keys from the Fool's belt and let himself hope he might escape. That he might find home.

'Thanks for everything, Questions,' Karl said. 'I hope you get to go on all those adventures.'

She smiled.

Karl crept through the crowd, keeping his hood down. He stood in front of the administration building doorway and noticed a parchment of himself stuck to the wall. It offered a reward of fifty gold coins for his capture.

He had to look back at Sabrinia's table and he caught her eye. He smiled, a mixture of relief, thanks, and sadness that their lives were on different paths.

She smiled back, then looked down.

Karl spotted the woman from the entrance, Syla, staring at him. He turned and rushed into the dungeons.

A TORTURED SOUL

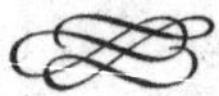

Oaf pulled the iron garden gate back and forth. His breathing matched the movement and the creaking soothed him. He was calm; ready for revenge.

In the middle of the garden was a recently constructed statue of Arazod wrestling a dragon. The four imposing columns around it gave the garden a fake, grand atmosphere, and nothing flowed from the symmetrical water features of children.

Oaf didn't care for it, or for anything he'd seen in Flowforn. Nothing beat the sand and sea air of his birthplace, Reech.

Laughter burst out of an alley. Oaf clenched his fists and crept over.

'Brilliant!' a drunken woman slurred to her small, hairy husband.

The man spat on the ground. 'For all his frowning, that Lord Ragnus must have a good sense of humour to have brought this with him.'

They laughed at a sculpture of a grinning cat riding a dragon, made from purple-black rock. Oaf's eyes widened and a sick feeling filled his throat…

* * *

THE FALL OF THE OAF

On the west coast of Flowfornia, where white, sandy beaches were pimpled with purple-black, shiny rocks, was the village of Reech. The rocks were believed to be chunks of an even bigger, magical rock that had fallen to Hastovia from the sky. That's why they called them the sky rocks of Reech.

Eighteen Oafs inhabited the beach village, which was strange, as they couldn't swim, so you'd think they'd get as far away from the water as possible. But no, they loved the rocks of Reech too much and passion came before sense. You see, while the Oafs were big, brutish creatures, those big brutish hands didn't exist to destroy. They existed to create. To sculpt.

One of the most obvious characteristics of the Oaf was that they all looked the same. Brown eyes, grass-green solid frames and no hair. The differences were only in size, and each Oaf had a unique feature to tell it apart from another.

They would pound away at rocks for many sunsets. Smash, smash, smash to get the shape. Scratch, scratch, scratch the detail. Sculptures of kings and queens so perfect they had more of an aura than the real ones. Octo-eagles so detailed you'd think a live one was about to burst out of its rock shell and whip you with its feathery tentacles. Weapons, buildings, boats, dragon-scorpions and meals; the Oafs sculpted anything that came to mind.

Hundreds of pieces of rock art surrounded ten sculpted rock huts, each elevated on four rock pillars. The Oafs loved to look down at their creations and out to sea. To the unfamiliar eye, Reech looked intimidating and haunting, but to those who knew, Reech was beautiful. A village sculpted with love.

Cecil was only eleven and not yet ready to sculpt, but one of his great joys was watching his mother, Boofa, craft the most magical pieces. Maybe it was because she was his mum, but he felt as if the gods let a bit of themselves flow through her and into the sculptures.

As the years passed, quiet little Reech became busy little Reech. Travellers from all over Hastovia came to look at the sculptures. Some loved what they saw. Some feared what they saw. But always, every single time, someone wanted to buy one particular sculpture that they considered to be Boofa's finest work – The Charmer; a grinning cat riding a dragon.

Boofa turned to Cecil. 'We've sculpted dragon-scorpions and not missed a scale, hair on the legs, or point of the tooth. We've sculpted castles where you can see the people in the windows. We've even sculpted strange vessels with flames shooting out of them that we jokingly say will propel us into the sky one day. But no, everyone goes crazy for the sculpture of the grinning cat on a dragon that we made in half a sunset when we ate too many rotten berries and got fuzzy.' She laughed at the ridiculousness.

Cecil smiled back. He was happy if his mum was.

'Oh well. I guess art is subjective.' Boofa hoisted Cecil onto her hump, her unique feature, and walked around the beach. Cecil touched his unique feature, a horn growing out of his right shoulder.

Travellers offered gold, but the Oafs had rocks and sculpted their own homes. Travellers offered feasts, but the Oafs ate sand, berries, fruit and leaves. Travellers offered land, but the Oafs were content living on the beach. However, they believed creativity was something to share, so Boofa told all who wanted The Charmer the same thing, 'If you alone can lift it, you can take it.'

Cecil loved it when someone tried. All the Oafs would gather as another cocksure traveller limbered up, postured to the crowd and inevitably failed. This was the way of life in Reech. Sculpt, sculpt, sculpt, eat, sleep, watch a traveller fail and leave, get back to work until the next visitor would arrive and fail too. The Oafs began to love The Charmer for the fun it brought them.

That soon changed.

Cecil was fifteen and at an age when he should be sculpting, but he struggled for inspiration. While fetching rocks from the snowy clifftops, he casually threw one down and it narrowly missed an armoured stranger riding a Cyclops. The stranger's cold stare instantly found Cecil, who raised an apologetic hand, but the stranger's expression did not warm. The man turned his eyes back to the path and the Cyclops continued to trudge through the snow. Cecil had seen all kinds of visitors and all kinds of eyes, but the stranger's eyes had only hate in them. Most visitors came in the hot season, but the stranger was here at the harshest time.

Cecil returned to see the stranger step off his Cyclops. What struck Cecil was his skinny frame stacked with muscles that tried to burst out of his leather armour.

The stranger left his tired Cyclops and strutted towards Boofa while she organised rocks. 'Which is the one everyone comes to see?' he asked, looking through Boofa at the sculptures.

She didn't like arrogant folk, so just nodded towards The Charmer and continued organising.

The stranger approached the sculpture. 'Ha! I can see why everyone loves it. A grinning cat riding a dragon. Genius! I'll take it.'

Everyone stopped what they were doing. A wry smile crept over Boofa's face.

Cecil itched to say the words and ran up to the stranger. 'If you alone can lift it, you can have it!' he declared.

All the Oafs cheered.

The stranger's eyes darted around Cecil, yet his mouth remained still. Cecil worried he was about to be attacked, but the stranger simply removed and folded his cloak, set it down and sat on it. 'It's time we gave it a new home.' The stranger turned to his Cyclops and whistled. It stomped towards him as quickly as it could, which was slowly. It stopped in front of the stranger and bowed. 'Get me that sculpture,' the stranger commanded.

The Oafs gathered.

The Cyclops planted its feet in the snow. It stretched its arms, got a firm grip on The Charmer with its giant hands, bent its knees and with an almighty roar…

Nothing.

The stranger cocked his head. 'Correct your technique.'

The Cyclops readjusted its stance and bent its legs a bit more. It strained, and its feet slid back.

'Maybe you should tell it to stop,' Boofa said, concerned.

The stranger tutted at her. 'Focus,' he casually told his Cyclops.

Its grey face darkened, its legs trembled and its veins throbbed as though trying to burst out of its skin to wriggle away.

'Stop!' Cecil shouted.

'Make it stop!' Grifta, the elder commanded, slapping his tail against the snow.

The stranger brushed snow off his trousers. The Cyclops' breathing slowed. Its body collapsed onto the floor, head slumped against the sculpture. The stranger pointed for the Cyclops to go back to Reech's entrance. It dragged its exhausted frame through the snow.

'Very well.' The stranger stood. 'I didn't want it to come to this, but I am the strongest living being in all of Hastovia, and now you will be able to say you witnessed that strength.' He approached the sculpture, ran his finger along it and nodded. 'No longer will they come here to see these sculptures. They will come to pay respect to the legend of my power.' He stretched his thighs, then his arms.

'Just get on with it,' Grifta called out.

The stranger narrowed his eyes at Grifta. He squatted and wrapped his muscular arms around The Charmer. There was total silence as even the Oafs thought this could be the moment someone lifted it. If there was one thing the stranger did well it was creating expectation. He steadied himself and...

Failure.

'What?' he said to the sculpture, pointlessly. He barged it. 'How?'

'Typical. All that confidence followed by pure disappointment,' Grifta tutted.

'I never fail! What sorcery is this?'

Boofa rolled her eyes.

Grifta chuckled. 'These are sky rocks. Not as light as the pebbles you play with. Now visitors will hear of another failure. What's your name?' Grifta prepared to scratch it into the Statue of Failure, depicting a man crying, unable to lift a feather. Names were carved all over it.

The stranger refused to answer.

'Fine. You'll be Lord Grass Arms.' Grifta carved it on the forehead of the Statue of Failure. He turned back to the stranger. 'You should know, the Oafs are the strongest beings in all of Hastovia; we just don't need to show off to the world about it.' Grifta lifted The Charmer with ease and put it on top of a small, sculpted hill. Pride of place for the joy it had brought Reech.

'No!' The stranger ran to The Charmer and tried to lift it using a different technique. There was the Jermalian technique where power comes from the calves.

Failure.

There was the technique made famous by the Barmashin tribe, where it's all in the elevation from the shoulders and channelling power through the chest.

Failure.

Then there was the Believers' technique of believing something was weaker than you. It explained why the Believers never won a war.

More failure.

It became tiresome. Soon only Cecil watched. He wished the stranger would leave, but he kept trying. This was obsession.

In the time the stranger spent failing, Boofa sculpted a tree and a table, while Grifta sculpted the stranger trying to lift The Charmer, but made the stranger chubby.

Finally defeated, the stranger wiped the sweat from his brow, stopped and stared at The Charmer.

'Thank you for visiting our village,' Boofa said.

The stranger dragged his feet back to his discoloured Cyclops.

Cecil couldn't hide his smile.

The stranger stopped and turned back. 'I want to stay and learn from you.'

Cecil willed Boofa and Grifta to reject him.

The stranger fell to one knee. 'Teach me to be strong like you. To sculpt like you.'

'Don't do it, Ma,' Cecil whispered.

'Why should we teach you?' Boofa asked.

'Because gifts like yours are given to be shared.'

'I don't like him,' Cecil whispered.

Grifta leaned into Boofa. 'He's right, though. We can't deny sharing our talents with those who want to learn. It would be shameful.'

Boofa nodded.

'But he *is* the worst being I've ever encountered,' Grifta added.

'Maybe sculpting will bring him the joy he's been missing,' Boofa suggested.

Why were they even discussing this?

'Very well!' Grifta said. 'You may stay. And Boofa shall be your teacher.'

Boofa gave Cecil an apologetic look.

The stranger smiled.

Twenty sunsets passed and Cecil still couldn't think of anything to sculpt. Boofa told him and the stranger, 'Let your first sculpture tell you it wants to be sculpted.'

Cecil wasn't sure what that meant, so he didn't sculpt a thing, while the stranger attacked the rocks daily.

During breaks, the stranger wandered around the village and asked everyone questions. 'So why do you love sculpting so much?' he asked Grifta. 'Why don't I ever see any of you swim?' he asked Boofa. 'Why don't you use your strength to take over all of Hastovia?' he asked Cecil. However, while the Oafs loved sharing, they were guarded about why they did or didn't do certain things. They always gave him generic answers, but that wouldn't stop him. Daily he asked the same questions. Daily he was disappointed.

Likewise, the Oafs had questions for him. 'Where are you from?' they asked, and he replied with a cocky, 'Hastovia.' He smiled, but never gave the real answer.

'What is your name?' they asked.

'Names mean nothing. Actions mean everything,' he said, and then moved away.

Cecil noticed Boofa was happier than she had been for a while. Teaching brought her great satisfaction, even if the student was the stranger. She'd show him: smash, smash, smash, pound, pound, pound, scratch, refine, tweak. He would then attempt it: Smash, stop for breath, smash, sit down for a moment and tend to his cut hand, pound, lie on the floor in agony. Oafs were born with hands tough enough to take this kind of punishment.

Over ninety sunsets of frustration passed for the stranger, as his sculptures never turned out the way he wanted. He tried to sculpt himself, but either the nose was too thin, the muscles were too small, or the face was too unwelcoming.

Cecil watched from his bedroom as the stranger sat on the beach and stared out to sea. Cecil struggled to think of something to sculpt. 'More than two hundred sunsets and nothing.' He admired the glorious creations of the village. The royalty, the beasts, the novelties, and his favourite, The Knight With No Name. When dragon-scorpions roamed the land, The Knight

With No Name was the one who drove them deep into the ground. Cecil had always wanted to be a hero like her.

He thought of Boofa's words. *Let your first sculpture tell you it wants to be sculpted.* The words whirred in his head. He saw Boofa go to console the stranger. He followed and hid behind the sculpture of the dragon-scorpion.

'It's not working,' the stranger said.

Boofa softened. 'You have to stop making it an obsession and let it just be an expression.' She sculpted a tiny bird from a pebble.

'That sounds like a great quote to carve into a wall, but I don't understand.'

'Obsession is a poison. You need to let it go before it consumes you.'

'Walk with me,' he requested.

Cecil followed, hiding behind sculptures, trying to blend in as much as a hefty Oaf could. He overheard them speak about life, their dreams, and what they hoped for Hastovia. Cecil actually felt sorry for the stranger.

'Thank you for taking me in, Boofa,' the stranger said. 'I have learned a great deal and wish I could be as strong as you all, but it isn't to be.' He showed her his trembling hands. The scars, lumps and deformities.

In that moment, it came to Cecil.

The following sunrise, everyone gathered in the centre of Reech to marvel at Cecil's creations. His mother beamed as the stranger slid the rock fists onto his hands. They were perfect; soft enough to move, yet hard enough to smash with. Cecil had found harmony between opposites. The stranger got straight to work.

He and Cecil became great friends. All the scary things about the stranger became normal. The stranger taught Cecil how to ride a Cyclops, while Cecil showed him hazel berries – a berry that felt amazing when rubbed into the skin. The stranger fell in love with hazel berries. When he wasn't sculpting, he'd be lathering it on himself.

One day, the stranger helped Cecil gather rocks from the cliffs. He couldn't lift them, but he had a good eye for finding them.

'Over here, Cecil!' he shouted from beyond a sculpture of a bearded Oaf pointing back to Reech.

Cecil stopped in front of it. 'We're not meant to go beyond the beards.' The Oafs had sculpted themselves with beards to see what they might look like with some form of hair.

'Why not?' the stranger asked.

'It's just something we were told when we were little.'

'Don't you ever want to explore?'

'We don't need to. Hastovia comes to us.'

'Some of Hastovia. Come on, the rock is only a little bit further.'

Cecil wasn't sure.

'It's just beyond those trees,' the stranger reassured him. 'It's the biggest rock I've ever seen.'

He wasn't exaggerating. It was majestic. As well as being the biggest it was the shiniest. It would keep the Oafs sculpting for a long time.

'I think I see another one.' The stranger ran off before Cecil could shout after him. Cecil shrugged and readied himself to lift the rock when he saw it.

Hungry eyes, hungry face, hungry mouth, and a horn in the middle of its head ready to skewer him. Cecil had only seen one in sculptures, but now he was face to face with a horned wolf. Cecil's legs froze. The beast moved closer, rolling its lips to present its huge, jagged teeth. It growled and leapt at Cecil. The stranger's rock fist smashed its side. It hit the floor, got to its feet and fled.

Cecil collapsed…

* * *

'HOW COULD you lead him beyond the beards?' Boofa blasted, tending to Cecil, shaken and groggy.

'I didn't know,' the stranger protested.

'Those bearded Oafs are to keep us from going where it's dangerous,' Grifta added.

'It's okay,' Cecil said. 'I chose to go. And he saved me. I got greedy wanting the bigger rocks.' He nodded at the stranger.

The stranger smiled appreciatively at Cecil.

Boofa calmed herself. 'I suppose we should be thankful to you, then.'

The stranger had won their trust and, as days passed, unanswered questions were answered. 'So why do you love sculpting so much?' he asked Grifta.

'Because it's all we know. We're not the brightest. We're not the fastest, and we can't cook. We tried once and accidentally poisoned a king. Now we stick to what will bring us no harm.'

The stranger absorbed the answer.

'Why don't I ever see you swimming?' he asked Boofa.

'Look around you.' She put a friendly arm around him. 'How well do you think we can float?' She smiled.

'I can teach you,' the stranger offered.

'You've more chance of lifting a sculpture,' Grifta called out.

The stranger let himself chuckle.

'Why don't you use your strength to take over all of Hastovia?' he asked Cecil.

'We can't intentionally kill. We love life too much,' Cecil replied.

'Isn't that a waste of being the strongest people in Hastovia?'

'Mum says a waste is doing nothing but evil with your gifts. If you look through all of history, no Oaf has ever purposely killed another being. Sure, an Oaf may have sat on a small creature by accident, but Mum says the preservation of life must always come before a desire for death.'

The stranger nodded.

Finally, he completed the sculpture of himself. The face was friendlier, the muscles were bigger, and he stood proud on top of what looked like the whole of Hastovia. Despite being more pleasant, he still had a warped view of himself.

The Oafs applauded him.

'Thank you for everything,' he said to Boofa and Cecil. 'I arrived an arrogant idiot, but I leave—'

'An arrogant idiot who can sculpt,' Grifta joked.

The stranger smirked. 'I'm sad to say goodbye.'

Cecil frowned.

'But I shall return with a gift.' And with that, he climbed onto his Cyclops and rode away.

That year in Reech was as normal as could be, but Cecil missed his friend. Whenever he heard the creaking of wheels, or the thudding of a creature, he would run to the village boundary to join Boofa. 'Is it him?'

His mother would shake her head. Cecil concluded that the stranger would never return.

Two hot seasons later, while Cecil and Boofa gathered rocks, a light humming carried in the air. It grew louder and louder, closer and closer.

Boofa peered over the edge of the cliff. 'That's not normal.' She caught Grifta's eye. He gestured for her to stay where she was.

The humming became rumbling. 'Look!' Cecil called out.

Boofa ran over and Cecil pointed her to a line of visitors on the horizon, easily over fifty of them.

'I'm going down,' Boofa said. 'You stay here.'

'But I—'

'Stay here, Cecil. And if anything happens, run.' Her wrinkled brow warned him and she descended.

Cecil desperately wanted to follow, but he didn't want to add to the stress. He noticed some of the visitors pushing cloaked boxes, and a carriage at the back of the line. 'Mum!' he called out, but she was too far. The line arrived at the village entrance. Cecil watched the Oafs gather behind Boofa and Grifta.

Boofa's worry became a grin. The stranger had returned.

Cecil beamed and climbed down the cliff.

Grifta stepped towards the stranger. 'We've missed you... umm... I can't believe we still don't know your name.' He extended his hand to the stranger, who folded his arms.

Cecil stopped on the sand and hid behind one of the pillars that held up his home. The coldness had returned to the stranger's eyes.

'I'm now known as Lord Ragnus.' He smirked. 'Apologies for the delay in returning. I had to work hard to bring you the ideal gift, which the Fools have helped me to gather.' He nodded to the sheet-covered boxes that the small, ugly, grey Fools stood behind.

'You didn't have to do that.' Boofa smiled.

'Nonsense. I wanted to.' Lord Ragnus turned towards the carriage. He nodded.

'Open!' a whiny voice shouted.

The Fools removed the sheets and opened the boxes.

Horned wolves.

Cecil's heart raced. A dozen horned wolves chased screaming Oafs around Reech, attacking in packs. A horn pierced an Oaf's stomach. Teeth ripped a chunk from an arm. Everywhere Cecil looked, blood dotted the sand.

Some Oafs ran for the sculpted boats on the shore, but horned wolves savaged them before they could untie them.

Lord Ragnus stalked Boofa and Grifta towards the sea. 'I would've returned sooner, but forming alliances and armies takes time.'

Boofa caught Cecil's eye. Her look told him everything he needed to know, but he crept to the next pillar, wanting to help.

'We took you in,' Grifta said, his eyes red with anger.

Lord Ragnus and a line of horned wolves forced the Oafs further into the sea. The water was up to their chests.

'You did, and I am grateful. However, I have a dilemma. As long as you live, I will never be the strongest being in Hastovia.'

Grifta marched out of the sea and towards Lord Ragnus, but a horned wolf pierced Grifta's calf. His scream stopped any more Oafs from being as brave and he fell onto his hands and knees.

Lord Ragnus stood above him. 'I'd like to show you a skill I learned from the Boulder Tribe while on my travels.' He put one hand on Grifta's head and the other around his neck. 'Sometimes, killing is too good for people.' He twisted Grifta's head.

Grifta screamed.

'Stop!' Boofa yelled.

Lord Ragnus released Grifta, letting him catch his breath, then grabbed him and twisted his neck again. 'You see, when you don't submit, your inner strength fights back, like a powerful energy. You know you're going to die, but you still want to give everything. So, I take you to the maximum point of pain, and the energies collide and…' He twisted a fraction more. Blood replaced the white in Grifta's eyes and flowed from his mouth.

He screamed and disappeared in a puff of smoke.

Cecil threw up on the sand. He moved behind a sculpture of an octo-eagle. What could he do?

Lord Ragnus kneeled on the sand and picked up a small creature with a big head and little legs. He placed it on his palm. 'Hello, there. It's your inner strength that is your curse and turns you into this thing.' He closed his hand and, with a crunch, Grifta was gone.

Boofa placed a hand over her mouth.

Lord Ragnus wiped his hands on his trousers, then he and a line of horned wolves advanced towards the Oafs in the sea. Some backed off and were swept away.

Boofa stepped towards the horned wolves. Cecil watched, hoping, crying.

'Stop this now!' Boofa ordered Lord Ragnus. 'Call them off! You can have your title of strongest, your sculptures, whatever you want. Just leave us in peace.'

Wolves tried to drag Boofa under the water using their teeth, but she pushed them away. 'We never leave here, so nobody will ever know you're not the strongest apart from us.'

Lord Ragnus looked as if he were considering her words. He stepped towards Boofa. Cecil hoped a part of his friend was still inside this cruel being.

'I'll know,' he said. 'Like you told me, obsession is a poison.' He clenched his rock fists; the rock fists Cecil had made him. 'Consider me incurable.' He smashed Boofa in the stomach.

She struck back, but he bashed her away. Each time, she'd come back a little bit weaker and he'd punch her further into the sea.

Cecil willed himself to help her, but his legs wouldn't move.

Lord Ragnus grabbed Boofa's head. He held her under the water until the thrashing stopped.

Cecil stared at the sea, hoping she'd come back up, but she didn't.

The only thing breaking the deathly silence was horned wolves ripping at Oaf flesh.

Lord Ragnus admired the sculpture of The Stranger. He turned to the carriage. 'The Charmer is that one.' He pointed to it.

Laughter came from the carriage and a whiny voice spoke. 'Bring it with us!'

A swarm of Fools wrapped ropes around it and struggled to pull it into a cart.

'There's one more Oaf. There.' Lord Ragnus pointed at Cecil, and then he and the horned wolves chased him. Cecil sprinted to the cliff and climbed up while the horned wolves ran up the path. Fear drove Cecil beyond the bearded Oaf sculpture and through Reech Forest. The footsteps and growls closed in.

Cecil came to a stream. He knew Lord Ragnus wouldn't stop until he was dead. He bit into a tree to contain the pain and ripped the horn from his shoulder. He dropped the horn and blood poured down the right side of his chest. He faced the stream. With no idea how deep it would get, he made his choice and ran through it. Sadly, he was mistaken. It was a river. The current carried him away. His arms flapped and he struggled for air. The only thing going through his mind was the image of his mother's last attempts at survival. Water filled his body and everything around him faded into darkness.

He regained consciousness, washed up on the edge of Reech Forest. Cecil went from town to village and camp to castle, hoping he would find Lord Ragnus, but due to Oafs having no sense of direction he kept ending up in the same places. He settled in a tavern to wait until information came to him. The entire time, he thought about his creation being used to kill his mother. He vowed to never sculpt again, to find Lord Ragnus, and to be the first Oaf to kill another being…

* * *

THE TAPPING of tiny feet jogged Oaf out of his memory. A tortured soul scuttled by him. Oaf pinched it and lifted it to his eye. He remembered Grifta and his bottom lip trembled.

The tortured soul's face had female features and her little legs continued running, but stopped when she realised she was getting nowhere.

'Please don't eat me!' she said.

Oaf set her on his palm. 'Don't worry; I'm full of berries.' He stroked her head with his index finger. 'You got a name?'

'I don't remember. I'm a tortured soul,' she said.

He walked back towards the gardens.

'I overheard that beaked idiot say the only way tortured souls turn back to normal is if someone says their real name to them, and I might remember some things in time.'

'Hmm… Is your real name… Granilio?'

'Let's wait and see if anything happens.'

They waited. Nothing.

'I guess not,' she said.

'I can't think of any other names at the moment. For now I'll call you… Tortured Soul.'

Tortured Soul smiled, but it faded. 'You'll 'ave to call me dead if I don't get in some liquid soon. Bein' transformed like this comes wiv drawbacks.'

'I'll take you to a stream,' Oaf said, but heavy steps grabbed his attention.

'Oh no, it's the nut job,' Tortured Soul said.

'Who?' Oaf's body tensed.

'The big miserable fella wiv the stone fists.' Tortured Soul coughed up water. Her eyelids twitched.

Oaf stepped forward.

Lord Ragnus and his Cyclops emerged from the alley. The sudden sound of horns led them away from Oaf.

A hot energy rushed through Oaf's body. This was the showdown he had waited for. He'd experienced this in his mind thousands of times, all against different backdrops, from snowy mountains to burning deserts. He'd say no words. He'd just smash Lord Ragnus in the face and pummel him to death in the name of all those he had hurt.

Oaf followed Lord Ragnus, but a cough drew his attention back to Tortured Soul. Her colour drained from a pale, ghostly blue to a rotten old grey. 'Don't mind me. I'll be fine.' She coughed up little dusty puffs of air and her skin cracked.

Oaf's breathing quickened. He carried on, but another cough

stopped him. As much as he wanted revenge, he couldn't let an innocent creature die when he could do something about it. For Boofa, he would put saving a life before ending one. He watched Lord Ragnus head back to the courtyard. He'd waited seven years for revenge. Now he'd have to wait a little bit longer.

THE EVIL WITHIN

Sabrinia couldn't understand why Karl was in Flowforn. She had instructed him to get as far away as possible, and worried he had made a stupid decision. She needed to get to him.

She tried to drown out the droning Fool horns, and Arazod was on his fourth bowl of tortured souls.

She rubbed her head. 'My dear...' She touched Arazod's arm. 'I've a bit of a sore head. I think I need to lay down.'

He spooned another tortured soul towards his beak, but the spoon wouldn't fit, so liquid splatted off his feathers. 'Yes, I'll come with you.'

She shook her head. 'I think it's best you stay, to keep the people company. It'll help you win their love.'

He scratched his feathers. 'If that is what my future bride wishes, then okay. But before you go. It's time!' He clapped, triggering a more energetic tune from the Fools. He turned his stool to face the centre of the courtyard. 'Look, look.'

Sabrinia dreaded what it might be time for.

Lord Ragnus, wearing steel armour, marched into the middle of the courtyard and waited for silence.

'You get to see him in action,' Arazod said.

It was among the last things she wanted to see, right after Arazod eating, Arazod talking, and... Arazod. How could she spend her life like this? She had to, for her people. She tried to blink the negativity out of her mind.

A Fool shepherded ten trembling Flowfornians and one of Proster's brutes towards an array of weapons, laid out in front of Lord Ragnus.

Sabrinia's eyes widened.

'It's okay,' Arazod said. 'He won't kill them. He's just going to hurt them a bit. For entertainment.' He wheezed. 'Tomorrow they can return to following their dreams.'

Sabrinia couldn't take her eyes off the helpless Flowfornians, people who just wanted to live peacefully.

'Attack me,' Lord Ragnus demanded.

Proster's brute picked up a mallet and stepped forward. 'Come on.' His voice quivered. 'There are ten of us. We can take him.' He swung the mallet. Lord Ragnus caught it in his rock hand. With his free hand he punched the brute in the gut. The brute fell to his knees and vomited blood.

Sabrinia's toes gripped the insides of her shoes. Her eyes filled with anger.

'Who's next?' Lord Ragnus asked.

The other Flowfornians ran away.

Arazod laughed.

From the corner of her eye, Sabrinia caught Arazod staring at her, waiting for approval, but she remained frozen, horrified, wishing there was something she could do.

'Behemoth Fool!' Arazod yelled. 'Bring it out!'

A six-foot Behemoth Fool, wide as two people, wheeled a large, cloaked cage into the courtyard. The Behemoth Fool's lips were squashed against its face and its nose was so flat you couldn't call it a nose. It pulled the cloak off the cage to reveal a

Lionbear taller than Lord Ragnus. The hairy, muscular beast roared. The sound shook Sabrinia's bones.

The crowd backed away.

The creature's scratch marks were all over the cage bars. Sabrinia swallowed her sadness.

'Release it, then get out of the way,' Arazod commanded.

Lord Ragnus stood in front of the cage. The Behemoth Fool unlocked it and fled.

The Lionbear leapt out at Lord Ragnus and dug its claws into his armour, knocking him off balance.

Sabrinia hoped the creature would slice him into chunks.

Lord Ragnus steadied himself and pushed the Lionbear away. It shook its head, grunted and leapt again. Lord Ragnus grabbed its arms and slammed it against the ground. He drove its head into the pebbles, then lifted it to its feet and punched it in the stomach.

It buckled to its knees and whined.

'Quite the fighter, isn't he?' Arazod said.

'Quite...' Sabrinia pressed her hands together to stop them shaking.

Lord Ragnus raised his fists either side of the Lionbear's head, ready to crush it.

Flowfornians turned away.

Sabrinia's heart raced and she stood. 'No!' Her neck was hot and sweat formed on her forehead.

Lord Ragnus turned to Arazod, who looked at Sabrinia's face, and then turned back to Lord Ragnus and shook his head.

Lord Ragnus sighed, changed his stance, and simply kicked the Lionbear to the ground.

'Remove it!' Arazod waved it away.

The Behemoth Fool chained the Lionbear and lifted it back into the cage.

Arazod applauded. 'With him on our side, we're unstoppable.

Now follow me.' He leapt off his stool and waved the circle of Fools to open.

Sabrinia dragged her legs behind Arazod to the covered, rectangular structure at the foot of the King's Tower. She cast her eye to the Lionbear, battered and barely breathing.

'This is your… is for you,' Arazod said.

She didn't want whatever it was.

The Fools pulled the sheet away, revealing cages. Twenty of them, with iron bars twelve feet high.

Sabrinia stared.

'This way, instead of a stu—' he wheezed, '—stuffy dungeon, we can look at the prisoners as they rot here—' he struggled. 'It's more of a spectacle. And we can throw things down at them, because I've put holes in the top of each cage. There's even a points system. Ten for hitting the prisoner on the head, twenty if you can injure them.' His beak curled into a smile.

Sabrinia had not received such a bad gift since Karl had given her a rock, thinking it was a two-headed turtle.

Karl… She needed to find him.

'Thank you.' She smiled to mask her concern.

Arazod pointed to a hole in a room at the top of the King's Tower. 'I've had my… my…' he struggled. Sabrinia wished he'd just write things down. 'Quarters opened to look down on them.'

'That's nice.' She wanted to change the topic. She pointed to a fat Fool sat on a cart. Flab covered it from head to toe, and rolls of its loose skin hung over the wood. With every slow breath its paunch would ripple, and it groaned. 'Is that Fool okay?' Sabrinia asked.

'That's the Birth Fool. It spits out eggs that these useless things come out of. We probably need to make Fools faster.' Arazod called out. 'Fools! Speed up the birth!'

Several Fools ran up to Birth Fool and pounded its stomach.

Birth Fool retched and cried.

'It looks distressed,' Sabrinia complained.

'It's used to it,' Arazod replied. 'Faster!' he commanded the Fools.

The Fools hammered at it.

Sabrinia stared, wishing she could help the Birth Fool.

Arazod coughed. 'I'm not even sure how the Fools came to be. One story says they were created by a mage. Another says they were people who were cursed. He wheezed. 'Doesn't matter. Father took them and now they're mine.'

Of course it didn't matter to him.

A rubbery, gooey, grey egg stretched Birth Fool's mouth to its limit, then fell out, bounced down Birth Fool's stomach and settled on the ground in front of Arazod. The egg cracked open, revealing a tiny Fool with one leg.

'Ugh. A dud.' Arazod kicked the creation away.

Sabrinia gasped. The tiny life cried and squirmed on the pebbles.

'They come in random forms. Sometimes these dim Fools you see everywhere. Sometimes conjurers, big Behemoths, and then these pointless little ones that can't do anything.'

'You never know what it might grow up into with the right care,' Sabrinia said.

Arazod shrugged. 'I don't have the energy for that.' He turned to a Fool. 'Chuck it in the sea,' he ordered.

Sabrinia's throat burned.

'Get another egg,' Arazod commanded more Fools. They rushed over and pounded Birth Fool's stomach.

Birth Fool looked desperate for rest, but couldn't communicate, probably due to the fat clogging its throat. It made a whistling noise, failing to squeeze words out.

There was nothing redeemable or likeable about Arazod. 'I think I need to go for that rest, my dear.'

Arazod nodded as a woman whose limbs were covered in markings approached holding a parchment with Karl's face on it.

'I've found your criminal,' she said.

Arazod's face darkened.

Sabrinia had to buy Karl some time. Whatever he was doing, he was in grave danger.

THE IDEAL CELLMATE

Karl rushed through the dungeon. He looked over his shoulder, worried he was being followed.

He examined the doors. 'One A, One B, this should be easy. Hold on, Two F? This is a terrible numbering system. What kind of idiot?' he muttered to himself.

He crept to a corridor that joined onto his. Hargon sat half way along it, painting.

Karl waited until Hargon lowered his head to dip his brush in the paint palette, then he snuck across. He wished he could have said a proper goodbye to Sabrinia.

He spotted barred cells on his right, and ones with wooden doors on his left that must have been the old luxury cells.

SQUAWK.

Peezant flapped above him, wearing a shiny new anklet.

'Be quiet!' Karl said.

'You'd find what you're after a lot quicker with my assistance.'

'Well then stop flapping around and help me find Two B.'

Peezant opened his beak. 'Pay.'

'I'll have nothing left,' he whispered.

'But I need a new accessory to go with my anklet.' Peezant posed. 'If you're struggling for funds I'll accept an eye.'

Karl huffed and grabbed a handful of gold. 'Not like I'll need this where I'm going anyway. They probably don't have stupid rules like having to use gold to buy nonsense we don't need.' Karl rammed gold into Peezant's mouth. 'Talk.'

Peezant let the tension hang in the air. Karl wanted to strangle him.

'Two B is next to Two A, naturally. Idiot.' And with the most useless piece of information ever revealed, Peezant flew away, leaving Karl both angry and poor.

Footsteps approached. Karl looked at the nearest cell, Two J. He fumbled with the keys; his hands shook. He could barely read the faded labels that Arazod had nibbled. 'Damn pigeon!' He found the key, unlocked the dark cell and rushed in. He lay against the wall and pulled his hood over his head. Two Fools walked past.

Karl exhaled. Time to go.

Chains jangled. 'Hello, Karl.' Proster stepped out of the dark corner.

BIRD FOOD

'**I** saw him enter the castle,' the woman said. 'He attacked two of your Fools.'

Arazod's feathers fluttered.

Sabrinia raised her arms to gesture caution. 'Are you sure it was him? He has a very common face, boringly so.'

The woman nodded confidently. 'It's him. He entered that building.' She pointed towards the dungeons.

Arazod puffed his chest out and lifted his axe, ready to go.

'Wait, my dear,' Sabrinia warned. 'This makes little sense. Why would a man who escaped the dungeons come running back to them? It would be one of the most idiotic things a person could ever do.'

'I saw him,' the woman said.

Sabrinia tutted. 'I think this is a case of someone trying to claim the reward through dishonesty.'

Arazod's beak twitched.

'I do not lie!' the woman claimed. 'Go and see for yourself.'

Sabrinia shook her head and held Arazod's arm. 'I think she's in too deep. She started a lie and now she's stepping further into it. But, I'm willing to forgive her. We should let her return to the celebrations and pretend this little incident never happened.'

Arazod crossed his axe over his chest. 'I don't like liars. Fools! Seize her!'

The Fools grabbed the woman.

Sabrinia bit her lip, she didn't want the woman to be punished, especially in whatever way Arazod saw appropriate. 'I'm sure she's learned her lesson.'

Arazod kicked dirt at the woman. 'You shouted at my future wife, and while she has a headache. Unforgivable! Fools, lock her up.'

The woman pleaded, but the Fools dragged her away. 'Wait! Her! He was with her!' She nodded towards the courtyard's far wall, where Questions, unaware, sat against the bricks writing in her book.

'Fools, hold her here.' They stopped and held the woman.

Arazod approached Questions and Sabrinia followed, hoping to help her friend.

'Questions, where have you been recently? I haven't seen you,' Arazod asked.

She looked up at him. 'Should I have been in the castle?' Not a lie, and not the truth, just a question, completely unhelpful to Arazod. Questions put her book away and stood.

Sabrinia offered her a reassuring smile.

'Have you seen Karl?' Arazod asked.

'Have I?'

'Yes, have you?'

'Have I?'

Arazod's beak twitched. 'Yes, have you?'

'Have I?'

Thankfully, he didn't seem to understand that she was saying yes.

'Why can't you give a normal answer?' he yelled.

Questions' eyes welled up. 'Do I wish I could?'

Sabrinia wanted to hug her.

Arazod scratched his talons against the pebbles. 'Questions, we're going to play a game.' He lost control of his breath, as usual. 'I'm going to give you an answer, and you give me the question that gets that answer.'

Questions glanced around, seemingly as confused as everyone else.

'My quarters,' Arazod said.

'Have we started?' she asked.

'What?'

'Is that your first answer? Or are you going to tell me about your quarters?'

'We've started!'

'And do I do the questions?'

'Yes! Answer the question.'

'Do I answer the question?'

'Question the answer! You know what I mean. My quarters...'

Questions bit her lip as though working it out in her head. 'Am I being slow?'

'Yes!' Arazod's face reddened. 'My quarters, is the answer!'

Questions smiled and clicked. 'Where does his highness hide his scroll of Beaked Babes?'

Arazod's feathers flapped. He leaned in and whispered, 'Any more lies like that and I'll have you fed to the horned wolves.' Arazod straightened himself. 'Okay, how about, the gardens?'

She nodded. 'Where does his highness go to weep when nobody compliments his newly preened feathers?'

Arazod grabbed Questions' face and dug a claw into her cheek. 'No. More. Lies.' Tears formed in Questions' eyes.

Sabrinia pulled her away and rubbed her shoulders. She turned to Arazod. 'She's just playing your game, my dear.' It sickened her to call him anything nice, but every move had to be cautious.

Questions smiled at her.

Arazod took a deep breath. 'Questions—'

'Who am I?' Questions scratched her palm.

'I haven't finished!' Arazod said. 'Karl.'

'Who is not very clever?' she said.

'Karl!'

'Who is weaker than a leaf in the wind?'

'Karl!'

'Who doesn't wash his hands after using the toilet bucket?'

Arazod's neck feathers fluttered. 'Okay... how about... Karl does?'

'Who believes that trees come from Cyclops eggs?'

This went on for some time...

After saying 'Karl is,' 'Karl does,' 'Karl wishes,' 'Karl likes,' and every other possible combination, Arazod tired, finally.

'KARL IS!' he said for what must have been the seventy-fourth time.

Questions hung her head. 'Who is looking for Cell Two B?' Her face turned white and she looked at Sabrinia apologetically. It wasn't her fault her people couldn't lie.

'Finally!' Arazod inhaled. He gestured to the woman with the markings. 'Well done. Lord Ragnus will reward you.' He smirked and rushed towards the dungeons.

Sabrinia followed. 'I'll join you, my dear.'

Arazod stopped and stared at her. 'You need to rest. You have a headache.' He continued on and shouted. 'Fools! Seize Questions.'

Sabrinia's heart sank.

A DOOR AWAY

'Why aren't you trying to kill me?' Karl asked Proster. 'It's making me nervous.' He was sure the air would be leaving his lungs about now, but Proster seemed defeated.

Proster's shoulders slumped, his muscles looked smaller and there was no anger on his face, just bruises and cuts. 'No point.'

Karl could still hear conversation along the corridor. He approached Proster apprehensively. 'What have they done to you?'

Proster retreated to the wall and sat down. 'That feathered idiot wanted me to build him a statue, and I made the beak a bit too big.'

Karl shook his head. 'Not the most forgiving ruler, is he?'

Proster hugged his knees. 'Why didn't you say sorry?'

Karl waited for the coast to clear. 'What?'

'You smashed my tower. The designs, the structure, the combinations and layout. That was my legacy tower, and you wiped it out in a morning and then just left.' Proster sighed.

It hit Karl that while he was casually trying things and failing

– a burnt intricate cake here, a wonky rare axe there, a broken legacy tower – his actions and lack of care had consequences.

He swallowed. 'I am really sorry. I was just so ashamed, because honestly, Proster, I'm rubbish at everything. I'm amazed I've stayed alive this long.' Karl approached Proster with the key. 'I'm so sorry.'

Proster shook his head. 'Leave me here.'

Karl ignored him and unlocked his chains. 'That beaked lunatic will probably do something really weird and humiliating to you, so get out of here. Plus, when Sabrinia gets rid of him, your legacy can be knocking down all his statues and rebuilding this place properly.'

Proster stared at Karl. He stood and extended his hand.

Karl shook it, still worried Proster would rip his arm off.

They waited for silence and went their separate ways.

Karl rushed to the end of the corridor and finally found Two B. He frantically searched the keys and found the one to freedom. The key clicked in the lock and he pushed the door open.

There was a cupboard, a painting of a two-headed woman surfing on a spiked ant while blowing a horn, and some wooden crates. Karl wondered where the portal might be. He lifted the crates and looked behind the painting. He wasn't even sure what a portal was meant to look like.

'Search every room and cell!' Arazod's voice boomed.

Karl closed the door, but it was only lockable from the outside. He searched behind the cupboard.

Nothing.

The corner of the room had faded stonework. It had to be there. He scratched at the mortar, certain there was something. He searched the room for an object to bash at the stones and found a candle holder.

The cell door swung open and claws grabbed the back of Karl's head. 'I've been looking for you,' Arazod said.

Karl's skull stung. As he tried to shake Arazod off, he glanced at the corner once more. Something shimmered.

He broke free, but Arazod's Soul Bleeder pressed against his neck. The blade smelled of old victims.

'I could cut through your bones right now,' Arazod said. 'But a straightforward execution is too good for you. I know the perfect...' he gasped.

'Way to lose weight?' Karl suggested. If he was dead he was dead.

'Punishment!' Arazod replied.

THE DEAD LANDS

Karl stared at the chipped, wooden wheels of his cage as they rolled through the light blue sand. He couldn't believe this desert was part of Hastovia. While the forests swelled with dying leaves and trees, this place glowed under the orange sunrise, and blue sand stretched as far as he could see through his sweat-drenched eyes.

A Behemoth Fool pulled Karl's cage, where Questions somehow slept peacefully, while another pulled Arazod's carriage. They trudged through the burning sand on their two-foot high wooden blocks, while discussing why the sand was blue.

One reason was that when people died, their souls turned to a blue dust and settled here. Another was that the monstrous Ice Dragon was buried in the Dead Lands and its spirit forever glows a piercing blue, shining up through its sandy grave. A further theory was that it was just blue and people shouldn't think about it too much.

Arazod guzzled water and let it spill over his feathers. Karl longed for a drop.

How could Questions sleep through this? Did death not bother her?

Karl recalled the shimmering brick work of Cell Two B. His route home. He was so close.

He picked at the rope that bound his wrists and ankles, but achieved nothing. He tried to shake free to release the cloak they had cruelly left on him, the fabric now heavy with sweat, making it a boiling blanket.

Arazod played with the dungeon keys, now hanging on a chain around his neck. He bit the head off a small hairy creature and chomped it down, then threw the rest of the body onto the sand. The carcass burned down to the bone, and Arazod grinned at Karl.

Four sunsets like this. Arazod staring, grinning, chomping.

Karl watched him for a moment. 'Why do you keep smiling like that? It's creepy,' he asked through dry lips.

'I'm just very excited about you dying,' Arazod said.

'Why don't you just slice me up with your Soul Bleeder? This seems like a lot of effort.'

'I considered it.' Arazod coughed. 'But I think you deserve eternal suffering, and Lord Ragnus told me this place is good for it.' His wheezing became more violent and his smile disappeared behind panic.

'That's what you get for being mean,' Karl said. He was unsure of what awaited him and Questions, but he wished his brain would stop guessing. He imagined they would be tied to planks on pillars an inch above the sand so the grains would burn them slowly to really stretch out the suffering. He tried to think of happier things, like Sabrinia's face, or his imaginary parents, but sadness prevailed.

'Stop!' Arazod wheezed. 'Stop!'

Both Behemoth Fools stopped.

'Have you realised you actually quite like me?' Karl said.

'This air...' Arazod gasped. 'Can't breathe! Back. We have to...'

he told the Behemoth Fool pulling his carriage. He pointed to the one pulling Karl's cage. 'But you keep going.'

Karl had noticed the heat thicken as they had progressed. It was like a huge hot hand grabbing his face. 'What a shame you won't be joining us. I was looking forward to a farewell hug.'

The Behemoth Fool turned Arazod's carriage around.

Arazod pointed to the Behemoth Fool pulling Karl's cage. 'I expect—' he wheezed. 'A full description of his pain. The begging...' he coughed. 'The crying—' he wheezed. 'Don't return until they are both in the pit.'

Pit? Karl swallowed, imagining being thrown in a sand pit where his flesh and bones would disintegrate.

'Must throw them in pit.' The Behemoth Fool nodded, the order registering in its eyes with a yellow flicker.

'Wait, Arazod. Don't you want to personally see me die? Wasn't that the whole point?'

'Looking at your face,' he wheezed and coughed, 'you're... you're already dead.' He turned to the Behemoth Fool. 'Toy with them too. Make it painful.'

The Behemoth Fool nodded, absorbing the order.

Karl watched Arazod's carriage fade into the distance along with his tedious wheezing.

Questions woke up. She took in the surroundings and her eyes danced. 'Are these the Dead Lands?'

'It seems that way.'

'Is this where there was a great battle between warriors and a dragon?'

'I don't know.'

She poked her head between the cage bars. 'Is this where there was once a thriving kingdom of inventors?'

'I have no idea.'

'Is it true that everyone who is brought here dies?'

'I hope not.' The cage wheels were so deep in the sand that it had to be dragged.

Questions turned to Karl, no doubt to ask another question. 'Is it true that the sands are so hot they eat through skin and bone if you stand still?'

Karl huffed. 'Doesn't it bother you that we're prisoners?' He tried to shake the image of the creature he had watched burn.

Questions looked as if she was considering his question. 'Is it true that—'

'Shut up, Questions!'

The cage jerked, stuck.

'Quiet back there!' the Behemoth Fool ordered. It lifted the cage over its head. 'I wouldn't worry about the burning sands. You're getting cast into the POES.'

'POES?' Karl questioned.

'It stands for Pit of Endless Screams.'

Karl wasn't sure which of the words bothered him the most.

Questions whispered, 'Did the creature say endless creams? Are we having cream?'

'It said screams, Questions! Screams!' Karl closed his eyes and took a breath. 'We're going to be pushed into a pit, where I'm guessing we will die. The endless screams bit probably means it's pretty deep; maybe endless.'

Questions frowned, but she bit her lip as if she wanted to know more. Karl prayed she wouldn't ask.

'Do we eat cream first?'

Karl banged his head against the cage bars and groaned.

'Does that mean yes?'

Karl felt like eating the scorching sand to melt himself from the inside.

They descended a sandy slope to what looked like the edge of the desert. Blue sand flowed around rocks and over a cliff like a stream into a waterfall.

But, it wasn't the edge of the desert. It was one side of the largest hole Karl had ever seen. It was uneven and cracked, as though a giant creature had stomped through the ground with their castle-sized boot.

The Behemoth Fool stopped on some rocks, dropped the cage by the edge of the cliff and unlocked it. 'Just sit here, quietly, and I'll push you in in a moment.' The Behemoth Fool pointed to the rocks, tossed them a rug, and rummaged through its pockets. 'The rocks are hot, but apparently not as deadly hot as that sand.'

Questions pulled the rug over the rocks and they sat.

Karl thought it might not be so bad to be thrown in. At least he would feel a breeze. 'I'm sorry I got you into this, Questions.'

She smiled. 'Am I glad you did?'

Her bravery was admirable, and weird.

The Behemoth Fool took a long gulp from its water pouch and stood in front of the pit. Water ran down its belly and splatted the rocks.

Karl wanted to cry, but he couldn't spare the liquid.

'Must toy with them,' the Behemoth Fool repeated its order.

'Do you have to?' Questions asked.

'Have you ever thought of not doing what Arazod says?' Karl added.

'Must toy with them.' It fumbled through its satchel and pulled out a dagger.

Karl and Questions shuffled back to the edge of the rock. Karl worried they would be thrown into the pit in smaller pieces, but the Behemoth Fool threw the dagger into the pit and held its hand to its ear.

Karl and Questions listened out for an end to the drop. Nothing. Definitely endless.

The Behemoth Fool smiled. 'Good toying, right?'

Karl had to look over the edge. The pit blended from sand and rocks into endless darkness, with the faintest blue glow from the depths.

The Behemoth Fool took a glass bottle of lotion. 'Thought I'd lost this. Can never be too careful in this heat.' It patted some on its head, and then extended the bottle to Karl and Questions. They looked at the Behemoth Fool blankly.

'Sorry. Just a little joke…' It waited for a response. 'No? Boring people.' It huffed and searched for something else in its satchel.

Karl touched his rope-bound ankles to the sand. It ate at the rope, but the heat burned a layer of Karl's skin. He bit his bottom lip to contain the scream. He pulled his legs away, the rope now loose, and tied one end to a spoke on a cage wheel. He covered his ankles with his cloak.

The Behemoth Fool gave up looking through its satchel and huffed. 'Toying is done. Now it's time for throwing.'

'Why can't I hear any screams?' Questions asked the Behemoth Fool.

'A pit doesn't scream. It's a pit. *You* provide the scream when you're pushed in,' the Behemoth Fool explained.

'But then it's not really endless, is it?' Karl held his arms to the sand, burning the ropes that restrained his wrists.

'Look, it's just the name, to make it sound more terrifying than something like, say, "The Big Pit."'

'Would you be annoyed if you were a visitor?' Questions asked.

The Behemoth Fool clenched its jaw. 'No, so—'

'Why not?' Questions asked.

The Behemoth Fool stared. 'Must throw them in pit.' It stepped towards them.

Karl broke free of the ropes around his arms. He grabbed the other end of the rope tied to the spoke and charged. 'Bravery!' He smashed into the Behemoth Fool's stomach of solid muscle. Pain shot through Karl's neck and shoulders, but he held on, trying to push.

'Must throw them in pit.' The Behemoth Fool lifted Karl into the air.

'Questions, push the cage!' Karl ordered.

She lifted her rope-bound legs, bent her knees and kicked the cage. It rolled over the cliff edge.

The Behemoth Fool looked down and lost its balance. The rope connected its thigh to the cage.

Karl shook free and retreated to Questions.

The Behemoth Fool fought the weight pulling it into the pit. It tensed, but the wooden blocks on its feet slid along the rocks. One of them broke off its foot and fell into the emptiness.

'I'm sorry. I wish there was another way, but you'll keep coming for me,' Karl said.

The Behemoth Fool's eyes watered. 'Must… throw them in pit.' The Behemoth Fool slammed its palm onto a rock. It tried to undo the knot on its thigh with its other hand but couldn't.

Karl untied Questions. 'Don't look.'

'Should you turn around?' Questions' eyes darted around Karl's face.

'I'd rather not look either.'

'Is the Fool fine?'

'What?'

A smash. Karl turned. The cage was in pieces on the rocks, and the Behemoth Fool an inch away from him.

'Must throw them in pit.' The Behemoth Fool hoisted Karl into the air.

'No!' Karl kicked.

Questions pulled Karl's leg, but the Behemoth Fool swatted her away.

A wave of sand formed on the horizon, but the Behemoth Fool was consumed by its task.

The wave broke and took the shape of a creature.

Oaf.

He slid on his sculpted rock shoes and knocked the Behemoth Fool down.

Karl fell towards the edge of the pit. His shoulder slammed against the hot rocks and he faced the terrifying endlessness.

'Oaf!' Karl groaned through his relief, clutching his throbbing arm. He scurried behind his ally.

The Behemoth Fool lunged at Karl, but Oaf knocked it down.

Oaf pointed to the broken cage wood. 'Tie some to your feet,' he told Questions and Karl.

They did as ordered.

'Now tie him up.' Oaf restrained the Behemoth Fool on the rug while they used Questions' ropes to tie its arms and legs.

'When we're gone and safe, we'll send a parchment to Flowforn to tell them it's here,' Karl said. He looked into the Behemoth Fool's eyes. 'Why don't you try to fight Arazod's orders?'

It shed a tear, unable to live outside of its curse. 'Must throw them in pit.' It tried to bite Karl. 'Must throw them in pit.'

Karl hung his head. The Fools didn't even get to choose a path. Maybe if it had any control over its mind, this Behemoth would've wanted to be a cook, a builder, or a singer.

Oaf put a hand on Karl's shoulder. 'Come on.'

They left. Even with wood tied to his feet, hot sand stung Karl's toes.

They arrived at the top of a sandy slope. Questions and Oaf slid down the other side, but Karl stopped and turned back.

The Behemoth Fool, free of its ropes, followed, agony on its face. With each step, blue sand burned into its exposed foot.

Karl shook his head, his heart heavy. He removed his cloak and dropped it. He turned and walked away.

He caught up with his friends. 'Thank you, Oaf.' Karl squeezed him. 'I take it you didn't get your revenge?'

Oaf shook his head. 'I missed my chance, and then he was surrounded by Fools again.' He handed Questions a waterskin to drink from. She gladly gulped from it.

'I'm sorry,' Karl said.

'It's okay. Him and Arazod want you dead so will hunt you, and the Fool army will be split to look around. If I stick with you, my revenge will come.' He smiled.

'I feel used, but I can live with that.'

Questions passed Karl the waterskin and he finished it.

'Meet Tortured Soul.' Oaf took a glass bottle of water from his leather vest, containing Tortured Soul. She smiled.

'Ugly little thing, isn't she?' Karl said.

Tortured Soul spat at Karl, the spit hitting the inside of the bottle.

'Charming.'

Oaf put her back inside his leather vest.

'What's your real name?' Questions asked Oaf.

'Cecil. But I'm the last of my kind, so I want to be known as Oaf.'

* * *

Six sunsets later, back in the safety of the tavern, the euphoria of evading death had evaporated. Karl needed to figure out how to get into Cell Two B. He rested his head against the bar. By now, Arazod would know he was alive.

Bar Witch wiped shelves with a damp cloth.

Questions watched her. 'How old is this tavern?' she asked.

'Old.' Bar Witch evaded eye contact.

'Why do you have so many empty jars on the shelves?' Questions waited to write the answer in her book.

'I save them for when I need to put the brains of people who ask too many questions in them.'

'Why?'

'Because… Karl!'

Karl waved Questions over. 'Join me,' he said for her own good.

'Are you okay?' Questions asked.

'There's no way I'll ever get back into Flowforn, Questions.' He took the tiny sock from his pocket and stared at his embroidered name. 'I'll never find out who I really am or how I ended up here.' He shook his head. 'I want to know my parents… what it's like to be loved without judgement, or just—'

'Karl,' Frong called from his and Sags' table. 'There is another option.'

Karl turned to them. 'Other than Cell Two B?'

'No, but for how to get in there. There are always other options. It's just that the first is always the least dangerous.'

'Nothing feels too dangerous when you have a death sentence hanging over you.'

'I guess it then comes down to how you want to die,' Frong said. 'I personally would opt to die in battle against a never-before-seen monster. I want to be the first to discover it, then if it kills me, I'll die honoured. Then I'd like to have a shroud listing all the places we adventured to wrapped around me. Then—'

'If you don't give me my options soon I'll die of boredom.' Karl raised an apologetic hand. 'Sorry. I'm very stressed. Just please tell me what I need to know.'

'Very well.' Frong rolled his eyes.

'Thank you.'

'But only if you give my back a trim.' Frong smiled.

Karl stood. 'I'm not in the mood for this.' He walked away and opened the door. 'Oaf?'

Oaf sat by a bush while Tortured Soul jumped from leaf to leaf. 'Is it Gwendy?' Oaf asked Tortured Soul.

Tortured Soul shook her head and continued jumping.

'Klob?' Oaf guessed.

'Stop it. You'll never guess my name!'

Oaf pounded the floor and huffed.

'Oaf, I need a favour,' Karl said.

'Not now,' he replied. 'I've got it. Boompi?'

'Nope,' Tortured Soul said.

Oaf scratched his head.

Karl's shoulders fell. He left Oaf to it and went back inside.

Frong waved him over. 'I was only joking, Karl. That honour is reserved for Sags.'

Sags grunted.

'Have a seat,' Frong said.

Karl took slow breaths, approached the stool and sat.

Frong smiled at him. 'On one of our many adventures, about eighteen thousand sunsets ago. Or was it twenty-five thousand and forty-three?'

Karl shut his eyes and rubbed the sides of his head.

'Never mind. There are many magic relics that grant power.'

'Magic relics?' Karl wished he was back in the past, living in Flowforn where he didn't have to think about death or weird creatures or relics.

'Hastovia is full of them,' Frong said.

'Why didn't you say before? I could find some power and obliterate Arazod and just leave without torment.'

'That is precisely the reason why...'

Karl scratched his cheek, ready for the inevitable story.

'Hastovia was created by eight gods, as far as we know. They were all born from the energy of Mother Hastovia and all possessed great power, unique to the energy they came from.'

Karl nodded, questioning whether any of this was true.

'But after the beauty of the world wore off, they got bored, so they created people and creatures of all sorts as a gift to Mother Hastovia, and they roamed Hastovia together. It was wonderful. But as the numbers increased, the less time the gods could spend with all the people to help them. So, they bestowed gifts and created items to assist them. Items for anything from creating tunnels to being able to breathe under water.'

Questions took her book, quill and ink from a pouch on her belt and scribbled everything down.

'For example, people were getting cold, so Pyralus, the god born of wind and flame, gave one woman a gauntlet giving her the ability to command fire, and she used it in the cold seasons and to cook. But, like most beings with power, it corrupted her, and she harmed others and turned on the gods.'

Karl shook his head. 'What happened?'

'The gods assisted people to defeat her, then punished her as an example, then they fell out with each other. Some gods tired of the needs of the people and wanted to destroy them, while others wanted to protect them. They were after all, their children. A war broke out between the gods, and there was division.' Frong sipped his ale. 'Those who wanted to protect were driven into hiding. The gods who wanted to destroy soon learned they couldn't; it was too painful to watch. So, they exploited the greed of their creations. They placed powerful relics in treacherous locations, where people who wanted them could find them at their own risk and then they would be responsible for their own downfall. Part of the gods hoped that those who found the relics would use them for good, to redeem themselves and build a harmonious world.'

Karl frowned. 'How do you know all this?'

'I read a lot.' He directed Karl to a wooden chest next to the table. He opened it – it was full of books and orbs. He lifted a book out titled *The Godly Godsfolk*; a leather-bound book etched with the carving of a tree, and with more pages than Karl cared to ever read.

'Wow,' Karl said.

Frong put the book back and slammed the chest shut. The dust fired into Karl's face.

'And I speak a lot, and I have travelled.' He picked some old meat out of his beard and took a bite. 'The gods have never been seen since, but there are people with more knowledge than me. And everything you see or have heard of in regards to magic… All of it came from the gods, and how we who live used their relics.'

Karl huffed. 'So I need to go and risk my life now?'

'You need the Hat of Invisibility. The King of Alseed had a god create it for him so he could hide when anyone invaded. A coward's relic, really, but his home was the most invaded for nine hundred sunsets in a row.' Frong scratched his beard. 'If you possess the hat you can enter Flowforn undetected. Considering you're a man who is being looked for, being invisible is likely your best solution. It's in a tower just a little way south of here. Or was it to the north? It may have been east. Hmm… Memories. Ah yes, it was east.'

'I'll find it. It's a tower. It will be tall,' Karl said.

'Actually, no. It's a reverse tower. So you go all the way up five thousand feet of Mount Alseed to then go a couple of thousand back down the tower that hangs off the edge of it like a fang. You can only see it from the coast so looking up won't help. It was built by the rock people of Alseed to deter invaders and allow—'

'Less history. You're sure it was east?'

'More southeast.'

Karl shook his head. 'I'll find it. Then it'll be simple enough to find a little hat.'

'It's not that simple. We couldn't find the hat.'

'Why not?'

'Because it's invisible.' He nudged Sags and laughed. 'You can't find what you can't see.'

'Don't worry, I'll find it somehow.' Karl stood. 'I have no choice.'

WASTE OF LIFE

Karl, Questions, Tortured Soul and Oaf travelled through the unknown for three sunsets to the southeast corner of Flowfornia.

On their travels, Karl had seen flies with teeth bigger than his own, vibrant flowers with combinations of colours he couldn't have imagined, and had eaten berries and leaves that may or not have made him unwell. At one point he was certain he saw a horned woman eating another horned woman by a lake, but he tried to forget that. He never knew whether the next thing would be beautiful or horrific. This kind of life was probably amazing to travellers and bandits, but with a death sentence over his head, Karl found it annoying. He was thankful for his friends, though. With Oaf accompanying him he even managed to rest, and Oaf was an extra pair of ears to handle Questions' thirst for knowledge.

The coastline came into view over the plains and the unfamiliar smell of sea air cleared Karl's nostrils. He couldn't believe the sea went so far. He'd only seen it in paintings; in person it was both stunning and menacing.

They walked along the shore and the demonic structure crept over the horizon. It hung off the top of a brown mountain like a giant, rocky, splintered fang, pointing at the violent sea below, where swirling winds bashed waves into each other like watery bulls locking horns.

Karl thought if Mount Alseed could see, it would probably look down at them and laugh, saying, 'Ha! Look at you puny people, aren't you puny?' Then it wouldn't say anything else because it had poor conversation skills.

They dragged their weary bodies to the base of the mountain and Questions dropped to her knees. 'Why would someone build a tower on top to only go back down?'

'Because some people like to make my life hard.' Karl studied the steep mountain for a path up. A few trees poked out of the rocks at odd angles, having no place on the mountain, a bit like him in Hastovia. The remnants of old wooden homes made the place eerier than it needed to be.

'Why do people want to make your life hard?' Questions asked.

Karl's shoulders sunk. He didn't want to enter into another nonsense chat, so he ignored her. 'There's no clear way up.' He sat on a rock and leaned forward, trying to release the tension in his back.

Oaf took a sip of water from his waterskin. 'There's probably a trail around the other side of the mountain, but that's far away.' He studied the mountain and pointed to a ledge, about twenty feet high with a thin tree covered in vines. 'Looks like a path up there. I could throw you to that ledge and then you drop a vine down for us.'

'It's a pretty big distance.' Karl doubted Oaf could throw him that far.

'I can do it,' Oaf assured him.

'But more importantly, if you miss will I survive?'

'You might break something, but you'll be alright. It's roughly three and a bit average-sized people high. You might die if it was more than four.'

Karl shuddered. He stood and psyched himself up. 'Are you sure you can lift me, though?'

Oaf chuckled.

Karl clenched his fists, summoning his courage. 'And I'll definitely be okay?'

Oaf nodded and stepped towards him.

'Wait! Not yet.' Karl took long breaths and shook his limbs. 'By roughly three and a bit people, do you mean roughly below, or roughly above?'

Tortured Soul popped out of her bottle. 'Get on wiv it.'

'I agree.' Oaf grabbed Karl around the waist and then bent his legs.

'Wait! I'm still—'

Oaf launched Karl.

Karl shouted the entire way up and crashed into a tree.

'Are you okay?' Questions asked.

'Yeah… Just about.' He trembled.

'Now pass us a vine,' Oaf called up.

One slip and Karl would fall back the way he came. He grabbed the top of a vine wrapped around the tree. He slid down cautiously, taking the vine with him to untangle it. 'Here.' He dropped it to them.

Oaf grabbed it. 'Thanks.' He pulled the vine to check it was secure. The tree ripped out of its rocky home and narrowly missed Oaf.

'Oh,' Karl said.

'I can throw Questions up and take the long way,' Oaf said.

Questions aimed a smile up at Karl.

'You know what. Keep her with you,' Karl replied.

Questions bit her bottom lip and looked at the ground.

'I'll see you at the top,' Karl said.

* * *

KARL WALKED for so long that by the time he reached the summit the sun had moved from over the Dead Lands in the east, to the southern sea. Karl's thighs throbbed and it felt as if Peezant had pecked them the entire way. He rested on the rocky ground and stretched his legs, hoping for relief, but he spotted a sword-wielding Fool. Karl scurried behind a rock and studied the situation.

The Fool jumped around a tiled opening on a slant, clearly the entrance to the reverse tower. Tall stone totems surrounded it, with carved faces of what Karl assumed were once rulers of this mountain.

The Fool looked at all the points of the summit in turn. It gazed at the solitary tree to Karl's left, which leaned so far over the mountain edge it looked like it was trying to jump off it. Then the Fool looked at the sharp rocks opposite Karl, then checked around the totems, diverting its eyes back to the path.

Karl wondered if he should wait for the others, but there could have been more Fools on their way.

He crept after the Fool's gaze. He passed the tree and then crawled behind a rock. The Fool took a break and practised manoeuvres. When it turned back to the mountain path, Karl pushed through the thigh pain, ran and rolled into a crevice near the totems, evading the Fool's spin. All he had to do was wait. He caught his breath and closed his eyes for a moment.

He opened them.

The Fool stood above him, pointing its sword at him. It grunted.

'Hi there,' Karl said. 'I'm just relaxing in this comfortable rock hole. Care to join me?'

The Fool gestured for Karl to stand, so he did.

'I mean no harm. I just love exploring, and that pretty door in the mountain looks like a fun place to explore.'

'There's nothing down there. I'd know. I had a look,' the Fool said.

'Well, if there's nothing down there you won't mind me entering?'

The Fool raised its sword. 'Nobody can enter. Arazod has ordered us to search and guard all caves and towers, and to kill a man named Karl and deliver his head. Are you Karl? You look like him.'

'No. I'm… Derlik.'

The Fool released a disappointed grunt. 'I lost the parchment with a likeness of him sketched on it and am going by memory.' It shrugged. 'I needed to blow my nose, you see, and then the wind carried the parchment off the mountain.'

'It happens.' Karl scratched his neck. 'If I meet a Karl I'll be sure to send him your way.'

'Arazod also said if we find any magical treasures to bring them back. You got any?'

'Sadly not.' It wasn't good news for anyone if Arazod was hunting more power.

Karl stepped towards the entrance, but the Fool blocked his path.

'I told you. I have orders.' It scratched a line in the rocks. 'The moment you cross that line, I have to kill you. It's nothing personal.'

'I understand,' Karl said.

The Fools followed orders so obediently, but what if Karl could make something feel like part of the order? He remembered an incident from his childhood. Sabrinia was punished for setting fire to King Sastin's clothes and her toys were confiscated. To cheer her up, Karl made her play with imaginary items, and they had more fun than they ever did with real toys. 'Well, if I can't go in there, I'll just look for invisible secrets around here instead.'

'What? Invisible?'

'Didn't you know? There are invisible treasures all around. This is the Land of Invisible Loot.' Karl grabbed nothing out of the sky. 'A golden fly! These are so rare and meant to be really tasty.' He pretended to eat it. 'Oh that's incredible. Like someone is cuddling my intestines.'

'My intestines want a cuddle!' the Fool moaned. It picked up nothing from the ground and held out its hand. 'What's this?'

'That's nothing,' Karl replied.

It grabbed at the air and showed Karl its palm. 'And this?'

'That's also nothing.'

It tried again. 'This?'

'That? Well that is…'

The Fool's eyes lit up, hopeful.

'Still nothing.' Karl walked to the mountain edge and felt the air with his foot. 'Oh wow! I knew it! It's actually the start of an invisible bridge! It must curve around to a cave in that lower part of the mountain. I bet there's loads of treasure. There might even be the legendary Golden Pig.'

'Golden Pig?'

'Surely you've heard of the Golden Pig? It's rumoured to live in a mountain cave, with meat so tasty that anyone who eats it can never feel sadness. It even regenerates so you can eat from it every day. Maybe you should take a look.'

'But I've been ordered to stay…'

'Technically, you're still guarding by searching potential hiding places. This Karl character may even be down there. It would be easy for him to live there forever.'

'Hmm.'

'And Arazod did say to take magical treasures back.'

'Good point.'

'Think of how pleased Lord Ragnus and Arazod will be if you take the Golden Pig back with you. Lord Ragnus might even smile.'

The Fool stepped forward then stopped. 'Must kill ugly Karl.

Must return his head to Arazod. Must guard. Must bring magic treasure back.' It stepped back behind the line.

Karl huffed, annoyed that the orders seemed to be ranked by importance. He leaned on the rock on the edge of the cliff. He had to do the only thing he could to move the Fool from near the entrance. He hoped he could then outsmart it to run into the tower. 'I'm Karl...'

The Fool's expression dulled and its eyes glazed over. 'Must kill ugly Karl. Must return his head to Arazod.'

'You said that already.'

It ran at him, its sword drawn back. 'Must kill ugly Karl.' It swung. Karl ducked behind the rock and the Fool's sword smacked against it and fell to the ground.

While the Fool nursed its sore wrist, Karl ran for the tower entrance, but the Fool grabbed his shirt, then pounced on him and bit his neck.

Karl screamed as its teeth sunk deeper, trying to rip Karl's head off his shoulders.

Karl felt dizzy. Weakened, he fell back, smacking the Fool's head against the rock.

The Fool fell off Karl, and he rolled away.

The Fool stumbled near the cliff edge, dazed and rubbing its head.

'I'm sorry,' Karl said as he shoved the Fool off the mountain. It disappeared beneath the water, chewed up by the crashing waves.

Karl buried his face in his hands and took a deep breath. Was this how it had to be? Take lives or lose his own? His chest tightened. He sat and stared at the infinite sea. The Fool was like him, a prisoner in Arazod's world.

Karl listened to the wind and he cried. He would wait for Questions and Oaf and wished he had from the start. He vowed to never kill another Fool.

He tore a piece of his sleeve off and patted it against his stinging, bleeding neck.

In the distance, a large, bird-like creature with tentacles flew towards the mountain. It seemed that waiting would only lead to him becoming a snack.

He picked up the Fool's sword and made for the tower entrance. He had to get home and escape this awful land.

SHARED EXPERIENCE

Oaf and Questions pushed their tired bodies up the ever-winding mountain path.

'Is it Lomboni?' Questions asked Tortured Soul, who floated on the water in her bottle that Oaf carried. Questions loved trying to help Tortured Soul to return to her true self, and she was sure this was the name that would do it.

'Nope. You're not gettin' anywhere. I'm goin' bed,' she said.

Oaf put her back in the pouch inside his vest.

Questions dragged her feet.

'Do you want to stop for a bit?' Oaf asked.

'What about Karl?' How could they stop when he was waiting for them?

The summit seemed to get further away.

'You have to look after yourself, not just Karl,' Oaf said.

'What if he's in danger?'

'We don't need to stop for long,' Oaf assured her. 'And if we turn up exhausted we won't be much help.'

Questions nodded. They sat against rocks and absorbed the silence, gazing out towards the east of Flowfornia. Beaches, forests and castle ruins all the way up to the Dead Lands.

Oaf stared at Questions. Was he going to say something? Why was he just staring? Should she ask him something? 'Can I ask you a question?' Questions asked.

'Of course.' Oaf smiled.

Questions took her book and quill from her pouch, thinking about what she wanted to ask, but would it upset him? 'Why did Lord Ragnus kill your people?'

Oaf took bread from his pouch.

Was he annoyed? Should she have asked a simpler question like, what's your favourite food? Or, do you like the night sun?

Oaf tore a piece of bread and offered it to Questions, leaving himself barely a mouthful. 'Because Lord Ragnus only knows hate. I heard that when he was nine, some travellers asked to stay in the village he lived in, and while the villagers didn't want to accept the travellers, his mother welcomed them. They deceived her and stole all the village's crops, costing them trade and food. The villagers didn't like the poorer way of life and blamed Ragnus' mother, tortured her in front of him. Every day they would whip, wound and do whatever else they thought of to her and make him watch. They crushed her fingers, and bent her legs in ways they shouldn't bend, all in front of him. Then they'd heal her to start again. It went on for too many sunsets. They told him he could end her suffering by killing her, otherwise they would continue. After one year of saying no, he put her out of her misery. But, he had to do it with just his hands. He was never the same.'

Questions shook her head. Why did such cruelty exist? The weight of sadness pulled at Oaf's face. Questions didn't write anything down, giving him her full attention.

'When he was with us he showed signs of goodness. But then he set horned wolves on us.' Pain left Oaf's body through a long breath.

Questions knew that breath; she had breathed it.

'He beat my mum into the sea until she disappeared.' Oaf stared into the distance.

Questions' eyes welled up. 'Can I dedicate a page in my book to your mother?'

Oaf looked confused. Was he insulted?

'That would be really nice,' he said.

Questions smiled. 'What was she like?'

'Erm… She was kind, smart, and the best sculptor in Reech.'

Questions wrote a description down, all in the form of questions.

Oaf smiled warmly. 'She cared about life… She used to put me on her hump and run around the beach…' Oaf choked up.

'Have I upset you?' Questions asked.

'In a good way. You've made me remember her properly, instead of at the moment she died… There was a lot more to her life than how it ended.'

Questions placed her hand on his.

'Thanks,' Oaf said. 'I guess you know how it feels.'

She nodded and rubbed his hand.

SCREECH.

A brown eagle the size of two Oafs, with three white, feathery tentacles hovered above them.

'Watch out!' Oaf warned.

It swooped at them and swung its tentacles. Oaf pushed Questions out of the way. A tentacle slapped against the rocks.

'Octo-eagle,' Oaf said. 'They used to fly over Reech in the hot seasons on their way to the mountains. Watch out for the tentacles.'

'What do we do?'

The octo-eagle screeched again.

'We run.'

They sprinted up the path.

The octo-eagle descended on them.

Oaf jumped on Questions and shielded her. The creature's talons tore strips off his leather vest.

Oaf pointed to a narrow crack in the mountainside. 'There.'

The octo-eagle screeched and dived, but Oaf pushed Questions into the crack and blocked her. Their bodies pressed against each other.

'What are you doing?'

'Just stay in here.'

It reminded Questions of her father standing in the doorway, blocking the icy winds from freezing her. She feared it would end the same way.

A tentacle whipped Oaf. His body jerked and he groaned.

'Are you okay?' Questions asked. Why was his face twitching?

Oaf nodded. 'Just a bit paralysed from the neck down. Take Tortured Soul.'

Questions reached into Oaf's vest and took Tortured Soul's bottle and placed it in her own pouch.

The octo-eagle hovered, studying how to get its meal. It landed on the path and poked its head into the crack. It screeched and bit, but couldn't quite reach Oaf. Its beak scratched Oaf's back and it whipped him.

Oaf's face jolted.

Questions felt Oaf's breath quicken, and his eyes reddened. 'Are you going to die?' What could she do?

The octo-eagle wrapped a tentacle around Oaf's face. It dragged him, but Questions pulled Oaf tight to her. She strained, but was no match for the muscular tentacles. The octo-eagle nearly had Oaf within eating range.

Panicked, Questions felt around the rocky wall and broke off some loose stone.

The octo-eagle craned its head through the crack. It opened its beak and screeched.

Questions threw the rock into its mouth. It choked and

coughed. It stumbled and bashed its face off the ground. It lashed at its throat with its tentacles, then fell off the mountainside.

'Are you hurt?' Questions asked Oaf.

He foamed at the mouth. 'Its tentacles... They... paralysis. I'll be okay... a... while...' he struggled to say.

'Why did you hurt yourself to save me?' Questions wiped the saliva from Oaf's mouth.

'Why not?' Oaf answered.

Questions smiled. She realised their bodies were still touching. 'What do we do now?'

'Leave me here. I'll move when I can. But you need to help Karl.'

TOWER OF TORMENT

Karl dragged his heavy legs down the stone steps that seemed to never end. The brown rock walls were only illuminated by occasional, window-like holes, through which the wind created a hellish whistling, as if he were inside a giant, out-of-tune flute.

Agonised faces were carved into the rock. Karl worried they would come to life and attack him.

The dead Fool crossed his mind, and probably would until Karl died.

Karl poked his head through one of the holes. Mount Hastovia pierced through the clouds in the north, and the Dead Lands to the east looked like a tiny mound of sand. Karl had no idea what anything else was, but it astonished him how limited his life had been within Flowforn's four walls. He understood what Sabrinia had said about feeling insignificant against the land's grandeur, only, he didn't feel part of anything bigger. He felt more irrelevant.

He sat to catch his breath and studied one of the faces in the wall. One eye was half closed and the mouth was twisted.

Karl removed the bloody sleeve from his neck. He left it on

the step, touched his wound and grimaced at the stinging. He ripped his other sleeve off and covered the laceration.

Something breathed and it wasn't him. 'Questions? Oaf?' he hoped.

'Who dares descend me?' an authoritative voice boomed from everywhere and nowhere.

Karl's eyes settled on the face in the wall. 'Are you alive? Were you the victim of some evil? Is there some annoying quest I have to fulfil to free you from your rock prison and get the Hat of Invisibility?'

'Stop talking to the wall, idiot. I, the tower, Alseed, address you.'

'What? How is a talking tower even possible?' Karl shuddered. 'Are you a god?'

'No, I'm a tower created by people given power by the gods.'

'And this face definitely isn't alive?'

'No. It is just part of the design. Atmospheric, you know? Now, if you don't mind, when you continue your journey, maybe don't stomp so heavily. And take that nasty rag off me!' Alseed moaned.

Karl huffed and picked up his bloody sleeve. 'Just tell me where the Hat of Invisibility is… please.'

Alseed whistled, ignoring Karl.

'Okay. Well how about this?'

Karl stomped hard and fast, but all that did was hurt his ankles.

'Idiot,' Alseed said.

Karl pressed his head to the wall and sighed.

The tower giggled. 'Stop that, it tickles.'

Karl sighed against the wall again.

'I said stop!'

Karl persisted and scratched the wall.

'Stop it! You'll make me sneeze!'

'Then tell me what I need to know.'

A great gust blew down the stairs and smashed Karl against the wall. The sword flew out of his hand and down the steps.

'I warned you,' Alseed said.

Karl struggled to his feet. 'Where is the Hat of Invisibility?'

'Silence.'

Karl grabbed onto the rim of a hole and tickled the tower. Another gust blew but Karl held on. He tickled the tower again.

'Okay! Okay. At the bottom. The bottom! Obviously. Throne room,' Alseed said.

Satisfied with its cooperation, Karl continued his journey. 'You're not going to sneeze me out are you?'

'Do you know anyone who can control their sneezing?'

'Good point,' Karl said.

Karl dragged himself through the doorway to the round, rocky throne room at the bottom of the fang. The room was more of a semi-circle, because the wall opposite Karl was gone. It was a deadly exit to the sea. The throne faced it, as though the king of this place would sit and watch people be thrown or blown to their deaths.

The wind slapped Karl's face with a stench he could only describe as death, rot, and old toilet bucket. A lonely pedestal with nothing to show stood next to the throne, as if it had grown out of the ground. It had a stone backboard, presumably to stop the wind blowing the Hat of Invisibility off it. Karl's sword shone at the foot of the pedestal.

He retrieved his weapon, and then the familiar sound of flapping and squawking distracted him. Peezant swooped in, killing Karl's hopeful mood.

'I can help you get the hat!' Peezant threw his new silk scarf around his neck to show it off.

'It's clearly on that pedestal. Otherwise it wouldn't make sense to have one. Now get your beak out of my business!'

'Appearances can be deceiving. If you give me—'

Karl grabbed Peezant by the face and held him close. 'Get

someone else to fund your wardrobe.' He flicked Peezant's beak and threw him out of the hole.

Peezant regained his composure and hovered.

Karl glared at the feathered fury-bringer. 'Don't try to tell me you know more than me. The hat is obviously on this…' Karl thrust his right hand onto the pedestal. It felt as though he'd dipped his fingers into a bowl of sticky beans.

Peezant laughed.

Karl grimaced. 'Why's it moist?' He rolled whatever it was around his fingers.

'It's the stinkiest piece of dragon dung in aaaaaaalll of Hastovia. You can thank the dead Invisible Dragon for that. The ruler of this tower used to throw it at people before kicking them out to sea.' Peezant laughed louder. 'The smell is impossible to wash off! Enjoy!' Peezant flew away. His laughter carried as he disappeared into the distance.

Karl shook his hand off, but the moisture consumed it and it wafted the hellish odour around. Karl retched. 'Tower? Mr. Alseed? Where's the hat?'

'In here.'

'I know that… but where exactly?'

'If you can't figure it out you don't deserve it.'

'Don't make me tickle you.'

'You want to risk being blown into the sea? Then go for it.'

Karl huffed. 'Useless.' Karl moved around slowly and waved his arms to feel for the hat.

Alseed chuckled.

Karl, embarrassed, stopped.

'No, no, please carry on,' Alseed said.

Karl remembered in Flowforn he used to walk down the alleys with Sabrinia and they'd hit walls with a stick. Obviously, it wasn't the best game. He'd hit a wall. CRACK. He'd hit another wall. CRACK. He'd hit a hanging carpet. THUD.

If he threw the invisible dung around the room and

listened, when it hit something that wasn't stone it might sound different. Worth a try, and his hand already smelled horrific.

He scooped a handful of dung in his right hand and threw it in a general direction.

SPLAT.

He took another handful and threw it at a different wall.

SPLAT.

He stuck his hand in the dung to get more. He felt it under his nails and shuddered. He spun around and threw it.

THUD.

It alerted him to the top of the wall to his immediate left. He felt around the wall and grasped at air. Finally he got hold of something wedged where wall met ceiling. He pulled on it, revealing a statue of a tiny rock warrior, its face covered in scratches. He stroked whatever he had pulled off the statue and a green, unimpressive hat materialised. 'Success! Finally, I can go home.'

The fang tower vibrated.

'You didn't think it would be that easy, did you?' Alseed replied.

'Oh no...'

On both sides of the entrance, two six-foot rock warriors broke out of the stone, each armed with a rock spear. They had no mouths, and dark dents for eyes.

Karl ran for the stairs, but a wall shut off the path. 'This seems bad.' Karl turned back and held his sword out.

'Now it's your choice. Die by sea, or by spear?' Alseed said.

Karl backed towards the exit to the sea. He considered his chances of survival if he fell. He wouldn't. 'Is there a third option?'

One rock warrior stalked him, while the second struggled to move its right leg. They were incredibly slow.

Alseed huffed. 'Sorry about this. They've not battled in a while so their limbs are a touch stiff. I don't mean to delay the inevitable.'

'How considerate.' Karl shook his head.

The first rock warrior neared, while the second tried to move.

Karl pulled the Hat of Invisibility over his head. Everything calmed and came into sharp focus. He waved his hand in front of his face and watched the trail of air it left with each motion.

'You do realise they can still see your clothes?' Alseed said.

'Oh...'

The rock warrior swung its spear at Karl's head. He ducked and the spearhead smashed against the wall.

Karl slashed at the rock warrior, but his sword bounced off its body and out to sea. The shock jolted his wrist. He frantically removed his shoes and trousers.

The rock warrior thrust its blunted spear at Karl. He fell out of the way and removed his shirt, becoming fully invisible. 'Ha. How are you going to get me now?'

The rock warrior searched the room.

Karl waited until it was by the hole and then pushed it, but it wouldn't budge.

Karl strained. 'Why won't you move?'

'Your arms are too puny,' Alseed said.

The rock warrior elbowed Karl in the jaw. He fell next to the pedestal, and one of his teeth rattled against the floor as blood poured from his mouth.

The rock warrior approached the blood that dotted the floor. It was about to stomp on Karl, but he rolled out of the way and in front of the entrance.

'Nowhere to run, little man,' Alseed teased.

'Just be quiet!' Karl spat blood and then realised that was stupid. He removed the hat and was naked.

Alseed laughed.

'Come on, swing at me,' Karl goaded his opponent, but the

other warrior kicked him and winded him. He dropped the hat by the pedestal.

Karl strained for the hat, but his enemy swept it away with its spear. It drew the spear back and lunged. Karl dodged and the rock warrior's momentum took it into the blocked entrance.

Karl ran for the indent in the wall that the first rock warrior had emerged from. He tickled it and pushed himself as far into it as he could.

'No. No!' Alseed moaned. 'No!' A sneeze broke off parts of the blocked entrance.

'Stop!' Alseed pleaded.

Karl tickled the wall again. The sneeze cleared the entrance and hurled Questions through it. The rock warriors fell.

'Questions!'

She was unconscious, wrapped around the pedestal.

The hat was caught against her foot. 'Questions! Get up and grab the hat!'

She stirred and her hand twitched.

'Questions! Wake up!'

The first rock warrior closed in on Questions' prone body.

'Questions, the hat. Quick!'

The rock warrior lifted its fist above her head.

Karl knew Questions was secure enough around the pedestal to survive the sneeze, but the hat...

He shut his eyes and scratched the wall.

The sneeze carried Karl's clothes and the Hat of Invisibility out to sea.

The gust flung the first rock warrior against the wall. Chunks of its arms and legs broke off and it landed at the edge of the room. The second rock warrior smacked into the throne. Its arm came off and spun along the stone. Questions remained wrapped around the pedestal.

Karl's eyes narrowed. He got up and dragged Questions into the indent in the wall and held her. Her arm bled.

'Please!' Alseed begged.

'You had your chance!' Karl's chest tightened. He didn't want to end another life, even if it was a pile of rocks.

'Please don't make me kill my sisters!' Alseed pleaded.

'You should've thought about that before you ruined my chance to get away from this place!'

'I'm sorry. I'm sorry…'

Karl touched his fingers to the wall. He stared at the rock warrior on the verge of falling out to sea, took a breath and lowered his hand. Killing them wouldn't bring the hat back. 'Will you let us leave here in peace?'

'Yes. I promise,' Alseed said.

Karl huffed and removed his fingers from the wall.

'Thank you,' Alseed said.

Karl dragged Questions' limp body towards the entrance to the throne room.

The rock warriors crawled towards their homes in the wall.

Questions stirred. 'Are you okay, Karl? Did I save you?' She sat up.

'Yes…' Karl gritted his teeth. 'Yes you did.' He would've said no, but worried it would lead to more questions.

'Where are your clothes?' Questions asked.

Karl's eyes welled up. He had entered the tower looking for an item of clothing, but instead had lost all of his. Struggling to say the words, he pointed to the sea.

'Did you find the Hat of Invisibility?'

He pointed to the sea again.

'Shall we just go down and get it?' Questions asked.

Karl sat on the floor and stared into the distance. 'I just need a moment, Questions.' He placed his hands over his genitals. He hated everything in the world.

'Do you want my clothes?' Questions asked.

'No. Thanks. Just… please… a moment.' His life was nothing.

'What's that horrible smell?' Questions asked.

Karl closed his eyes, wishing the rock warriors had crushed him.

WHEN TO GIVE UP

'*P*ull up a stool,' Frong told Karl.

Karl adjusted the leaves Oaf and Questions had fashioned into clothing that barely covered him. He dragged a tall stool towards Frong and Sags. 'Can I please have one of your lovingly made ales?' Karl asked Bar Witch.

'One gold piece,' she said.

'My gold is somewhere in the sea with all my clothes and the Hat of Invisibility. I can go outside and ask Questions and Oaf, but each time I move the leaves scratch against my sensitive bits.'

Bar Witch took a breath and dipped a cup into a bucket behind the bar. She walked over and gave it to him.

'Thanks.' Karl took a sip.

'It's from the spillage bucket,' she said.

Karl swilled the liquid in his mouth. He swallowed and smiled, hiding how much he hated the taste.

'What is that stink?' Bar Witch asked.

'It's Invisible Dragon dung.' Karl held up his offensive right hand. 'I don't suppose you have some way to get rid of it?'

Bar Witch shook her head.

Karl sighed. 'I've nearly died so many times. And now Arazod has sent Fools to find relics, hunt me, and guard ancient sites until they find what's in them.' He sat at a height that made Frong and Sags visibly uncomfortable with what was in their eye-line, but he didn't care anymore. 'I can't go through all that again...' He shook his head. 'The idea is I go home to avoid death and find out who I am, but to do that, I need to risk my life? It's pointless.'

'But we both know you're not going to give up, don't we?' Frong smiled.

Karl bit the skin around his thumb. Frong was right, but it didn't make Karl less terrified. 'Please tell me about those other relics? I promise to listen patiently.'

Frong smiled with a hint of pride. 'My stories just take getting used to. Then you won't be able to get enough of them, I can assure you.'

Bar Witch raised an eyebrow.

Frong turned to Sags. 'You ready to do this?'

Sags grunted in agreement.

Frong opened the wooden chest and took out two rectangular items wrapped in velvet. He handed one to Sags. 'Haven't looked at this since... Marlens.' They toasted and waited a moment.

'What is it?' Karl asked.

'It's our Journal of Adventures.' Frong and Sags removed the velvet, revealing two halves of a book. They clicked them together, then opened the book on the table. There was an etching of the three adventurers. Frong and Sags were young, happy and energetic next to Marlens, a smooth-faced witch with short red hair. Tears formed in Frong's eyes. He turned the pages.

'I'm sorry...' Karl said.

'There's the blood of the frog-badger,' Frong said, trying to keep it together. 'It was... formulated to burrow into mountainsides and create caves for people to take shelter when we had four thousand sunsets of rain. You could probably use it to make a path through the ground and into the castle without being detected.'

Bar Witch raised a finger. 'Oh, what about the wings of the Tree-Cyclopsi? They sounded fun.'

Frong nodded. 'They are a splendid creation. Not like normal wings, as they're not made from feathers, but the leaves of a magical tree. They have a real strength, and glow beautifully.' He turned the pages. 'There's the relic of persuasion, granting even the most socially incapable the gift to manipulate.' He raised an eyebrow at Karl.

'What?' He didn't get what Frong was hinting at.

Frong ignored him. 'Then there are the blade fish scales, from a pool in the waxy mines, which give the wearer a protective shell, shielding them from the toughest of magic. There are plenty.' Frong picked up a dry, hard, bone-snake skin shaving from a bowl and took a bite out of it, underlining his point.

Hope filled Karl's body. 'Why didn't you ever keep anything? Isn't the point of adventuring to keep something?'

Frong shrugged. 'We kept the memories and the shared experiences.' He and Sags exchanged a loving glance; Karl smiled at the warmth they showed each other.

'We loved the thrill of completing the adventure. Plus, these things are where they are for a reason. If we took them, someone would come after us, desperate for power.'

Karl understood.

'Your best chance is Lake Shizneh. It holds the wings of the Tree-Cyclopsi.'

'Is it because it's the least dangerous?' Karl asked.

Frong's eyes said otherwise. 'It's too treacherous to guard, so likely no Fools await you. Past a certain point the lake tries to grab you and swallow you. Only the really greedy go there.'

Sags grunted.

'Did he say there's an alternative?' Karl asked.

'No. He said the wings would be good because you can fly into Flowforn at night, avoiding any Fool patrols.'

'You got all of that from a grunt?'

'When you know someone, you know someone.'

Karl thought about Sabrinia. She was probably suffering in Arazod's company. 'Why can't Sags speak anyway?' Karl asked.

'He cut his tongue out.'

Sags showed Karl his half tongue and wiggled it.

Karl grimaced. 'Why would anyone do that?'

Frong chuckled. 'One of the tribes we met said that if they use a tongue in a potion it could bring Marlens back from the dead. Sags didn't hesitate to chop it off, but it turned out the tribe was wrong, so we ended up with a tongue soup.'

'That's awful!' Karl said.

'It happens. Soup wasn't bad, though. You should count yourself lucky. He's better like this. When he talked he'd just go on and on and on.'

Karl smiled, fully aware of what that was like.

Frong ripped several pages from the Journal of Adventures, rolled them up and handed them to Karl. 'I wrote everything we know about the lake here. It was thousands of sunsets ago so might be worthless. Otherwise, this is your survival guide.'

'Why are you being so kind?' Karl asked.

'Because you're going to promise me that if you get the wings, you'll take Sags for an evening flight around all of southern Flowfornia before you disappear.'

Sags clapped, excited.

Karl nodded, knowing he would likely forget that promise. 'Deal. And thanks again.'

Bar Witch returned and threw Karl a sack. 'Clothes.'

'Thanks.' Karl steadied himself, touched by the kindness they all showed him when they had no obligation to.

Frong extended a hand. 'If you don't make it back, it's been nice talking to someone from Flowforn who isn't so utterly awful.'

LAKE SHIZNEH

Karl wore ill-fitting orange clothes meant for children and waved a fly away from his face. Bar Witch assured him the clothes were the only spares she had, but he was certain she was playing a joke on him.

He looked at what must have once been hilly grassland, now covered in thick, dark green sludge. 'So I guess this is Lake Shizneh.' The tops of trees poked out of the mess, grasping for that last bit of air. From the haunting majesty of Mount Alseed, Karl now faced Hastovia's toilet.

A slow whirlpool with green arms pulled everything from old shoes to dead bodies into it. It was a sort of belly of the lake, feeding the filth so it could spread, and the slime rose and fell as though the lake breathed.

Karl swatted another fly away from his stomach, where his top refused to meet the trousers. The gentle wind blew the taste of waste into his mouth and up his nostrils. If there was a competition for the rankest, foulest-smelling thing ever, he'd vote for Lake Shizneh. He retched, covering his mouth and nose with the hand he had put in dragon dung. He threw up and decided he'd vote for his hand instead.

'Is it true the stream from near Flowforn carries all waste here?' Questions asked.

'Considering there are dead bodies and Arazod is ruling Flowforn, I'll say yes.' Karl grimaced.

Oaf caught up. 'Is your name Boingo?' he asked Tortured Soul, sat on his shoulder.

'Nah. Not doin' anythin'.'

'Is your name Crumbon?' Questions asked.

'I might not have a memory, but I know that ain't even a name,' she said.

Questions pointed at the thick branches and treetops poking out of the sludge. 'Is that how we get across the lake?'

'It looks unnecessarily dangerous, so I guess so.' Karl hoped that this would be the last deadly place he had to visit.

Among the bony remains of those who had failed to make it across, Karl spotted a Fool consumed by the green. 'Looks like Frong was wrong about Fools coming here.' A parchment in the Fool's hand had the likeness of Karl on it.

The entrance to the cave was across the lake. 'Why a cave?' He huffed. 'Can't they just have these relics on show as a nice display in someone's home?'

They ventured forward until the grass met the thick lake liquid.

Karl took the pages Frong had given him and stepped closer to the muck. He read:

> The lake surprised us by how big and dirty it was. And when we say big, we don't mean big like a kingdom, but big enough to surround a castle. It made us discuss the word big as we thought of a way across...

Karl slapped the pages with the back of his hand. 'His guide is just a conversation with himself!' Karl scanned the pages, searching for something useful, and as he spotted the words "Getting to the cave entrance," a green arm rose from the lake and snatched the pages. 'No!' Karl reached for them and lost his balance.

Oaf grabbed the back of Karl's collar and yanked him back.

Karl held his eyes shut, annoyed to have lost his guide.

'Better the guide than you,' Oaf said.

Karl nodded. 'Thanks.'

Oaf pointed to a hillside, far away from the stench and danger. 'I'll meet you back there.'

'What? Why?' Karl asked.

'Those branches won't hold me.'

'Are you sure?' Karl stared at the branches that definitely wouldn't hold Oaf.

'Sorry,' Oaf said.

Tortured Soul leapt out of her bottle and onto Oaf's shoulder. 'I can help Karl and Questions. This green stuff won't bovva me. I'm too light to sink, and too quick to grab.' She jumped on the filth and ran around, proving her point. 'Plus it keeps me moist.'

'I don't think so,' Karl replied.

'Come on. I can go ahead and warn you of any dangers and stuff.'

'Please, Karl, she might remember things,' Oaf pleaded.

Karl stared at Tortured Soul's sad little abnormally shaped head. 'Fine, you can come.'

Tortured Soul grinned.

'Good luck.' Oaf walked away.

'Bet we come back and he's having a nap,' Karl said to Questions. 'Okay, Tortured Soul, what do—'

Tortured Soul was gone, running along the green muck, having the time of her life.

Karl shook his head. 'I guess I have no choice.' He moved his foot towards the first branch, but Questions stopped him. 'Do you want me to go first? Do you want me to make sure it's sturdy?'

'I guess that makes sense, but please be careful.'

Questions stretched out her leg. Karl felt guilty for not going first, but she was right.

The branch wobbled under her weight. She placed a hand against the top of the tree for support and climbed up.

'Good work,' Karl said.

Questions moved to the next branch.

Karl cautiously followed. 'Now let's speed up so we don't get swiped.'

Branch by branch, tree by tree, they advanced over the stench. Karl found his rhythm. It was slow enough that he didn't lose balance, but not so slow he got caught. Questions was far ahead now.

'Stop!' a Fool holding a spear shouted behind Karl. 'No one is allowed to…' It looked at its parchment. 'Ugly Karl!'

'Just Karl is fine.'

The Fool's eyes glazed over and it chased him. 'Must kill ugly Karl, and return his head to Arazod.'

Karl sped up, but slipped and just about steadied himself. He looked back, relieved to find the Fool wasn't moving swiftly.

It wobbled on every branch and seemed stuck between being frozen by fear, but compelled to complete its task.

'Stop,' Karl said. 'Go back, you'll fall in.'

It wobbled, and ungracefully made its way onto the next branch. 'Must kill ugly Karl, and return his head to Arazod.'

Karl couldn't do anything. The Fool swayed, edging towards the next branch. Karl refused to watch. Questions waited on the other side, the sympathy clear on her face.

Karl continued, the Fool's repetition of its orders filling the silence, until it spoke no more and Questions looked away.

Karl made it to land, tormented by another Fool wasting its life.

'Are you okay?' Questions asked him.

'No,' Karl replied. He couldn't understand why his death meant so much to Arazod. Karl's life had meant nothing to anyone for nineteen years, and now it meant something in the worst possible way.

'Do you think the lake is one giant creature?' Questions asked. The thought had crossed Karl's mind. 'I hope not.'

'How are caves made?' she asked.

'Don't do this now,' he said, aware she was only trying to distract him from what had just happened.

'Are they made by things trying to get out of somewhere? Or are they made by things trying to get into somewhere?'

'Please…' Karl lay on his back and shut his eyes.

'Do you think Oaf is okay?' Questions asked.

'I don't care, I'm resting.'

'Can you open your eyes?' Questions' voice quivered. She poked him.

'Give me a moment, will you? I need my heart to calm down.' Liquid splatted against Karl's cheek. 'Stop dripping whatever you're dripping on me, Questions. It's not funny and it smells,' he whined.

'Why don't you tell the dripper that?' Questions said.

'The dripper? No…' Karl's voice cracked. 'I'm going to open my eyes, and there's not going to be a weird scary thing here, okay? Eyes about to open.' He opened them. A bubble with an eye stared at him. Karl shrieked and sprinted into the cave.

WASTE-FILLED WONDER

hey crept through the dark, narrow, chalky cave. Everything Karl touched left a dusty stain on his hands, but he was relieved that the eye thing had left them alone.

'Oaf is probably eating some berries around now,' he moaned, saying anything to drown out the fear.

The cave led them deeper until they couldn't see anything in front of them, or the green glow of the lake behind.

'Why have you stopped?' Questions asked.

'Because I can't see, Questions.'

'Does stopping in the middle of darkness make your eyes work better?'

'No, Questions! It doesn't! I'm just collecting my thoughts.'

'Are we lost?'

Karl huffed. 'We'd be lost if we knew where we were meant to be going! So no. We're not lost.'

'Help!' Tortured Soul screamed, bumping into Karl's leg.

A green glow closed in behind them; the bubble.

'Of all the ways to die, I'm going to be suffocated by a stench bubble.' Karl clenched his fists.

The bubble stopped in front of them and they waited for it to make its move. Questions approached it.

'No, Questions…' Karl said.

The bubble wiped itself on Questions' face, tickling her, and then it indicated to Karl with its eye.

'What's it doing?' he asked.

'I reckon it wants you to follow,' Tortured Soul said.

The bubble's eye moved up and down to nod.

'Just make sure it don't gobble me up,' Tortured Soul added.

'Do you think it wants to be our friend?' Questions asked.

'It wouldn't be the smelliest friend I ever had,' Karl replied.

The bubble floated towards Karl's dragon-dung-scented hand, rolled its eye around, and then gave off an eye sneeze.

'Looks like you're the pongiest chum it's ever had, though!' Tortured Soul said.

Questions laughed.

'Great, we've got ourselves a jester. We should take it back to Arazod to see if it can make him crack a smile in that stupid little beak of his.'

The bubble's eye welled up.

Karl shook his head. 'It seems the glorious one has already left his mark on this part of Flowfornia too.'

The bubble sped ahead and they followed its glow until they came to an opening.

They stepped into what must have once been an underground paradise, now overrun by sludge dripping through holes in the cavern walls.

'Wow!' Karl stared ahead. It was the most dominant tree, bigger than any Karl had seen in Flowforn Forest. Green sludge hugged the skeletal branches on one half, turning the brown into a dead grey. The other half shone so brightly that Karl had to squint. Beams of light burst through cracks in the rocky ceiling and illuminated the red, yellow, and orange leaves. Whatever created Hastovia had chosen this tree to be the most beautiful in the world, then for some reason hid it from everyone.

'Is the tree dying?' Questions asked.

'I don't know, but it doesn't look healthy,' Karl replied.

The tree roots pierced up through the soil and created ten normal-sized trees in a perfect circle around it. Half of them mirrored the beauty of the tree, while the others struggled for life.

Karl's eyes traced a tree root, which cracked through rocks in the north wall and escaped into the world above.

A waterfall poured through a large hole and flowed into a clear stream. It split off and fed directly into fountains to the south and east of the tree. The western fountain overflowed with sludge.

Questions approached the southern fountain and ran her hand over the tiles, carved with bald, but hairy bodied, one-eyed people with wings.

Tortured Soul jumped into the water while the bubble, vibrating, stared at the tree.

Karl entered the circle of trees and joined the bubble next to the bony remains of what must have been small creatures... or children. Another pile of bones was at the base of the tree along with spears. Dead Fools.

Karl touched the tree's bark, smooth as skin. It vibrated and rippled. He rubbed his hand over it then poked it. The bark moulded around his finger, but he wasn't scared. It was as if it communicated with him.

'Do you think the tree is part person?' Questions asked.

He'd met a talking tower, so it was possible. He knocked on the tree and it vibrated. He knocked again. It vibrated again.

'Do you think that's a bad idea?' Questions asked.

'It's probably been ages since something has been here. If it is part person, it just needs a bit of waking up.' Karl smacked the tree. 'Come on.' The vibrations sped up and the tree shook.

The bubble shot back into the cave.

'Maybe you were right, Questions.' Karl and Questions stepped away.

Branches shook from the top of the tree all the way down. The tiniest, frailest thing poked its head out from behind the trunk. It was a bald, naked, little old man with wings. It had one eye on its berry-sized head and was a shrivelled version of the creatures on the tiles. Karl imagined it was the kind of creature a king or queen would give their spoilt child as a plaything, only for the child to torment it.

'Are you who I get the wings from?' Karl asked.

The creature flew in front of his face, spat in his eye and flew several feet back.

'Horrid little thing!' Karl wiped his face.

'Shall I look through my book?' Questions asked.

'If you think it'll help.' Karl edged closer to the creature.

Questions skimmed through the pages.

Karl readied his fingers to pinch the creature by the wings. 'Okay, let's try—' It whizzed behind Karl's head. He turned around and the creature kicked his ear then flew away. 'This is annoying.' He chased the creature, but couldn't catch it.

It flew up and sat on a branch. 'Enough,' it said in a deep voice reserved for larger beasts. 'I ask three questions. If correct, you ask me question. If wrong, I eat.'

'You eat, in general? Or you eat… us?'

'I eat.'

'That doesn't answer anything!'

'Favourite number of mine, what?' the creature asked.

'You're joking, right?'

'You're joking not number.'

'Wait! That wasn't my answer. Hmm… Twe…' Karl studied the creature's face for a hint. 'Se… Foouu…'

'Is it six?' Questions stood next to Karl, book in hand.

The creature laughed then stopped. 'You correct.' It disappeared into the leaves.

Questions showed Karl a page with a drawing of the creature. It had no name.

Karl took the book and read. 'Does the creature like the number six?' 'Have I met three of them on my travels?' 'Are they always near filth?' He smiled. 'Very impressive, Questions.' He flicked pages back and forth. 'But where's the rest? It's got two more questions.'

Questions shrugged.

'Your dad didn't finish it, did he?' Karl asked, sympathetic.

Questions shook her head and Karl handed the book back to her.

'Thanks,' Karl said. The leaves rustled. 'Come on then. Next question.'

The creature burst out of the leaves and placed two egg-shaped pieces of fruit, one black and one red, on the grass in front of them. 'One good. One deadly, but one time good. Which?'

Karl, baffled, scrunched his face.

'Shall I do this for you, Karl?' Questions stepped forward.

Karl put his arm across her. 'You've done enough for me.'

'Did I tell Sabrinia I would do anything to help?'

'Yes. So you can help by not doing this.' Karl picked up both pieces. 'So one good. One deadly, but one time good? Whatever that means.'

The creature rubbed its belly, mocking Karl.

'Is it you?' Karl asked the black fruit. 'Or is it you?' he asked the red.

'Fruit no speak, idiot man,' the creature said.

Karl tutted. 'So one is completely fine. The bad one that is one time good probably means it's a mystery fruit.' Karl had no idea what he was talking about. 'I'll trust instinct.' He took a bite out of the black one before he could convince himself not to.

Questions gasped.

As soon as Karl's teeth pierced the skin, his head inflated to six times its size and thudded against the grass.

'Am I dead? Is this death?' Karl tried to lift his head off the ground but couldn't. 'I'm dead aren't I?' His brain felt hot and his legs jumped around his anchored head.

'That's amazing!' Tortured Soul said.

'No, it isn't!'

'Are you okay, Karl?' Questions tried to lift his head.

'No, Questions. My head is the size of a small boat and my brain is hot. This is the opposite of okay!'

The creature laughed.

Karl cried. 'You must be very happy with yourself.'

'Congratulations. Eat other fruit.'

'Congratulations? Congratulations!'

'Good one turns you big head. Deadly one, good for one time when you big head. Antidote to big head. If eat without big head, head shrinks, crush brain and eyes. Small head make dead.'

Karl tried to move his head but gave up. 'What's wrong with you? Why can't we just talk instead of this death game?'

Questions fed the fruit to Karl. His head shrunk back to normal size.

He rested, relieved to be alive. 'Thank you, Questions.'

The creature chuckled.

Questions tapped her head as though remembering something. 'What did Father tell me in his story?' She turned away.

'Question three...' the creature announced.

'I don't care anymore! Where are the wings?' Karl stood and picked up one of the spears. He threw it, but missed the creature. The intent was clear, though.

'You provoked this!' Karl picked up another spear and threw it. The creature dodged and settled on the grass. It growled at Karl.

The creature's eye reddened and swelled.

'Did you attack it?' Questions asked Karl.

'Maybe.' Karl, regretful, stepped back.

The green sludge poured out of the western fountain, moved towards the creature and slid up its body and into its mouth.

The creature grew to twice Karl's size. It shot green ooze out of its eye, which splatted by Karl. An arm grew out of the slime and swiped at him.

'Questions, if you can remember anything else, now would be good.'

Questions took cover behind the east fountain, hopefully thinking of a solution.

Karl dodged slimy green hands and eye shots. 'Questions! Tortured Soul! A little help!'

Tortured Soul ran up to the creature. 'Halt!' she shouted.

The creature stopped and blinked at her.

Tortured Soul screamed and ran away.

Useless.

Karl prepared to dodge more slime shots. Was water the answer? Maybe he needed to push it into the fountain.

The creature sucked the leaves off a branch and turned to Questions.

Her eyes widened. 'Karl, can you block its belly hole?' She ducked sludge that hit the fountain.

Of course. The creature could only shoot from its eye because it discharged a thicker, green, sand-like material from its belly hole.

Karl clenched his fists. 'Hey, disgusting unhygienic thing. Here!' The creature turned around. Karl charged, but it back-handed him into the fountain. It dragged him by his foot, lifted him and slammed him against the ground. His bones ached.

Questions ran to help, but took a punch. Her head bashed against the fountain tiles.

The creature pinned Karl, used one hand to force his mouth open and gushed ooze into it. Karl coughed and struggled until sludge overflowed from his mouth. His breath was stuck and his body weakened.

Everything blurred. Tortured Soul bit the creature's heel, but was swatted away.

Karl's chest burned. His brain begged him to move, but his body refused.

Questions ran behind the creature, reached around and jammed her book into its belly hole. The creature squirmed. It swung its arms back, but she held on.

Karl's arm regained some life. He hammered his chest and stomach until he coughed up mess. He rolled onto his side and puked up a puddle of it, trying to breathe again.

The creature flew several feet off the ground and lined itself up with the tree. It grabbed Questions' arms so she couldn't let go. She would be crushed against the bark.

The creature flew backwards.

Karl jumped into Questions and pulled her leg. It knocked the creature off balance and it hit its head against the tree. They all fell, and Karl helped Questions to hold the book in the creature's belly hole.

The creature groaned, coughed and gargled. It writhed around and withered until it was so small it burst into specks of coloured dust. Questions grabbed her book and held it close.

'Are you okay?' Karl took large breaths.

She nodded. 'Are you?'

'I think so.' They sat on the grass, battered and exhausted.

The bubble returned.

'Nice of you to help,' Karl said to the bubble.

It ignored him and floated towards the tree. Slime receded from the branches. The bubble popped and turned into specks of coloured dust.

Questions grabbed Karl's wrist.

The coloured dust joined together and reformed. 'Please don't be another monster,' Karl moaned.

A three-foot, bald, orange, one-eyed creature stood before them. He had a single spot-sized hole for a nose, and wore no clothes. Pointy orange hairs from the neck down covered his body and he had majestic, leafy wings.

He gazed at Karl and Questions. 'You did it… thank you.' The creature rubbed his cheeks. 'How's my face?'

'It looks like a face,' Karl said.

The creature ran to the fountain to check his reflection. 'Phew, still smooth as a silk sheet.'

'What are you?' Questions asked.

'I'm Scrath. Elder of the Tree-Cyclopsi.' He approached them.

'And that slime-shooting beast thing?' Karl asked.

'The Putrid Valotaur.'

Questions jotted it in her book.

Scrath looked at the mess. 'This is what we're meant to stop from happening.'

Six other bubbles with eyes entered the garden. They gathered around Scrath.

'Family!' Scrath said.

The bubbles materialised into wingless Tree-Cyclopsi, thrilled to return to their old form. One turned into a one-eyed girl, only a foot and a half tall. She hugged Scrath. 'Daddy!'

'Wob!' Scrath beamed. He turned to Karl, Questions and Tortured Soul. 'Thank you for saving us. You are true heroes.'

'Heroes?' Karl smiled at Questions.

Scrath looked at the tree. 'Oh no! If the Heart of Hastovia perishes, so will all the other trees in the land.'

'Why?' Questions asked.

'It feeds the soil. Trees won't be able to grow.' Scrath shook his head. 'It's our job to keep this place clean.' He turned to his people. 'Tree-Cyclopsi. Let's do what we were born to do.' Scrath strained his eye, flew up and sucked the sludge from one of the smaller trees. The filth was processed into hair that sprouted from his already congested body.

The tree showed signs of returning to its bright, glowing form, and the other Tree-Cyclopsi helped to remove the slime.

'What happened to make this place so gloomy?' Questions asked.

'All I remember is Arazod coming here. He climbed towards the cave so I flew everyone up into holes in the cavern and we hid.'

Scrath pointed to the tree. 'He stood in front of the Heart of Hastovia and kept shouting, "Give me wings", but we ignored him.'

'A wise move,' Karl said.

'He folded his arms and he waited, for many sunsets, always demanding the wings. All we could do was watch dirt from Flowforn and the rest of Flowfornia build up, unable to clean it.'

Karl hung his head, guilty that he, like his fellow Flowfornians and King Sastin, had been part of the problem.

Scratch continued. 'Arazod still waited, obsessed, until the dirt became the lake that ate our homes and gave birth to the Putrid Valotaur, born of extreme filth.' He shook his head. 'Arazod only left when it became too dangerous for him to stay. He commanded Fools to wait at the foot of the tree, and they did, until they starved to death or were killed by the beast. It pained us to watch the trees suffer. And finally, when the Fools had died and Arazod was gone, we emerged only to be turned into bubbles by the Putrid Valotaur.' Scrath rubbed his eye. 'Arazod was willing to let pain come to this beautiful tree, all for some wings.'

Karl turned to Questions who winced. He clasped his hands together and turned to Scrath. 'Erm… I'm afraid I come with the same request as Arazod, but with a less whiny voice and no threats.'

'I'm sorry. But people abuse the gifts the gods left to this land. They always have a selfish motive.'

'I don't.'

'What do you plan to do with the wings?'

'I plan to leave Flowfornia.' It felt more real.

'Travelling? Sounds pretty selfish.'

'It's less about being selfish and more about survival.' It still sounded selfish.

Scrath shook his head. 'These wings were a gift from the Heart of Hastovia.' He patted the tree. 'It was left to us by one of the gods, Naturais.'

'I don't suppose the tree has any other gifts to give?'

'Actually, it grants wishes, so you can wish for a pair.'

'Amazing!' Karl said.

'But only once every two hundred and thirty-six years,' Scratch replied.

'Two hundred and thirty-six years!?' Karl moaned.

'It's more of an average. We are granted a wish whenever there is a day where nobody, anywhere, hurts anyone else. And on average, that's every two hundred and thirty-six years.'

'It wouldn't happen to be time for a new wish, would it?' Karl asked.

'Sadly not...' Scrath said. 'We're about two hundred years away. And with Arazod roaming the land, the average has gone up. It used to be every thirty-three years.'

Wob stroked her dad's leg and he held her hand.

'Well then, I guess that's it.' Karl rested against a miniature tree.

Tortured Soul jumped on his shoulder and stroked his cheek with her head. The gesture confused Karl, but he was too sad to stop her.

'All I want is to go home to find my parents and learn who I really am.' He longed for the closeness between Wob and Scrath. 'I'm sick of having a death sentence over my head. Back home might be a thousand times worse, but at least there's a chance there. Here I'm just a corpse that walks.'

Wob tugged on her dad's leg hair and looked him in the eye.

'Oh. Alright!' Scrath said.

'Alright what?' Karl asked.

'I have the power to grant *my* wings to someone else.'

'Why didn't you say?'

'I wanted you to be honest. And people tend to be honest when they've got nothing to gain. I tested you!' Scrath smiled.

Karl wanted to complain, but clenched his jaw.

'All these wings have done is attract the wrong kind of attention. You can have them,' Scrath said.

'Thank you!' Karl trembled. 'Thank you so much.'

'But. Do you promise to use your wings responsibly?' Scrath asked Karl.

'Of course.'

He raised a finger. 'Do you promise to use them for good and not evil?'

Karl nodded. 'Yes. For my definition of good.'

'Do you promise to help all those in need?'

'Yes. Yes. Come on.'

'Okay. Let's do this!' Scrath and the Tree-Cyclopsi stood in a circle around Karl.

'The procedure is pretty basic,' Scrath said, 'but we'll put on a show for you because you seem nice.'

They hummed, and a branch stretched out from the top of the Heart of Hastovia and stroked Karl's head. Feeling awkward, Karl joined in the humming, but his timing was off. He wasn't sure what the branch was doing. Twigs stretched around his face and grabbed him underneath the chin. The branch retracted swiftly and swallowed Karl into the tree.

He could barely breathe as his body was flung from side to side. Leaves and twigs scratched him and a blur of orange, brown and green surrounded him. He spun until the leaves parted, showing him the rocky ceiling. He worried he was going to be flung at it.

Karl's back tingled and heat built up in his shoulder blades. Air shoved him out of the tree and he fell towards the ground.

'This seems cruel,' he said.

Questions held her hand to her mouth, but wings of orange-brown leaf burst through Karl's top and helped him to hover.

His heart raced. 'These are amazing!' Karl tried to get to grips with his new body parts.

Scrath held Karl's shoulders to stop him zipping around. 'These are the only wings we can grant until we get another wish. They are transferrable to others more in need. So if you find someone more deserving, let us know.'

'I can't see that happening,' Karl said.

'Okay, Tree-Cyclopsi. Let's rid our home of this filth.'

They all went to split off, but Karl interrupted.

'Before you do your eye thing… is there any chance you can remove the stench from my hand?'

Scrath smelled Karl's hand, ran to a fountain and threw up in it. 'Oh my! That is horrible! What kind of person puts their hand in dragon dung?'

Karl huffed.

The group returned to Lake Shizneh, now a thriving, hilly grassland with a small lake in the middle. The Tree-Cyclopsi sucked up muck, reducing the green ooze to tiny pools. Straw huts and trees that were twenty feet under the liquid were free, albeit in need of repair and a good scrub.

'I hope Oaf had a nice rest,' Karl said.

There was Oaf, beyond some trees, half in the ground, stuck in some sinking sludge.

'Oaf, are you okay?' Questions took a step back.

'No, Questions, don't—' Questions jumped in after him.

Oaf held her up enough that her head wouldn't sink.

'Have I been stupid?' Questions coughed.

Oaf chuckled. 'No. You've been brave.' He looked at Karl. 'Thought I saw Lord Ragnus so ran after him… My eyes were messing with me.' He craned his neck. 'Been here a while.'

Tortured Soul jumped on Oaf's shoulder while Karl looked around for a branch or anything to pull them out with.

'Are you okay?' Oaf asked Questions.

She smiled. 'Are you?'

'Thanks for trying to save me,' Oaf said.

Tortured Soul tried to nudge Oaf towards the side with her head.

Karl found a large enough branch, but he didn't have the strength to pull them out. 'You know what. Let's just wait until the orange things get here and do their eye magic suck thing.'

And that's what they did.

THE JOY OF MISERY

Sabrinia stood on a cliff edge, gazing down at the still, glass-like seawater in Flowforn Basin, the place her father had died. She imagined him sitting at the bottom of the cliff, laughing with Lombus and heaving fish into his mouth. She promised herself that when Flowforn was safe, she'd sit there and eat some fish to celebrate his memory.

She turned to Arazod. The sun sparkled against the dungeon keys hanging on a chain around his neck. He tossed his axe in the air and caught it. He seemed mesmerised by the Witches Split, a viscous waterfall to the north, said to have been created when witches battled and their magic split the ground.

Arazod smiled. 'Such a pleasant sight, the sea smashing against the rocks, isn't it?'

Of course he was entranced by it. It was violent.

Sabrinia considered jumping off the cliff. Why did saving everyone have to be her responsibility? 'Have any of the Fools caught Karl and Questions?' It was a question she asked every sunrise since she had learned they had escaped the Dead Lands.

Arazod frowned. 'Not yet, but I'm confident they will soon.'

He coughed. 'Don't worry, I've demanded they be instantly executed.' He shrugged. 'Hopefully they've starved to death by now. Or been eaten by beasts.'

Sabrinia wished she could do something. She hated that Arazod wore her father's cloak. Father… he would know what to do.

Arazod coughed. 'Now, we need to name—' He gasped and pointed down.

'This cliff?' She found herself finishing more of his sentences. He thought it was because couples do that, but she was just bored. 'It already has a name, Celinor's Sentence. It's where Queen Celinor used to sentence people to death in the early times of Flowforn. She heard there was a curse over the cliff that damned those pushed off it to never cross into the realm of the dead.'

Arazod nodded. 'Well, we need to rename it now that it's mine, and the name needs to scare people.'

Of course it did.

He stepped towards the edge and continued speaking, but Sabrinia shut out the noise. Her neck tensed and her head throbbed. She could push him. It would be easy – just one big shove, or kick to the back and she'd enjoy watching his one working wing flap and fail to save him. She wanted to see his head smash against one of the rocks, any rock. It didn't matter as long as he died.

She couldn't go through with it. Lord Ragnus would destroy everything. The point was to marry Arazod so Flowforn felt like his kingdom. He would never let destruction come to a place he called home. But the thought of marrying him and being bound to him for eternity made her want to poke hot arrow points into her eyes.

Maybe if she pushed him it would inspire her people to swarm Lord Ragnus. She stepped towards Arazod and raised her palms.

He turned to her and studied her stance. 'Are you okay?'

She lowered her arms. 'Yes. I was just going to rub your shoulders… you look cold.'

He smiled, turned around and rolled his shoulders. 'Oh. Go ahead.'

She rubbed his shoulders and gritted her teeth. She wished she had claws to dig into his feathery flesh and tear it from the bone.

'I've got it. The Wrath of Arazod!' He applauded himself.

She stopped rubbing. 'Perfect.'

He took her hand in his claw and turned to her. 'So, I'm thinking we get married in seven sunsets.'

'Why so soon?' Sabrinia enjoyed the frustration in his eyes, but she knew she couldn't stall forever. Her last excuse was that the suggested day was exactly ten years since she had lost her first cuddly Lionbear toy, so the next ten sunsets would be dedicated to mourning and not right for marriage.

'Because I can't wait to make you my wife,' Arazod said.

'And I can't wait to be your wife,' she forced. 'But seven sunsets from now is bad. It's the anniversary of the day Flowforn first created toilet buckets, and we don't want to share our wedding with that, do we?'

Arazod sniffed. 'Why do I feel like you're stalling?'

Because she was. 'I'm not. But our souls are going to be bound, in life and death for all eternity…' She almost choked on the lump in her throat. 'I want the moment it happens to be perfection.'

Arazod smiled. 'Eight sunsets from now, then.'

'Let's see in a few sunsets' time. Perfection is hard to plan.'

His beak twitched and he nodded. 'Very well. If it's what you want, our souls will be bound together when it is truly special, but soon.'

Sabrinia smiled. 'Thank you.'

'Now… Showtime!' Arazod declared.

She bit her lip, fearful of what that meant.

Arazod led her past the quiet crowd of Flowfornians and back to their table, on a platform facing the cliff. Arazod's part of the platform was, of course, slightly higher. Flowforn Forest and the castle stood in the background, with the bendy white trees of Herbis Forest to their right.

Arazod gestured for Sabrinia to sit and then he faced the crowd. 'Let today mark the first—' he wheezed. 'Arazod Fest!' He placed his axe against the table.

The Fools played their horns out of sync. Lord Ragnus applauded, so everyone followed his lead.

'I'd like to dedicate this event to my not-too-distant future wife, Princess Sabrinia.' Everyone cheered.

She smiled; proud she still had their love.

Arazod sat and winked at Sabrinia, but he couldn't wink, so his face just scrunched and contorted.

'What are you doing?'

'I'm winking.'

'That's not a wink.' She couldn't hide her disappointment.

'Yes it is!' He tried again and failed. It looked as if something was exploding in his head. If only it was.

'Wait, watch.' He tried a few more times, but it just got worse. 'Better?'

'Yes,' Sabrinia lied, wanting to look anywhere else.

Arazod addressed the crowd. 'Before we—' Arazod struggled and huffed. 'Begin. I want you to have your say.'

Sabrinia leaned forward. Hargon, standing by the platform, looked as confused as she felt. Was Arazod changing? Was her plan working?

'I've heard rumours of people being worried about what life is like under my rule. So, if—' He gasped. 'If you want to raise any issues, do. This is, after all, a free kingdom.' He smiled at Sabrinia and failed to wink again.

He was softening.

Arazod waved his arm in the air. 'If you have a quibble, form a line.'

Everyone shuffled into a line.

Arazod grunted and waved for Maladin, a goblin, to step forward. 'What can I help you with... Mister... strange... gobliny thing?'

'That's Maladin,' Sabrinia said. 'One of our bakers.'

Arazod gave half a shrug.

Maladin trembled. 'Your... Your Highness. While I... I admire the statues of you... your glorious self. There seem to be... a lot. One became two. And two is now ten. While beautiful... they block the sunlight from... from coming into our rooms. Plus, we need... we need to spend resources on new bakeries. There are lots of extra mouths to feed... with all the Fools. Erm... please consider allocating more resources to us bakers.'

The other bakers nodded.

'Thank you for raising your concern, Mal... Mel...' Arazod looked at Sabrinia.

'Maladin.'

'Yes. That.'

'He'll think about it,' Lord Ragnus said.

Maladin, sweating, walked away from the line.

'Wait! Wait,' Arazod called. 'I've thought about it.' He stood.

Sabrinia shuffled in her seat.

'I'd like you to submit—' he gasped, '... a written request, and place it in my Realm Improvement Box.'

Sabrinia relaxed.

Maladin bowed his head. 'Thank you. Thank you so much! Where can... I... I find this box?'

'Lord Ragnus. Show him where the Realm Improvement Box is.' Arazod's beak curled into a little smile.

Lord Ragnus grabbed Maladin by the back of his neck and dragged him towards the edge of the Wrath of Arazod.

Flowfornians backed away.

'No, no!' Maladin pleaded. 'I'll just work harder. I promise!' He dropped to his knees.

'Stand,' Lord Ragnus demanded.

Sabrinia leapt out of her chair. 'Stop!'

Lord Ragnus turned to Arazod.

Arazod huffed. 'You can't do this again, future wife. He needs to express himself.'

'But… but Maladin is one of our best bakers. You just… You can't kill him.'

Arazod's beak twitched. 'Very well…'

Lord Ragnus clenched his fists. Maladin closed his eyes.

Sabrinia took slow breaths.

Arazod's eyes narrowed at her and he scratched his feathers. 'You choose someone, or it's bye bye baker.'

Her mouth fell open. 'What?'

The crowd gasped.

'Not including me, Lord Ragnus or any Fools.' He smiled. 'Not that you would choose me.'

'But—'

'You want people to follow their dreams. Lord Ragnus dreams of throwing somebody off the Wrath of Arazod, don't you?'

'Among other things, yes.'

Arazod shrugged at Sabrinia. 'So choose someone.'

There was no reasoning with such muddled logic.

None of her people made eye contact with her. Hargon nodded, volunteering.

Sabrinia straightened herself. If Arazod wanted fear, he would have it. She would threaten the thing he truly wanted. 'I choose me.' She remembered Karl's selflessness in the dungeon.

Arazod's smile vanished. 'Wha… you can't…'

'I choose me!' She walked towards Lord Ragnus, her arms out, offering herself to be thrown. With each step it became more real. She stood in front of Lord Ragnus and her neck stiffened. Why wasn't Arazod stopping it?

Lord Ragnus grabbed Sabrinia under her arms, lifted her and held her over the cliff edge. He looked her in the eyes and smirked. Her feet dangled and her heart pounded. At least she would see her father.

'No!' Arazod commanded. 'Put her back on land! Back on land! Land!'

Lord Ragnus took a deep breath, looked into Sabrinia's eyes with pure hatred and then placed her back on land.

'But you said I could choose,' Sabrinia said, her heart still racing.

'And now I'm saying your choice is bad.'

'Well… if he's not going to throw me, he shouldn't throw anyone.'

Arazod stared at her and nodded, then hung his head.

Some in the crowd smiled.

'Return to me,' Arazod said.

Sabrinia walked back and sat, her body still trembling. 'Thank you,' she said.

Maladin's eyes shone at her, full of gratitude.

'Changed my mind!' Arazod nodded to Lord Ragnus, who took Maladin under the arms and launched him off the cliff.

'No!' Sabrinia leaned forward.

Arazod raised a finger to silence everyone so they could listen to the scream. It stopped for a moment before a splash. Arazod clapped, sat, rested one of his talons on the table and leaned into Sabrinia. 'Sorry, I can't look weak in front of them. Otherwise they'll never love me.'

He had no idea what love was.

'Now, who is next to raise an issue?' he asked.

The line turned back into a crowd. Arazod smiled at Sabrinia. She swallowed her hatred and closed her eyes, trying to shake Maladin's scream from her mind.

'This is the kind of free kingdom—' he coughed, '… that will make our lives easier. Otherwise, we'll always be dealing with nonsense complaints.' He mimed people chatting too much.

Sabrinia stared into the distance.

Arazod scratched his cheek. 'Also, thinking about you dying just then, it made me realise. I want us to be remembered as the greatest rulers of Flowforn, so we must be the last.'

Sabrinia nodded, not listening.

'Fools, on one knee!'

They dropped to one knee.

'If I die, before you kill yourselves, you are to kill Princess Sabrinia so she can join me in death. Then, burn Flowforn to the ground so we are its final rulers.'

burn Flowforn to the ground and kill Princess Sabrinia so she can join me in death.'

The order registered in their eyes.

The words shook Sabrinia out of her slump. She had no idea how she was going to protect her people now.

Arazod turned to her. 'And if you die, I... It will be too difficult, so I'll have to destroy all things to do with you.'

Her heart felt as if it was trying to eat itself.

Arazod turned to the crowd. 'Time for the fun to begin! The rope pull! I'm going to break King Sastin's record.'

Fools carried a long rope to an area of grass and mud. They poured buckets of water on themselves, rolled around on the ground and created a muddy patch.

'You're going to marry—' Arazod gasped, '... a record breaker.'

He was like a child desperate to please a parent.

Sabrinia bit her lip. Maladin had travelled all the way from Basnar, across the southern sea to live in Flowforn, having heard about its great way of life.

Arazod removed King Sastin's cloak and handed it to Sabrinia. He strutted over to the rope. 'King Sastin once beat three Cyclopes. I will now beat a larger number of beings to set the new record.'

A rotund scribe unrolled a scroll, ready to alter it.

'Bring me my opponents! They are the fiercest warriors from the town of Lugas.'

Two Fools dragged a chained line of eight filthy, hungry children. They stumbled to the rope, some coughing, probably full of sickness.

Sabrinia covered her mouth.

The children lifted up the rope while Arazod encouraged the crowd to applaud. He removed the keys from around his neck and placed them on the grass behind him.

'Give us the count, future wife.' Arazod smiled at her.

She took a breath. Everyone watched her. The words hung in her throat.

'Go on,' Arazod encouraged.

She stood and with no enthusiasm or pause between the words, said, 'Three two one pull.' She sat and stared ahead.

The children tried, but they were too weak and weary.

'Is that your best?' Arazod threw the rope from hand to hand and laughed.

The crowd groaned.

'Fine, I'll put them out of their misery. Little runts.' Arazod tightened his grip, but something like an eagle knocked him beak first into the mud. His feathers were now a dirty brown.

Sabrinia could have sworn she saw Karl hiding up a tree, but when she looked back there was nothing.

Pockets of laughter broke out from the crowd. The children won. They collapsed.

Sabrinia grabbed a handful of meat and bread and hid it in her cloak. She approached Arazod and dropped the food by the children. 'Are you okay?' she asked him, diverting his eyes from the children eating.

'They cheated!' Arazod scowled.

Lord Ragnus joined Sabrinia in helping Arazod to stand. He handed Arazod his axe.

'All of you, get back to the—' Arazod gasped. He swung his axe. 'Castle! Go!' He swung again. 'Leave me! Leave me!'

Everyone apart from Lord Ragnus and Sabrinia departed. 'You go too.' He got up. 'I need to be…' He gestured alone.

RELEASE THE PAIN

Arazod wept. He didn't want anyone to see or hear it.

Arazod's father had once described his crying as a concoction of horrible noises that nobody should ever have to hear. Then he threw Arazod into a pit. Each day, Sarzo would unleash a new hell on Arazod, from snakes with stingers to imps with a burning touch. Sarzo would watch, and he only freed Arazod once he had learned to hold back his tears.

Arazod approached the platform and stared at it. He took deep breaths, then brought his axe down and chopped through the table. His body tensed. He screamed and chopped the chairs, other tables, and the platform itself, until his feathers were damp with sweat and his breathing laboured.

Nothing impressed her. She was like his father, judging every action, every word. He did what she asked, but it wasn't enough.

He walked away and leaned on one of the soft trees of Herbis Forest. He was done doing things her way. When he returned to the castle he would make her choose a wedding day and stick to it.

Something moved in the leaves behind him. Whatever it was, he'd slice it in half.

He turned around, axe ready, but only saw trees. A large hand clamped his face and swiped him into the woods.

FOR A FRIEND

Karl and his friends stood under a statue of King Sastin that marked the beginning of Flowforn's land. The castle poked over the horizon.

The relief of being so close was mixed with the sadness of goodbye.

'Well, I guess this is it.' He smiled at Questions. 'You've been my hero.'

Questions smiled back. 'Am I sad to say goodbye?'

'So am I.' He hugged her. 'I'll tell Sabrinia to come and find you by this statue.'

Oaf extended his hand.

Karl shook it. 'I'm glad we met. And they'll still be looking for me, so I hope you get what you want. Just… be careful.'

Oaf nodded. 'Good luck. I hope the portal takes you somewhere nice.' He took the bottle containing Tortured Soul out of his pocket, but she was asleep. 'Tortured Soul, do you want to say goodbye?'

She didn't move. Oaf shook the bottle, but it made no difference.

Karl chuckled and shrugged. 'Thank you, both.' They were so brave and inspirational. 'Stay safe.'

And that was it. He flew towards the castle.

He landed on top of the castle wall. He'd never appreciated Flowforn until he was forced to flee, but it was different. The old drunk who threw potatoes at people wasn't in her usual spot by the tavern. Worse yet, the tavern was closed and boarded up. Arazod's statues poked their beaks into every silent alley and the flags flapped with Arazod's smug face.

Karl swooped down to a washing line and stole clothes more suited to an adult. He flew up the Lookout Tower to what he thought was Sabrinia's open window, not realising he was at the King's Tower. Lord Ragnus stood in a steel tub and coated his leathery scarred back with moisturiser. Karl grimaced and flew away, finding Sabrinia's actual room.

'You're alive!' Sabrinia threw her arms around him. 'And Questions?'

'She's fine.' He held her tight. 'She's waiting for you by a statue of your father outside the back wall.'

'Thank you.' Sabrinia pulled away and looked at his wings. 'Much has changed.'

'Given to me for saving a species.' He smiled. 'I hope you enjoyed me knocking Arazod into the mud.' He flapped his wings, and was so excited to see her he held her face, but as soon as his dragon-dung-scented right hand neared her, she retched. 'Sorry! Invisible Dragon dung.'

Sabrinia wiped tears from her eyes.

'I'm so sorry,' Karl said. 'I can't wash it.'

'It's not that. Arazod is missing.' She sat on her bed. 'Lord Ragnus found his axe, but no sign of him. We think he's been taken.'

'Then it's over. Let's celebrate! Where do you hide the ale? And don't pretend you don't have any. I bet you've a secret stash to help you tolerate that feathered cretin.'

'No. You don't get it. He told the Fools that if he dies they are to burn Flowforn to the ground.' She buried her head in her hands.

'Oh… But hold on. Even if he dies in many years, it makes no difference.' Karl shrugged.

Sabrinia nodded. 'If I marry Arazod, this is his home. And as time passes, who knows, he might soften and call off the Fools. Maybe I can get to him.'

'But there's no guarantee of that.'

'That's why I've been stalling the wedding, wishing for another solution to come along, or hoping I could at least find something good in him to make the situation less awful.' She lay back on the bed. 'I know princesses rarely ever marry for love, but I hoped I could at least feel something other than disgust.' She shook her head. 'But it's not about me; it's about saving the lives of my people.'

'I don't know if you've noticed, but he seems to be making their lives miserable. They've closed the tavern.'

She stood, grabbed a flask of crushed berry juice from atop the chest of drawers and poured two cups. 'I have to believe that marrying him will calm his appetite for destruction and that things will improve.' She handed Karl a cup. 'He keeps killing no matter how many lands he claims. But he's never had love, or what he thinks is love.' Sabrinia drank and walked to the window.

'Because he's too unbearable.' Karl joined her, careful to avoid being seen.

'The situation is dire, yes. But where there are only bad options, I've chosen the least terrible.' She sounded so lost.

Karl offered an understanding nod.

'Do you have a better option than hoping?' she asked.

'Get your people together to fight the Fools and Lord Ragnus.' Karl drank and placed the cup on the window ledge.

'I thought about that for a moment. I even thought about

pushing Arazod off a cliff. But we wouldn't stand a chance.' She pointed to Hargon down by the outdoor cages. He had a bucket on his head while three Flowfornians hit it with sticks.

'I could fly to another kingdom and ask for help?'

'Nobody will help us. Father cut off alliances because he saw too much betrayal. That's why he tried to make Flowforn a place that didn't need anyone.'

'So you're going to bind your soul to that tyrant and wreck not only your life, but even your death?'

'If I can fix the future for hundreds, hopefully, then I don't matter.' She took a breath. 'I should have reminded myself of that and just gone through with the wedding sooner.'

Her selflessness amazed him. Sacrificing herself for the happiness of others who likely wouldn't do the same.

Sabrinia studied Karl's face. 'With your new wings, you could go and search for him.'

He bit his lip, unable to think of words that didn't sound harsh.

'But you won't, will you?'

'It's just… in the dungeons is the portal back to my home. I saw a piece of it.' He could finally find out who he was. If his parents were alive, he would have a home. He showed her the keys. 'I swiped them when I knocked him down.'

'I understand. You have to look after yourself and find out who you are. There is no guarantee this chance will come again.'

Her tone poked at Karl. He tapped his foot on the wooden floor. 'Good. Glad you see it that way.'

BANG, BANG, BANG.

They looked at each other, eyes wide.

'Hide,' Sabrinia whispered. She turned to the door. 'I'm coming!'

Karl looked in a cupboard. Too obvious.

'Hurry!' she said.

BANG. BANG.

'Hold on, I'm coming!'

Karl remembered he had wings and flew outside.

BANG. BANG. BANG. BANG.

He pressed his back against the tower bricks to stay hidden from the Fools below. He listened intently.

Sabrinia's door creaked open.

'Hello,' she said politely.

'One of the Fools saw a person fly in here,' Lord Ragnus said.

'A person? No. They must be imagining it.'

Items crashed against the floor. Was Lord Ragnus harming her? Karl tensed, ready to fly in and attack at the slightest sound of pain.

'If you're holding a cup of juice, whose is that?' Lord Ragnus asked.

Karl's cup of juice rested on the window ledge.

'I've left it on the ledge to cool, for later,' she said.

Lord Ragnus' hand landed next to the cup. His shadow crept over the window frame. He popped his head out, but Peezant flew in front of his face and into the room, thankfully diverting his attention.

'What are you doing?' Lord Ragnus asked.

'What are you doing?' Peezant replied. 'Did you knock my perch over?'

A strained squawk burst out of the room.

'Did you fly in here from the ground earlier?' Lord Ragnus asked.

Peezant made a useless noise.

'What?' Lord Ragnus demanded.

'It would probably help him to answer if you released his beak,' Sabrinia said. 'You know, beak moving leads to words.'

Peezant squawked. 'I flew up here. I flew!'

'And I was cooling the juice for him,' Sabrinia added.

Peezant flew up to the cup and dipped his beak in it. His body got stuck in it and he and the cup fell out of the window.

Idiot.

'I'm going to search for Arazod,' Lord Ragnus said. 'I'll burn anything that raises my suspicion.'

'You don't have to burn things,' Sabrinia said. 'Just ask questions, be polite, and people will likely help.'

Lord Ragnus chuckled. 'Maybe I'll just burn anyone who irritates me.'

Fools in the courtyard and as far as Karl could see dropped to one knee.

Karl flew to the top of the tower and hid behind Arazod's statue. A Fool hammering stones dropped to a knee. 'Must find Arazod,' the Fool said. 'Somewhere with rocks.'

Karl flew back down and Sabrinia poked her head out of the window to call him back in. She sat on her bed and Peezant returned and perched on her shoulder.

'Thank you, Peezant,' he said.

'I didn't do it for you,' Peezant replied.

'He's great, isn't he?' Sabrinia stroked him.

'He's a joy,' Karl said with a false smile.

'He's really smart too. Understands all the languages of all the creatures in Flowfornia, don't you? Yes you do.' Sabrinia kissed Peezant on the beak.

Karl shook his head.

Peezant smiled.

Karl thought he should make an effort. After all, Peezant had saved him and Sabrinia loved him. 'So, Peezant, how do you find having wings?'

Peezant looked at Karl, blinked, and then flew away.

Sabrinia laughed and then took Karl's non-smelly left hand. The warmth of her fingers relaxed his body. 'I hope Lord Ragnus finds Arazod before too many people have to suffer. Good luck finding out who you are, Karl.' She smiled. 'I'll miss you.' She opened a drawer and took a rock with two little faces carved into it. She showed it to him.

'It's the rock I gave you for your twelfth year of birth!'

'The one you thought was a two-headed turtle.'

He smiled. 'You've carved little faces into it!'

'Yes. Sadly it is still no closer to being a two-headed turtle.'

Karl chuckled.

'I want you to take it.' Sabrinia placed it in Karl's hand.

'I can't do that; it's yours.'

'Please? Something familiar for you to take to the new world, to remind you of us.'

Karl smiled. 'It would be impossible to forget you.' He placed the rock in his pocket and studied Sabrinia's face. Her heart was so kind.

He put the keys down on the chest of drawers. 'I'll go and look for the idiot.'

Her eyes widened. 'Really?'

He nodded. 'I owe you more than you could ever understand.'

'Thank you.' She hugged him. 'Thank you so much, Karl.' Her eyes shone. It was the first time she had looked at him with hope more than pity. 'Good luck, and be careful. It's—'

'I know. It's every kind of weird out there.'

THE RED MOUNTAIN

Karl stood on the edge of the Wrath of Arazod. He scanned the clear water for feathers, blood, or any sign that Arazod had been disposed of. He'd know if Arazod was dead, though, because the Fools would be marching back to Flowforn to destroy it.

He lifted his head and the sun warmed his cheeks. He flew down to Flowforn Basin to get a closer look. Nothing but strange, colourful fish.

'Somewhere with rocks.' A mountain? A cliff? A cave? Was it a rocky shore, or just some rocks? Arazod hadn't given the best clue. Karl thought it was as useful as saying "under the sky", or "outside of Flowforn".

He flew back up to the others.

Oaf stood at the entrance to Herbis Forest, which stretched to the northeast. All Karl knew was from Questions' book, that the white trees were bendy. They could be moulded and would gradually return to their original position. Oaf made shapes out of them while Questions and Tortured Soul guessed what they were, which wasn't what Karl would call helping the search.

'Is it bread?' Questions asked.

Oaf shook his head.

Karl lowered to his knees to search for talon marks.

'Do you love Sabrinia, Karl?' Questions asked.

'What?' Karl said.

Tortured Soul spat on the ground. 'You would've dived head-first through that portal if you didn't love her. You reckon by helpin' you might get lucky.'

'Put her back in her bottle!' Karl told Oaf.

Oaf grinned at Karl.

'Stop it.'

Oaf's grin widened.

'I'm helping because I'm one of the good people. It's what good people do. Now, help me find this place with rocks.'

Oaf pointed to some bent trees. 'Those bent trees look like a bottom.' He wasn't wrong.

Karl shook his head. 'Questions?'

'Where would you be if you were lost or captured?' she asked.

'That's not helpful in any way whatsoever.'

'Where would you go if you were Arazod?' Questions smiled, somehow proud of her strategy.

Oaf raised a finger as though he had something better to contribute. 'If you were Arazod, would you rather fly or be invisible?'

Karl huffed.

'I reckon he's invisible and is just pervin' on everyone,' Tortured Soul added.

This continued for a while. Karl questioned whether he was stupid for not thinking like them.

'Does Arazod prefer night or day?' Questions asked.

'Quiet! All of you!' Karl paced.

They let him think for a moment. Smoke rose from the south-east of Flowforn Forest. 'That's probably Lord Ragnus introducing himself to people.'

Oaf's eyes widened and his smile vanished. He stormed towards the smoke.

'Oaf?' Karl called out.

He was gone. The mere mention of Lord Ragnus was enough to shut down all reason.

Tortured Soul looked around, confused.

Questions stared after Oaf. Her legs shook.

Karl turned to her. 'Sabrinia said you'd help me in any way you could, right?'

She nodded.

'So help me by going after him.'

Questions smiled, full of thanks.

'But only if you take that thing with you.' He pointed to Tortured Soul.

'Rude,' Tortured Soul said.

Questions took Tortured Soul in her hand. 'Will you be okay on your own?' she asked Karl.

'I've got these.' Karl flapped his wings, showing he had complete control over them. 'Arazod's clearly been nabbed by some pathetic bandits who live in a cave and think they can ransom him off for a quick bag of gold. I'll find him, swoop in, grab him, and fly away. Easy. Now go.'

Questions hugged him.

'I guess this really is the last time I see you,' he said.

Questions hugged him again.

'Thanks,' he said.

Questions and Tortured Soul left.

A lump formed in Karl's throat. She was a genuine friend.

He exhaled and searched for clues. He found himself thinking, *If I was Arazod, where would I go?* He cursed Questions and Oaf for putting those stupid questions in his mind. It did make him chuckle, too.

He studied the bent trees and realised they weren't meant to resemble a bottom.

'This is going to be easy,' he announced to the air, thinking it cared.

Behind the trees he spotted a feather. Further into the forest another feather, followed by more feathers.

He followed them until the ground became muddy.

The victory he had prematurely celebrated was now a disaster. He stood in a footprint so huge it could only belong to a monster.

Karl flew over a trail of feathers and footprints in the thicket of Herbis Forest until he came to four giant tree stumps illuminated by the night sun. They were in front of the Red Mountain and their bark was a decaying, rotten green.

Karl stared at the entrance to the mountain. A roar burst out of it and shook him to the bone. He edged closer. Growls, low hums and a language he didn't understand stopped him from entering.

He flew to the top of a stump for a better view of the area, hoping for another way in, but saw no such thing. He gazed at the sky, took some seeds from his pocket and tipped his head back to drop them into his mouth, but a demonic shriek shook them out of his hand.

He braced himself.

A shadow with wings and a long nose consumed him. Heavy, gruff breaths made Karl's legs shake. 'Please don't be a dragon.' He turned around.

Peezant burst out laughing.

'Peezant! Don't ever do that again!'

'You should see your stupid face!'

Karl threw seeds at him.

'Did you like my impression of a dragon?' Peezant asked.

'No. I found it immature. Now help me find a better way into the mountain before Arazod is killed.'

'I do know the best way in, but you know the deal,' Peezant said.

Karl was ready. Sabrinia had packed him off with more gold. He took a pouch from his pocket and slammed each shiny piece down. 'Here, here, here, here, here. Now, I'll have my bowl of information.'

Peezant looked at the gold, then at Karl. 'I hate to disappoint you, but I don't want gold.'

'What?'

'I want hair.'

'Hair?'

'You've got a nice head of it and it's good for the stomach.'

Karl buried his face in his hands. 'Just do what you have to do.' He felt the hair rip from its scalp bed. His cries included, 'Be gentle!' 'Stop pecking my brain!' and, 'I feel bleeding!'

Peezant finished.

'So how do I look?' Karl touched patches on his head.

'Lovely.' Peezant wiped hair off his beak and tried to contain his laughter, which didn't reassure Karl. 'Follow me,' Peezant said.

The two of them flew to the bottom of the giant stumps.

'Ah, so a secret entrance in the stumps. Very clever.' Karl untied the string from around his trousers.

'Nope.' Peezant pointed a wing to the entrance of the Red Mountain.

Karl folded his arms. 'I know about this entrance. The deal was you help me to find a better way in.'

'This is the only entrance I know about,' Peezant squawked.

Karl gritted his teeth.

'Bye then.' Peezant was about to fly off.

Karl grabbed him.

'What are you doing?' Peezant flapped and struggled.

Karl tied the string around Peezant's legs and bound him to his wrist. 'Sabrinia said you speak all the languages in the realm.' Karl smiled at Peezant. 'You're coming with me.'

REST IS IMPORTANT

Karl glided through flame-lit, pale-red rocky tunnels. It was typical that he had these lovely wings, yet the beasts decided to live inside a mountain.

Each distant growl reminded him that this was a terrible idea.

Peezant pulled against Karl and pecked at the string.

Karl whispered, 'Relax. I can't be saviour to a tyrant *and* have to keep watching a parrot with an attitude problem.'

Out of the tunnels, dwellings stretched all the way up to the top of the mountain. The impressive structures were like big rock igloos. The red rocks made the lair more intimidating, which wasn't necessary, as whatever lived here had already perfected intimidation.

Peezant flapped.

'Stop it!' Karl searched for cover.

'Untie me or I'll shout.'

'You'd get us both killed?'

'Yes.' Peezant smirked.

'Fine. Have it your way.' Karl grabbed Peezant's beak in his dragon-dung-stained hand until Peezant passed out. Karl stuffed Peezant into his trouser pocket.

Muffled growling neared and Karl hid behind the curved wall of a dwelling.

The beasts were large and hairy, as solid as tree trunks and more than twice Karl's size. Their spiked teeth and scythe-like claws confirmed what they were.

Karl was in the lair of the Lionbear.

The beasts carried an iron pot big enough for Karl to sleep in, and he feared they had already cooked Arazod. He followed stealthily and hid behind another Lionbear's home. He peered into the dwelling and was thankful it was empty, so entered. The stench of damp hair invaded his nostrils. He fought the urge to retch and poked his head out of the window-shaped hole in the structure.

The Lionbears placed the pot by a rock cage on the edge of a path overlooking what must have been a long drop to death.

Karl never thought he'd be glad Arazod was alive, but there he was, shaken, weeping, blindfolded with his arms rope-bound, and with patches where he'd shed his feathers.

One of Arazod's captors shook the cage.

'Do you know who—' Arazod wheezed, '… I am!' He coughed. 'Let me go. I need open air for my bre-eee-eathing!' His whining echoed through the hollow mountain.

The Lionbear shook the cage again. The other laughed.

'Fools!' Arazod called out. 'Somewhere with rocks, a cage, and loud creatures! They smell bad!'

The Lionbears growled in their native tongue. Karl tried to understand what they were saying from their gestures, but it was useless. Karl took Peezant out of his pocket. 'Peezant. Peezant. Wake up.' Karl shook him.

Peezant stirred. His eyes widened at Karl.

Karl covered Peezant's beak with his clean hand and whispered. 'If you make me think you're going to get us caught, I'll do it again.'

Peezant's chest puffed up and down and the anger in his eyes eventually faded, so Karl removed his hand.

'I'll never be able to wash that smell off!' Peezant moaned.

'You deserved it. Now, what are they saying?'

'Untie me and all knowledge shall be yours.'

'If you don't tell me what they're saying I'll put you to sleep, tie you up and leave you here. Then a Lionbear will find you, and it will eat you.'

Peezant folded his wings, accepting defeat. He listened in. 'She's complaining about the way Hastovia is today and what they'd do to change it… Stuff about the environment…'

'What about him?'

'He's moaning about being hungry because Lord Ragnus keeps taking all the hazel berry from their stumps.'

Karl's eyes widened as if he'd solved a great riddle. 'So, when Sabrinia said Lionbears are being sighted all over Flowfornia, it's because they're having to go looking for food.'

Peezant rolled his eyes. 'Well done.' Peezant held his wing to his ear. 'She's saying she doesn't even like eating meat. It gives her a bad temper and messes with her bowels.'

The Lionbear couple picked up the pot and threw its thick, sticky contents all over Arazod.

He released a shrill cry.

Peezant shrugged. 'But times are tough. They're marinating Arazod to eat in the morning.'

The Lionbear couple left the pot and walked back the way they came. Karl climbed out of the window and hid behind a dwelling closer to the Man-Hawk. 'Arazod,' he whispered.

He couldn't hear him, but he shook his blindfold off. 'Fools!' Arazod called out. 'Find me! I'm inside a red mountain with Lionbears!'

Karl leaned in further. Sweat trickled down the back of his shirt. 'Arazod.' Still no response.

Karl picked up a rock and aimed it next to Arazod, but accidentally hit him on the head.

Arazod's head shot around to see Karl. Anger turned into disappointment.

Karl, offended, turned to Peezant. 'He should be thankful! If someone came to save me from something, I'd be flattered.' Karl threw a couple more rocks in anger, his poor aim failed to achieve the desired result.

Peezant pecked Karl's ear to get his attention.

'Ow!'

'If you untie me, I'll fly over to Arazod, study the cage, then come back and we can figure out a plan,' Peezant said.

'No. I can't trust you.'

'I promise I won't deceive you.'

'Really?'

'Do I have the finest beak in Hastovia?'

Karl raised an eyebrow. 'I've only seen bits of Flowfornia, and Hastovia seems quite a lot bigger, so I'll say no.'

'The answer is yes. Plus, I'm small enough to do it undetected.'

Karl considered it. Peezant had a point. 'And you absolutely, won't fly away?'

'I swear on my feathers. We're a team now. Friends until the end. Brothers in battle.'

Karl smiled. 'Brothers in Battle… I like that, or Winged Warriors.' He untied Peezant from his wrist. 'I think we'll make a great—'

Peezant flew back the way they entered.

'… team.' Karl huffed and stared. His fury rose as Peezant disappeared through the tunnels. A parrot's promise is worthless.

Karl took a deep breath. 'Come on, Karl. Think, think, think.' He scratched a sharp rock against the dwelling wall to mark the layout and his plan. From where he stood, dead ahead was Arazod. Behind the cage, a drop. Karl outlined the path to his right, leading to more Lionbear homes. It seemed to be quiet up there. To his left, fires burned, where he assumed most Lionbears were. He'd have to avoid that area.

Karl studied the layout, then sat back against the wall and thought about how tired he was. He tried to keep his eyes open, but before he could plan anything his eyes drifted.

A hairy hand closed in.

A DESPERATE PURSUIT

The stars shone above Questions and Oaf as they walked over hills towards the source of the fire. Oaf powered onwards while Questions dragged her feet, carrying Tortured Soul in the glass bottle of water.

'Can we stop?' Questions asked. They came to the charred remains of an old farmhouse.

Tortured Soul popped her head out of her bottle. 'Yeah, I'm shattered from bumpin' around as she tries to keep up.'

'No stopping until I find Lord Ragnus.' Oaf's eyes were red with tiredness, but his desire for revenge seemed to energise him.

Tortured Soul drifted. 'Come on, this is a good… patch… to kip on… for the night…'

'No.'

Questions struggled to push a statement out of her mouth. It wouldn't materialise and she could only make strained noises. 'Will you have the energy to fight when you find him?' She hung her head and wished she could make a stronger point. Every time she failed to make a statement she remembered the day her people perished; the day her father froze to keep her alive.

Oaf softened. 'Maybe you're right.'

Questions rested her elbow against an old, disused well.

'I want to be at full strength when I find him,' Oaf said.

Tortured Soul hopped out of her bottle. 'I'll find some scraps for a fire.' She dragged herself towards the bushes behind the farmhouse.

Oaf grabbed some branches from a nearby tree. 'Have you ever been able to make a statement, Questions?'

She shook her head and looked at the burnt grass. 'Are you annoyed with me for not being able to speak properly?'

Oaf frowned. 'Of course not. You speak perfectly.'

Questions' hands tingled. Nobody had ever said that.

Oaf piled the branches on top of each other. 'Are you annoyed with me for wanting revenge so badly?'

Questions thought for a moment. 'Do you think it's dangerous to be obsessed?'

Oaf sighed and rubbed his head.

'Have I upset you?' Questions looked for a good patch of ground to sleep on.

'No. Just made me think about something. My mum once said, "Obsession is a poison. You need to let it go before it consumes you."' Oaf reached up and grabbed leafy branches. 'Here.'

Questions took the branches to use as cover and smiled.

Tortured Soul dragged tiny twigs in her teeth. 'Does this help?'

Oaf grabbed the twigs, but they broke in his massive hands. He looked apologetically at Tortured Soul who stared, open-mouthed at her hard work, now crushed.

Questions slept with a smile on her face. She dreamed she was in a huge wooden library with sunlight shining through a hole in the roof.

There were books on every topic imaginable. Books were always happy to answer her and never judged.

She studied a sketching of a castle in the shape of a demon's face. She looked up and her eyes filled with tears. Her father, Quizmal, stood in a doorway to another part of the library.

'Is that you?' she asked.

'Have I missed you, too?' He smiled, turned and walked into another room.

Questions' heart swelled and she followed him through messy stacks of books that made her feel smaller and smaller.

A crackling sound filled the air, and her father sat on top of a giant book.

'Can you give me a hug?' he asked.

'Can I?' She walked towards him, but the smell of ash shot up her nostrils and he faded into a smoky image of himself.

'What's going on?' She reached for him and held him, but he felt weak. She closed her eyes. 'Do I love you?'

'Do I love you, too?'

When she released her grip and stepped back he was gone, and the giant book opened onto a page that showed Inquiso before the final frost.

'Fire!' a voice called.

Books fell all around her, their covers smacking off the wooden floor. Smoke rose from them.

'Fire!' the voice called again.

The library collapsed around Questions, and the books opened with flames shooting out of the pages. Questions tried to escape, but the fire was everywhere. She collapsed.

When she opened her eyes, she was back in reality, with Tortured Soul's bottle pressed against her face.

'Fire!' Tortured Soul yelled.

Questions' heart raced. She scanned the farmhouse and the tree. 'Where's Oaf?'

'Fire! Fire!' Tortured Soul repeated.

Oaf was gone and flames gobbled up trees. Questions gasped.

* * *

SHE FOUND OAF SAT, his shoulders slumped, staring at a huge mound of ash. Fire raged in the distance and all that remained was the sign on its pole:

This is a tavern. If you haven't already figured that out by the generic tavern look of the place then you aren't welcome

Tears formed in Questions' eyes. 'What happened?'

Oaf shrugged.

'Where are… they?'

Oaf shook his head. He stood up and walked over to a pile of burnt wood.

'Do you think they escaped?' Questions asked.

'I hope so.' Oaf touched the sign. It fell onto the pile, kicking up a puff of ash and dust. Oaf huffed. 'I could've stopped this… If we didn't rest, I could've stopped it.'

They all stared at the destruction.

Oaf clenched his fists.

'Do you blame me?' Questions asked.

Oaf looked away. 'I'm going to find Lord Ragnus, but on my own. I don't want you two getting hurt.'

'Can I please come with you?' Questions protested.

'Yeah, we're a team,' Tortured Soul said through her bottle.

'No.'

Questions tried to say what had been on her mind, but her throat clenched and she made strained noises again.

Oaf looked at her and waited. 'What are you trying to say?' He tensed.

Questions whimpered. Lines jumped around in her head. *Do you know I love you? Is this love?* They weren't quite the same as saying 'I love you'. Throughout history, since the first time the queen of the Soil Dunes told a snake, 'I love you,' and married it, people had made so much of it being three little words. Any more, any less, or any variations just seemed like a disappointment.

Questions stared at Oaf's impatient face and she gave up.

Oaf nodded at her. 'Sorry.' He turned and ran towards the fire.

Questions watched, wishing she had the words to stop him.

A CAGED BIRD

A Little Lionbear licked Karl's dragon-dung-stained hand. He didn't move for fear of the lick becoming a bite and was surprised she didn't retch or wince. She must have only been a child, but was still nearly as tall as him. She didn't seem as ferocious as the others, but Karl wanted his hand back before she proved him wrong. 'There, there,' he whispered. 'It's my hand. Now, please don't make any noise.'

The Little Lionbear smiled and poked Karl's head, knocking it off the wall. Pain shot through his skull. Her strength was terrifying. He rubbed his head and stood up.

The Little Lionbear shuffled, agitated.

'Do you want some gold?' Karl took some gold from his pocket and waved it around. 'Look, gold, wow. Meaningless, shiny nonsense.'

She shook her head.

'Do you want some seeds?' He showed her a handful. 'Yum, seeds.'

She shook her head again.

'Well then, you're out of luck. I'm not a damn merchant.'

She pulled on Karl's hand.

Karl tapped his head against the wall. 'Why won't everyone just leave me alone?'

The Little Lionbear laughed.

'No, hitting my head isn't a game. It's to show how annoyed I am.'

The Little Lionbear pointed to the wall.

'No. I don't… ugh.' Karl knew there was no point. He hit his head against the wall again. 'Brilliant. I'll break my head before tomorrow.' Karl banged harder until the Little Lionbear giggled.

'Great. You've had your fun. Now go away.' He waved her off, but she pointed to the rock by Karl's feet.

'Really?' Karl handed the creature the rock, but she pointed at Karl's head. 'I suppose I deserve this for cracking Arazod in the skull.' Karl held the rock high above his head and dropped it. Pain jolted through his cranium.

The Little Lionbear laughed.

Karl dropped the rock on his head again. 'As far as games go, you Lionbears are a bit restricted in here, aren't you?'

The Little Lionbear was focused on the flight of the rock. Karl moved it from side to side to see what she would do. 'You like this, don't you?' Her eyes never shifted from the rock.

Karl threw the rock in the path's general direction. 'Oh no, look what I've done completely by accident.'

The Little Lionbear ran to retrieve it.

'Yes, off you go, idiot.' Karl turned back to Arazod. A Guard Lionbear sat, cross-legged by the cage. Karl nearly cried at the sight of the beastly, hairy obstacle he'd have to overcome. He cursed himself for falling asleep.

The Guard Lionbear rested a hand on the pot of marinade. The key dangled from a chain on his wrist.

Karl thought he'd fly around the guard, dizzy him, grab the key, free Arazod, and then fly them both away. He could do it. He had overcome a Fool, outsmarted a tower, and overwhelmed a Valotaur. He launched himself out into the open, was grabbed mid-flight and chucked in the cage with Arazod. The sound of the lock clicking hammered home that Karl had failed.

'Congratulations,' Arazod scratched his face with his rope-bound wrists. 'I bet you're glad to have evaded death.' He wheezed. 'This is a vast improvement.'

'Hey. If I was dead, who would be here rescuing you?'

'Oh, is this a rescue?' Arazod gestured to the cage. 'Is this what rescue looks like?' He coughed.

'One step at a time, Mr. Pigeon.' Karl smiled, enjoying that they were equals. He sniffed. 'What is that stench?'

'It's this sticky sauce.'

'You reek. We may be in the same boat, but yours is a lot smellier.' It pleased Karl that something smelled nearly as bad as his dragon-dung-stained hand.

The Guard Lionbear showered Karl in the same, stinking, warm liquid. 'Argh!' Karl shuddered.

The beast dragged the pot away to where Karl imagined the rest of the beasts were.

Arazod smirked at the gloopy mess.

'What is this grim mixture?' Karl wiped it from his eyes.

'The chunky lumps are crushed bones—' he wheezed. 'What gives it the runny texture is the boiled skin of a Cyclops, and the sticky bit is the stomach acid of a wovel mixed with honey.'

Karl's face dropped. 'I won't even ask what a wovel is.'

'It's a puffy, circular, stupid creature that hovers. It's made purely of fat and feeds on any and all dung. I thought I'd wiped them out.'

Karl sighed. Of course he'd tried to wipe them out.

'I don't recall you having wings,' Arazod said.

'Just a little something I picked up on my travels,' Karl replied.

Arazod's eyes narrowed.

The Little Lionbear approached Karl, presenting the rock.

Karl grabbed it and threw it towards the dwellings, but with his wonky aim it only landed a few feet away. 'Go away!'

The Little Lionbear retrieved it and returned.

'No. It's not a game!' Karl aimed to throw the rock to the left, towards where the activity was, but the rock went to his right, towards the dwellings.

The Little Lionbear ran to get it. When she came back, the Guard Lionbear returned and growled at her. She scurried away, and the Guard Lionbear sat on the ground.

Karl turned his attention to the lock.

'Good plan. Play with the lock. I wish I'd thought of that,' Arazod said.

'Relax. I was just checking. By trying things, eventually something will be the solution.'

'Don't converse with me until you—' he wheezed.

'Until I what?' Karl mocked.

'Figure out how we're going to escape!' Arazod moved to the opposite side of the cage, a mere shuffle away. He hummed, but it turned into song. *It's tough being the greatest King...'*

Karl's eyes widened. 'You've got to be joking,' he muttered. Suddenly the Pit of Endless Screams seemed attractive. Arazod's voice scratched at Karl's brain.

'Especially when—' the wheezing kicked in.

'Especially when you're angry at everything?' Karl suggested.

Arazod kicked at him. *'Especially when people want to take everything!'* Arazod steadied himself. *'So what if I destroy villages and kingdoms...'* he coughed. *'Here and there.'*

'And everywhere,' Karl said under his breath.

'I personally think that my laws are...' Arazod struggled.

'Horribly unfair?' Karl threw in.

'Very, very fair.' Arazod took a deep breath. *'People see a Man-Hawk but inside I'm a sweet Man-Dove...'*

Karl stifled a laugh. He had never met anyone with such a lack of self-awareness.

'Like everyone else, all I want, is...' he tried to catch his breath.

'All of the death?' Karl added.

'*Love,*' he concluded.

Karl sighed, relieved it was over.

'*Love, loooooove.*' Singing became wailing.

Lionbears roared from afar. Karl assumed they were saying, 'Shut your beak.'

The Little Lionbear returned with the rock, but Arazod's voice seemed to have created a small barrier of ear-abusing pain she couldn't break through. At least there was one positive.

Arazod finally stopped. He sniffled, sadness in his beady, evil eyes.

'Karl,' Arazod said, his tone almost friendly. 'Why are you here to rescue me?'

Karl shrugged. He couldn't tell the truth. 'I overheard that you were missing and I'm sick of running.' He scratched his wrist. 'I thought if I found you, you'd let me make a deal.'

'I'm listening.'

'I want this death sentence you've got hanging over mine and Questions' heads to be gone. Call the Fools off.'

Arazod nodded. 'Very well. Get me out of here and I'll call off my Fools. You can live your lives in peace outside of Flowforn.'

'And...'

'And?'

'You and Lord Ragnus will leave Flowforn and never return.'

Arazod fixed him with a look that suggested he try again.

'Okay. How about, Questions can go back to living in Flowforn, and before I carry on with my life away from it, I can get some of my old things from Cell Two B?'

'Like what?' Arazod pressed.

'You know, things like clothes... mementos.'

Arazod folded his arms.

'Like, erm... ashes.'

'Ashes?'

'The ashes of my dead childhood pet.' He instantly regretted the words. 'In a crate. The remains of my fish… Fuzby. I want to scatter them into the sea.'

'Very well.' Arazod grimaced. 'Now untie me.'

Karl hesitated.

A voice echoed from the entrance. 'Must save Arazod.' Three Fools entered the lair and walked towards the cage.

Arazod turned to see them and moved to the front of the cage. 'The deal's off.' He nodded at the Lionbear. 'Kill it and bring me the key,' he commanded.

Yellow flickered in their eyes, registering the order. They charged at the Lionbear, spears and swords ready. The Lionbear kicked the first in the head; the crack reverberating around the mountain.

Karl winced.

The Lionbear punched the second. Its head bashed against the rocky ground and its eyes rolled into the back of its head. The third Fool thrust its spear at the Lionbear, but it bashed the spear away, raised its claw and sliced the Fool's neck open. The Fool fell to its knees. Instead of trying to stop the blood flowing from the wound, it tried to stand to attack again, but collapsed.

Arazod's face wore a look of disappointment more than sadness at the loss of life.

The Lionbear dragged the bodies towards the fire-lit part of the mountain.

Arazod turned to Karl. 'I accept your deal.' He held out his rope-bound wrists.

'Maybe not just yet.' Karl took deep breaths. 'Doesn't it bother you when Fools die?'

Arazod shrugged. 'I'll just make more.'

It was that easy to not care.

Arazod returned to his corner of the cage. 'Now, solve our problem.' He went to sleep.

* * *

KARL HAD a plan in his mind, but Arazod's sleep-wheezing knocked it out of his head for the fifth time.

Karl held Arazod's beak shut with his thumb and forefinger. He thought it would be funny to wipe some of the dragon dung that stained his hand on Arazod's beak, so he did. Arazod's beak twitched.

The Lionbears were all asleep, but that didn't help, because one of them had the key.

Karl tried to fan out his wings, thinking he had the strength to fly the cage to freedom then worry about unlocking it, but the horrible goo stuck them down. He ran his hand through one wing, but the marinade was too thick to comb out.

Karl rattled the cage, unsure what that would do.

He needed to swipe the key from the Guard Lionbear. He had an idea and poked the lazy Man-Hawk.

Arazod lay still.

'Hey.' Karl pushed him.

Nothing.

Karl flicked Arazod's beak.

Arazod woke with a start, murder in his eyes. 'What was that?'

'A big flying… thing. Just whooshed in here. Smashed you straight on the beak, but I scared it off.'

Arazod's eyes shot around, looking for it.

'Seeing as you're awake, would you mind singing me a song to help me fall asleep?'

Arazod's beak tightened. He looked as if he wanted to peck Karl's eyes out.

'I'm serious! Please, your highness. I'm struggling to fall asleep and your voice is so, so soothing. Some rest will inspire my escape plan.'

Arazod beamed. 'Well if you're serious, then of course! I have two songs suitable for night time. Feathers of Freedom, or Pecks Passing In The Breeze.'

'Feathers of Freedom!' Karl said enthusiastically.

Arazod took deep breaths. *'My feathers are sooooft, their bright-ness is brighter than light, you see.'*

Karl heard grumbling.

'My feathers are powerful, for you they are too mightyyyy.'

Aggressive Lionbear noises filled the air.

'If you touch my feathers, you will feel joooooooy.'

The collective aggression grew. Karl smiled.

'But I told you not to touch them, so now I'll slice your face off.'

A Lionbear slammed its fist on the cage. Karl saw no key, but noticed a wound on her face. She pressed her mouth against the cage bars and tried to bite Karl.

'Hey!' he moaned.

The Wounded Lionbear lifted the cage into the air. The Guard Lionbear swiped the cage out of her hands. They growled, pushing and shoving. The Guard Lionbear placed the cage down and stood in front of it.

The commotion brought the Little Lionbear out, and finally Karl had his plan. He called her over. She sneaked up to him and gave him the rock. Karl nodded approval.

'Can you throw?' Karl asked Arazod.

'I'm the greatest thrower in all of Hastovia.'

'I mean genuinely. Not through some contest of fear where people let you win.'

Arazod stared at him. 'I'm the greatest thrower in all of Hastovia.'

Karl huffed. 'Fine. You can't be worse than me.' Karl untied Arazod and handed him the rock. 'Hit that big angry beast in the head.'

'What?'

'They're obviously upset with each other, so we start a fight, then who knows? Like I said, one step at a time.'

Arazod puffed his feathers out. 'With such careful planning—' he wheezed, '— how did we fail to kill you so many times?'

'I'm all about instinct.'

The Lionbears turned away from each other as though in the middle of some pathetic lovers' quarrel.

'Try to hit her really hard. Like, really hard.' Karl directed Arazod.

'Don't give me instructions!' Arazod lined up the shot and did a few practice motions.

'Today,' Karl said.

Arazod tutted. He launched the rock. It went straight up onto a ledge above the Wounded Lionbear. Completely useless.

'That wasn't even hard!' Karl moaned. 'I can't believe I'm locked up with the one person in all of Hastovia with a worse throw than me.'

'It's this sticky rubbish, it affected my—' he struggled, '... technique.'

Karl took his shoe off. 'Right, I'm going to do it.'

Arazod snatched the shoe from him. 'I'm King.' Arazod wheezed. 'So that shoe is my property and I'm going to throw it.'

'King of the Shoes. How far you've fallen.'

They wrestled for it and in the struggle Karl spotted the Little Lionbear throwing the rock down on the Wounded Lionbear's head. The pained roar drove the Little Lionbear away.

Karl and Arazod let go of the shoe, no longer wanting to claim it.

The Wounded Lionbear charged at the Guard Lionbear and knocked him down. They rolled around, punched, scratched and growled.

'So, is this fight for our entertainment?' Arazod asked.

'Hey, if we're dead by sunrise, I'll be glad I saw it,' Karl replied.

The Wounded Lionbear rolled out of the Guard Lionbear's grip and swiped the cage. She held a helpless Karl and Arazod above the drop.

'Okay, so maybe I didn't fully explore the consequences,' Karl said.

The Guard Lionbear looked as though he was going to charge at them.

'No. That's a stupid idea,' Karl said.

The Guard Lionbear knocked them all off the path; Karl and Arazod's cage sandwiched between the two hairy beasts.

'Is this stage two of the plan?' Arazod mocked as they fell towards the rocky ground and everything faded.

* * *

WHEN KARL REGAINED CONSCIOUSNESS, Arazod stirred. Their eyes met and they were horrified to find they were cuddling.

'Get off me!' Arazod pushed Karl away.

'You get off me!'

'Your arm was—' he gasped, 'clearly around me.'

'Well, I could feel your beak nuzzled against my nipple!'

'Don't. Touch. Me. Again.'

It was hard to move. Their cage was bent and dented, making it even harder to get out of and any key would be useless now. Worse yet, they were wedged between the mountain wall and the unconscious Wounded Lionbear.

The Guard Lionbear was next to her, slumped against a rock. Blood ran down his shoulder.

Arazod paced the limited area of the cage. 'Why don't you use your fancy new wings to get us out of here?'

'They're stuck down by this death juice.' He noticed a crack in the cage ceiling. 'Maybe we can knock this open.' He hit it again and again. 'This must be made of an extremely heavy mineral. Probably the heaviest type of rock in all of Hastovia.'

Arazod scoffed and knocked Karl to the side. He tried to force the ceiling open but also failed. 'Maybe you're right.'

The Little Lionbear, rock in hand, looked down at them from where the cage once was. She descended. Karl was worried she would fall, but she seemed to be an expert climber. She approached the Wounded Lionbear and was about to poke her.

'No, no, no.' Karl waved his hands frantically, but the Little Lionbear really wanted to get past the Wounded Lionbear to give Karl the rock and continue playing what Karl viewed as the worst game created by anyone ever.

'Your stupid little friend is going to get us eaten,' Arazod said. 'Tell her to go and play with some poison.'

'She might be strong enough to get us out of here.' Karl pointed for the Little Lionbear to walk through a gap between the Wounded Lionbear's feet and the mountain wall. The Little Lionbear smiled and walked to the gap.

Karl smiled at Arazod. 'A little love goes a long way.'

Arazod rolled his eyes.

The Little Lionbear was almost through, but stopped at the Wounded Lionbear's left foot. She looked over at Karl, smiled, and lifted the rock.

'No!' Karl shouted, then held his mouth, worried he'd stirred the beast.

The Little Lionbear frowned, but still had the rock lifted over her head.

'It's okay,' Karl whispered gently and gestured. 'It's okay.'

'Useless little waste of life,' Arazod elbowed Karl aside. 'I've—' he wheezed, 'commanded enough idiots.'

'I don't think she's a fan of the aggressive approach.'

'Quiet,' Arazod said. He waved at the Little Lionbear.

She waved back.

'Good, stupid creature. Now...' Arazod pointed to the cage ceiling.

The Little Lionbear mimicked Arazod's gesture and pointed to the mountain ceiling. 'No. You. Idiot. The cage ceiling, not the mountain ceiling. Come here.'

The Little Lionbear stared at him, but didn't move.

Arazod clenched his claws and waved them at the Little Lionbear. 'Idiot!'

She hissed at him.

'Congratulations,' Karl said.

'Stupid thing needs to learn to speak our language!'

'Yeah, it's clearly the Lionbear's fault. We're in her home, how dare she not speak *our* language.'

Arazod fixed his beady eyes on Karl.

Karl offered a warm smile to the Little Lionbear. He waved her over and she stepped towards the cage, thrilled with herself. She handed Karl the rock.

He smiled at her and tapped the rock against the cage ceiling. She leapt on top of the cage, and unable to reach the rock in the gap, she pulled the ceiling open.

Karl grinned at her and aimed the rock as far away from the Wounded Lionbear as possible. It narrowly missed her face, and the Little Lionbear ran off to fetch it.

Arazod jumped onto Karl's back. 'Fly me out of here,' he ordered.

'Wings. Stuck. Remember?'

Arazod groaned.

'After you, your highness,' Karl said through a false smile.

He gave Arazod a boost out of the cage, and rather than help Karl out, Arazod made his way around the Wounded Lionbear.

Karl struggled to climb out and fell over the top onto his back, stirring the Wounded Lionbear, but luckily not enough. He made his way carefully between the beast and the mountain wall.

Arazod waited next to the Little Lionbear who offered him the rock. He ignored her and she sniffed his feathers.

'Sniff me again and I'll stuff you and put you on my wall,' he said.

The Little Lionbear sniffed him again.

Arazod kicked at her.

'Stop it...' Karl stood between them. 'Thank you,' he said to the Little Lionbear and stroked her head. She licked Karl's dragon-dung-stained hand.

Arazod grimaced.

'This looks a lot weirder than it actually is,' Karl said.

'Let's go!' Arazod snapped loud enough to be authoritative, but low enough to not alert the Lionbears.

A path of uneven rocks protruding from the mountain walls ascended like ledges towards a small, natural crack, where the starry night illuminated the red. It was too small for a Lionbear to follow them.

'I guess it's better than going back through their home.' Karl ruffled the Little Lionbear's hair. 'Goodbye, little friend.'

She frowned and tried to hand him the rock, but he shook his head apologetically. 'If we meet again we'll play more.'

Karl and Arazod rushed towards the first ledge.

Karl turned back. The Little Lionbear's sad eyes touched his heart. 'Oh, go on then.' Karl picked up a rock and waved it at the Little Lionbear. Overcome with emotion, he forgot how bad he was at throwing. The rock smashed the Wounded Lionbear in the eye.

A pained cry echoed through the mountain. The Wounded Lionbear's eyes blazed with hatred aimed only at Karl.

'Idiot!' Arazod ran.

Karl followed. The Wounded Lionbear shoved the Little Lionbear against the wall and chased Karl.

Arazod was long gone, hopping up the rocks to freedom, while Karl's lack of fitness showed. His wings wouldn't flap. He took an age to climb and was sapped of energy. He struggled towards the exit and leapt for the final ledge. He hung, tried to pull himself up, but he only presented himself to the Wounded Lionbear. She stood beneath him, growled and scraped one of her claws along the rocks.

Karl was sick of feeling like he was about to die and resigned himself to being sliced in half, but Arazod pulled him onto the ledge as the Lionbear's swipe scratched his ankle.

'You saved—'

Arazod pulled him through the crack. The Lionbear forced her arm through and felt around, but Arazod raked his talons down her hand.

She roared and they listened to her descend the ledges.

Arazod stood over Karl and looked at him in the same way he did in the dungeon.

Karl swallowed. He stared at Arazod's claws. The night sun shone on them like a warning. They were sharp enough to drive through his skin.

Arazod stretched his arm out and helped Karl to stand.

OVERSHARING

Karl and Arazod stood naked in a star-lit stream below the Red Mountain and washed the foul marinade off their bodies. Their clothes dried on a stick, hanging over a fire.

Karl sat in the water and watched the blood from his ankle mix with it. He inhaled nature's revitalising scent, then noticed the flames lick and swallow their clothes. He squeezed his eyes shut.

'I thought you said you knew how to make—' Arazod coughed. 'A controlled fire?'

'In my mind I've made many fires.'

Arazod stared at Karl.

Karl shook his head. 'It looks easy when others do it.'

'Idiot!' Arazod kicked water at Karl.

Karl stood and walked over to what used to be clothes. He picked up the singed, two-headed turtle rock that Sabrinia had given him.

'What's that?' Arazod asked.

'Just a present from a good friend.' He tucked it into the join of his wings.

Arazod nodded 'Can you… just…?' Arazod gasped, straining to clean his good wing. 'There's a bit I can't reach.'

Karl nodded, approached Arazod and used his fingers to comb sticky filth out of his feathers. 'A bit weird, this, isn't it?'

'We'll just leave out—' he wheezed, '— these details. We fought all the Lionbears and escaped.' He inhaled. 'We're heroes and that's that.'

Karl liked that thought. He fanned out his wings, finally clean. He didn't trust Arazod, but then again, he had learned through his time with Frong, Questions, and Oaf – not so much Bar Witch – that vulnerability and talking could bridge most gaps. Most.

Arazod gazed at Karl's wings.

Karl scratched his cheek, debating whether to ask what was on his mind. 'So, umm… if you don't mind me asking… what happened to your wing? You obviously don't have to answer that.'

'I know. I don't have to do anything.' Arazod walked over to the burnt clothes to see if he could salvage them. He picked up his armour, now useless. 'But I will…' He turned to Karl. 'It was my father. Supreme Man-Hawk Sarzo. He got…' Arazod gasped and kicked ash, '… annoyed with me always flying off and exploring. He was strong and fearsome, but having children—' he wheezed, '… gives you a weakness.'

Karl nodded.

'And because he was scared I'd get kidnapped and used against him, he snapped my wing so I couldn't fly away.' Arazod tried to move his broken wing but it twitched. 'He died in an accident…'

Karl looked at the water flowing around his feet. 'Sorry…'

'Happiest day of my life,' Arazod added.

Karl felt sorry for him. While he longed for his parents, Arazod probably wished he had never met his father. 'Thanks for helping me,' Karl said.

'How else am I supposed to get back to Flowforn?' Arazod joked, but probably wasn't really joking.

Karl smiled. 'You know. I prefer it when you're not trying to kill me in weird and painful ways.' Karl stepped out of the stream and flapped his wings dry.

Arazod let out a feeble chuckle and pointed at Karl's wings. 'They're impressive...' He scooped a worm off the dirt and dropped it into his beak.

'That's because they're magical. Not bad, eh?'

'No. Not bad at all.' Arazod scratched his working wing. 'Karl...'

'Yes?'

'When you're done looking in the cell, maybe you'll want to come to—' he struggled, '— my council meeting? You know, before you're banished again.'

'Me, giving ideas on how to run things?' Karl knew once he was in Two B he would be gone. 'I'd be honoured.' It didn't stop him feeling important. 'Before I'm banished again I'd also like to say goodbye to Princess Sabrinia, if that's okay? To thank her for her kindness towards me throughout my life.'

Arazod stared at him. 'Let's see.' He seemed distracted. 'Do you know what she likes?'

'What?' Karl asked.

'What she likes? For enjoyment?' Arazod asked. He looked smaller than Karl had ever seen him. Outside of a forced marriage, Arazod had no hope.

Karl saw no harm in offering him a crumb. 'Her favourite game is a childish one, but that's why she likes it. We used to play it as children – three-word-monster slayer.'

'Three-word-monster slayer?'

'Yeah. You get three words. For example, magic, cave, and bread. You have to come up with a monster based on two of those words, and a way to defeat them with the third.'

Arazod nodded. 'Maybe I'll ask her about it.'

Karl smiled. Arazod would have to do more than play a game to make Sabrinia see him as anything other than a lunatic, but Karl had been surprised by Arazod's openness. Maybe there was hope. 'Ready to take a ride?'

Arazod seemed lost in a thought.

'Arazod... Ready?'

Arazod snapped out of his thoughts. 'Yes. Just... I need to use those bushes.'

Karl nodded. He waited for Arazod to relieve himself, and was sure he heard him muttering something, but was too distracted by thoughts of freedom. The struggling was almost over.

MAKE A DIFFERENCE

Sabrinia rested on her bed and stared at the painted ceiling. It was a scene of her father cradling her, with Peezant covering his genitals. She was disturbed that it would either be the image above the bed she would soon be sharing with Arazod, or the last image she ever saw.

She wondered what her and Arazod's babies would look like. Would she give birth to a child or an egg? Would they even sleep in a bed or would he make a nest on top of one of the towers?

She heard a scratch against the bricks outside her window. Cries of, 'Ow,' 'How can you be so weak?' and 'You're scratching my beak!' drew her to investigate.

Karl held Arazod and hovered below. He struggled to fly high enough to get through the window.

'Karl! Arazod!' Sabrinia called out, excited.

Karl strained. 'I told you we should've just walked in.'

'It's not as dramatic!'

'But less painful.'

'You have no sense of flamboyance!' Arazod moaned.

'Why are you both naked?' Sabrinia asked.

'I set our clothes on fire.' Karl tried to lift Arazod that little bit higher, but only succeeded in scraping Arazod's face against the brickwork.

'It burns!' Arazod complained.

Sabrinia pulled them up. They covered their nakedness with their wings.

Sabrinia got them each a feminine robe from her cupboard.

'I wanted to surprise you and fly in like a hero.' Arazod put the robe on and ripped the back to get his wings through. Karl did the same with his.

Sabrinia hugged Arazod. It wasn't a loving hug. It was one of relief, and she hoped he wouldn't sense it. 'Were you harmed?'

'Just some Lionbears. But we handled it.' Arazod leaned in for a kiss, but she turned her cheek, which he pecked and accidentally cut. She held in the pain and wiped the blood away.

Karl sat on Sabrinia's bed. 'You know, the only reason the Lionbears are being sighted is because the bushes and tree stumps they get their berries from are being stripped.'

Sabrinia stared at him, hoping he'd take the hint and get off the bed, but he didn't.

Arazod placed his working wing around Sabrinia. 'I'll see to it that the woods and bushes around their mountain are made sacred and untouchable.'

Sabrinia smiled at him. She'd perfected looking pleased while analysing his actions for something more sinister.

'In fact, I'll tell—' he gasped, '— Lord Ragnus now. Fools!' Arazod shouted.

Three Fools ran into the room. They saw Karl and drew their daggers. 'Ugly Karl!'

Karl backed towards the window.

'You are not to kill Karl or Questions!' Arazod commanded.

Yellow flickered in their eyes and they put their daggers away.

Karl looked as if he might cry. Just like that, he and Questions were free, but Sabrinia wouldn't let herself get excited.

'Go and find—' Arazod struggled and hit his chest. 'Go and find—' he wheezed.

'Lord Ragnus?' Karl suggested.

Arazod nodded. 'Yes, Lord Ragnus.' He waved the Fools away and noticed the keys on the chest of drawers.

'I found them at the site we last saw you,' Sabrinia explained.

Arazod accepted and took the keys back. 'I'll be in my quarters.'

'Wait. What about Cell Two B?' Karl asked.

'I want to hold our meeting first. So tomorrow, after...' he took a huge breath, '... we've discussed ways to help Flowforn. Then you can visit your storage cell.' Arazod turned and exited.

When he was out of sight, Sabrinia threw her arms around Karl. 'Thank you, thank you. I knew you wouldn't let me down.' Karl squeezed her.

'Karl.' Arazod poked his head back around the door.

Sabrinia's eyes widened. This was the kind of hug she knew Arazod wanted. The kind she would never give him. She released Karl.

'Maybe you won't be banished,' he said.

'What?'

'Maybe you will live—' he wheezed, '— in Flowforn again.'

'Really?' Karl said.

Arazod nodded and left.

Sabrinia closed the door and turned to Karl. 'You need to go, now!'

'Why?'

'He's being even stranger than usual.'

Karl took her right hand in his left. 'Sabrinia, we've just been through a life-threatening experience together. It's bonded us and I think it has melted away a lot of that hatred. Me and Arazod are now friends.'

'He'll peck your eyes out while you sleep.'

'He's not that bad. And this council meeting tomorrow is a great way to help people before I go.'

Was he insane? 'The council is just him and Lord Ragnus.'

'I'll be fine.' He seemed sure there was good in Arazod.

'I know he's up to something.'

'Hey. What is it you said?' He let go of her hand. 'If I can fix the future for hundreds then I don't matter.'

'You've changed your view.'

'I've been chased by Lionbears, Fools and rock people. I've been covered in sludge, dragon poop, and thought I was going to die seven hundred times. What has it taught me? That there's a lot to be scared of and the world is weird. But, I've also learned that the world outside of Flowforn has been ignored for too long and we need to be part of it. You were right when you told me that if I don't look beyond these four walls, then I'll only ever know myself within them. Give Arazod a chance. Maybe he's been trapped in his own four walls.'

'Are you sure?' she asked. 'We'll break the door down to Two B and get you home before sunrise.'

'What's one more night? I'll voice my concerns and then leave knowing I've set things on the right path and helped you. Being from another world has made me feel part of something. And if my parents are there, I want to be able to tell them I did something good before I left.'

'Alright...' she said, full of doubt.

SPECIAL TREATMENT

Karl grinned, energised. He, Arazod and Lord Ragnus walked through the courtyard.

Karl took it all in for the final time. The sun felt that little bit warmer, as though it wanted to give him a hug before he left. 'That was incredible. I never knew those meetings were so open.'

'We'll consider all of your ideas,' Arazod said.

'Particularly the one about me no longer using Lionbear food for my moisturiser,' Lord Ragnus scoffed.

They stopped by one of the open outdoor cages. 'What do you think of these?' Arazod asked.

Karl shrugged. 'While a bit ominous, they're very inventive. I'm sure problems will come up, but I guess you deal with them as you encounter them.'

Arazod smirked.

Lord Ragnus punched Karl in the chest. Karl flopped onto the cage floor. His heart pumped as if it was going to explode.

A Fool rushed in and chained Karl's ankles to the bars. The Fool left and Arazod locked the cage door.

Karl tried to shout something brave at Lord Ragnus, but pain squeezed his bones whenever he tried to form a word.

Arazod watched Karl struggle. 'I should've been more...' he gasped, '...specific. When I said you could stay in Flowforn, I meant rot in it.' He wheezed. 'Now excuse us while we go and see what's so important about Cell Two B.'

Arazod and Lord Ragnus left.

Karl tried to stand. He needed to stop them finding the portal, but the crippling pain overpowered him. He collapsed and pressed his face to the floor, groaning, hoping for some relief.

ON THE OUTSIDE

Sabrinia rushed towards Cell Two B. Her hands shook and her breathing quickened. Surely he wouldn't leave without saying goodbye.

'My Princess!' Arazod called out, with Lord Ragnus and the band of Fools by his side.

She steadied herself and smiled through the worry. 'Hello, darling.'

Arazod strutted up to her. 'I wanted to ask you. What's your favourite game?'

'Game?'

'Yes. Your favourite game. Perhaps something you played with friends while growing up. What is it?'

Sabrinia shrugged. 'I've never really been the sort of person to play games.'

Arazod's eyes filled with sadness. His beak twitched and that sadness became anger.

Sabrinia clenched her fists to stop her hands trembling.

Arazod stepped towards her, his beak an inch from her chin. 'So, what are you up to down here?'

Lord Ragnus grinned.

'I… umm… I was just…' She turned and ran.

'Fools…' Arazod swallowed. 'Get her.'

Three Fools tackled her. She tried to shake them off, but Lord Ragnus reached down and grabbed her. He slung her over his shoulder.

She pounded his back, but it was solid and hurt her fists.

'I'll shatter your face!' she yelled at Arazod, who stared at her. 'I'll rip your beak off and stab you in the eye with it.'

Lord Ragnus walked her through the entrance to the court-yard and slammed her onto her back. 'While I admire your aggression, you're not in a position to do anything.'

He dragged her over the pebbles and threw her into the cage next to Karl's, where he lay in a crumpled heap.

Sabrinia found her breath. 'You tell that feathery little moron I'm going to shred his one good wing!'

Lord Ragnus walked away.

Karl turned to her, his eyes full of sympathy.

She glared at him. 'You idiot. You should've just gone last night.'

'I thought—'

'You thought… that's the problem right there.' He should've just gone.

'You're the one who agreed to marry that cretin,' he replied.

'I'm trying to do what's right for everyone!' It was exhausting.

'Look at me,' Karl mocked her voice. 'I'm Sabrinia, I put everyone before myself, which is why I'm marrying a crazy pigeon.' He reverted to his own voice. 'Which is actually worse for everyone!' He coughed and pressed a hand to his chest.

Rage burned in Sabrinia, but she didn't want to speak to him.

Karl raised his palms. 'Okay, that was a bit much. Sorry.'

Sabrinia put her head in her hands.

Karl shuffled up to the cage bars. 'I was actually starting to like him. He even told me about his dad snapping his wing.'

She shook her head at Karl. 'And you believed him? He killed his father, and all the Man-Hawks, because he was born with a defective wing. He couldn't handle feeling inferior and being mocked, so made sure he was the only Man-Hawk, and therefore the most powerful. You idiot!'

'Okay. I feel a bit stupid now. But I think if you had that kind of information you should have offered it up before sending me to save him.'

She took slow breaths.

'Sabrinia?' Karl said.

Arazod approached Sabrinia's cage. He tapped his axe against it and looked at the ground, his bravado gone. 'I don't care if a mountain looks too cold, your hair smells too hair-like, or it's the anniversary of when a feather brushed your feet.' He swallowed. 'In three sunsets you will be my wife—' he wheezed. 'And as soon as our souls are bound and it is written in history, I will execute you, so your soul can stand by me and watch me destroy everything you love until the day I die.'

HOW IT FEELS TO FLY

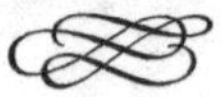

Karl, sweating, sat against the cage bars. Every breath was like a knife twisting in his chest.

He hadn't seen Sabrinia so angry since they were seven, when he threw her toys into a well thinking the water would transform them into giants. They just sank and disappeared forever.

Karl scratched a red pebble against the two-headed turtle rock, trying to create shell lines. His hands ached and he hoped it would distract him from the pain, but had no such luck. 'Look.' He offered the rock to Sabrinia, but she wouldn't face him. She was probably thinking about the marriage she never wanted; about how she would die and how her soul would have to follow Arazod. 'I'm sorry, Sabrinia. I'm sorry the responsibility falls on you.'

She huffed and turned to him. 'You're right, Karl. I was stupid. All I did was keep everyone alive but miserable, and what difference has it made?' She shook her head. 'What was I supposed to do? Every option was awful.'

Karl placed the turtle rock by the bars to Sabrinia's cage.

She half smiled and sat by the bars next to him.

'If there's anything I've learned, Sabrinia, it's that nobody knows what to do with anything. We're all just getting by, hoping any mistakes we make aren't fatal.'

Sabrinia blinked, clearly confused and uninspired.

Karl took a breath. 'What I mean is, Flowforn was about to be burned down and everyone slaughtered, but you stopped that happening. Yes, people are miserable, but at the time, in *that* moment, you did what you needed to do to save them.' He offered his non dung-stained hand through the bars. 'I'm sorry for what I said before. To me, you're a hero.'

She held his hand and squeezed it. 'I don't feel like one.'

Lord Ragnus approached. 'How sweet.'

A Fool opened Karl's cage, locked a chain around his neck and handed Lord Ragnus the other end of it.

Karl released Sabrinia's hand and stood.

'Leave him,' she said.

'I don't think I want to.' Lord Ragnus stared at Karl, as though deciding how he was going to hurt him.

The Fool unlocked the chain that secured Karl's ankle to the bars. It seemed he now belonged to Lord Ragnus as a pet.

Karl turned to Sabrinia. 'If this is my end, thank you for being the good part of my life.'

She stood and reached out her hand. 'Wait.'

Lord Ragnus yanked the chain, pulling Karl by his neck.

'Can I ask you a question?' Karl said.

Lord Ragnus pulled the chain again. 'You can. But you should be very careful what you ask.'

Karl nodded. 'Have you had an argument with your smile?'

Lord Ragnus whipped the chain sideways, cracking Karl's head off the bars.

He flopped to the ground.

* * *

WHEN KARL REGAINED CONSCIOUSNESS, he was slumped in the corner of a room. He recognised the painting of the two-headed woman surfing on a spiked ant while blowing a horn. He was in Cell Two B, opposite the corner to freedom.

Lord Ragnus stood next to him, while Arazod poked his axe through the debris of crates, his eyes puffy. 'What is so important about?' He coughed.

'Prayer?' Karl said.

Arazod struggled some more. 'About—'

'Talking through our problems?' Karl needed to get to the corner.

'This room!' Arazod finally managed.

'I told you. It's my storage.'

Lord Ragnus effortlessly lifted Karl to his feet. 'Stand when you address your king.' He pushed him into the centre of the room.

'There are no dead fish ashes.' Arazod caught his breath. 'I tasted all the ash. None of it is dead fish.'

Karl grimaced.

'What is it about this room?' Arazod demanded. 'Are you hiding a magical relic?'

Karl shrugged.

Arazod drove his axe handle into Karl's stomach.

He fell to one knee. 'What's... wrong... with you?' He stumbled past Arazod.

Lord Ragnus whacked Karl in the ribs.

Karl collapsed. He lifted his head and looked at Arazod. 'I'd rather *you* kept hitting me.'

'Is it this painting?' Arazod pressed the painting of the two-headed woman surfing on a spiked ant into Karl's face.

'That's my greatest fantasy. What's yours?' Karl strained.

Arazod smashed the painting over Karl's head.

Karl groaned and retreated into the corner. He scratched at the stones behind his back, trying to loosen one.

'What are you doing?' Arazod asked.

'Nothing.'

Lord Ragnus whacked a crate board across Karl's face.

Karl whined, clutched his face and curled up.

Arazod held his axe to Karl's neck. 'What's behind there?'

Karl beat his heel against the stone floor, trying to fight the pain.

'May as well investigate.' Lord Ragnus dragged Karl out of the way and bashed through the stone.

'What is it?' Arazod asked.

'Nothing…' Lord Ragnus replied.

It couldn't be.

'Just more wall, then the back of the castle.'

Karl looked, hoping they just couldn't see it, but tears filled his eyes and his body weakened. All of his struggling and the pain he'd gone through; it was all for nothing. The other world he had imagined and the parents he had created in his mind, who held him, conversed with him and loved him, became nothing.

'You have one last chance, Karl.' Arazod scraped his axe against the floor.

Karl gazed emptily at the hole in the wall. His sense of purpose abandoned him. If there wasn't a portal, then what was he supposed to do? Who was he? What was he fighting for? He was back to being Karl, the Flowfornian loser with no tribe.

Arazod and Lord Ragnus towered over him.

'You brought this on yourself,' Arazod said.

'Wait! Wait…' Karl begged. 'I have got something to say.'

Arazod stared at him.

'If you're going to turn me into a Tortured Soul, I hope you choke on me.'

Lord Ragnus booted Karl in the head.

* * *

KARL HUNG UPSIDE DOWN from a tree, several feet from the grass. He tried to move his wings, but another chain was wrapped around his upper body and pain shot through every muscle he tried to move.

The stunning sunshine blazed. Its beauty contradicted Karl's situation. Part of him wished his body would give up and die.

He recognised the entrance to the Red Mountain. Fools rolled boulders in front of it.

Lord Ragnus, as miserable as always, approached Karl and brought his stretched, muscular face closer. 'We wanted to show you what we thought of your suggestions. You see, I like my moisturiser and can sell it for quite a sum, but I don't care much for Lionbears.'

'Am I supposed to be interested in what you have to say?' Karl spotted Arazod, who nodded to some Fools.

They dragged the Little Lionbear, chained up, to the front of the stumps. Her face was bruised and swollen. Scratch marks ran down her back.

'No!' Karl tried to shake free, but only achieved more sharp pain.

The Little Lionbear groaned, her eyes red.

'Let her go!'

Lord Ragnus grabbed the back of Karl's head. 'Now you get to see me smile.' He grinned. Even that looked miserable.

Lord Ragnus approached the Little Lionbear. He bashed her in the stomach and kicked the back of her knees. She buckled. He raised his stone fists either side of her head.

'No! Don't!' Karl shook, desperate to break free.

Lord Ragnus' fists came down, followed by a whimper and a crunch.

* * *

KARL SAT, chained and crying on the edge of the Wrath of Arazod. He couldn't shake the sound of the Little Lionbear's end. Such a playful and joyful creature crushed in an instant.

Lord Ragnus yanked the chain. 'Get up.'

A group of Fools dragged a sack along the grass and rocks. Someone struggled inside. They untied the sack, revealing Scrath, his wrists bound by ropes.

'Come on! Let me go! I've barely had a chance to enjoy being myself again,' he cried.

They handed him to Lord Ragnus, who grabbed him around the throat and tossed him in front of Karl.

Arazod pointed at Karl's wings. 'Give me those.'

Scrath looked at Karl, seeking an answer, but Karl could only offer a deflated shake of the head.

'I don't want to do it.' Scrath puffed his chest out, raised his bound wrists and clenched his fists.

Karl wondered what power the Tree-Cyclopsi had that they hadn't shown him. Was Scrath going to turn into a giant beast and eat Arazod and his idiots? That would be great.

Lord Ragnus backhanded Scrath with such force that he spun into the air and landed on his back.

Karl winced.

Lord Ragnus lifted Scrath by his face and held him over the cliff edge. 'Do as his highness commands.'

'Bu... ne...' Scrath was a dazed mess.

'Just do it,' Karl said. 'Do as he says.' There was no point in fighting.

Scrath strained a muffled, 'Okay,' from his clamped face.

Lord Ragnus slammed Scrath down by Karl.

'And don't even think about taking the wings for yourself...' Arazod wheezed, '... and flying away.' Arazod nodded to three Fools who readied their dart shooters.

Scrath struggled to stand. 'This is going to hurt,' he warned Karl.

'How badly?' He didn't really care.

'What hurts a lot?'

Everything he'd been through. 'Realising you will never know where you're from, or why you even exist, or who your parents are.'

Scrath touched Karl's shoulder. 'Probably similar.' He moved around and placed his hands on Karl's spine.

The wings pulled at Karl's insides. 'AAAAAARRRGHHHH!' His back tensed, as if something was trying to burst out of it, but the rest of his body wanted to pull it back in. He pounded the ground and contorted. The wings vanished and his body flopped. Blood warmed his back and he pressed his face to the ground, sweating, breathing heavily.

'Is that it?' Arazod asked. 'No ritual? No chanting? No—' he wheezed, '— no show?'

Karl raised his head. 'I got… everything. Humming… A circle.' He coughed. 'A tree that did a weird head grabbing thing. I'll never forget it.' Karl smiled. The only joy he had left was in annoying Arazod.

'Give me the wings, but make it epic,' Arazod demanded.

Scrath stood up straight. He looked to the sky, stretched his arms out and vibrated, faster and faster.

'Chant!' Arazod demanded.

Scrath chanted a load of meaningless, fast nonsense.

'Jump up and down!' Arazod commanded.

Scrath jumped up and down. He touched Arazod's back. The wings transformed his existing ones into fully working, new, leafy wings. Arazod inhaled.

'My airways. They're… they're clear!' he announced. 'Clap!'

The Fools clapped. Lord Ragnus nodded.

'I'm just going to get familiar with these,' Arazod told Lord Ragnus. 'You have your fun with that one.' He pointed at Scrath. 'But I'll be back for him.' He pointed at Karl. He snatched a sword from a Fool and flew off, swinging his axe and the sword through the air, hacking at trees.

Lord Ragnus stepped towards a retreating Scrath.

Karl grabbed Lord Ragnus' ankle. 'Run!'

Scrath fled into the woods, evading the Fools' darts.

Lord Ragnus booted Karl's shoulder.

The Fools chased Scrath and Lord Ragnus strolled after them.

Karl crawled away, but Arazod landed in front of him. 'These are incredible. Now I can fly over everything and monitor everyone whenever I like.' He swung his Soul Bleeder through Karl's chains.

'I think it's time I made sure you died. Now, rise for your king.' He threw the sword by Karl.

Karl struggled to his feet and stared at the curved steel blade.

'Pick it up,' Arazod said.

Karl lifted it, but he was so broken it just hung from his limp grip.

Arazod narrowed his eyes and swung his axe.

Karl swung the sword to counter, but the Soul Bleeder sliced through it.

Arazod raked his talons down Karl's wrist. Karl dropped the sword.

Arazod swung his axe again. Karl fell towards the edge of the cliff and heard the waves crashing below.

Arazod stared at Karl and drew his axe back. He smiled. That damn, smug smile.

Karl summoned what little strength he had and forced himself to his feet. He was no longer scared; he was just exhausted. He looked Arazod in the eyes. 'Wouldn't you rather torture me?' He spat blood. 'It lasts longer, is more fun for you and is a better anecdote than chopping me in half. Plus, this all seems a bit—'

'A bit what?' Arazod's eyes widened.

Karl stood as tall as his beaten body would allow. 'Extreme. You pigeon-brained, overly aggressive little idiot.'

Arazod dropped his axe and kicked Karl off the cliff.

Karl let the breeze take him towards the relief of death. His final thought was that he hoped Sabrinia would be okay.

SAVE THE DATE

The sun cast tree shadows onto Questions' ash and tear-stained face. She scraped through the remains of the tavern, hoping to find some clue to confirm that her friends were alive. Her focus masked her annoyance at herself.

'Why can't I speak like normal people?' she moaned.

Her hands were criss-crossed with cuts from all the jagged bits of wreckage. She booted a burnt plank, releasing a puff of ash that made her retch. 'What's that smell?'

Tortured Soul sniffed around. 'I recognise that. It's burnt horse-mole hair.'

Questions trembled, remembering Sags' feet. 'Is the smell mixed with the smell of a person?'

'Nope. Just the hair.'

Questions scratched her stomach. 'Do you remember anything else?'

Tortured Soul's eyes rolled around. 'Nope. Nothing. Just that smell.' She rubbed her head against some splinters.

Questions gazed into the forest. 'Do you think we should go and find Oaf?'

'He told us not to.' Tortured Soul licked the ash.

Questions bit her lip. Where could Oaf be? Wasn't Oaf against Lord Ragnus and a group of Fools unfair? Did he care about what happened to him after he killed Lord Ragnus? Was the problem with revenge that all planning was up to the point of getting revenge? Did any thought go into an escape plan?

'He's a big fella. He can handle himself,' Tortured Soul said.

'Do you remember when he got stuck in the sludge in Lake Shizneh?'

'Good point.'

'Do you think he's even thought about the danger?' She remembered when she first met him, bloody and beaten by several Fools. Her throat ached.

'If I was nutty mad, carryin' the rage of a lifetime in me and close to unleashing it… probably not, nah.'

Questions smiled, knowing Tortured Soul was on her side.

'Lead the way.' Tortured Soul jumped into her bottle, resting in the shade of a tree.

They followed the footprints through the woods until they arrived at a burnt down camp. Oaf's footprints became confusing. Feet faced each other, crossing everywhere and going around trees.

Tortured Soul jumped out of her bottle. 'Looks like a big ruck.' She ran around and nodded at a skid line. 'You reckon he knocked a Fool off its horned wolf here?'

Questions spotted blood on a rock. 'Do you think?' She put her hand to her mouth.

Tortured Soul blinked. 'No… no. He's too tough…'

Questions picked up a bloody piece of Oaf's leather vest. Her eyes filled with tears. Why didn't she stop him?

Tortured Soul walked up to her. 'I…' A drop of blood hit Tortured Soul on the head. 'Oi!'

Questions was a mix of relieved and terrified. Oaf floated upside down, about three people high, next to a tree, as though held by some kind of magic. His right arm dripped and dangled while the rest of his body looked as if it was being pulled towards the sky. Drops of his blood floated above him.

'Oaf!' Tortured Soul beamed.

Why wasn't he moving? What was keeping him in the air?

Underneath Oaf, a perfect circle of grass around unknown letters pointed to the sky while the surrounding grass was patchy and flat.

'Let's not get too close.' Tortured Soul called Oaf's name until he stirred.

'Ugh…' His eyes opened and he looked relieved when he saw them.

'Welcome back!' Tortured Soul said, while Questions smiled.

'Why am I looking down on you?' He realised where he was and panicked, but he couldn't move anything other than his right arm. 'Why can't I move properly?'

'What happened?' Questions asked.

'Last thing I remember is tripping up, hitting my shoulder on a rock and rolling, then I'm up here. Can you help me get down? I'd like to carry on with my revenge.'

Questions folded her arms. 'Do you promise to not go running off?'

He held his gaze on her, then his muscles tensed but he didn't move. He stretched out his right hand and grabbed a small twig, but all he could do was shake it and the branches it was attached to, making purple berries fall to the floor. He wasn't going anywhere.

Tortured Soul stood by Questions. 'I've seen this before. It's a rune trap.'

'How are you remembering things?' Questions asked.

'I guess I've lived longer than old Feathers normally lets tortured souls live.' She looked at the markings on the grass. 'But yeah… there ain't no way down unless someone,' she nodded at Questions, 'helps you.'

Oaf looked at her. His desperate anger fading behind defeat. 'I promise I won't go running off.'

Questions nodded. Was she being mean for depriving him of revenge? Would he understand that she was saving his life? 'What do I do?' she asked Tortured Soul.

'Hmm… You've gotta dig underneath and poke out the letters, but anything that gets near them starts floatin', so you've gotta be careful.'

Questions nodded and looked for something to dig with. There were lots of sticks, but none quite right.

'I'm remembering more.' Tortured Soul stared at Oaf. 'This trap is used for catching big, but not Oaf big animals. In fact, there's normally different kinds of traps in one area.'

Questions lifted a stick. A noose took her ankle and swept her into the air. Everything spun and rushed and she dangled from a branch, about ten feet from Oaf.

'I guess the promise doesn't count now,' Oaf said.

'Can you not talk to me?' Questions pulled herself up the rope to untie it, but couldn't reach. She swung her body to turn away from Oaf.

* * *

AN UNCOMFORTABLE SILENCE filled the evening air. Questions refused to look in Oaf's direction.

'Gooboo?' he said to Tortured Soul, trying to guess her name.

'Stop it! You'll never get it,' she said.

'Ziki?'

Questions wanted to join in, but wouldn't give him the satisfaction. Instead, she added to the map of Flowfornia in her *Is This the Book of Tales?* Writing upside down was difficult, but it was better than letting Oaf feel like things were okay.

Tortured Soul kept trying to run up the tree to free Questions. She admired her effort, even if it was of no use.

'Oi, sulky, chuck me down my bottle. I'm gettin' dry,' Tortured Soul told Questions.

Questions took the bottle from her inside pocket and dropped it onto the grass. Tortured Soul stood the bottle up using the tree for leverage and bit the lid off. 'I ain't gonna bovva tryin' to help until you two are friends again.' She took the lid in her mouth and jumped inside the bottle, closing it behind her. She went to sleep.

Leaves rustled in the wind and battled the silence.

Questions spotted some plump, purple berries and hunger crept in. She swung back and forth, but they were out of her grasp. With each swing she got closer, but she'd reached the limit. She strained and stretched and groaned.

The branches shook and she turned to see Oaf pulling on a twig that shook the branch. 'What are you doing?' she complained.

He kept shaking, bouncing her more and more.

Why was he being so cruel? She wanted to scream at him, but then a berry hit her. Then another one, until it rained berries all over her and she caught them.

Oaf stopped shaking the twig. When the rope settled, Questions' hands and mouth were painted with berries. She aimed an appreciative smile at Oaf and stuffed her face, struggling to eat upside down.

'Do you think I'd be more understanding if I knew more about revenge?' she asked through a mouthful of berries.

'We've got time, so ask all the questions you want,' Oaf replied.

Questions swung back and forth. 'Umm, does revenge make you see things in funny colours?'

'No.'

'Do you hear angry music in your head?'

'No.'

'If revenge was any being who would it be?'

'I've never thought about it like that. But… it would be Lord Ragnus. Angry and just… selfish. Shutting everything else out for what it wants.' Oaf frowned as though ashamed of himself.

Questions continued her interrogation, asking whether revenge existed in the air, and if it was possible to make revenge-flavoured cakes and what Oaf thought they might taste like. Without either of them saying the word sorry, they were friends again.

'Tortured Soul!' Oaf called out.

'Can we ask you a question?' Questions shouted.

Tortured Soul opened the lid and sat on the rim of her bottle. 'Go on then.'

The circling wind blew a leaf towards Oaf. It caught in the magic and floated in front of his face. 'Why would someone want to catch big but not me big animals?'

Tortured Soul searched her mind for a memory. 'Well… it wouldn't be to torture. Pits cover that market. You can leave things in there to starve and can add scary stuff, for a laugh. Weird folk pay top gold to pick things to throw at victims in pits. So yeah, you ain't in danger of that.'

'That's a relief,' Oaf said.

'Yeah. Magic traps and nooses are used to catch food… Oh…'

A howl pierced the night. The colour drained from Oaf's face and he shut his eyes.

Bushes rustled and growls neared.

'Are you okay, Oaf?' Questions asked.

'I know that howl…'

'Help!' Tortured Soul shouted.

Four horned wolves emerged from the thicket and charged at her bottle. Tortured Soul jumped into her bottle and closed it. The wolves knocked it between them, trying to open it.

Oaf tensed, opened an eye and then shut it again.

'Oaf, can you do me a favour?' Questions asked.

He nodded and opened his eyes.

A horned wolf placed its horn under the bottle and flicked it against the tree. The crack alerted the other wolves to a potential way in.

'Can you say they're just little cuddly creatures? Can you say it over and over?' Questions asked.

He nodded. 'They're just little cuddly creatures. They're just… little… cuddly creatures. They're just… HAIRY KNIVES WITH EYES AND LEGS!'

Questions swung towards Oaf. 'Do you want Tortured Soul to get eaten?'

'No.' He shut his eyes again.

'Can you open your eyes?'

Oaf nodded. He slowly opened them. 'It's staring at me. It could snack on my calf, then feast on my body. For dessert it would probably skewer my fingers, eyes, ears, and toes and cook them over a fire. I can't do it, Questions!'

Tortured Soul stumbled around her bottle. 'Speed it up!' she shouted. The wolves knocked the bottle some more.

Questions reached for Oaf's free hand. 'Can you help me?'

Oaf stretched his fingers out.

Questions' fingertips pinched Oaf's. She pulled herself until she was grabbing his wrist. 'Can you pull?'

He did, and rather than pull him out, he pulled Questions towards him, but her rope was at its limit and her method began to work. Oaf's arm moved out of the magic field, then his head, followed by his other arm.

Questions groaned; her body ached from being stretched.

A horned wolf flicked Tortured Soul's bottle against the tree. The bottle smashed and she fell out.

'Do I believe in you?' Questions asked.

'I guess so,' Oaf replied.

'Do you believe in you?' Questions groaned through the pain.

'No,' Oaf said.

With one last pull he was free, and Questions' noose whipped back into position. Oaf fell between the wolves and Tortured Soul. He got to his feet, his legs wobbling. 'Please don't eat me, please don't eat me.' He stepped back.

A berry hit a horned wolf on the head. It growled up at Questions and stood on its back legs. She showered them all with berries, and they howled and whined.

Oaf spread his arms. He stepped forward and roared at them.

'That's it!' Tortured Soul said, spurring him on.

Oaf took slow steps towards them and they backed off just as slowly. He waved his hand at them. A horned wolf jumped at him. He smashed its jaw with his forearm. Several of its teeth fell out. It whimpered and ran away.

Another wolf leapt at Oaf. He backhanded it into a tree. Its horn wedged in the bark. It used its legs to push free while a third horned wolf sunk its teeth into Oaf's ribs.

Questions wished she could do something.

Oaf fell to his knees, but he pried the beast's mouth open, then hurled it by its jaw into the magic, imprisoning it in the air. Another horned wolf approached.

Oaf showed no fear.

It turned and ran away with the others, leaving the trapped wolf.

'You did it!' Tortured Soul said.

Questions grinned and shook her rope.

'Yeah. Yeah… thanks to you two.' Oaf looked at his bloodied torso. 'That's not good.' He collapsed onto the muddy grass.

'How am I supposed to get down?' Questions asked.

'We'll figure that out when this one gets up.' Tortured Soul put leaves on Oaf's wound and patted them down with her head. She jumped on Oaf's cheek, but he wouldn't awaken.

'Did you hear that?' Questions asked.

'What?'

A gentle whistling.

Tortured Soul hid behind a tree.

A hairy-faced, muscular woman, carrying ropes and dressed in steel armour approached. She noticed the wolf in the rune trap. 'You idiot. Not again.' She raised her hand towards the trap, the letters in the grass glowed and the wolf dropped gently. It ran for Oaf, but the woman grabbed it by its horn. 'Go away.' She shoved the creature back and it ran away.

She unsheathed her dagger from her belt and poked Oaf with it. 'Ooh, this'll feed 'em for a while.' She looked up at Questions. 'You'll do as a snack.'

'Can you let us go, please?' Questions asked more out of hope than expectation.

The woman laughed. 'Sorry… They pay me generously to train the horned beasties on my farm.' She pinched her nose and blew it, filling her palm with sticky black mess. 'Think I'm allergic to the damn fur monsters.' She wiped her hand on her behind. 'Now, this is going to hurt.' She took a throwing axe from her belt.

'Why?' Questions asked.

'Because falling hurts.' The woman threw the axe and it cut the rope.

Questions fell and her body thumped against the ground. She groaned.

'See.' The woman approached, kicked Questions onto her belly, stood on her back and tied her ankles to her wrists. The woman stank of damp animal hair.

She stomped over to Oaf and tied the rope around his ankles.

Oaf pulled his knees to his chest, dragging the woman forwards. He grabbed her around the throat and sat up. He thumped her on the top of her head, knocking her unconscious.

Oaf stood, grabbed the dagger and cut Questions free. He helped her up and pressed a hand to his wound. 'Questions. I promise I won't go charging after Lord Ragnus. I'll wait until the moment is right.'

She hugged him.

Oaf searched the woman for any items they could use, but found nothing. Questions tied the woman's arms and legs, making sure she wouldn't follow them.

A Fool emerged from the bushes and walked towards them. Then another, and another, until there were too many to count.

'Oh no...' Tortured Soul said.

Oaf braced himself for a fight. 'I'll distract them. You two run.'

Questions clenched her fists and stood next to him.

'If you won't go, at least take this.' Oaf handed her the dagger.

The Fools closed in. Questions readied herself to stab one, desperate not to.

The Fools ignored them and continued walking north.

'What's going on?' Questions asked.

Oaf ran next to a Fool and grabbed its arm.

'Must return to Flowforn...' It tried to shake free. 'Must stand guard at the wedding in two nights. Move, otherwise I'll be late.' It swung a fist at Oaf but he grabbed its hand.

The Fool tried to bite him.

'Does that mean Karl found Arazod?' Questions asked.

'Looks like it.' Oaf released the Fool.

It walked on. 'Need to protect the castle for the wedding, and help with Princess Sabrinia's execution.'

A knot formed in Questions' stomach.

FROZEN FRIEND

They walked along the sandy cliffs that looked over the west coast of Flowfornia, hoping to avoid the forest fires that lit the night. Although the wind blew sharp sand into Questions' face, there was less chance of running into anything unfriendly.

'How are we supposed to save her?' Questions asked.

Oaf shook his head and wiped sand out of his eyes. 'Us two can't take them all on.'

'Three,' Tortured Soul said from her new home, an old water-skin attached to Questions' belt.

'Sorry, three,' Oaf corrected.

Questions stopped, sat down on the edge of a cliff over-looking a secluded beach and wept. 'Do you think Karl is dead?'

Oaf sat next to her and put a hand on her shoulder. 'I don't know. I'd like to think he isn't. That he made it home and is meeting his parents about now, telling them about his adventure.'

Questions nodded. She had experienced so much that sitting on the edge of a cliff didn't bother her. The white of the night sun illuminated the endless sea. 'Why do people enjoy looking far away?'

Oaf stared at the horizon. 'Because it's peaceful? Or maybe because it's looking away from the pain.' He huffed.

Questions nodded. She didn't want to think about Sabrinia being executed. The world would be a much unkinder place. She placed her hand on Oaf's and felt comfort.

He looked into her eyes. She rested her head on his shoulder and for a moment the world wasn't so bad.

Oaf stood and walked towards a sandy slope. He reached for a yellow flower with glowing blue specks.

'What are you doing?' Questions asked.

'I want to give you something nice.' He stretched his arm out, but couldn't reach it.

'Is it okay if you don't?' She clasped her hands, worried he'd slip.

'But I want to.' He lost his footing and stumbled forward, but steadied himself. 'See, I'm fine.' He stood on one leg and smiled, showing he had control, but then his smile faded and his eyes widened. The sand beneath him gave way.

Questions gasped and ran over, her heart thumping. 'Are you okay?' She stared into a dark, rocky, sandy hole. At the bottom, broken pieces of wood. 'Can you say something?' Was he hurt? Why wasn't he speaking?

'I'm fine!' Oaf's voice called.

Questions' heart relaxed.

'It's a tunnel! A bit of a painful one, but climb down!'

She climbed down and emerged on a secluded beach flanked by rocks. The only way here would be via the sea, or the unorthodox route they had taken.

Oaf handed Questions the flower, dotted with blood from his cut arm. She smiled and attached it to her belt, having never received anything like it.

When she raised her head, she noticed the night sun's rays hugged the waves and shone upon a washed-up dark bump of some kind.

Oaf shuddered. 'What is that?'

'Is it a body?' Questions asked.

'I think yes, but I hope no.' Oaf grimaced. 'I guess we should check.'

Tortured Soul jumped out of her waterskin and onto Questions' shoulder.

They crept over to the body. As they neared it became familiar. The dark hair, the thin frame.

Questions put her hand to her mouth. 'Is it?'

Oaf dropped to his knees, swallowed and turned the body onto its back.

A smile was frozen on Karl's dead face.

Questions buried her face in her hands.

Oaf tapped Karl's cheek, but nothing happened. He listened for breath, but there was none. 'I can't believe it.'

Tortured Soul fell back into her waterskin. 'I can't look at this.' She closed it.

Questions turned away.

'Get away from him!' a powerful voice boomed. A shrivelled lizard in a silk robe approached atop a humped horse. The lizard leapt out of her saddle and swung a flaming twig at Oaf and Questions, forcing them back. Her tongue flicked the white hood of her robe off and her worn face suggested she was so old that age no longer mattered. 'Everything that drifts to this shore is mine,' she said.

'We just want to bury our dead friend.' Oaf kept one eye on the bony, weary-looking horse.

'Dead? He's not dead,' the lizard claimed.

Oaf huffed. 'Look at him! He's not breathing! I'd say that counts as pretty dead!'

Questions nudged Oaf and pointed towards the base of the cliff. A rocky arch led to a torch-lit village, populated by creatures that seemed frozen in time, in lifelike positions.

'If he's not dead, what is he?' Oaf asked.

The lizard pointed to a cliff way in the distance, towering over the rocks that kept the beach a secret – the Wrath of Arazod.

'Anyone that falls from that cursed cliff ends up petrified so they don't move on to the realm of the dead. Luck would have it that they wash up here.' She stared into Oaf's eyes. 'Petrified expressions are ones of sorrow and regret, because on the way down they think about their loved ones, the things they'll never get to do, and the mistakes they made to be in the situation of being pushed off a cliff.' The lizard dramatized the process, jumping and flapping her arms. 'The moment they feel the most fear and pain, their hearts beat such a powerful, regretful beat.' She pounded her chest. 'BOOM! The curse gets them, and their bodies freeze. Although this one is rare. He seems to have found a glimmer of happiness in his moment of pain.'

Oaf and Questions exchanged a baffled look.

The lizard moved Karl's arms and legs. 'Their limbs can be moved with some effort. But the faces, they're frozen forever.'

The lizard dragged Karl by the arms, towards her horse.

Oaf grabbed Karl's legs.

The lizard struggled against his strength. 'I told you, he's mine!'

'How about I just take him?' Oaf puffed his chest out.

'Won't get far.'

'Why won't we get far?' Questions asked.

The lizard dropped Karl. 'I'm the only person who can cure him.' She folded her arms. 'So, if you want to take away a stat-uesque companion, go ahead.'

Oaf huffed and let go of Karl's feet.

'You're welcome to stay for dinnies and a chattie. But bring him with you.' The lizard strode off and dragged her humped horse by its neck. 'The name is Morcoli, from the Entertainers of Jaspol across the southern sea. If you haven't heard of us before, you have now. Lucky you.'

Questions leaned into Oaf. 'What do we do?'

Oaf shook his head. 'What choice do we have?' He lifted Karl onto his right shoulder and they followed.

Morcoli bored them with the history of each grubby wooden building. 'The washing hut is where Ms. Green Hands lives. She was a snake-toad that was found three years ago. I called her green hands on account of her green hands being the unique thing about her.'

Oaf wished for silence.

Morcoli continued, 'She had an affair with King Crab Claws, who isn't a king. He runs the inn that has no roof, which is ironic considering most people stay at an inn because they want a roof over their heads.'

The humped horse stopped. 'Come on, stupid!' She kicked its knee. It whined and hobbled on.

Questions stared open-mouthed at Oaf. She had read about humped horses. When a horse was young, Jermalian warlords would cruelly cut the skin off their backs, and then attach a saddle that had two large hump-like stones, one on each side of the saddle. Then the skin would regrow around the stones, giving the horse its humps. It was so archers could sit alongside riders when they went to war.

Morcoli chained the humped horse to a stone post, then nudged its bowl of food far enough so it couldn't reach it.

Questions bit her lip.

Along the steps up to Morcoli's house was an army of petrified knights from Jermal, blades at the ready. They must have been from a war long ago. From afar this village would look well defended.

Questions studied the sad, petrified faces. Part of her hoped to see Frong, Sags, and Bar Witch, as at least it would mean they weren't completely dead, but instead she saw dud Fools, the bald woman from the engagement party and Maladin, a baker from

Flowforn. He'd been manipulated into cleaning a petrified Cyclops' foot.

Jars of herbs and potions lined the walls of Morcoli's wooden kitchen. There was a wooden worktop to match the wooden interior and the bedroom door was shut.

'Put him in that chair,' Morcoli requested of Oaf.

Oaf set Karl down in a rocking chair and folded Karl's limbs to fit.

'Your strength is remarkable.' Morcoli held her gaze on Oaf a bit too long. Her long tongue licked her eye.

Oaf grimaced.

'Let me just get his dinnies.' Morcoli walked outside.

Tortured Soul popped out of her waterskin and looked up at Questions. 'I'm staying in here. I've remembered that I hate these needy, entertainery types. Night.' Tortured Soul retreated into her waterskin and closed it.

Oaf stared at the village below. 'Let's hear what she has to say about curing Karl.'

Morcoli returned with a bowl of thick, sloppy, white liquid. She spooned it into Karl's mouth, but most of it ran down his chin.

'So, how do we get our friend back?' Questions asked.

'We're kind of in a rush. We've got to save someone from being executed,' Oaf added.

'Well… the potion to save your friend here takes half a day to prepare.' Morcoli massaged her brow with her tongue. 'So, I guess the best thing you can do is have dinnies with me. Keep a lonely old lizard company.' She looked at Oaf, who turned to Questions.

Oaf approached the exit. 'It's okay. We'll wait out on the beach and return when Karl's ready.'

'Well… If you have dinnies with me, maybe I can cure a lot more people for you… Help you on your mission to save your friend. An army might be of use when it comes to stopping an execution.'

Questions' eyes lit up.

* * *

QUESTIONS STARED at the chalky black soup in the bowl, but no matter how long she looked at it, it didn't become any more appetising.

Oaf stirred his, avoiding tasting it, too. They exchanged a smile. 'I guess it'll give us energy for the road back to Flowforn,' Oaf whispered. He swallowed a spoonful of the grainy liquid and grimaced.

Morcoli watched Oaf. 'It is remarkable how large and muscular you are.'

'Thanks.' Oaf didn't look at her.

'If you know how to cure everyone, why do you leave them petrified?' Questions asked, shifting Morcoli's gaze from Oaf.

'People get pushed off cliffs for a reason. If I cure them I end up endangering myself if they're crazy.' She wiped Karl's mouth with her finger. 'You're the first people to ever come for someone, so I'm making an exception.'

It sounded innocent enough, but Questions saw darkness stir in Morcoli's yellow-red eyes.

'What do you do with them?' Oaf asked.

'I perform scenarios.' She smiled. 'And I'm working on a play that they will help me bring to life.'

Oaf raised an eyebrow.

'It's called *Captain Brave and the Lionbear*.'

'What's it about?' Questions asked.

'It's about a lizard who falls in love with a Lionbear, but her village won't accept the creature. However, the Lionbear wins them over through helping. But then, a jealous villager who hates his presence and loves the lizard, starts a fire, blaming him.'

'Is that a bit sad?' Questions asked.

'No! He is banished, but Captain Brave leaves her village to find him, breaking free of the oppressive attitudes. It's beautiful, about the power of love.'

It sounded quite good. Oaf swallowed more soup.

'However, the Lionbear dies of illness, wind-stricken in the cold seasons. Captain Brave decides to preserve the tragedy in a play.' Her eyes narrowed. 'None of the Entertainers of Jaspol will take her play, so she leaves for new shores.' A smirk flashed over her wrinkly face. 'She takes it to all the towns and castles in Flowfornia, but she is shunned, ridiculed!'

'I feel a bit sorry for her,' Oaf said.

'With nowhere to turn, Captain Brave settles on a beach and stumbles across a pile of petrified bodies and decides to give them a new life.'

Questions relaxed in her chair, her fingers and toes tingling.

Morcoli continued, 'She builds them a village where, having been judged her whole life, they don't judge her, and they live happily ever after.'

Oaf's slurping sounded louder, a thankful distraction from the tale.

Morcoli stood. 'She waits for the day a petrified Lionbear comes into her life. Day after day, sunset after sunset, year after year, only knights, villagers, and idiots.'

Questions stared at her bowl and struggled to keep her eyes open. Her jaw felt numb.

Morcoli pointed at Oaf. 'Until she finally sees an Oaf, one of a kind, and decides she will make the Oaf her new Lionbear... and marry him.'

'What?' Oaf slumped forward, and his head smashed the bowl in his lap.

'Hey, what have?' Questions' neck stiffened and everything faded.

* * *

THE WORLD WAS blurry and Questions couldn't move. She couldn't tell how much time had passed. There were dots, colourful dots. Why so many dots? She was on her side facing the wall.

A tune… Was that whistling? Was Morcoli whistling?

Her heart beat loudly and slowly. It was as though she was somewhere between life and death.

A pale blur moved through the haze like a ghost. 'We will be together in the morning, my love.' It looked down at what must have been Oaf. 'Now I must sleep to look my best.'

The blur moved away and snoring filled the air.

What was going on?

Something bumped around in Questions' throat. Was she choking? Was this the end? Her insides tightened, the only feeling she had, but then something flew out of her mouth and her eyes focused that little bit more.

Vomit streaked the wood next to her and Tortured Soul stood in front of her eyes.

'Shh,' Tortured Soul said. 'That weird thing gave you some sort of sleepy soup.'

Questions groaned. Her arms tingled and her toes moved. She almost cried, so glad to regain movement.

'Can you say anythin'?' Tortured Soul head-butted Questions' nose.

Questions lifted her head off the wood. 'Is Oaf okay?'

'He's out of it. You have to pretend you are too and strike when the freak least expects it.'

Questions, her head full of clouds, put her head back down.

'Clean this up first!' Tortured Soul said. 'And find me new liquid before I flake.'

Questions cleaned the mess and found Tortured Soul a glass bottle and filled it from a water bucket.

'Moving up in the world!' Tortured Soul boasted and jumped in.

Footsteps came from the closed room.

Questions rolled Tortured Soul's bottle under the wooden worktop. She returned to her position.

Morcoli opened the door and looked into the room. 'Best tie you up, just in case.'

* * *

QUESTIONS, rope-tied from head to toe and pretending to be unconscious, slumped against a petrified frog-woman on the beach. The orange sunrise coloured her face while the cool breeze tickled her cheeks.

Morcoli, dressed in a blue, gem-encrusted gown, positioned all the petrified beings inside a circle of candles around a shiny, circular stone that rested on a plinth. Karl held a broadsword over the stone, and Oaf, propped up by three frozen knights, had one of his limp hands on the stone.

Morcoli scooped more soup from the bucket and spooned it into Oaf's mouth. 'When the Cutting of the Stone is complete, we will share one life, one soul, one love, one skin.' Morcoli's arms trembled.

She approached Questions, who held her breath. Morcoli poured more horrible liquid into Questions' mouth, but when Morcoli turned, Questions spat it onto the lizard's back.

'My gown!' She turned back and lifted her hand to strike, but Questions barged a petrified knight on top of her, knocking her to the sand.

'Get it off me!'

Questions hopped behind the petrified frog-woman and barged it on top of the knight. She shoved and kicked as many petrified creatures as she could until Morcoli had no hope of escape.

Morcoli shouted from under the pile, but Questions ignored her.

She sat back, thankful Oaf was safe.

Tortured Soul ran out of Morcoli's home and climbed into Oaf's mouth. Oaf vomited a river of the foul soup all over Karl's face, but he remained still.

'Why isn't it working?' Questions' hands trembled.

'Dunno.' Tortured Soul climbed into Oaf's mouth again. He vomited more liquid onto Karl's face and his daze returned to normality. He took a moment to readjust, then coughed.

'Sorry, Karl.' Oaf pinched a cube of vomited bread from in between Karl's bottom lip and lower teeth. Oaf turned to Questions. 'Thanks for saving me.'

She smiled and waved with her bound hands.

Oaf took the broadsword from Karl and cut Questions free. He looked over at the pile on top of Morcoli. 'I've got an idea.'

They lifted enough creatures off Morcoli's body so that Oaf could tie her up. He carried her back to her home and put her in the rocking chair. 'Now, we need you. So please cure our friend, and the rest of these people.'

Tortured Soul stared at the jars of herbs and potion bottles.

'Are you remembering something?' Questions asked.

'I don't know,' she said.

Morcoli said nothing.

Oaf huffed and folded his arms. 'They can be our army to free Flowforn, and we'll see to it that you have somewhere to host your plays. There will be plenty of real people to see your work and keep you from being lonely.'

Red filled Morcoli's eyes and she cackled. 'I don't know any cure! I used one of the oldest manipulation techniques. Tell people you have something they want, and they'll do pretty much anything depending on how badly they want it.'

Oaf stared at her. He took slow breaths and clenched his fists. He hung his head.

Questions, overcome with rage, stomped over and forced Morcoli's soup into her mouth until she passed out.

Oaf took a sack and filled it with all the jars of herbs, potions and a loaf of bread.

The group left Morcoli's door and returned to the hole they came through. Oaf threw Questions up it. He tied the humped horse to his back and climbed out of Morcoli's village of misery.

The group mounted the horse, with Karl laying over the back of it. Questions held the sack of jars that hopefully contained the answer.

DREAM CRUSHER

razod perched on his statue on the King's Tower and abused all of Flowforn with a night of singing. Sabrinia stared up at him from her cage, her eyes sore from crying, wishing she could stomp his beak into the pebbles.

She dabbed her unwashed face with a wet cloth, not caring that water dropped onto her blue gown. She threw the cloth back in the water bucket she'd been permitted. Arazod didn't want his future wife looking dirty and he'd told her to cheer up, but since he had described how he had killed Karl, Sabrinia had forgotten how to be cheery.

A Flowfornian man, Valees, the blacksmith, scrubbed the beak of Arazod's statue. Exhausted, he fell to his death with a thud and crack, in front of Sabrinia's cage. A spear-wielding Fool who held the keys to the cages didn't even flinch.

She covered her mouth and closed her eyes, disgusted that legs could bend that way. She chose this for her people. She may as well have pushed him.

Valees had lived in Flowforn since before Sabrinia was born. He was the only survivor of a battle at sea and had lost his family.

He had once told Sabrinia that in Flowforn he had found a place that felt like home again.

'*My wings will wrap around you...*' Arazod screeched.

Prisoners shouted, 'Shut up!' and, 'Boo!' Arazod had picked the wrong audience. People resigned to death tended to speak honestly.

'Responsibility,' Sabrinia mumbled and shook her head. She hated that word. When her father took her to Flowfornian villages he told her that her responsibility was to bow and wave. She was never much of a bower. Once she bowed too aggressively and accidentally head-butted Princess Elma of Rispa. King Sastin had to give Rispa more gold than he could spare in order to avoid an incident. Since then, Sabrinia was limited to just waving, as long as nobody was within arm's reach.

She studied the cage for something, anything that could help her. It was hopeless. She stared at the two-headed turtle rock and sighed. She put it in her pocket.

Hargon swept the alleys and she caught his eye. She smiled at him, hoping he'd help her.

He shook his head, fear in his eyes, and swept his way out of sight.

What did she expect? Everyone lived in fear.

She kicked the bars. 'Stop that awful screeching! I would rather have my ears boiled than listen to your horrible voice!'

It worked. Arazod stopped and flew into his quarters.

Hargon poked his head back around the corner and swept his way to the cage.

'What do you want?' the Fool said.

'I just want to clear this body. Keep the place tidy for our great leader.'

'Hurry it up then.'

Hargon put his broom down and grabbed Valees' legs. He groaned, pretending to struggle. 'Any chance of some help?' He winked at Sabrinia.

'No,' the Fool replied.

'Come on,' Sabrinia said. 'Show the weakling how it's done. He needs the guidance of someone stronger.'

The Fool grunted. It put its spear down. 'That's not how you do it!' the Fool told Hargon and grabbed Valees under the arms and lifted him. 'Then you drag.' The Fool dropped Valees.

Hargon nodded. 'Can you show me again, please? Just so I'm clear.' Hargon kneeled and placed a hand on his broom.

The Fool huffed. 'Fine. Last time, idiot. Grab under the arms, like this.' The Fool bent to pick Valees up from under his arms.

Hargon smashed the broom over the Fool's head, knocking it out.

The other prisoners cheered. Hargon signalled for them to be quiet.

Shaking, he grabbed the keys. He unlocked Sabrinia's cage and the cages of all the others. 'Right, we're going to need—'

The other prisoners fled.

Hargon sighed and then turned to Sabrinia. 'Follow me. There are about thirty Fools guarding Flowforn Arch so you need to find another way.' He reached into his pocket and handed her a slab of dirty meat with dry edges and spots of yellowing decay.

Sabrinia smiled, both disgusted and appreciative. She took it, knowing she would rather eat some dirt outside of Flowforn.

They crept across the courtyard towards the alleys. They took cover behind King Sastin's statue. Sabrinia drew strength from his face.

Hargon whispered. 'You have to hurry before the Fool wakes up or the others see it.'

Sabrinia regretted leaving her people, but staying was no use to them. She had to rebuild the alliances her father had broken, even if it meant begging and giving up land. 'I'll return with help.'

Four Fools guarded the alleys by the Lookout Tower.

'They're everywhere,' Sabrinia whispered.

Hargon looked back at the Fool by the cages who stirred. 'Good luck, Princess.' Hargon walked towards the Fools.

'Stop. We'll find another way.'

He was already near them.

'Why aren't you sweeping?' a Fool asked.

'I don't feel like doing it anymore.'

The Fools looked at each other and laughed.

Hargon mocked their laughter, kicked some pebbles at them and ran. They chased him towards Flowforn Arch.

Sabrinia crept into the alleys and looked back. The Fool guarding the cages blew the alarm horn.

She ran and weaved her way through narrow paths, taking cover in the shadows she knew well from playing games as a child. She spotted the old brewery at the end of an alley. She could jump from one of its upper-level windows onto Flowforn's back wall and out.

She sprinted towards it, but that familiar, loathsome drum and horn music filled the air. She hid around the side of the brewery and waited for the sound to pass. She looked through a crack in the boarded-up window and felt sick. There was a pile of butchered bodies with faces that resembled Karl's.

She turned and slammed into the solid frame of Lord Ragnus. Her jaw throbbed.

Lord Ragnus stared at her and shook his head. He grabbed her around the throat. 'She's here.'

Arazod flew down. 'What are—'

Peezant swooped and pecked Arazod's cheek.

'Peezant, no!' Sabrinia cried, wanting him to avoid pain.

Arazod whined, grabbed Peezant and snapped one of his wings. Peezant fainted.

'Monster!' Sabrinia swung a punch at Arazod, but Lord Ragnus caught her fist.

'I should snap his neck too.' Arazod handed Peezant to a Fool.

'Now, future wife, what are you doing out of your cage?' Arazod stroked Sabrinia's face.

Her chest felt hot. 'I came to find you so I could tell you, there is no way I am marrying you, and you are to take your idiots and leave Flowforn, immediately!'

Arazod looked at Lord Ragnus. 'She wants us to leave. She wants *us* to leave.' He appealed to the Flowfornians who watched from their homes. 'Well, I guess we should probably just respect her wishes and go.' He laughed.

Lord Ragnus chuckled.

'I could never love you,' she said.

His beak twitched. 'All that matters is the history books saying we married.'

'But *you* know I don't love you.'

'No, I don't.'

'Then I'll say it again. I don't—'

Arazod covered his ears with his wings. 'La la la la la...'

'I DON'T—'

'LA LA LA LU LI LALA LI—'

'NOBODY WILL EVER LOVE YOU!' She was exhausted.

The feathers under Arazod's eyes trembled and his chest deflated. He uncovered his ears. 'Chain her up in my quarters,' he told Lord Ragnus.

Sabrinia tried to shake free, but Lord Ragnus' grip was too strong.

Arazod grabbed her face, dug his claws into her cheeks and drew his beak close. His stale breath entered her nose; an unwelcome invasion, like his presence in her life. Blood ran down her cheeks and she gritted her teeth. 'Fools, separate all the couples and families. If I can't have love, nobody will.'

HOME...

It was the morning of the wedding. Oaf stirred and woke up with his face pressed against the back of the humped horse's head. He wiped his mouth on his hand and noticed waves caress the white sand.

The humped horse's heavy footprints marked the otherwise spotless beach. Oaf nudged Questions, who lifted her head from his back. Karl was still slumped over a hump. Beyond him, they could no longer see the Wrath of Arazod.

'Where are we?' Questions asked.

'I don't know.' Oaf took some bread from inside his leather vest. 'It's the last of it.' He tore some for Questions, and dropped a tiny piece into the sack of jars where Tortured Soul was. Oaf looked at the last bit of crust. He sighed and held it by the humped horse's face. 'There you go, Humpy, you need it more than me.'

Humpy wrapped her tongue around the crust and swallowed it.

'Did you give her a name?' Questions nibbled her bread.

'When you fell asleep I got bored, so I spoke to her. Felt

strange her not having a name.' Oaf patted the side of Humpy's neck. 'She's one of us now.'

Questions pointed to the northeast, where Mount Hastovia crept above cliffs. 'Are we going the wrong way?'

'I don't know,' Oaf replied.

The beach curved around a cliff. As more sand came into view, Oaf dug his heels into Humpy's side to stop her. His bottom lip quivered.

'What's wrong?' Questions asked.

It couldn't be. A weathered, stone sculpture of a bearded Oaf pointed towards a village of more sculptures.

Reech. Home…

Some sculptures poked out of the sea due to the receding coastline, and three sculpted row boats were partially buried under the sand, but it was pretty much the same old Reech. Just without the passionate sculpting, without visitors, without life.

'This is my… was my… Reech.'

They jumped off Humpy and Oaf entered his old rock home. He stared out over the village and Questions joined him. They watched Humpy roll around in the sea. Oaf remembered looking out of the same window at his mother while she spoke to Lord Ragnus. The memory was poisonous. 'We can't stop. We have to keep going.'

Questions grabbed his wrist. 'Do you want to rest before we go on?'

He shook his head. 'No. We need to hurry.'

Questions held his hand and looked him in the eye. 'Do you think you need to stop?'

Oaf exhaled and nodded. 'Thanks. But once Humpy is ready, we have to carry on.'

Questions pointed to a sculpture of a humped Oaf holding a baby. 'Is that your mother?'

Oaf's resistance broke and his eyes filled with tears.

They sat on the beach and Oaf told Questions the story of his last sunsets in Reech. She asked no questions, never took her eyes off Oaf, and offered him her sleeve to wipe his tears on. When he'd told her everything, he showed her the sculpture of The Stranger.

'I'm surprised he didn't take this with him.' Oaf picked it up and walked towards the sea. 'Maybe he wanted to leave a symbol of what he did here.'

Questions stood next to him.

He wanted to hug her, just to release a fraction of the pain.

Her attention shifted. 'Did you see that?'

'It's just the sun dancing off the sculptures,' Oaf said. 'I got used to it as a little Oaf.'

Questions nudged him. 'Can you hear that rattling?'

'It'll be nothing.'

'Could you check, please?'

'If it stops you being scared.' Oaf put The Stranger down. 'Where do you think it's coming from?'

Questions pointed to a crack in the base of a cliff; the cliff Oaf used to climb.

Oaf dragged himself past the sculpture of the Knight With No Name and the dragon-scorpion. He poked his neck through the crack.

'It's just a cute little bone-snake.' The noise was its bony frame clattering against rocks as it tried to manoeuvre. 'I'll free it, then we should go.' Oaf reached in.

'What's this red, webby stuff?' Questions asked.

'Hold on, I can't see.' He turned around.

Questions studied a bright red, sticky web, which clung to the sculpture of Grifta.

'Don't know...' Oaf watched her for a moment, amazed at how curious she always was.

Questions ran her finger along the web over Grifta's face, around his neck like a scarf and down his torso then along his tail. The web stroked the sand until it disappeared beneath it.

Questions checked her book. She opened the sack of jars. 'Are you okay, Tortured Soul?'

'Yeah. Just rememberin' somethin',' she mumbled. 'I need to concentrate.'

Questions nodded and closed the sack. Oaf turned back to his task. The sand beneath him shifted.

Humpy whinnied.

'Everything okay?' Oaf asked.

'Can you help me?' Questions called out.

'Yeah, hold on.' He reached for the snake, but it squirmed away.

'Can you help now?' she sounded worried.

'Got it!' Oaf turned around with the bone-snake in hand. From the sand, two large black pincers emerged. Oaf placed the bone-snake down. 'Best you go now, little friend.'

Questions backed away as a horn, then a dragon's head on a muscular, serpentine neck, followed. Almond-shaped eyes glowed icy white, and large nostrils took long, slow breaths.

Questions pulled the dagger from her boot.

A large body with black and red scales like plates of armour shook off sand. Eight hairy, thin black legs pushed the rest of the creature above the ground. The tiny, three-clawed feet looked like they shouldn't be able to hold its weight, and its long, thick tail threw sand into the sky, revealing a circular stinger with two long, curved spikes either side of it.

'Run, Questions! Up the cliff.' Oaf reached his arm out and waved her to come to him.

The dragon-scorpion grabbed Karl by his foot. Its stinger sprayed a red, stringy liquid over him. Questions sprinted towards Oaf, but the beast's other pincer bashed her and her dagger into the sea.

'No!' Oaf yelled and ran towards the beast to get its attention.

Humpy galloped over to Questions and she pulled herself up.

The dragon-scorpion encased Karl in a body-hugging, sticky coffin and tossed him onto the sand.

The monster charged at Oaf, whacked him with a pincer and knocked his head against a sculpture. Oaf slumped, dazed and breathless, and struggled to get back to his feet. Everything tumbled and looked blurry.

The dragon-scorpion approached Karl and spewed a clear solution over him. Steam rose off Karl's red casing.

Questions pulled him away. 'Can you go away?' she yelled at the beast.

It stalked her back towards the water, then swept her legs with its tail and towered over her, baring its crooked, pointed teeth.

Oaf pushed against the sculpture, trying to get to his feet, but he fell back down.

Humpy leapt over Questions and stood between her and the monster. She flared her nostrils, turned and kicked the beast in the face.

It shrieked and pinched Humpy's neck, slicing it open and releasing a flood of blood. Humpy collapsed.

Questions screamed and shuffled back, but she had no chance of escape.

Oaf had to get to her, but muffled whispers confused him. Was he losing his mind?

The creature seemed confused too and it turned around. The whispers came from all directions.

Two tiny, robed creatures with brown sacks over their heads grabbed the dragon-scorpion's front legs. Two more grabbed the back legs. They pulled until the dragon-scorpion was secure, struggling with its pincers and loose legs. It fought and slashed with its tail, but it was stuck. A fifth creature threw a spear, piercing the dragon-scorpion's left eye. It released a demonic shriek. Red-black blood ran down its face and around its mouth.

The dragon-scorpion jumped onto its pincers, shaking its

tormentors off. Oaf concentrated to stop everything from sway-ing. He stood and leaned on the sculpture, waiting in case he fell again.

The monster whipped the spear thrower into the sea, then leapt at Questions and balanced on its tail. It was like a hairy black and red sun with wiry tentacles. Its shadow covered Questions, who slithered backwards while the creature's stinger pulsated.

The beast squealed and leaned back.

Oaf grabbed the sculpture of the Knight With No Name and bashed the creature's tail, knocking it down.

It shot hot orange lumps from its stinger that burned white sand next to Questions.

'Leave her!' Oaf smacked the sculpture against the dragon-scorpion's head. It tried to pinch Oaf, but a golden sword sliced its pincer.

It shrieked and a hooded woman cut its arm off.

Oaf punched the beast in the mouth.

It growled, grabbed Humpy's carcass and dragged it into the sand to a world below, leaving a trail of blood.

Oaf, exhausted, fell to the floor and stared at Humpy's blood.

Questions exhaled. 'Are you okay?'

Oaf nodded.

'Those monsters are pests.' The woman placed a hand on Oaf's shoulder and removed her hood, revealing brown eyes, brown hair and a travel-worn, muscular face of around forty years of age. 'Quick, before he's cooked.' She rushed to Karl.

Questions gasped.

'This is how the dragon-scorpions kill their victims.' She made an incision along the red wrapping around Karl's body. 'It coats them in this webbing, then spews that hot mess, which gets absorbed by it and slowly cooks what's inside.' She peeled the casing off Karl's body. 'Makes the meat peel off the bone nicely – not that I've tried it.'

Questions and Oaf uncovered Karl's face. The woman hesitated when she saw it.

'Will he survive?' Questions asked.

'Seems… Yes, he should.' She stared.

Karl's face was red and most of his clothes had burned.

'Thank you.' Oaf put the Knight With No Name back in her place.

The spear-throwing creature returned from the sea and removed his sack.

'Hello there,' Scrath said.

Questions grinned and hugged him. The other Tree-Cyclopsi approached and removed their sacks.

'Why did you have a sack on your head?' she asked.

'I told them to,' the woman said. 'I'm Larnela. The costumes were just for effect in case we ran into bandits. Someone with a sack on their head is far scarier than someone with a face.'

'Especially one as lovely as mine,' Scrath added.

Oaf's face fell. 'Where's Tortured Soul?' He opened the sack and put his hand to his chest. He took her out. 'You okay?'

'Yeah. Why? Did something happen?'

'Just a battle with a dragon-scorpion.'

'Oh… Okay. Can you put me back in? I'm a bit busy.'

'Sure…' Oaf put her back and shrugged.

'Come with us,' Larnela said. 'I've got a cave not far away, depending on how you define far.'

'We need to keep going. We have to get back to Flowforn by tonight,' Oaf said.

'No chance. It's at least three sunsets away,' Larnela said.

'What?' Questions gazed into the distance.

'So we can't save Sabrinia…' Oaf hung his head.

'You can get there tonight if you take one of my boats.'

'Can we?' Questions grabbed Larnela's hand.

She nodded. 'The rapids will get you to the edges of Flowforn

Forest swiftly, but there's every chance you'll be thrown from the boat and drown.'

Oaf looked at Questions. 'We have to try.'

She smiled back at him.

Larnela shrugged. 'Well, then you'll have a moment to get patched up and eat, so come on.'

Oaf nodded. 'I'll catch up…'

'Are you sure?' Questions asked.

'I just need a moment.'

'Make sure you're not followed,' Larnela warned. The others left with her.

Oaf stood waist deep in the sea, in the last place his mother took a breath. He was sure he felt her spirit hug him, but it was probably the warmth of the sun. He missed her touch, the way she made him feel more than he was, and her peaceful energy. He gazed at the sunlight reflecting off the calm water. The rows of sculptures behind him made him feel tiny. He wiped his eyes, took the sculpture of The Stranger, looked at the face and twisted Lord Ragnus' head off. He threw the rest of the sculpture as far as he could and watched it sink. He held Lord Ragnus' sculpted head in his hand and smashed his fist into it.

BACK IN THE ROOM: QUESTIONS

Questions thought the brown clay cavern was cramped but cosy. Everyone ate fruit and traded stories about what had happened and how they'd ended up there, apart from Larnela. She had gone to gather fish and more fruit.

Scrath explained that the Tree-Cyclopsi had to flee Lake Shizneh when Lord Ragnus chased him. He told them about Karl sacrificing himself to help him to survive, and that Arazod now had the wings.

Tortured Soul ignored everything. All Morcoli's jars of herbs and potions seemed to jog memories and Questions thought it best to leave her to it.

'Don't forget to jump in your water bottle from time to time,' Oaf told Tortured Soul.

'Yep,' she replied.

'Let me go,' a tied-up Fool moaned. 'Must guard the castle! Must help with the execution.'

Oaf jammed a cloth into its mouth.

Scrath nodded at the Fool. 'Lord Ragnus got fed up with chasing us and knocked this one out for no real reason other than he's a very, very angry man. We thought it'd be best to grab it just in case, but now we're not really sure what to do with it.'

The Fool strained against the ropes.

Scrath gestured to six Tree-Cyclopsi. 'This is our army for stopping Arazod. Not counting Wob, of course.' He placed his hand on her head. She was barely up to Oaf's knee.

'I can help!' Wob protested.

'But you won't,' Scrath replied.

Oaf blinked. 'Well, it's more than just me, Questions and Tortured Soul, so thanks.'

Larnela entered and placed a bucket of fish on the table.

'Larnela, will you join our fight?' Scrath asked.

She shook her head. 'I've spent my life running away from trouble. I'm not going to go chasing it.' She blew her hair out of her face. 'If you need me I'll be resting in my room.' She exited.

'What about the rude people?' Wob asked.

'Ah, yes. They complain that we interfere with their relaxation.' Scrath shook his head and pointed to a hole. 'They're through there. Maybe you'll have better luck with them.'

Oaf sucked his tummy in and squeezed through the tight cave. Questions noticed his face brighten and she followed.

Bar Witch stirred fruit into ale in a hole. Was it really her?

Frong rested his head on Sags' shoulder and they drank. Questions couldn't believe it.

Oaf smiled at Frong, who stood, realised how drunk he was, then sat back down. 'Aren't you a sight for old, diseased eyes?' He grinned, his beard filthy.

'How are you alive?' Questions asked.

'Charming.' Bar Witch continued stirring.

'You know what she means,' Oaf said. 'We thought you died in a fire.'

'Ah, that.' Frong pointed at Bar Witch. 'Clumsy broom knocked a lantern over when we all got too drunk. We didn't notice the fire until we were very much in it. Had we been sober, we may have thought about putting the fire out, but we ran instead.'

Sags grunted.

'Yeah. It did Sags a favour.'

Sags showed his now less disgusting foot, got up and walked without his limp.

Questions beamed.

'Burnt all the dirty hair and most of the other filth, so he's his old self again. If we'd known fire did the trick we could've cured him long ago. It turns out dragon phlegm made his foot immune to burning, so he could withstand the heat needed to cure him of all the other filths, then the phlegm peeled off quite nicely.'

Sags grunted.

'We kept running until we could rest a night without seeing a Fool and ended up here...' He drank some more. 'You know, I feel sorry for the Fools. Can't be much of a life being cursed to follow orders.'

Oaf looked at the ground.

'Where's the idiot?' Bar Witch asked.

Oaf shook his head.

'Can you please come with me?' Questions asked.

Questions took them to Karl and hoped they could help.

Bar Witch poked Karl's face.

'So, do you think you can cure him?' Questions asked.

Bar Witch put a hand on Questions' shoulder. 'I'm sorry, love. He's petrified. Magical ale I can brew, and weird tricks I can perform. Curing the petrified, though, that's for the gifted ones.'

Scrath looked at his Tree-Cyclopsi apologetically.

Tortured Soul was oblivious to it all, mumbling. 'Human toe. Worm-fish blood. Sweat of the frog-bee.' Was she going mad?

'What about you two?' Questions pointed at Frong and Sags. 'Are you the greatest adventurers? Is there a relic that can help him?'

Frong took a swig of his ale. 'We were the greatest as a three, but as a two, we're honestly more useless than great.'

Sags released a sad grunt and held Frong's hand.

'Yeah,' Frong replied.

'What did he say?' Questions asked.

'He wishes our old pal Marlens was here. It was her that got us through most adventures with her planning and potions.'

Tortured Soul coughed, then coughed some more. She stumbled into the jars. 'My head!' She spewed lumpy water all over herself and anything close by.

Questions ran over to her. 'Are you okay?'

'Her bottle! Liquid!' Oaf grabbed it and poured water on her.

'My head! It stings!' She exploded into a grey mess.

'Where's she gone?' Questions asked.

Tortured Soul was reduced to a puddle of grey liquid.

Oaf dropped the bottle of water and stood. Tears flooded Questions' eyes.

Oaf pulled her tight to his chest. 'I...'

'Why do bad things keep happening?' Questions said.

Oaf released Questions and tried to scoop the grey mess into the bottle.

Frong kneeled by him. 'I don't think that will work, friend.'

Everyone waited for someone else to say something, but what was there to say?

Coughs filled the air, and a pasty woman with a casual manner emerged from behind a rock. The sack of jars covered her naked body.

'Don't cry, Questions and Oaf. You should be chuffed you don't have to lug me around no more.' She pulled on her red hair.

Questions stared, open-mouthed.

'Marlens!' Frong ran over and squeezed her, as did Sags. They were a mixture of overjoyed and confused.

'You know it,' she strained from Frong's hug.

'But you died,' Bar Witch said.

'Nope. Just got massively tortured.' She adjusted the bag to be more comfortable and hugged Bar Witch. 'When the ledge collapsed in that volcano I ended up in some cavern. That stone-fisted madman found me, and when I wouldn't tell him where the Boarbrick Sandals were, he tortured me pretty badly. Not the friendliest thing to do.'

She swiped the ales from Frong and Sags and threw them away. 'What are you doin'!?' She turned to everyone else. 'These fellas used to be thin and motivated!'

Questions chuckled, and her heart swelled with joy.

'Thank you. For everythin',' Marlens said to Oaf and Questions. She held Questions' hands. 'The breath from a true friend. That's the missin' ingredient.'

Questions smiled. She'd been through so much with Karl.

Sags grunted and grabbed a glass jar.

'Why are you makin' noises?' Marlens asked.

'He hacked off his tongue thinking it would bring you back,' Frong said.

She touched Sags' cheek. 'You always were a bit dim, weren't you?' She smiled. 'But also the sweetest.'

Sags grunted acceptance. He held the glass jar to Questions' mouth.

Marlens nodded. 'A big breath please. Think of all the lovely things.'

Questions closed her eyes. She thought of everything she had experienced with Karl: when he listened to her questions about stars and the Dead Lands, even though he had no answers. His terrible ideas that got them into trouble, and how they had evaded death at the Pit of Endless Screams and the Tower of Alseed. When he ate the fruit that enlarged his head. She laughed. He had grown from someone terrified by everything, to someone who faced everything head on, albeit still terrified. He had brought Oaf, Tortured Soul, and the other wonderful creatures into her life. Her book was bursting with love. She choked up, and also thought of the kindness Sabrinia had shown her. She breathed into the jar and fogged up the glass.

Sags sealed it.

'I have so many questions, Marlens,' Frong said.

'Questions can wait. Right now, we have our petrified pal to save.' She turned to everyone. 'I need two buckets, a fire, an iron pot, six branches, water, a spoon, and three fish.'

'Three fish?' Bar Witch asked.

'I'm hungry.'

Marlens' process was hypnotic. There was certainty in every action. She boiled four branches in the iron pot full of water. She poured worm-fish blood into one bucket and frog-bee sweat into the other. She cut the human toe in half and put a half in each bucket. She bashed the buckets together, and then used the last two branches to stir each. When a skin-like layer formed on one of the mixtures, she removed it and placed it in the other, swung that bucket by the handle, then poured its contents into the iron pot. She stirred with both branches until they boiled down, and then dropped the jar of Questions' breath into it. The mixture glowed sky blue.

Marlens smelled it, smiled, took the back end of a spoon, dipped it in the pot, blew on it a few times and then poked it up Karl's nose. 'Petrification starts in the heart, but ends in the brain, so we need to unlock it.'

Questions held her breath.

Marlens sat back. 'Next we wait until...' she took a bite out of her fish, '... now!'

Nothing happened.

'What?' Marlens tapped her fingers. 'It's the right mix. I don't know what's gone wrong.'

'Is my breath bad?' Questions clasped her hands. Did thinking of the others while she breathed mess it up?

'Maybe you're just rusty is all, Marlens,' Frong said.

'I don't get rusty.'

'Does this mean he's… dead?' Questions asked.

Black mucus washed out of Karl's nostrils. He groaned.

Marlens clicked. 'Ah, it just takes longer 'cos he's naturally a bit weaker than most.'

Karl's body spasmed and he jerked up. He looked around the room. His chest rose and fell. 'Hello everyone… Everyone?'

They all smiled, thrilled to have him back.

The shock of everything hit him and he collapsed.

A DIFFERENT LIFE

Karl opened his eyes.

Oaf's big face smiled down on him. 'You're okay… you're okay.' Oaf squeezed him. He explained everything, and then explained it again, but slower.

'Thank you all,' Karl said sombrely.

'Why are you still in Hastovia?' Questions asked.

Karl sighed. 'There is no portal.' He remembered the wall; the hopelessness.

'Nonsense,' Frong said. 'The legend of the useless woman of Two B has been told for thousands of sunsets, and the story has always remained the same. The sign of a true tale.'

'Karl's right.' Larnela emerged from her rocky room. 'There is no portal in Cell Two B.'

'Well, then how did the idiot of Two B just vanish?' Frong asked.

'She escaped.' Larnela's eyes scanned Karl from head to toe.

He wasn't sure if she was looking at him with suspicion or romantic interest. He assumed it was the latter.

'But my sources are very reliable,' Frong said.

'What are they?' Larnela questioned.

'Journals and travellers.'

'Drunk travellers,' Bar Witch pointed out, as though that were a good thing.

'Drunk travellers,' Frong corrected. 'More keen to share than any normal person, and often more revealing in the nature of their conversation.'

'Well, my source is pretty reliable too.' Larnela poked an apple with her sword, drew it to her mouth and took a bite. 'The Two B idiot, as you call her, is me.'

Karl wished they hadn't revived him. It confirmed his worst fears. Not only was there no portal in Flowforn, but there was likely no portal anywhere.

Frong waved a finger. 'But what about the stories that spread through the land of monsters and portals?'

'Made up to spare embarrassment.' Larnela grabbed a spear and skewered some fish. 'Grab a stone to sit on, and whatever you want to eat.'

Karl, numb, stared at the cave wall.

Larnela ran her hand over the fire. 'I didn't escape through a door to another world. I walked out thanks to the guard.' She turned the fish over the fire. 'He watched the door all the time, so obviously he got bored and we got talking. And well, we fell in love.'

It all made sense; much more sense than a portal. The familiar feeling of worthlessness washed over Karl. He was just a random baby found in a heap of Lionbear dung.

Larnela turned another fish. 'He freed me and we fled, but we were chased by my lover's former friend, another guard named Ludan. He was ordered by King Sastin to find and kill us.'

Karl's eyes widened. 'King Sastin was a hero. He'd never do that.'

She scratched her cheek. 'King Sastin became a hero only after he'd done many unheroic things and learned from them.' She shrugged. 'He was desperate to prevent word getting out that

Flowforn couldn't hold its prisoners. The embarrassment would be huge and people would leave, scared they weren't protected from idiots. He didn't want anyone to ever leave. His vision would die.'

'But the portals?' Frong said.

'A cover story. It justified mages and knights looking around the realm for us. Otherwise people would start asking questions.'

Larnela removed the fish and placed them on the rock table. She chopped them into pieces for everyone.

'I'm sorry, Karl, I was so sure...' Frong said.

Karl shook his head. 'Don't worry, Frong. You gave me more hope than I've ever had. For a while I had possibilities. I felt like somebody.'

Scrath clenched his fists. 'You are somebody. You're the somebody to lead us against Arazod and Lord Ragnus.'

'I'm not.' Karl swallowed the sadness.

'Who's going to help us to save Sabrinia?' Questions asked.

Karl hung his head. 'I... I don't know... I'm not the hero you're looking for.' He left the cave.

Karl sat on a rock, stared at the night and listened to the waves. He wished he'd been killed rather than petrified. What was the point of his life? To keep running from a weird tyrant? It didn't seem like much of a purpose. Failing at every job that existed wasn't much better, either.

Oaf untied a boat from a rock. 'We've got a wedding and an execution to stop, Karl.'

The others stood next to him.

'I can't...'

'What about Sabrinia?' Questions asked.

'I wish I could do something for her, but we'll just add to the body count. I fought Arazod and I was hopeless. I'm going to find a cave of my own and live out my days in peace. I'm done with danger. And near death, well, I don't want to be close to that ever again.'

Questions put a hand on his shoulder. 'Did Sabrinia give you a good life?'

She tried to. He couldn't look Questions in the eyes.

Oaf glared at him. 'After everything we've been through, you want to give up?'

He saw no other way and hoped they'd realise the same thing. 'I'm sorry.'

Oaf huffed. 'I guess deep down you're a coward.' He frowned and climbed into the boat.

Questions stared at Karl, but he had nothing to say. Her shoulders fell and she joined Oaf.

Karl sniffled. They had done so much for him, but he had nothing to offer. He was a burden.

He watched them all get in the boat and row into the distance. 'Good luck and be careful. It's a strange world out there,' he muttered to himself.

A FRIENDLY CHAT

Karl dragged his feet along Reech's coast. The night sun hugged the sculptures and made them seem real. He sat on the shore and watched the boat full of people who had made him feel more than useless disappear towards Flowforn. *Be safe. Thank you for the adventure.*

He would only get in the way. He had imagined saving Sabrinia countless times, but when he thought about it realistically, he always died.

'Do you mind if I join you?' Larnela asked.

Karl gestured to the sand.

Larnela stabbed her sword into the sand and sat.

'How do you do it?' he asked her.

'What?'

'Live life on the run. I've not been great at it.'

She smiled. 'It's not something I ever wanted to do. As far as choices go, my options were poor. Run while death chased me, or stay in a room and die.' She chuckled.

'I know the feeling.' Karl wiped sand off his trousers, remembering being imprisoned.

Water washed around Larnela's sword. 'I ran to be with the person I loved. But as we got older, running got harder.'

'Does it ever get easier? I'm exhausted and it hasn't been very long.'

She lay back on the sand and looked up at the night. 'For a short time we got to live a normal life.'

'Really?'

'We found a village, around the time Sastin softened and called off his hunt. We had a home, got married, and...' Larnela choked up.

'What?' Karl asked.

'Nothing... We just got to be normal.'

Karl lay back. 'If Sastin called off the hunt, why didn't you go back to Flowforn?'

'Ludan.' She sighed. 'He refused to let there be an escape against his name and would cover his continued hunt with made-up missions to trick his king.' Larnela scooped sand up and let it fall through her fingers. 'I woke one night to a fire raging. My husband had disappeared to save himself.'

'What a guy...' Karl shook his head. 'At least you survived.'

Larnela sat up. 'We're in front of Ludan's grave...' She nodded to the sea then pulled her shirt up to show two long scars on her ribs. 'But I got lucky.'

Karl winced.

'I kept his sword as a memento of the years of suffering.'

'Well, if he's dead, surely you can stop running?' Karl rolled onto his front and propped himself up on his elbows.

'It's not that simple. The longer you run, the more people you end up having to run from. You get desperate and make enemies out of your need for food, shelter, water, and anywhere you stay you bring danger to. There are Ludans everywhere.' Larnela took a breath. 'You have to make big sacrifices. I...' She tried to say something, but stood up and pulled her sword from the sand.

'You what?'

'Doesn't matter...' Larnela wiped wet sand from her blade. 'You have friends and you can change this place, Karl, to stop people ever having to run again. I had no choice. You do.'

'But I'm not a hero.'

'Neither was the great King Sastin you worship.'

She had a point.

Larnela brushed sand off one of the sculpted row boats. 'Heroes aren't born, Karl, they become. And from the way your friends look up to you... I'd say you're their hero.'

'Are you just saying all of this to get me to leave you in peace?'

Larnela laughed and then looked down at the sand. 'Most of us want to do the right thing. We get it wrong sometimes, and what the right thing is changes, but we try again, and we keep trying until we sometimes get it right.' She pushed the row boat towards the shore.

Karl helped her. 'Why don't you come? Then you can help to stop the running too.'

Larnela shook her head. 'I may carry a sword, but unless I have to, I no longer have the strength or desire to swing it.'

'I get it...' Karl stepped into the boat and extended his hand.

Larnela shook it and smiled at Karl. She pulled him in for a hug and squeezed him. He wasn't sure what to do, so squeezed her back.

'Good luck, Karl,' her voice broke. She pushed the boat away from the shore.

Karl rowed for Flowforn. He wished he'd gone with the others so he didn't have to do all the rowing. He looked back at Larnela, who wiped her eyes. Maybe she had gotten sand in them.

NOT MUCH OF A PLAN

Karl's boat approached the rapids. He feared the chomping, watery teeth would crush his bones. He gripped the sides of the row boat and braced himself for the first, short drop.

He tumbled to the back of the boat. It spun, the bow facing backwards and the stern rising. Karl rushed to the middle to steady it.

Water smacked his face and blinded him.

'That all you can do?' he yelled, then realised the water wouldn't answer.

He coughed, every muscle straining to hold on. The water bashed him from all angles. He couldn't open his eyes.

He pressed his body against the boat.

He wished he had gone with his friends. Oaf would be steadying the boat, looking as calm as ever. Questions would be asking questions about water, and despite it being annoying, it would be a welcome distraction. Bar Witch would probably be cackling, telling them all they were going to die, while Frong would no doubt have a story about the first wave.

The boat hit a rock, flipped, and Karl crashed into the water.

He thrashed and gasped, but water hammered the back of his throat and shot up his nose. He fought and he fought, but the rapids swallowed him.

As he sunk, he imagined his friends. People who had given him strength and shown him kindness even when he didn't deserve it. They were his inspiration, and gave him energy he never knew he had. He would not die here. He kicked and pulled his arms through the water, breaking the surface. He took the biggest breath he could.

The boat threatened to abandon him, but he grabbed it and held on.

It dragged him over the final drop and into the calm of Flowforn Basin.

The base of the Wrath of Arazod was in view. Karl climbed on top of the capsized boat and rested there, his body battered. Each cough felt as if it would shatter his insides.

The gentler waves nudged the boat towards the cliff.

Soaked and panting, Karl dragged his feet up the hill towards Flowforn.

His friends appeared in the distance, under a statue of King Sastin. A pained scream from the castle pierced the night.

'Karl!' Oaf gave him an overly tight hug.

'I'm sorry for having a… moment. But dying does that to you.'

Marlens raised a hand. 'It wasn't death, it was—'

'A technicality,' Karl said. 'We need to save our world.'

'Can you convince them?' Questions pointed to Scrath and the adventurers.

'Convince them of what?' Karl asked.

'Some of us have been thinking,' Scrath said. 'Maybe we don't get involved in this.'

Others murmured in agreement.

Bar Witch nodded. 'There are battles and problems all over Flowfornia that Flowforn has never bothered with, so why should we rescue it?'

Scrath opened his palms. 'We could live where they've already destroyed. Less chance of being revisited.'

Karl shook his head. 'And how long do you think that will last?'

Nobody had an answer.

The Fool, tied to a tree, fought against its restraints. 'Must return to guard castle. Kill intruders.'

'Oaf, can you silence the prisoner, please?'

Oaf picked up some twigs and jammed them into the Fool's mouth.

Karl pointed towards the castle. 'As long as they rule, nowhere will ever be safe, because there's always a chance they'll come back. Especially now that the idiot can fly. You think he'll stop at Flowforn?'

Questions smiled at Karl.

Karl took a breath. 'We are the only chance this land has.' He shook his head at the cruelty of the situation. 'We can make it a place where nobody has to hide in caves, or in dirty taverns.'

'I cleaned that tavern once a sunset!' Bar Witch said.

'I didn't mean it like that. I was just—'

'Then why would you say it?' She folded her arms.

'It was just an example.' He wished he'd not said anything now.

'Well get a better one next time,' she said.

Everyone else nodded in agreement.

Karl sighed. 'Fine. I'm sorry... Your tavern was impeccably maintained. Can I carry on?'

Bar Witch shrugged.

'As I was saying... *We, together,* can save Hastovia. Sabrinia let Arazod take over, because Flowforn has an army of about three hopeless people, so she had no choice. We have a choice. We can hide, with destruction spreading around us, always scared we'll be next... or we can change things...'

Oaf smiled at him.

'Alone… that's exactly what we are. I know I was… I thought I needed to find another world and parents to feel like I belonged. But I found meaning in all of you.' He cast a glance at Bar Witch. 'Most of you.'

She spat at his feet.

He huffed. 'Together, we are so much more. So much stronger. And we can achieve anything.'

Scrath looked at his Tree-Cyclopsi and nodded.

'We have a group of people with so many different, albeit obscure and not always useful skills, that we are an army. An army of friends who want to make a difference.' He clenched a fist.

'Damn right!' Marlens put her arms around her rotund duo.

Karl pointed at her. 'We have adventurers that have seen most of our land and can easily break into anywhere.'

Frong raised a finger. 'It depends how you define "easily". The word has roots in—'

Karl pointed to Oaf. 'We have the strength to smash Lord Ragnus' joyless face in.'

Oaf nodded.

'And we have the smarts, speed, trickery and above all…' he looked at Questions and Oaf, '…heart, to overcome fear, doubt, and any creature that blocks our path!'

They all cheered. Questions beamed.

Karl raised a finger. 'Maybe let's not cheer. We don't want to draw any attention to ourselves.'

The others agreed.

'So, let's go and save this place from an irritating pigeon with anger issues.'

They all smiled, inspired.

'Do we have a plan?' Questions asked.

He frowned at the question. 'We need to split up. And that's kind of as far as I got. So now we consult the experts.' He turned to Sags, Frong, and Marlens. 'Ready for another adventure?'

* * *

KARL USED his nail to carve a plan of the castle into the dirt.

Marlens paced in front of the group and pointed to the gardens on the plan. 'Tree-Cyclopsi. You make some chaos here.' She poked at five points. 'These four columns, and the statue they form a square around. Pour what's in these jars on each target.' She showed them a jar of blue powder and a jar of yellow dust. She put them back in a sack. 'Make sure they mix. You'll have just enough time to get out of harm's way, so pour 'em onto the targets at the same time and run.' She threw Scrath the sack of jars. 'Be careful, I only got five of each, no spares.'

Scrath looked at the sack as if it contained all of their hopes of success.

'Bar Witch, you cause a distraction at Flowforn Arch,' Marlens said. 'It'll drag Fools away from the courtyard so we can climb in through the waste well wivout havin' to deal wiv too much grief. Divide and break in. Any questions?'

Questions raised her hand.

'Yes, Questions?'

'How are you feeling?' Questions asked.

Marlens shook her head. 'Any proper questions?'

Questions raised her hand again. Marlens ignored her.

Karl bit the skin around his thumb. 'What do we do once we're in the courtyard?'

'We improvise.'

'Improvise?' That didn't sound good.

'Every adventure has parts where you 'ave to go wiv the flow.'

Karl let it sink in. The unknown. Something he was never interested in, but now provided opportunity.

Oaf pointed to the tied-up Fool. 'As you heard, the Fools have been ordered to kill any intruders.' He looked at Karl. 'We need to try our best not to kill them. It's not their fault.'

Karl was proud of him.

They marched towards the castle, no longer as individuals with strange quirks, but as a group, an army with so many quirks the greatest scholars of the mind would throw away everything they had learned.

They split off in their various directions to begin their missions. Karl hoped they would all survive.

INSTRUCTION DESTRUCTION
(RENAME)

'**Y**ou're to stay here,' Scrath told Wob. He climbed a ladder of Tree-Cyclopsi and reached the top of the wall.

'But I can—'

'No, Wob. I can't put you at risk. Stay by that tree, please.' She was stubborn like her mother and he didn't want her to meet the same fate.

She scoffed.

Scrath scanned the gardens. At the opposite end was the path that linked it to the courtyard and alleys. Scrath had heard about how beautiful Flowforn's garden was, but reality disappointed him. The bright green grass he'd read about was yellowy brown. The statue of King Sastin wrestling a dragon had been altered so it was Arazod doing the wrestling. The majestic blue and white flowers he'd heard about had withered. It looked like part of an abandoned city.

Scrath took note of the Fools' movement along the lines of dying bushes and flowerbeds. Four Fools armed with spears moved along their paths at the same time. They would stop, look left, and return to point A, stop, look left again, and return to point B.

The bottom Tree-Cyclopsi, Brog, climbed to the top of the wall, and the rest followed. Scrath looked down at Wob, her eye full of anger, but he knew she'd understand eventually.

'If things sound bad, you run back home,' he told her.

She pulled on her neck hairs.

The Tree-Cyclopsi climbed down the other side and hid behind a fountain. Scrath worried their distinct appearance would get them all caught. Little one-eyed orange, bald creatures with hair from the neck down would receive a lot of attention, but he had to trust the plan.

Scrath mimicked an owl's hoot to see if it would alert the Fools. It didn't. He meowed like a cat. Again, the Fools didn't react.

'Perfect,' he whispered. He handed everyone their jars. 'Stop when you hear the owl's hoot. Go when you hear the cat's meow.'

'What if I hear something else?' Brog asked, ever the idiot.

'Then you do nothing.'

'A stop nothing? Or a go nothing?'

'Just carry on as you are unless you hear one of the noises I mentioned.'

Brog processed it. He probably still didn't understand.

Scrath pointed Grum to the northwest column. Grum made his move, got halfway and heard the hoot. He took cover behind a signpost to the admin building. On the cat's meow he made his way to the column.

Scrath sent Prob to the northeast without trouble, and Darf found the southwest column without incident.

Brog ran for the southeast column, the closest one. He got confused by the owl's hoot and ducked. He heard the cat's meow and looked around, scared.

Scrath used gestures instead.

Brog fell over. The jars bumped off the ground.

Scrath froze.

A Fool turned around, but saw only hedges.

Brog retrieved the jars and was close to his column. Just one more Fool to avoid.

The Fool turned away to patrol the entrance.

Brog made it. 'Yes!' Brog shouted, victorious.

Scrath slapped himself on the forehead.

Brog cursed himself and threw the jars into a bush.

The Fool turned and pointed its spear at him. Its expression turned.

Brog raised his arms. 'I'm sorry. I was just looking—'

'Kill intruders.' The Fool drove its spear into Brog's stomach. He looked over at Scrath, tears in his eye.

Scrath held his fist to his mouth. Four hundred years of life, gone. His legs trembled and his neck stiffened.

'Intruders!' the Fool yelled. 'We need more Fools to stand guard.'

OVER TO YOU

*B*ar Witch counted roughly thirty Fools, including Behemoth Fools, guarding Flowforn Arch. She bit her tongue. There was no way she could approach them; too many swords, clubs and daggers. She hid behind a tree and studied them. They scanned the surroundings.

Bar Witch tapped her chin. She rolled her eyes into her head and a blue glow flowed through her veins. 'Baldigotum!' A hairless, miniature goat leapt out of her cloak. She wiped the sweat from her forehead and tapped the goat's legs to get it moving towards Flowforn Arch. 'Good luck.'

The Fools chased the goat. It bleated and bounced, evading death.

Bar Witch caught her breath and smirked. Another Fool joined, then another, until six Fools chased the goat, swiping their swords and throwing their spears at it.

She shook her arms to relax and rotated her shoulders. Her eyes rolled into the back of her head again. The blue pulse burned her veins and left cracks in the skin of her arms.

'Grundimonus.' A hairy, whiskered mole-fish leapt out of her sleeve and into the soil. The ground vibrated and the mole-fish leapt up in front of the Fools. One tried to catch it, but it slithered out of its hands and back under ground, then leapt out behind it. Four more Fools joined in trying to grab it.

It wasn't enough. She needed to draw more Fools out. Bar Witch wiped the blood from her nose and rubbed the stinging out of her fingers. She clenched her fists and her heart raced. 'Come on, then.' This had to count. She took a breath, closed her eyes, and then they shot open and rolled into the back of her head. The blue pulse stung and stabbed at her insides. Her body tensed and she had to fight the urge to scream. She gritted her teeth and the cracks in her arms widened and blood poured out.

'Spikuswingnum.' Her stomach bubbled and the bubbles moved up her chest and into her throat. She opened her mouth and hundreds of snake-bees flew out. Their long, striped bodies slithered in the air and their tiny wings flapped. Their stingers moved side to side on the end of their tails.

The Fools waved their weapons and arms, fighting off the bites and stings. More Fools joined them.

Bar Witch smiled and fell to her knees. The pain consumed her and her body throbbed as if it could explode. 'Over to you lot… Don't mess it up.' She collapsed face first into the mud.

FATHER AND DAUGHTER

Scrath stared at his friend's corpse. He wanted to give up, but then Brog's death would be meaningless.

His people hid by columns, all terrified. What could he do? The number of Fools had grown and some were on horned wolves. There was no easy path to the column.

Wob joined him. 'I can—'

'What are you doing, Wob? It's too dangerous for you. Please.' He took her hands. 'Please, just stay behind this fountain.'

She pulled her hands away.

Scrath counted the Fools again. There were still ten, and three on horned wolves. The other Tree-Cyclopsi did their best to camouflage against the columns. 'Oh boy, Scrath. Looks like it's happening. First I'll take care of that column, then that leaves me roughly no time to get to the statue. Come on Scrath, be brave.' He took a deep breath. 'Wob, if anything happens…'

Wob was gone.

Scrath felt numb.

She leapt over a hedge and ran along the tiled rim of a water feature. Scrath was aware she was agile, but this was incredible.

Wob scooped up Brog's jars in her stride. Scrath's heart raced.

She headed straight for a collision with a Fool on a horned wolf, but spun behind the southeast column, dodging its gaze. She looked over at her father. He mouthed an apology and she smiled.

More stubborn than her mother, but just as brilliant. He hoped she was watching over them.

All that remained was for Scrath to get to the statue of Arazod wrestling a dragon, but the Fools had all angles covered.

'If I go from… no. Maybe I should… no.' There was no way.

Scrath moved then hesitated.

Wob looked at him, poured the contents of the jars on the column, and then stepped into the open.

Scrath's eye widened. His heart twisted and all the hairs covering his body stood on end.

'Fools!' She spread her arms, welcoming a fight.

Scrath stepped forward, but she shook her head.

The Fools turned their attention to her.

'Come and get me if your stupid little legs are fast enough.'

'Must kill intruders.' One of them walked over to stab her, but she dodged the knife, then another thrust a spear, which she sidestepped. A horned wolf tried to bite her. She kicked off a fountain and spun away.

Scrath's body shook.

Seven Fools chased her. She led them away from the central statue and Scrath took his chance. He made it and nodded to his fellow Tree-Cyclopsi. They all mixed the pastes onto the stone and ran.

When Scrath lifted his head, Fools chased Wob out of the gardens. He sprinted after her.

DON'T SPLIT THE PARTY

Karl, Sags, Frong, Marlens, Oaf and Questions waited, chest deep in the filthy, murky, waste well.

Karl fought the urge to vomit, but the smell was so foul he could taste it.

They'd listened to what felt like an eternity of Arazod's songs. Among the ear burners he screeched through were, *'Share this egg', 'Is it because I have feathers?', 'A tree does not maketh a nest', 'Let me beak your lover'*, and his final eardrum abuser, *'These wings are for huggin'.'*

Sags pulled at his ears, desperate for the singing to end.

Karl gazed up to the well entrance. Fools rested their hands on it, likely with their backs to it, looking out onto all areas of the courtyard.

Karl let filthy water run between his fingers. He held them in front of him, a mess of black and green lumpy waste. 'I can't believe this is what we let flow into the stream all the way to Lake Shizneh.'

'What's that?' Questions looked at the waste water.

Karl was sure he saw something too.

'It's just a dirt-fish,' Frong told Questions. 'They are born out of waste. Brains, hearts, everything. The largest one ever recorded was found in Gumton, a disgusting kingdom that used to stand tall on the island of Mornok across the Wilda Sea, far north—'

'Just stop it,' Karl said.

Frong nodded. 'Perhaps for later.'

Karl nodded.

Marlens secured some grips to ropes. She put her arms around Frong and Sags. 'It's excitin' bein' on an adventure again.' She felt around Frong's back and found an ale pouch in his armour. She tutted and threw it away.

Karl listened to the Fools at the top of the well. 'Hold on…'

'A bald goat, a mole-fish, and snake-bees,' one said.

'We'd better help. Must guard the castle,' another suggested.

'We'll keep guarding the castle here,' another stated.

Two sets of hands left the rim of the well, and the sound of shuffling pebbles under their feet grew distant. Karl listened out for the next part of the plan.

Marlens raised a finger. 'If the Tree-Cyclopsi have done their bit, then any moment now we should hear…'

Rumbling.

She smiled.

'What was that?' a Fool cried.

'Intruders. The gardens, now!' another ordered. All the hands from around the well disappeared.

Karl turned to his friends. 'Ready?'

They nodded.

Marlens threw her rope up and secured the grip. They all did the same. One by one they climbed until it was just Oaf and Karl.

'I made you something,' Oaf said.

He took out a beautifully sculpted black and purple stone shield from his sack. It had spiked sides and a hooked bottom. He handed it to Karl.

His body tingled from its touch. 'But you swore you'd never sculpt again.'

'I made this out of a sculpture of Lord Ragnus' face.' Oaf smiled. 'If my sculptures can help save everyone, I'll sculpt until my hands fall off.'

Karl put his filthy hand on Oaf's shoulder. 'Thank you.'

'Arazod's Soul Bleeder may be the sharpest axe in the land, but the sky rocks of Reech are the toughest material I know,' Oaf said.

Karl hugged him. 'If this ends badly… it's been a pleasure.' He admired the shield.

Oaf patted him on the back. 'It's called The Star of Reech.'

'It's perfect.' Karl turned and grabbed the rope, but Oaf stopped him.

'One last time?' Oaf said.

Karl nodded. Why not? Oaf threw Karl out of the well. His face skidded and burned along the courtyard pebbles and he regretted letting sentiment get the better of him.

There was chaos towards the gardens and Fools chased creatures at the arch.

Flowfornians in chains watched. Proster tried to chase a Fool, but the men he was chained to refused to indulge his thirst for fighting.

Peezant pecked at the chains that bound him to an outdoor cage.

A Fool looked at Karl. It was about to call out, but Frong drove his shoulder into its face, knocking it out. Karl's jaw dropped, marvelling at the power. Frong smiled and rolled his shoulders.

A Behemoth Fool blocked the entrance to the King's Tower, alongside a Fool armed with a spear, riding a horned wolf. They looked towards the commotion in the gardens.

'We've officially adventured into Flowforn,' Marlens said.

'Another fine plan executed to perfection,' Frong added. He

pulled Sags in and kissed him. 'Take that Flowforn!' Frong yelled at the top of his voice.

Sags grunted. They stood proud, taking it all in.

Karl couldn't help but smile.

'We're not done yet, though.' Marlens indicated to the Behemoth Fool. 'Looks like we've got to overcome a beast.' She took the rope and grip and threw the other end to Frong. 'You ready?'

'I've missed this.' Frong straightened his beard.

'Sags, you're up,' Marlens said.

Oaf climbed out of the well using the remaining ropes, then Frong and Marlens took them.

Sags ran up to the Behemoth Fool and its companion.

'Intruder,' the Behemoth Fool said, so Sags punched it in the face.

Karl's eyes widened, worried his friend would be crushed.

The Behemoth Fool blinked and clenched its fists. It roared, throwing its arms to its side in a display of dominance, accidentally smashing the Fool off its horned wolf. The Behemoth Fool chased Sags towards the well.

Sags dodged punches, moving as though he knew what was coming before it was on its way.

'How?' Karl couldn't understand his agility.

Frong and Marlens threw their ends of the ropes to each other and back, circling the Behemoth Fool in a well-practised routine.

Sags weaved and ducked more attacks, while Frong and Marlens threw the ropes above and below the Behemoth Fool's arms until its body was tangled.

Sags grunted to Frong and Marlens. He walked up to the Behemoth Fool and thumped it in the stomach.

'Must kill intruders.' The Behemoth Fool grabbed Sags and squeezed him against its muscular chest.

Karl grimaced.

Frong and Marlens ran around the Behemoth Fool and pulled

the ropes until the beast was covered from head to toe, with Sags bound to its body.

'Can he breathe?' Karl asked.

'You alright, Sags?' Frong checked.

He grunted.

'Why have you tied him up?' Questions asked.

Something moved under the ropes, accompanied by the uncomfortable clicking of bones. Sags' foot, followed by his leg, his other leg, his body, arms and head slithered out of a tiny gap in the ropes.

The Behemoth Fool tried to break free, but fell and struggled against the restraints.

'Strong work, Sags.' Marlens patted him on the back. He clicked every bone back into place. The others winced.

Karl was both impressed and disgusted.

Frong patted his shoulder. 'Circus time teaches you a lot.'

Karl waited for him to continue into a long story about their time in the circus, but he didn't. 'One for later as well?'

Frong nodded. 'Just that other Fool to go.'

The Fool mounted its horned wolf and pointed its spear at them. 'Charge!'

Oaf roared at the horned wolf.

Terrified, it ran away, taking the Fool with it.

A disruption came from Flowforn Arch. 'Help!' Bar Witch yelled.

Marlens turned towards the noise. 'Seeing as we never nab anything from our adventures, how about we claim Bar Witch as our magic relic?'

'I don't think she'll appreciate being called a relic, but she'd appreciate the gesture,' Frong said.

Sags grunted.

'Thanks... all of you,' Karl said.

Marlens hugged him. 'We'll come and help as soon as we've got her. Good luck.'

Frong stepped in. 'It's better to just say "go for it". Luck is something that isn't driven by mentality, whereas if you say "go for it", it motivates the person to push through fear and doubt. There have been studies since the beginning of history—'

'Just go.' Karl smiled.

The adventurers ran towards the commotion, passing the chained group of Flowfornian men.

At Flowforn Arch, a Fool speared the bald goat, while the Behemoth Fool caught the mole-fish and ripped it in half. The other Fools waved flaming torches at the snake-bees.

Scrath dragged Wob into an outdoor cage and closed it, shielding him and his daughter. Fools poked their spears through the bars, but they evaded them. They wouldn't last long.

All of this was to help Karl and Flowforn. A group of Fools spotted him, Questions and Oaf.

'Get them!' They charged.

Proster, chained and looking exhausted, dragged a reluctant line of fellow prisoners and stood between the Fools and the trio. 'Go on then, idiot,' Proster told Karl.

Karl smiled at him and rushed into the tower. He looked back for Questions and Oaf, but oncoming Fools fought them along a different corridor.

'Keep going, Karl!' Oaf shouted.

He had to do this alone.

A HAPPY OCCASION

Sabrinia, wrists and ankles tied with rope, stood next to Arazod at the front of the Great Hall. She refused to wear her red wedding dress, so Arazod had it tied around her, like a long scarf, over her undergarments.

Lord Ragnus stood by Arazod's side.

Gold carvings of old royal figures under messages of positivity lined the walls. They read more mockingly: "Pursue your passion", "Love who you are", "Don't let others stop you being you", "Dreams can become reality."

Wooden benches faced the large, golden Soul Candle, which never burned out. Sabrinia gazed at the tiny, uneven wooden entrance, which made the Great Hall more aesthetically disappointing than great. She hoped someone would burst through it and throw a spear through Arazod's head.

An old Warlock who looked and smelled like he'd been living in an ale barrel addressed them, his back to the candle. He was wearing a torn and stained silver gown. His fingers were covered in faded precious stones, and a tiny, white, pointy hat leaned off his head to complete his outfit.

He placed his hand on an orb on a plinth. Names formed in smoke within it.

Arazod clenched his fist. 'What do you mean you won't marry us?'

'She has to say yes without being restrained,' the Warlock replied nasally.

Arazod nodded to Lord Ragnus. He untied Sabrinia's wrists and ankles, gripped her head tighter than he needed to and made her nod.

The Warlock huffed. 'No. She has to *say* yes herself.'

'Not going to happen,' she said through the forced nods.

The Fool alarm sounded and Sabrinia smiled, hoping another kingdom Arazod had ruined was here for revenge.

Lord Ragnus released Sabrinia's head and turned to Arazod. 'It would help if you gave me full control of the Fools. I can assign them specific duties to counter whatever is going on.'

Arazod scratched his talons against the floor. 'I told you. When I get what I want you'll have your army. And I want Sabrinia to be married to me.'

Lord Ragnus smiled. Sabrinia could feel the frustration behind it.

'Understood,' Lord Ragnus said.

Sabrinia smirked. 'You know he'll never give you command of them, don't you? They're the only strength he has.'

'Quiet, you,' Arazod said.

Lord Ragnus cleared his throat. 'I'll go and investigate.' He left.

Arazod turned back to the Warlock. 'Look, I am the king, and I command that she is my wife. Why doesn't that mean anything? What's the point of being a king if people don't do as I say?'

Sabrinia, bored, shook her head.

The Warlock sighed. 'I don't think you understand. If Sabrinia doesn't want to marry you, I can't cast the spell of binding souls and cast your names into the History Orb.'

'I really don't want to marry him,' she said.

'Silence!' Arazod turned back to the Warlock. 'Surely it's about what I want?'

'Not when it comes to marriage. That's a two-way process in most kingdoms,' the Warlock replied.

'Hmm...' Arazod raised his axe. 'Will you marry us if I threaten to kill her?'

Sabrinia craned her neck. 'If you kill me I won't have to marry you, so go on, slice me right there. Take as many swings as you need.'

Arazod scratched his head. 'What if I threaten to kill *you*?' he asked the Warlock.

'If you kill me, you'll have to search Flowfornia for another Warlock to perform the ceremony. I get the impression you've killed most of them already, so you need me more than I need you right now.'

'Gah!'

Sabrinia and the Warlock exchanged a smile, relieved this wouldn't drag on.

'Fools!' Arazod screamed.

Two Fools brought in a struggling, exhausted Hargon, his face covered in bruises. One Fool held a knife to his neck.

Sabrinia's neck tensed and her heart raced. Hargon had been through so much with her.

Arazod gestured to the Warlock. 'Ask her the question again, and as we practised.'

The Warlock huffed. 'Do you wish to marry Arazod, Supreme Man-Hawk, heroic leader and conqueror of all?'

Arazod stared at her.

'Can you repeat the question, please?' Sabrinia asked.

'Don't do it, Sabrinia!' Hargon shouted. 'My life isn't worth it.'

Sabrinia hung her head. Was this really it? Bound to the most evil creature she had ever come across? She smiled at Hargon, admiring his bravery. Even in the misery that had hung over

Flowforn, she had seen hope in him, and great determination in others. Through pain she felt pride.

She gazed at the walls, the history on them. It would be reduced to rubble, but she would hold on to the flicker of hope she had seen in her people in such a crisis.

She nodded at the Warlock.

He took a breath. 'Princess Sabrinia, do you wish to marry Arazod, Supreme Man-Hawk, heroic leader and conqueror of all?'

She swallowed. 'Yes. I do…' Sickness threatened to leave her throat.

Hargon's head lowered. 'I'm sorry, Princess Sabrinia.'

Arazod clapped. 'We're married!'

The Warlock stepped to the side of the Soul Candle. 'Now step into its shadow.'

Arazod leapt into the shadow of the candle, while Sabrinia dragged her feet.

The Warlock held a hand over the flame until a black circle formed on his palm. 'Now hold your hands out and place them on top of each other.'

Arazod grabbed Sabrinia's hand and held it out under his claw.

The Warlock placed his hand on top of theirs.

The warmth ran up Sabrinia's arm, even though the rest of her body felt cold.

'In the light of the Soul Candle, I bind your hearts, your minds, and your souls. May you never be apart, and may you continue your journey together in the afterlife, spreading togetherness and love.'

He removed his hand and the shadow became light, shining on Sabrinia and Arazod's faces.

Arazod closed his eyes and grinned.

Sabrinia cried, wishing the flame would set her ablaze.

The Warlock touched the History Orb, and their faces formed

in it, their union documented forever. Their faces dissolved into cloudy letters, spelling their names.

'Congratulations. You are King and Queen, husband and wife, two beings with one soul. Live your lives to serve others, to—'

'Blah blah blah.' Arazod waved a hand at the Warlock. 'You can go now.'

The Warlock stared at him, shook his head, offered Sabrinia a sympathetic look and departed.

Arazod opened his wings. 'Ready to die, my queen?'

'I don't think she is,' a familiar voice said.

Sabrinia turned to find Karl stood in the doorway. 'Karl! You're alive!'

All of Arazod's feathers stood on end. 'I pushed you off a CLIFF! It was really HIGH!'

Sabrinia punched Arazod's beak and ran to Karl.

The Fools stepped forward. 'Must kill intruders.'

'No! Don't kill him.' Arazod's eyes narrowed. 'He's mine.'

The Fools stopped. Hargon ran to Sabrinia.

Karl stood in front of them and held his shield to his chest. He stared at Arazod. 'Let's make sure this is the last time we meet.'

Arazod chuckled and flew at him. He swung his axe, but Karl deflected the blow, knocking the axe out of Arazod's hands.

'How?' Arazod retrieved the Soul Bleeder and hovered. 'Capture her!' He pointed at Sabrinia.

'I think you should run,' Karl told Sabrinia and Hargon. He bashed his shield against the first Fool's head, pushing it against a bench. The second Fool grabbed Hargon. Sabrinia punched it in the face, knocking it over.

'Stay safe, Karl,' Sabrinia said. She and Hargon ran, but she turned back in the doorway.

Arazod struck Karl's shield again.

'This can't be!' Arazod moaned.

'Sorry to ruin your plans.' Karl blocked a flurry of blows.

'Come on,' Hargon told Sabrinia.

She wanted to help, but there was nothing she could do. She and Hargon ran up the stairs, but she had no idea where to go.

'Wife!' Arazod screeched. 'Don't hide from your husband.'

'Get back here you coward!' Karl shouted.

Sabrinia and Hargon turned a corner. A Fool tried to grab Sabrinia, but Hargon grappled it. It stabbed Hargon in the thigh. He yelled and fell.

'Hargon!' Sabrinia bashed the Fool's head against the wall. She reached for the dagger in Hargon's thigh.

'No... no,' he said. 'Thanks. I'm not ready to take it out yet. You should run. I'll be fine.'

Sabrinia nodded and stroked his face. 'Thank you. For everything.'

She turned and sprinted towards the end of the corridor.

'There you are!' Arazod flew after her.

RISING RAGNUS

Oaf searched the corridors, but couldn't find Karl or Questions. It was all the same – just bricks and doors.

A familiar voice boomed from outside. 'Why's it so difficult for you all to keep a bit of order?'

Oaf poked his head out of the window and looked down at the courtyard.

Lord Ragnus.

A hot energy filled Oaf's insides, desperate for release.

Lord Ragnus kicked a Fool. He threw Flowfornians out of the large tub of moisturiser where they stamped on hazel berries to make his lotion. A Cyclops dragged other Flowfornians towards an alley.

Oaf sprinted down the stairs. He watched Lord Ragnus relax, lost in a heaven of lubricant, his eyes closed, ignoring the chaos around him.

This was it. Oaf entered the tub, moisturiser up to his ankles. He could creep up and crush Lord Ragnus' skull, but he wanted him to know who was going to kill him.

'Stand,' Oaf said.

'What is it now?' Lord Ragnus sat up. His annoyed expression became a smirk. 'Cecil? I guess this means I'm not the strongest being in Hastovia anymore.'

Oaf stepped forward and clenched his fists, his nose a few inches from Lord Ragnus'.

'Do you need help?' Questions ran towards Oaf.

He turned to her. 'No, Questions...'

Lord Ragnus drove his elbow into Oaf's ribs, then punched the back of his head.

Questions leapt at Lord Ragnus, but he tossed her to the opposite side of the tub.

'Questions... no...' Oaf strained.

'Restrain her,' Lord Ragnus commanded his Cyclops.

It entered and pinned Questions to the tub wall.

Oaf tried to steady himself, but Lord Ragnus thumped the back of his head again. Oaf stumbled face first into the moisturiser. It couldn't end like this.

Lord Ragnus rolled Oaf over and lifted the back of his head in his left hand. 'I've been waiting an eternity for a decent challenge... What a disappointment.'

Oaf had failed. Years of pursuit and purpose, gone in a matter of brutal seconds. Worse yet, he had pulled Questions into his mistake.

Lord Ragnus turned to his Cyclops. 'Get the rest of this in carts and let's leave this dump. We'll get a boat to another land and sell it. Time to form an army a different way.'

Oaf had no strength left.

Lord Ragnus clenched the fist Oaf had created. He punched Oaf's cheek and cracked it.

'Say hello to your mother.' Lord Ragnus punched him again and the world darkened.

* * *

OAF'S HEAD WOBBLED. A voice tried to pierce through the darkness.

'Are you okay? Are you okay, Oaf?' Questions asked.

His eyes rolled around. He tried to focus on her face but struggled.

She poked and shook his head, but he couldn't respond. Words formed in his mind, but they made no sense and they wouldn't arrive to his mouth.

Questions rested Oaf's head on her lap and wept. 'Why does everyone I love have to die? Why couldn't I have died with my father?'

Oaf strained. The words moved slowly. 'You love me?' One of his eyes fluttered.

Questions blushed. 'Do you know I love you?' She looked down.

Oaf strained into a seated position against the tub wall. He smiled through the piercing pain in his cheeks. 'I love… you too. Lots.' He held her hands.

Questions looked at him, her eyes lit up. 'Does it annoy you that I can't say it like everyone else?'

Oaf shook his head. 'The way you say it… is perfect.'

She smiled and kissed him.

'I'm sorry for breaking my promise… running off.' His breath was slow. 'I'll forget… this whole revenge thing. I'm obviously not… very good at it.'

Questions frowned at him. 'Is that nonsense?'

Oaf wondered if he was still dazed. 'What?'

'Do you think the world needs less of Lord Ragnus'? Do you want to go and get your revenge?'

Questions stood and extended her hand to help Oaf rise.

* * *

OAF TOOK deep breaths and stumbled through Flowforn Forest. His face ached and his body struggled to keep going.

Lord Ragnus' whistling carried in the wind.

'Hurry up!' his miserable voice ordered the Cyclops pushing the carts.

Oaf caught up with the Cyclops, grabbed it and threw it out of the forest and in front of Lord Ragnus, standing on the edge of the Wrath of Arazod. Oaf recognised the cliff as the one Morcoli had pointed to from his village, as he could see a slither of the hidden beach on the distant shore.

Oaf pushed the line of carts out of the forest and emptied one of them onto the ground.

'Go and get what's mine,' Lord Ragnus commanded the Cyclops. It leapt to its feet and rushed at Oaf. Oaf lifted it and slammed its back against the rocks.

'Useless,' Lord Ragnus complained.

Oaf emptied every cart. Moisturiser covered the ground, flowed past Lord Ragnus' feet and off the cliff.

'It took me a long time to get all of that.' Lord Ragnus beat his fists together and charged. Oaf ran at him. Their solid frames crashed against each other, knocking them both down. They sprung to their feet. Lord Ragnus swung a fist but Oaf caught it. Lord Ragnus swung the other fist, but Oaf caught that too. Oaf tried to restrain him, but he was drained. Lord Ragnus forced his hands towards the sides of Oaf's head. 'I'll crush your tiny brain.'

Oaf feared the worst. His hands shook and his arms throbbed. He thought back to the brutality in Reech, to his creations being used for evil.

Lord Ragnus kicked Oaf in the stomach. Oaf released Lord Ragnus' hands and Lord Ragnus raised his fists either side of Oaf's head.

'I guess this is the end of the Oafs,' Lord Ragnus said.

Oaf pictured his mother and Questions; his strength.

As Lord Ragnus brought his fists down, Oaf moved his head

back, grabbed Lord Ragnus' wrists and pounded his stone fists together. He sculpted the weapons into one big block, binding his enemy's hands.

Lord Ragnus' smug expression faded.

'Not today,' Oaf said.

The expected epic battle was far from it. Lord Ragnus swung his bound fists down like a hammer, but took an uppercut. He fell back and his head smacked against the ground.

Oaf trudged to the edge of the Wrath of Arazod and swept moisturiser off it with his feet. He stared at his fallen foe, the reason his life had changed so much.

Lord Ragnus rose to his knees. 'What's wrong, Cecil? Can't finish me?' He smiled and moved closer to Oaf.

'Go away. You're done.' Oaf clenched his right fist and measured it at Lord Ragnus, but lowered it, struggling with his inability to destroy life.

'You forget that I know your people. I know you can't kill. It's not in your blood.' Lord Ragnus edged closer. 'And that dumb look of helplessness in your eyes. Exactly the same one Boofa showed before I buried her in the sea.' Lord Ragnus swung his arms up at Oaf, but Oaf stepped aside, grabbed Lord Ragnus by the throat, and punched him in the face.

He squeezed Lord Ragnus' throat tighter.

Lord Ragnus groaned. 'That's it, Cecil. We'll make a killer out of you yet.'

Questions stood by the tipped-over carts; concern, but acceptance on her face. Revenge was no longer Oaf's priority. Killing would not only end Lord Ragnus' life, but in some ways end his own. He wanted to avenge his mother, his people, but the best way to do that was to keep their values and way of life alive.

Oaf ripped the horn from around Lord Ragnus' neck. He dragged Lord Ragnus away from the edge of the cliff. He turned back towards it. 'I'm not going to kill you.'

Oaf lifted Lord Ragnus off his feet. He ran and flung him off the Wrath of Arazod. The arrogance in Lord Ragnus' eyes disappeared behind the emptiness of petrification.

DESTROY IT ALL

Karl stepped onto the King's Eye bridge from the Lookout Tower. All of Flowforn was below, from the cages to the gardens and beyond. Bar Witch and the adventurers tried to repel Fools, while Flowfornians led by Proster helped them. There were too many Fools, though. Karl closed his eyes, feeling the weight of responsibility.

Sabrinia hid behind Arazod's self-dedicated monstrosity atop the King's Tower.

Arazod flew above her. 'Why run from me? I'm your husband.' He swooped down, but she ran around the statue, evading him.

Arazod swiped his axe at Sabrinia. 'I'll destroy everything!'

'I don't mean to point out the obvious.' Karl gestured to the burnt woods to the south, damaged landscape to the north, and the smashed buildings around them. 'Have you ever thought about not destroying everything?'

'Briefly. But it seemed boring.' Arazod swooped at Karl and knocked him onto his stomach. If Karl fell off the bridge he'd become a human stain. He pushed himself to his feet.

Arazod caught Sabrinia and placed her on the beak of his statue. The slightest slip and she would die.

She swung a fist at him, but missed and nearly fell. 'Get back here you coward!'

'If I can't have love, nobody will.' Arazod laughed at Sabrinia. 'Now you get to see me cut him in half, then it's your turn. You'll wish you'd loved me to avoid all of this.'

'I could never love you, no matter how much I tried.' Sabrinia looked at Karl then turned back to Arazod. 'You are unlovable!'

Arazod's beak twitched. He flew at Karl, who blocked the axe, but was knocked over the railing.

'Karl!' Sabrinia screamed.

The curved hook of Karl's shield dug into the bridge. Karl moved his legs, frantically trying to get back on the King's Eye.

Arazod hovered by his statue and looked down at the battle. 'Lock them all up!' he commanded the Fools. 'I'm going to personally slice them one by one.'

The Fools funnelled everyone into the outdoor cages.

Arazod placed his axe down, grabbed a statuette of him feeding starving children and moved it towards the edge of the tower, no doubt to drop on people.

Karl swung a leg onto the bridge and rolled under the railing.

Arazod hovered.

Karl readied himself to throw his shield. He focused and squinted to sharpen everything. He pulled his arm back. With all he had left he added that bit of flamboyance and bravado that would make Arazod appreciate the showmanship. 'Die! You irritating flying rat!' He launched the shield. It cut through the air.

The prisoners, hopeful, open-mouthed, followed its flight.

Arazod simply moved.

Sabrinia ducked; the shield nearly beheading her.

'That's all you had left?' Arazod laughed.

The shield smashed the elbow of the statue's axe-wielding arm. It fell, creating a potential but risky route down for Sabrinia.

'You broke my statue!' Arazod fumed. He put the statuette

down and picked his axe up. He glared at Karl, nothing to defend himself with. 'For the last time, Karl. Die!' Arazod swooped at him.

Beak and axe closed in. Karl knew it was over, but had to try something. He clenched his fists, hoping to whack the tyrant out of the sky, but behind the heroism he knew it was folly. He met Sabrinia's eyes one last time. 'Sorry.'

'Karl!' Larnela stepped in front of him.

Metals clashed in a blur. Larnela turned to Karl, wounded from her shoulder to her stomach, her sword broken in half.

'Larnela! No…'

She collapsed into Karl's arms. Blood leaked out of her.

Karl kneeled and held her against him. He covered her wounds, but her life seeped through his fingers. 'Why?'

'Use this…' Larnela handed him the sword handle with the broken blade. 'He might have wings, but they just make him a wider target.'

Karl lay Larnela down, stood and faced his enemy.

Arazod swooped. Karl leaned back. The axe grazed his left shoulder, but he jammed the broken sword into Arazod's right wing.

Arazod yelped, dropped his axe and crashed head first into the railing. His struggling wing only slowed the inevitable collision with the courtyard pebbles in front of the cages.

Karl rested Larnela's head on his lap.

Sabrinia climbed down the broken statue arm. She removed the red dress tied to her and used it to cover Larnela's bleeding chest.

Larnela gazed up at Karl. Life barely flickered in her eyes. 'Karl… you did it.'

'Shush. Save your energy.' Karl pressed against her wound. 'Why did you sacrifice yourself? I could've taken him.'

She chuckled and held his hand, squeezing it weakly. 'It's… it's a mother's job to protect her child.'

Too many thoughts exploded in Karl's mind. 'You're...' He welled up; his head was hot and light.

'I failed once... Not again.' Larnela coughed blood.

Tears ran down Karl's face. He had her. She was here in his hands, a real thing. Not a vision, not a blue stone, not a story. An actual real person. 'M... Mum?' Saying it out loud made his heart swell.

He pressed his clean hand to her cheek.

She nodded. 'I'm so proud of who you've become.'

Sabrinia put a comforting hand on Karl's shoulder. Larnela's blood darkened the red dress.

'Why didn't you say anything when we spoke?' he asked.

'You had something bigger to deal with...'

'Bigger than you...' He shook his head. 'No...' Karl pulled her into his chest and wished he could transfer his life to hers. 'I don't want you to die...' He wanted to take in every flicker in her eyes.

She smiled, blood on her teeth. 'I died the moment I gave you up... but I had to. I couldn't let them kill you.'

'It's okay,' Karl said. 'It's okay, Mum.'

'I tried to find you...' Her breathing slowed.

'Please...' Karl's stomach twisted. Just another moment, that's all he wanted. Another sentence, another breath.

'Thanks for letting me live again.' Larnela's life stopped.

A pulsing hatred flooded every inch of Karl's being. He stared at Arazod's axe.

* * *

KARL MARCHED into the courtyard wielding the Soul Bleeder. Sabrinia and a limping Hargon followed him.

He approached Arazod's body; face down, his leg broken and wing wounded. The feathered villain stirred and Fools approached.

Bar Witch poked her head out of her cage. 'Cut his stupid head off!'

Karl pressed the axe blade into Arazod's back.

'Argh!' Arazod screamed.

'Tell the Fools to stop,' Karl said.

'Never!'

Karl pressed the axe deeper. Arazod's blood coloured the blade.

Sabrinia covered her mouth.

'I'll slice you in half before they get to me,' Karl said.

'Stop! Stop Fools!' Arazod groaned.

The Fools stopped.

Karl stared at the weapon in his hand and his prone nemesis.

'Karl…' Sabrinia said softly, concern in her eyes.

His mother's dead face flashed in his mind. 'Make me the leader of the Fools,' he commanded Arazod.

'What?' Arazod said.

'Make me the leader.'

'Never! Kill him!' Arazod commanded.

A Fool thrust its spear at Karl. He chopped the spear in half and touched the axe to Arazod's beak. 'Do it!'

'Stop Fools! Stop!' Arazod cried.

The Fools stopped.

'Are you sure you want this?' Arazod asked.

Karl pressed his foot to Arazod's head and pushed it into the pebbles. He could feel Arazod's skull on the verge of cracking and he enjoyed it. Just one stamp and he'd squash his miserable little brain.

Arazod screamed into the ground. Karl raised his foot enough to allow words.

'Karl is your new leader!' Arazod coughed. 'Karl is your new leader!'

Karl released his foot.

The Fools dropped to their knees and stared at Karl, the yellow flickering in their eyes.

Arazod laughed. 'See how you like leading these idiots. It's no fun. And soon, someone like me will come to take them from you,' Arazod warned. 'It's inevitable. Beings created to follow orders are very appealing.'

'I'm already tired of leading,' Karl said. 'I think I'm ready to rest. I command all the Fools to be free to think for themselves, and to never let anyone be their leader.'

'Oh...' Arazod had clearly never thought of that possibility.

The Fools looked at each other, worried. Their eyes flickered, registering the command. They stood up.

One Fool studied the surroundings. 'I'm going to fix what we broke.'

Other Fools nodded.

'Yeah, I'll help too,' another said.

'I need a sleep,' another commented.

'I'd quite like to eat leaves until I pass out. Then I'll think about helping,' one said.

'I want to build a boat and explore the world,' another added.

For the first time in their lives, they all made an independent decision. They threw their weapons down.

Oaf and Questions returned. 'What did we miss?' Oaf asked.

'An idiot being defeated.' Karl gestured to Arazod.

Oaf and Questions smiled.

Sabrinia faced the prisoners. 'Thank you all for saving Flowforn.' She sounded drained but also relieved.

Arazod mocked Sabrinia's voice from his vulnerable position. 'Thank you all for saving Flowforn.'

She took the two-headed turtle rock and bashed Arazod across the head. 'Best gift anyone ever gave me,' she told Karl.

Oaf ripped the cage doors open.

'What shall we do with him?' Questions pointed at Arazod.

'Scrath,' Karl said. 'Can you do that wing ripping thing to him, please?'

'It would be an honour and a pleasure.'

'And do it without any of that showy nonsense he wants.'

Arazod stared at Karl in that threatening way that meant nothing now.

'To whom shall I give the wings?' Scrath asked.

'Take them with you back to Lake Shizneh. The fewer people who know about them the better.' Karl's thoughts turned back to Larnela.

'Consider it done.'

Hargon limped towards them. Sabrinia turned to him. 'Let's get you patched up.'

Hargon smiled. 'Do you mind if we lock Arazod in the dungeons so I can paint him?'

'Be my guest.'

Karl and Sabrinia walked away from the spectacle.

'Wait!' Arazod yelled. 'I can make up for everything!'

His screams meant nothing and they walked on.

Karl returned to the King's Eye. He held his mother's dead face in his hands. 'You've made it so nobody ever has to run again, Mum.' He turned to see the people he'd shared this journey with.

Questions cried.

Sabrinia squeezed him. 'We'll give her a proper burial.'

'Thank you all,' Karl said. 'I've lived in Flowforn since I was little, but I never felt at home until I stepped outside and met you.'

Sags grunted.

'Yes, even you. You've all made me a better Karl. A Karl I like.'

The others smiled.

Karl took a breath and kissed his mother's forehead.

'Are you okay?' Questions asked.

He nodded. 'I'm better than okay, Questions. I'm home.'

WHERE JOURNEYS END

Karl, Sabrinia, Oaf, and Questions entered the Great Dragon's cave at the top of snowy Mount Hastovia. They stood in awe of the grand, demonic stalactites.

Oaf carried Arazod, kicking and wriggling, in a sack over his shoulder.

'Do you think the Great Dragon will eat us?' Questions asked.

A roar shook them and the sound vibrated in their bones.

Karl hesitated. 'I guess we'll find out soon.'

'We come to you asking if you'll take a prisoner for us?' Sabrinia shouted into the dark.

'He has breathing issues, a terrible singing voice, and is pretty bad company. But you can poke him,' Karl added.

Oaf dumped Arazod onto the ground and lifted the sack off him. He'd been crying. He'd tried to peck through the rope that bound his arms, but his beak was covered with a sock. This would be his hell; being prisoner to the Great Dragon, living in total darkness.

The Great Dragon stepped out of the black. He was a fearsome creature as long as a river and as black as the darkness he lived in, with spear-pointed teeth and angry, amber eyes. His loud breathing was enough to make everyone look at each other as though they'd made a mistake.

'I hope he eats us all!' Arazod said, barely audible.

Karl tightened the string on the sock and waited for the terrifying creature to speak.

'Ooh, isn't he a little treat.' The soft, excited voice surprised them.

'Where shall we leave him?' Sabrinia asked.

'Just dump my little pet in that circle of rocks there.' The Great Dragon pointed its face towards a rocky area covered in bones. 'What's his name?'

'Ara...' Karl stopped himself. 'Call him anything you like.'

'I'll go with Pidgy. Like a pigeon! Pidgy the pigeon!'

Arazod tried to complain.

'Sounds fitting,' Karl said. 'Thank you, Great Dragon. We'll leave you to get acquainted.'

The Great Dragon sniffed Arazod. 'I'm not sure when, but I think I will eat you,' the Great Dragon said.

Sabrinia bent down to face Arazod. 'Now when you die, your soul will follow me, and you'll get to watch me do good things, help people, and spread love until the day I perish.'

Arazod's eyes reddened.

The group retreated, ignoring his muffled screams.

Karl stopped. 'Actually...'

Arazod looked as if he was expecting mercy, but none was coming.

'Do you by any chance know how to get the smell of Invisible Dragon dung off my hand?'

'Easy breezy. Bring your paw here.'

Karl extended his hand. The Great Dragon's breath shook him. It licked his hand. Everyone grimaced.

'Thank you...' Karl felt a touch violated.

They left the cave and Karl slipped on a loose rock, falling off the edge of Mount Hastovia.

'Karl!' Sabrinia screamed.

He felt a squelch. When his friends looked over the edge and down at him they laughed. He lay in a huge pile of Great Dragon dung.

Sabrinia took a breath, relieved. 'Looks like you'd better go back in for a full scrub.'

Karl cried dry tears.

* * *

QUEEN SABRINIA STOOD in the courtyard and addressed her people, with Karl next to her.

'Friends. Thank you all for enduring the difficult times.' She looked at the statue of her father. 'It taught me a lot, about myself, my friends, and what it means to be alive.' She swallowed. 'My father was a wonderful king. But he made mistakes...' She choked up, swallowed and steadied herself. 'Flowforn is great... but it's not all there is. You need to see the world. Learn about other people and creatures, and we need to stop ignoring that there are lives outside of these walls.'

Bar Witch and the adventurers smiled.

'From now on, taking the Lionbear's hazel berries is illegal, punishable by probably being eaten by them... and we will work with the Tree-Cyclopsi to manage our waste.'

Scrath stroked Wob's head.

'And all are welcome to live in Flowforn. We will live our dreams, and help other people to achieve theirs... And where there is evil...' she looked at Karl, '...we will fight it with love.'

'And weapons!' Proster shouted from the crowd, his ribs bandaged. Others laughed.

Sabrinia chuckled. 'And yes, so we are better prepared, we will learn to defend ourselves, but I hope we never have to.' She sighed, wishing it could be different. 'We have stopped evil, for now. And should it return, we shall repel it again!'

Everyone cheered.

* * *

IT HAD TAKEN over a year to get Flowforn back to resembling its old self. They never bothered rebuilding the tavern. Instead, Bar Witch, Sags, Frong, and Marlens were given a new tavern within the walls, called The Adventurer. Flowfornians and visitors loved their stories, even Frong's. Bar Witch regularly wowed crowds with her tricks.

The adventurers toyed with the idea of exploring again, but this time bringing back relics so Flowforn could keep the peace. The Journal of Adventures was there for anyone to read, and Arazod's Soul Bleeder hung on the wall above the tavern bar. Their first collected artefact.

Karl did keep his promise to fly Sags around Flowfornia. He borrowed the wings off Scrath for an evening and they flew over every inch of land until Karl's arms couldn't take any more. Sags now regarded Karl as a true friend and woke him up every morning. Karl was not as keen on this new friendship. No matter if he locked his door or window, Sags would contort himself into Karl's room and be there on the edge of his bed.

Sabrinia, seeing how happy Questions was with Oaf, told her to go and be with him. Questions didn't want to leave her friend, but she wanted to keep the promise she made to herself to return to Brohl. They rebuilt Inquiso and Oaf sculpted them rock homes to forever beat the icy winds. Questions gave birth to little Oaf-Inquiso twins. They were only twenty sunsets old, but already stronger than Karl. They named the girl Boofa and the boy Quizmal.

Oaf provided homes for the Fools and taught those interested to sculpt. The Birth Fool had a comfortable dwelling where it could spit out eggs at a rate that didn't hurt. It had even lost a bit of weight around the eyes. Oaf also sculpted a fountain for stray tortured souls to live in while he tried to figure out their names and free them.

He made a special library for Questions with a room dedicated to *Is This the Book of Tales?* Questions' latest entry was a page on the friends she'd saved Hastovia with. As for The Charmer, Oaf took it from Flowforn and stuck it on a plinth in Reech, where nobody would ever move it again.

Marlens went with Oaf and Questions to the Village of the Petrified. They made a cauldron full of the cure for petrification, but they didn't know the true friends of the petrified to collect their breath and complete the mixture. They made a deal with Morcoli. They would send parchments to all kingdoms, and those who wanted could come to claim their friends and complete the cure to restore them.

Morcoli agreed, and was pleased to have Lord Ragnus, dead behind the eyes, dressed as a Lionbear. Oaf and Questions watched as Morcoli cut the stone with a petrified Lord Ragnus. Oaf imagined that Lord Ragnus' last thought when he fell from the Wrath of Arazod wasn't of regret or remorse, or how he would have lived a good life, it was probably that he wished he had punched Cecil just one more time and crushed his brain.

* * *

SABRINIA KEPT her promise to eat fish at the spot her father loved. She could see why he enjoyed it. It was peaceful and relaxing. She missed him, but felt lucky to live somewhere that would always remind her of him.

One night, Karl and Sabrinia visited Larnela's cave. Karl wanted to take her belongings and keep them. He placed her clothes in a basket, comforted by her smell.

He had so many questions. 'Who is my dad?' 'Do I have any brothers or sisters?' 'Why did you call me Karl?' And one that bothered him quite a lot… 'Why did you leave me in Lionbear poop?'

'I think this is for you,' Sabrinia said.

He turned to see the other sock with his name embroidered on it.

She handed it to him and his eyes filled with tears.

'I'm sorry, Karl… for my father's role in all of this…'

He shook his head. 'It's okay. His mistakes helped him to learn to become the great king he was, and it put me on this path.' He held her hands. 'I'm going to make her proud. Make her sacrifices worthwhile.'

Sabrinia placed her hand on his cheek. 'You already have.'

Her touch made things that little bit less painful. She moved her face closer and pressed her lips to his. He felt like things would improve, and that they had made Hastovia a better place.

The End.
Of book one…

More info on book 2 and 3 on the next pages!

RISE OF THE DEATHBRINGER

BOOK 2 IN THE KARL'S KINGDOM SERIES

Peace doesn't last. It's just a temporary break while war rests. They might as well rename times of peace 'war holidays.'

Karl and his friends have had their fill of conflict and are thankful to live whatever is considered a normal life.

But not too far away, a noble deed produces terrifying results, awakening a fearsome foe obsessed with unleashing a power so devastating it could destroy everyone.

Karl and his friends must find a magic relic, put their trust in the untrustworthy, and make sacrifices that could include their lives.

Hastovia needs some heroes.

'With the perfect balance of comedy and edge of your seat action, I couldn't put this book down'

Includes a bonus short story *The Rise of Ragnus*. The origin story of the stone fisted lunatic.

Get your copy from your preferred retailer: www.mark-boutros.com/riseofthedeathbringer

EXCERPT

RISE OF THE DEATHBRINGER

$\mathcal{A}$razod lay on the cold ground inside a circle of rocks – his bed. He stared at the stalactites on the ceiling, wondering if he'd imagined the sound. There were no Man-Hawks left to be shrieking. He'd seen to that, and if there was one, did he want to see them? Maybe he could get them to help him. Then he'd kill them once he was free.

Water dripped onto his feathers. He shuffled to his right but another drop hit him.

He grumbled. Three years in this miserable cave, living as the Great Dragon's plaything. He hadn't seen his reflection in all that time, but his feathers were filthy and he could see his ribs. His bones creaked whenever he moved and the closest thing he had to a bath was when the Great Dragon's dry, bumpy tongue licked him.

Arazod stared at the beast, roughly thirty feet high and about sixty long, black as the darkness he dwelt in and outlined by the faint glow of the night sun creeping into the mountain.

The dragon's spear-pointed teeth tore through the torso of a boar-hippo. The beast was pure power and death, yet all he ever did was eat, sleep and torment Arazod. What a waste.

Arazod thought about the long list of people he hated, but at the top of the list were two: Karl, who wouldn't die even when Arazod kicked him off a cliff, and Sabrinia, who refused to love him. All she had to do was love him and everything would be different.

Arazod sat up and released another demonic shriek, so forceful it hurt his broken wing. He'd take his chances with a Man-Hawk.

'What are you doing?' the dragon asked in a voice more suited to a small child.

'I like the—' Arazod wheezed, '—echo this cave provides.'

'Well, stop it. That noise makes my skin crawl, and you're disturbing my snacking.'

Arazod fixed his eyes on the dragon's scales. He wished he could grow to the dragon's size and sink his talons into the monster's flesh. He'd shred him and relish the warmth of dragon blood soaking his feathers while he ripped out the beast's insides.

Arazod missed having working wings and freedom.

'Are you hungry?' the Great Dragon asked.

'You know the answer.'

The dragon crunched through the boar-hippo's skull. 'I just like hearing you say it. Go on.' He flicked a sheet of boar-hippo skin onto Arazod's head.

'Agh!' Arazod whined and fought to remove the oily skin-blanket. He threw it down, his feathers a mess of grease and blood. 'Of course I'm hungry! I'm starving!' A waft of rotting flesh shot into his nostrils and he retched. He stared at the dragon with the rage reserved for his murder victims.

The Great Dragon laughed. 'You're cute when you're stressed.'

Arazod shuddered. 'I hope you choke—' he wheezed, '—to death on those bones!'

The Great Dragon raised his head from his meal, turned and brought his face closer to Arazod's.

Arazod raised a claw. The tension in his body turned to trembling fear. 'I didn't mean that…'

The dragon breathed on Arazod's face. The warm stench of devoured creatures clung to Arazod's feathers.

He swallowed his vomit.

'Clean my teeth,' the dragon demanded.

Not again. Arazod struggled onto his bony legs. His stomach twisted, desperate for proper food.

The Great Dragon rested his face on the rocky ground, opened his mouth and rolled his dull red tongue out, creating a fleshy path to more misery.

Arazod stepped onto the tongue and pressed his talons down, hoping to cause the dragon any kind of pain. It amazed him how the monster's teeth were the same size as him. That's how insignificant he had become.

The heat suffocated Arazod and served as a reminder that one puff of fire would be enough to cook him.

Arazod spotted some boar-hippo stuck between two lower teeth. He approached and pecked at the meat, dislodging it. He chewed some and forced it down despite his body trying to reject it. He was lucky it was somewhat fresh today. His stomach turned.

Arazod pecked some more meat out of the beast's teeth. 'All clean.' Arazod grimaced.

The dragon exhaled, knocking Arazod down his tongue and back into the circle of rocks.

The monster retracted his tongue. 'I've been thinking. I know I say it a lot, but tomorrow I think I will finally set you on fire.'

Part of Arazod was relieved. Death was preferable to this tedious routine.

'Time to sleep now.' The dragon lay down, closed his eyes and pinned Arazod under his claw.

Arazod stared up at the stalactites. If only one would fall and pierce his head – or, better yet, pierce the dragon's. A giant, sword-shaped rock sticking out of the dragon's skull, squashing an eye, would be a majestic sight.

A shadow moved in the cave entrance, but when Arazod focused there was nothing.

He closed his eyes, but when he reopened them his breath caught in his chest. Was he hallucinating? His sister, Ryza, hovered in the entrance, a haunting smirk on her beak.

She flew over to him. 'Hello, Little Arazod,' she whispered.

He smiled through the terror. 'Sister—'

'Let's get you out of here.' She grimaced at the stench, gathered the bones of the dead creatures and placed them under the dragon's claw, propping it up.

Arazod shuffled free, keeping his eyes on her. How?

Ryza shook her head; a disappointed gesture he had experienced too many times in the past.

Arazod stood. 'It will come looking for me when it wakes up,' he whispered.

'Just grab on,' she replied.

Arazod wrapped his arms around his sister's neck.

She flew them out of the cave.

Arazod glanced back and wondered whether he was safer staying where he was.

IN MEMORY OF...

BOOK 3 IN THE KARL'S KINGDOM SERIES

I can't say too much without giving away spoilers, but it's ready for purchase, and you'll get more of an insight into it at the end of book two.

Get your copy from your preferred retailer: www.mark-boutros.com/inmemoryof

THANK YOU!

Thanks for joining Karl and his friends. If you enjoyed reading and have a moment to spare, I would really appreciate a short review on the platform where you got the book. Your help in spreading the word and sharing is hugely appreciated and important as I have no marketing budget, so word of mouth is my hope. Also, if you don't leave a review, it empowers Arazod to sing some more and nobody wants that.

Sign up to my VIP club to get an **EXCLUSIVE, FREE** story, *The First Fool,* about how those little things came to be cursed to follow orders.

You won't find the story elsewhere, apart from through piracy, obviously.

You'll also get subscriber-only giveaways, contests, preview chapters, and other offers.

To join and to get your free story, head over to www.mark-boutros.com/crew

ACKNOWLEDGMENTS

Thank you to anyone who wants to be thanked. You deserve thanks. Thank you. Consider yourself thanked and acknowledged.